Voices on the Prairie

Jacque,
Thanks for all you
do to make the world a
better place!
Rick McNary

Rick McNary

D1607986

BLACK ROSE
writing™

ISBN: 978-1-61296-557-4

PUBLISHED BY BLACK ROSE WRITING

www.blackrosewriting.com

Printed in the United States of America

Suggested retail price $18.95

Voices on the Prairie is printed in Adobe Caslon Pro

This book is dedicated to my wife, Christine McNary.
Without her inspiration and insistence,
this story would never have seen the light of day.

Voices on the Prairie

Chapter One

As the morning sun lifted the blanket of night off the Kansas prairie, Sunny grabbed the saddle horn and swung her long legs over the big buckskin, Starbuck. Starbuck nickered but remained motionless as Sunny settled into the saddle, removed her worn Stetson and combed her fingers through her long brunette hair. The prairie whispered the morning's charm.

Starbuck easily navigated the prairie as cattle trails follow ancient game trails. A chill lingered as winter curtseyed and invited spring to dance on the prairie. This morning's sun was rectangular before it became round as it crested. Waving brome-grasses silhouetted against the sun like a phalanx of soldiers swaying across the horizon.

Sunny breathed deeply and sank even further into the well-worn saddle, a finely crafted trophy she won in high school as a champion barrel racer. She still liked to rodeo, but found the company of cows and horses more relaxing than people.

Starbuck shifted his weight waiting for a signal from Sunny who was mesmerized by the morning sun chasing long shadows across the waving prairie like a sparrow chases a hawk. The morning dew christened and a thousand sprinkles of light rippled in the breeze like sequins shimmering in a spotlight. His ears perked as a prairie chicken rooster boomed and furiously danced the mating ritual on the same spot as his ancient fathers.

Sunny slipped the fencing hammer into a scabbard then peeled the glove off her left hand to examine the puncture. She knew better than to wear buckskin gloves while mending fence, but the kind of gloves Daddy used to wear were too stiff. Reaching into her saddlebag for a bandage, she quickly doctored her throbbing finger. The only thing that hurt worse than a barbed-wire puncture - her Daddy said - was smashing your thumb with the fence hammer trying to drive staples into the hedge posts.

Dried hedge was a stubbornly hard wood that ranchers on the prairie discovered. The limbs of the abundant tree, also known as the Osage orange, made perfect fence-posts. Some posts were known to last in the ground for up to eighty years. But over time, the hedge was replaced by metal t-posts, which were much easier to acquire than the chainsaw-dulling hedge tree laced with malicious thorns able to puncture the soles of work boots.

Other pasture borders were lined with another pristine type of fence popular in the Flint Hills but one with origins in the Celtic Isles: loose stones stacked on top of each other. These picturesque fences had once been prolific, but massive machines gobbled up mile after mile of stone fencerows. They were ground into limestone powder then sprinkled on fields to enrich the soil.

Some ranchers chose to ride fence with four wheelers, but Sunny stubbornly resisted the temptation of time and chose, instead, to check them off the back of Starbuck. Her stubbornness came from her Daddy's best friend, Spook Masterson, who usually rode fences with her. Spook often said that his mother gave birth to him on a horseback and he hadn't felt comfortable on anything else since. He was at home today waiting on a buyer for a roping horse he trained. Spook could turn a green-broke five-hundred-dollar horse into a thirty-thousand-dollar calf-roping horse.

Spook took Sunny under his wing after her Daddy died and since he had no children of his own, she was like a daughter to him. Spook nicknamed everyone and chose the moniker of "Sunny" for her when she was six months old. He told her, "Yore mom done handed yore little britches to me but I was afeared of holdin' ya. Then ya smiled at me lik'n' I was your hero and the sun done started shinin' on my lonesome heart right then and there."

She couldn't make it on the ranch without Spook. She didn't like taking his help for free, but she had no resources to pay him for the work he did to help her keep things going. Even though he had everyone in town convinced he didn't have two nickels to rub together, he'd let her know that if she ever needed anything, he inherited a significant amount of money and was happy to help her out. His free labor she finally accepted because he convinced her it was to honor the friendship with her Dad. But she would never take his money.

Although her Daddy liked these wooden fence posts, some driven in the ground by her Grandpa sixty years before, Spook had a different opinion about them. "The onlys diff'rence twixt drivin' a staple into a hedge post and a stone post is that the stone post is a darn sight softer."

Sunny squeezed Starbuck into moving down the fence line with slow, deliberate, pouting steps of a horse made for action, not fence mending. Sunny raised a lot of foals in her life, but she knew she had a special horse on her hands when Starbuck was born five years earlier. It was more than just a strong pedigree and confirmation that made Starbuck special; it was the Perseid Meteor shower that dazzled the prairie sky the night he was born. Sunny sat on a straw bale in the corner of the stall watching out the barn window at hundreds of shooting stars while waiting to help the mare give birth.

She raised Starbuck from a foal and trained him to respond to simple pressure from her hands or knees rather than spurs or a quirt. Some cowboys wanted the jangle of a spur to goad their horses, but Sunny learned from Spook how to train the horse with simple pressure. Spook said, "Dem hosses are a dang sight smarter than most of dem jarhead cowboys with tobaccky juice drooling down their chin

9

and you don't need no gol dang spur the size of a hubcap to get a horse to do what you want. I'd like to sink a set of spurs into one of those cowpoke's skinny little hides one of these days so theys would know how it feels."

Starbuck could cut a calf away from a herd so fast he unintentionally unseated Sunny more than once. She raised him from a colt and knew his moods as well as she knew her own. He would rather be racing across the pasture after a calf to rope and brand than walk mile after mile checking fence. Sunny would too, but there was work to be done and miles of fence left to check.

Spring giving birth to summer was the only time of the year in the Flint Hills that Sunny felt at home in her heart. As Starbuck ambled, she wondered what it must have looked like to Zebulon Pike, the famous explorer who named these hills. How many wagon trains lumbered across these panoramas headed for the gold mines of California or the plains of Texas? Although it seemed like there was more limestone than flint, Pike wrote of "these flinty hills," and the name just seemed to stick. If you looked across the prairie, the outcroppings of rock were predominantly limestone, but there was also a base of flint that ruined many tires on these country roads. Daddy insisted that two spare tires be on the truck - one wasn't enough in these hills - and had his own tire fixing machine, one that Sunny still used on occasion.

While those sharp stones were cussed more than complimented by local ranchers and cowboys, they were vital product to the Native Americans. Arrowheads, tomahawks, knives, drills, and a variety of other Stone Age equipment still lay undiscovered across the vast prairies of the Flint Hills. She had a collection of these artifacts on her wall, neatly mounted behind glass and labeled as to the date and location of the find. In a land too rocky to farm, the prairie of the Flint Hills remains almost the same as it was for various Native American tribes of centuries past.

Some said that the birth of the American cowboy was in the Flint

Hills. After the Civil War in the late 1800's, folks who raised cattle in Texas and wanted to ship them to markets in Chicago and New York started driving thousands of longhorns up to the railroad in Abilene, Kansas. Texans soon discovered that the vast, rich grasses of the area were ideal for fattening their cattle so three-year-old bony steers as big as a horse and thin as a mesquite twig were shipped to Kansas and this ocean of prairie soon replaced the diminished bison with cattle and cowboys.

In Sunny's family, the succession of cowboys could be traced back four generations. Sunny's great, great grandfather took up the cowboy life after the Civil War. Passing the heritage from one generation to the next, she heard many stories of life on the prairie. Unquestionably her favorite ones were by her own Daddy of the times when he was only five and would go to Matfield Green, some thirty miles away, to help bring home a load of cattle from the railroad. Tied to his saddle so he wouldn't go to sleep and fall off his horse, he would start the long trek home behind a bunch of wild Texas longhorn steers.

Sunny's great grandfather homesteaded this portion of land and was astute enough to acquire more pasture so they had one of the bigger spreads in the area. But about ten years before her Daddy died, the market on cattle collapsed and just keeping the taxes paid each year was a real struggle. Although her brothers and Daddy wanted to sell all or portions of it, she fought, as Spook said, "Lik'n' a treed coon!" to keep the ranch.

Sunny gently breathed *Whoa* to Starbuck who immediately paused in his pouting gait. She rested her hands on the saddle horn and gazed across the sea of grasses rippling like a flag unfurling in the breeze. Early morning sunlight cast long amber shadows on the lee side of hills and glistened off yellow-breasted meadowlarks perching their songs on top of hedge posts. The breeze, like a gentle breath, resuscitated from slumber the regal ring-neck pheasant that squawked as it signaled its take-off from the earth. Plump prairie chickens, disturbed by the presence of the horseback intruder, dusted their russet coats in disgust and erratically fluttered to a safer distance.

Sunny drank in the gentleness of the morning like a cup of coffee cradled in her soul. She threw open wide her arms and spoke to the sun's rays from a poem she once penned,

You quiet spies with silent voices
Whisper in the ears of nature
Wake the lark and the hawk
Who trumpet their call to man.
You kindly spies
With intents and motives pure
Bring hope and life and warmth
Dispelling cold darkness from the land.
You gentle spies
Are welcomed by my cotton-tailed friends
Hearts are gladdened, Spirits lifted
As beauty replenishes the bland.

How could her brothers ever want to live anywhere but here? She gently squeezed her knees against Starbuck, invigorated by the brief doxology.

Although she rambled through these pastures many times, she kept alert. She occasionally stumbled upon remnants of various Native American tribes that dined upon the feast of this land. Near the northwest corner of their property a crystal clear spring fed a tiny creek that flowed year round. On the north side of the creek was a gentle rise in the hill with the type of southwest exposure the Native Americans favored.

One year, after a prairie fire parched the ground, she stumbled upon ancient tipi rings. Gathered to weigh down the bottom of a tipi, the round, river-smoothed rocks the size of large loaves of bread lie in nearly perfect circles.

As she wandered among the tipi rings, she saw, gleaming in the spring sunlight, a stone knife with perfect symmetry and a razor edge. She brushed the dirt off the shank and ran her fingers over the cold stone; she could almost hear the sharp click on one piece of flint chipping at the edge of another piece as a Stone Age father taught his son the ancient art of flint-knapping. How many animals were skinned with this knife? How many men were scarred by its razor edge?

She heard how the neighbors, the Clatterbuck family, found an old adobe oven and told the local agricultural agent about it. Within two days the state university sent out archaeologists who staked off the land with no-trespassing signs; soon, trespassers from as far away as Australia scavenged the area. Putting up "no-trespassing" signs, Grandpa used to say, was the same as putting up a "welcome" sign for some folks. No, this place was too special, almost sacred, for Sunny to ever let anyone tear it up; no one knew of her find.

What once was grazing land for buffalo, deer, and elk, now was sectioned off in large tracts and used to graze massive herds of cattle or horses. People in other states often owned thousand acre tracts and the days of the family ranch were slowly ebbing away. The Lonesome Star Ranch was in Sunny's family for over a century, but people she never met owned all the lands around the borders of their fences.

A few months earlier, the hills were ablaze with the annual fires as ranchers burned thousands of acres of grass. The Native Americans learned that when the prairies burned in the spring, green shoots of native grasses would soon spring up. For hundreds of years, this springtime rite was a way of life on the unchanged prairie. Sunny was checking to make sure none of the wooden fence posts got burned up in the fires. Sometimes they would char enough around the base to weaken them and when cattle leaned against them to graze, they snapped off like a knuckle popping.

April rains replenished the earth and grasses were coming to life. The black, scorched earth slowly gave way to a gentle haze of green as the brome and bluestem grasses slowly peeked their stalks above the ground. It was now May and the hills were covered with a carpet of grass almost a foot thick. Occasional bursts of wildflower patches splashed across the canvas of another day's dawn. Like confetti sprinkled on the breeze, myriad hues of daisies dotted swatches of heather blanketing in the sun.

As Starbuck ambled through the grass, a Killdeer flitted up from her nest and tumbled around as if injured. Acting like it had a broken wing, it would settle back on to the ground with a brisk walk. Sunny smiled to herself, knowing that it was only a ruse of a mother trying to lure them away from her nest of eggs somewhere near.

Her friends asked her how she endured the silence of the prairie, but she often told them that she thought the prairie was one of nature's nosiest places. The voices of the prairie were as varied as the wildflowers and, if one listened, would speak directly to the soul. Someone published a compilation of poetry about the Flint Hills which Sunny read so many times the pages were falling out. Her favorite one, by an anonymous poet, she committed to memory:

The wind lays soft against the prairie
And gives breath to the new day
This winding road I'm traveling on's a memory
Of a place I've been and a place I'd like to stay
But a Voice in the distant hills is calling
From the shadows, He whispers my name
And the winding road I'm traveling on will take me
To a place I'll never leave again.
A place where no one dies
A place where no one cries
And my heart finds its healing rest
In my Father's house, this journey ends
And the winding road no longer bends
And my heart finds its healing rest
From the winding road.

Sunny loved the voices of the prairie. Whether it was the mournful cry of the turtledove looking for its mate, or the piercing shriek of the red-tailed hawk circling overhead, the voices were as familiar to her as her own. She spent enough time listening to the voices to mimic them perfectly. A whistle of *Bob-White* could get a covey of quail to respond. She chattered back at the testy squirrels barking at her and Starbuck if they wandered too close to the cottonwoods guarding the creek banks.

Years of life in a ranch twenty miles from a town made Sunny familiar with the voices of the prairie. With each season came a cacophony of new voices, or at least different trebles from the same voices. Spring would bring the meadowlark and the thunderstorm; summer, the creaking rusty windmills in the burning south winds; fall, the rustling of cottonwood leaves limbering to the ground, but winter had its own unique voice both hallowed and horrifying. She huddled many nights under a comforter, cuddled up by the wood stove, as the prairie winter cried like a lover betrayed. Nothing felt quite as lonely as a long winter night wind moaning through the cracks and crevices of one's soul.

Starbuck perked his ears and turned his head towards the west. The prairie's voice interrupted her daydreaming with the distant rumble of a brewing thunderstorm. Looking west, she watched thunderheads build in the sky like a boiling cauldron in a chemist's lab. Lightning danced across the darkening sky, which grew menacingly gray and green under the canopy of churning white storm clouds. She saw the hail coming from miles away, marching slowly across the prairie splattering the grass flat as it came. Distant thunder like tympani drums began an erratic staccato. She knew she should head Starbuck towards home but was entranced by the beauty of the brewing storm.

There was something terrible and terrific at the same time in a spring thunderstorm in Kansas and today had all the ingredients of a ferocious storm. The weather was relatively warm and humid but she noticed the barometer dropping last night, then heard on the radio this morning that a cool front was moving through. Not only was that a recipe for a good thunderstorm, but could also trigger a few tornadoes.

The Flint Hills were also part of what was called, "Tornado Alley," a loose geographical description given to an area that was known for frequent and ferocious tornadoes. It was not uncommon to spot some remnant of a tornado lying on the prairie thirty or forty miles away from a town a tornado hit. She found car tags, check books, pieces of fiberglass insulation, and even a ladies purse. The lady was astonished when Sunny called her almost six months after the storm ravaged her home.

Weather forecasters warned residents to find cover in the basement or a community storm shelter whenever the sky grew menacingly black and green. But Spook said, "The best ways to get us durn Kansans out of our house is to sound the tornado sireen! Ever'body runs out'n their house on to the front porch to get a photygraph."

Tornadoes fascinated Sunny like an innocent child fascinated by a rattlesnake. Since she could see for miles across the prairie and spent much time outside, she gained a good feel for the storms that created tornadoes. She saw many wispy ropes of clouds snake menacingly from the sky. Some went back up before they touched ground; some kissed the ground lightly and dissolve; but occasionally a dark swath swirled up the dust and plowed across the ground gnarling anything in its path. Ugly and ominous, they were greatly respected, but stirred within her mysterious feelings of intrigue.

Although she liked to watch a good storm brewing in the sky, she also knew the damage it could bring. Winds that raced at sixty or seventy miles per hour could drop tall cottonwoods on her fence, or lightning could strike the cattle, or hail could destroy the crops. One bad hailstorm could wipe out an entire crop in fifteen minutes. A sudden cool breeze shivered across her tanned forearms.

Her thoughts were interrupted by another voice of the prairie; an unwelcome interloper reminding her there was no escape from civilization. The lonely whine of a single engine airplane could be faintly heard; another intruding voyeur invading her secret place. Although not surprised by its presence - the planes often flew low checking oil and gas lines since they were too lazy to do it from horseback - she was always annoyed by it. Normally, the planes would fly in a straight line, but occasionally they would circle a few times directly over her. Would a slingshot make them stop? Sometimes the pilot waved at her.

One plane that flew low enough she could read the letters and numbers on the back of the plane - 91886N - she memorized it and intended to call someone at the local airport to report it. It didn't come out as often as the ones to check the pipeline, but it flew around the pastures longer. It would sometimes circle over a section for a while and other times it would go back and forth from north to south like it was flying over imaginary grids. She assumed it was someone from the Governor's office since he owned several thousand acres of land adjacent to theirs. She never met him, but he asked Daddy to sell the ranch a number of times and that made her not like him. From what she heard about him, he liked to wear the gear of a cowboy and brag of being a *Kansas Rancher* with large herds of cattle, but he couldn't tell the difference between a bull and a steer.

Suddenly, there was a sputter; the constant drone sounded like someone swallowed wrong. She heard the nasally whine again, a cough, then silence. In the distance, she could see a glint of sunlight reflecting like a mirror from the airplane. She saw enough planes to know that this one was in trouble. The engine would start, whine again, then sputter and nothing but the meadowlark was heard on the prairie. The plane descended too fast as it rushed by Sunny and Starbuck, clipping the tops of the tall grass prairie.

"Oh, my gosh!" Starbuck flinched as Sunny shrieked against the sky, "It's going to crash!"

Chapter Two

Chris Conroy tucked the fly-fishing rod under one arm and reached inside his vest for the plastic box of flies. Fishing for trout was done best while standing in the river but a Colorado morning was hard on dexterity in the fingers. His stubby fingers made knot tying difficult enough; he didn't need the added aggravation of numb fingers. More than once he dropped a box full of flies into the swift moving water. Losing one of his hand-tied flies to a big rainbow was heartbreaking; losing one in a branch was annoying; losing a full box to the river was stupid.

Although the sun wasn't shining on the river yet, the air temperature above the water warmed up enough the little bugs in the water were starting to make it to the surface to hatch wings and fly away. Although this was their destiny, they had to make it past a few voracious trout. Chris never grew tired, even after twenty years of fishing almost every day of the year, of watching Mother Nature work her wonders. Minute eggs clinging to the river's bottom would morph from larvae into nymphs then finally struggle to the surface to emerge into a Caddis Fly or a May Fly. But isn't that life, Chris thought, to struggle and then be eaten by something bigger than you.

This is the *hatch,* and any trout fishermen worth his weight in waders lived for this part of the challenge to *match-the-hatch* as trout rose to their hand-tied mimicry of insects. Chris could tell by the size of the washtub ring on the surface the size of the fish below. As opposed to wet flies that were fished below the surface and usually out of sight, dry flies floated on top of the surface teasing trout to rise.

Chris loved fishing by himself, but guiding another fisherman was a good way to make a living. Although, there were some folks he would rather send down the river instead of helping them fish. He saw his fair share of dandies show up with five hundred dollar waders, four thousand dollar bamboo rods, and a three hundred dollar reel yet still, as his mentor, Ol' Harry, used to say, "Couldn't catch their butt with both hands." They would spout off the Latin names of the insects like entomologists and name-drop about famous fly-tiers as if they were friends. However, it took Chris about five minutes to determine if he was a *dunker*, a person you'd just as soon dunk in the river as fish beside.

Chris met Ol' Harry Whithers on his first trip back into the mountains many years earlier. Chris was backpacking in the Indian Peaks Wilderness and a late spring snowstorm barreled over the Continental Divide and he barely made it out. He waded through the snow with his bear-paw snowshoes wondering if he was going to make it out alive. He finally smelled the wood smoke coming from Harry's cabin and suffering with hypothermia, Chris knocked at the new wood door on the old log cabin. Harry took him in and warmed him up and, from that time on, treated Chris like a son.

After Chris thawed and Harry made him some eggs and bacon on his old wood cook-stove, Harry explained the new door was there because a bear busted down his old one the week before.

"I'd a killed that bear with my bare hands if he would still have been there when I got back. Do you know how hard it is to get a new door all the way up this mountain when you're eighty years old?" Harry growled. "I got my gun loaded and I'm going to shoot the first bear I see even if it is out of season."

Harry taught Chris to fly-fish using a fly rod made from bamboo from the Tonkin range in China. The finest of rods, the master rod builders take bamboo reeds and split them into small shafts that they plane down into six triangular tapered pieces. Chris still had Harry's rod hanging above his fireplace in the cabin.

Harry taught Chris that trout weren't quite as bright as scientists and fishermen believed. While most fly-tiers strained to get the perfect imitation of the insect the trout, Harry made some of the most awful looking flies Chris had ever seen. One looked like a hairy, feathered, turquoise bug the size of a large beetle that exploded. Chris has never seen anything in nature that closely resembled that bug, but Harry caught fish when others got skunked.

"A trout is a sucker for something new," Harry quipped. "But if you're trying to imitate something he eats every day, then you gotta be perfect. But this old ugly blue bug is something he ain't never seen before and he's just got to try a bite of it. Kind of like a woman trying out new lipstick."

Chris cried at Harry's funeral. There were still days he looked down the river expecting to see that old man standing there waving his rod like a maestro conducting a symphony. As he put away his equipment for the day, he would look at the old rod hanging above his fireplace and whisper, *'Nother fine day, Harry, standing in the water waving a stick.*

Chris paid his dues as a guide and was now more selective. Then, he would take anyone willing to pay for his services and left the cabin each day with absolute fear that he wouldn't help anyone catch a fish. But he gained a reputation as one of the best and, if you were a trophy hunter, then Chris Conroy was the man you hired. He held the state record for the biggest cutthroat.

Standing beside him in the river that day was a trophy hunter - a man who cared little about what things cost as long as he could have something to brag about, a man whose fish grew in length with each story repeated. "I don't lie about the size of my fish, I just remember big," he said.

Ron Moore walked into the Orvis store and purchased every expensive piece of clothing and gear related to fly-fishing. A typical dunker, Ron bragged about how much he paid for this, how rare that was, and how much he was willing to tip if Chris could help him catch a state record fish. To Chris, holding the record was more important than some hundred-dollar tip from this loudmouth so he intentionally stayed away from the honey-holes. Not that it really mattered; it took a far better fisherman than Moore to bag a big Brown. But there was always beginners luck and Chris didn't want to risk it.

Moore bragged to Chris about his elevated position in the state government in Kansas and all his connections. Chris nodded his head and tied on another fly for Moore. Chris wondered why people who could afford thousand dollar fly rods couldn't tie their own flies.

"Did I ever tell you about the time the time the Governor and I went fishing in Scotland?" he asked. Chris heard the story every year *ad nauseam*.

"Well, the Scots are mighty uppity about their fly-fishing and if you don't do everything just like they say, they won't let you fish," Moore grumbled again, but Chris just nodded. It was five years since Moore went to Scotland with Kansas Governor Dane Richards. For a fish being dead, Moore's seemed to grow about an inch a year.

Chris pointed Moore to a deep, green eddy formed behind a big boulder. He knew there was at least a twenty-inch rainbow lurking in there and saw him flash a few times earlier that morning. He stood close to Moore's backside as he raised the rod in the air and whipped the line back and forth like a crazed person swatting at a wasp with a pixie stick.

With the crystal clear water of this freestone creek in the mountains, trout had sharp enough vision to see the line above the water, especially if the sun was shining. Moore had terrible form for casting and spent most of his effort false casting. Whipping the line back and forth above him, he either caught the fly in a bush behind him or you could hear the "thunk" of the line hitting the pole and wrapping itself up in a tangled mess. Chris had a two-minute rule: if you couldn't untangle the mess in two minutes, he cut it off and tied a new one on. And when Moore finally did get the line to land on the water, it made such a splash that any self-respecting trout within fifty yards headed for cover.

Chris knew Moore had little chance at the big one lurking behind the rock. The old rainbow didn't get to be big by being stupid. The younger 'bow might bite, but not the big boys. If you were going to catch him, you needed to be sly and maybe even sneak up on the stream

"Come here, big boy," Moore mumbled as he splashed the line across the eddy, sure to frighten even the dumbest 'bow in there. "Come to daddy. Come on, take that ol' fly, you know you want it. What's that you say? That ol' fly not good enough for Mr. Trophy Trout? Well, how 'bout I just give you a rest and come back with a better fly?"

Chris remembered the conversation with his wife about raising his rates this year and guys like Moore were the reason. If Chris had to spend all day on the river with a goober like this, he wanted good money.

Chris looked at the eddy forming behind his own legs. Two large cutthroats decided he was a good place to hide. With Moore deep in conversation with an uncaring trout, Chris lost himself for a few minutes in the world that swirled behind his legs. The bigger cutthroat got the best position near his legs and rested in the slower current waiting for food to drift by. With minimal movement of his tail, he moved into the current and digested a little midge, then slipped back.

Down the stream, fishing in a long, dark pool by himself, was Dane Richards, the Governor of Kansas. Chris wondered how in the world these two ever became friends, but he fished with enough famous people through the years to learn that some relationships like the one between Moore and Dane were based on things besides trust. Maybe one donated large sums of money, or the other helped the one get elected, or maybe there was a distant family connection of uncle so-and-so's first cousin what's-his-name and there you are stuck fishing a beautiful freestone mountain stream with someone you don't even like. Chris watched Dane the night before around the fireplace in the lodge as Moore relived stories of past fishing trips. Dane smiled and nodded his head, but seemed to be lost in thought, mesmerized by the sapphire blue flames dancing on the pine logs. Chris couldn't remember who said that politics made strange bedfellows, but whoever it was, must have been talking about Moore and Dane.

Chris looked down the river to watch Dane fishing. Chris read people as well as he read a river and he learned quickly not to call him *The Great Dane*, which is how Moore would introduce him. Chris saw a flicker in Dane's dark brown eyes like the flash of a rainbow turning its side; it wants nothing to do with you or your lousy imitation.

Dane cut a rustic figure standing knee-deep in the mountain stream coursing the fly rod back and forth with masculine elegance. Moore looked like a maniac swatting at wasps but Dane looked like a maestro conducting the London Philharmonic.

Gently, Dane raised his arm extending the rod to a vertical position and lifted the line softly off the water imperceptible and silent. With a gentle, deliberate motion, Dane moved his arm to a nine o'clock position then abruptly stopped letting the line sail mildly by and unfold soothingly on the water, the fly floating down as light as a feather.

Exploding out of the dark green depths of the eddy, a twenty-four inch rainbow snatched the fly before it hit the water, arching and twisting, the multi-hued colors glistening in the spring sun. Splashing back into the river, the fish dashed downstream stripping the line off Dane's reel. One wrong move and the fish would be gone so Dane just let him run, careful to keep the tip up and the line relatively taut.

While Moore was muttering to phantom fish upstream, Chris admired Dane playing the fish. Dane was fishing a #20 Pale Morning Dun which would barely cover the fingernail of your pinky finger.

Dane slowly reeled the line in tight then the drag on his reel screamed as the trout headed for deeper water.

For twenty minutes, Chris watched Dane struggle with skill against the will of the fish. Chris had a camera handy to take photos of the men and their fish and waded down the stream to get a picture. Dane slipped his hand into the water and gently grabbed the trout by his lower jaw. With a hemostat in his other hand, he removed the barb-less hook from the fish's mouth.

"Thanks anyway, Chris," Dane let the fish go, "but that was too good of a fish to take a picture of. That old boy is going to get a lot bigger and smarter in the years to come; I look forward to challenging wits with him. The best photos are the ones that stay in your mind."

Their conversation was interrupted by the piercing shriek upstream. Moore was holding up a twelve-inch rainbow like it was a trophy. Between the noise of the river and the shrill of Moore, Chris was almost certain he heard Dane whisper, "moron" as Moore slipped and fell headlong into the river.

Chapter Three

Dane Richards felt fully alive in a trout stream. Knowing full well to distance himself from the circus up-stream, Dane found his favorite spot well below Moore's thrashings. Moore didn't realize his splashing around in the river in turn helped Dane because it dislodged bugs attached to the rocks. Nymphs and midges floated down to where Dane was standing and the trout would gorge themselves. Dane tied on imitation midges and nymphs and floated them along with the creatures Moore busted loose; he caught even more fish.

Dane let Moore think he was getting the better deal by fishing upstream in the "honey-hole" that Moore called it. Dane knew big ones hid below those big rocks and hoped that Moore would catch one someday, but his bungling would keep him from catching a fish above twelve inches.

Even though Dane knew Chris was getting paid for guiding Moore, he appreciated the dignity with which Chris treated him. Not once did Chris treat him with any disrespect, although he was certain to have shared some of the blunders with Jennifer when no one was around. Dane noticed Chris moved a little slower than normal when Moore fell in the river; it wasn't deep enough for too much danger of drowning, although if anyone could drown in a foot of water, it would be Moore.

Dane didn't have much of a choice when it came to being friends with Moore – he made a promise to his father-in-law, Jim Moore, when he was dying with cancer to look out for Ron, Moore's only son. Jim was a wise old man and knew that what his son lacked in common sense and smarts, he tried to compensate with arrogance and attitude. Jim liked Dane and knew Dane would keep a tight rein on Moore as well as help find a niche for him in the family business that Dane took over instead of Moore. Jim worked too many years building a business to entrust it to someone like Moore who, as Jim said, didn't have the sense God gave a goose when it came to running a business.

The old man transitioned it to Dane before he died, but it was met with hostility from Moore. They created a new title for him, gave him a newly remodeled office complete with a pretty secretary smarter than Moore, bought him a new company car each year, and gave him a relatively unlimited expense account. They convinced him of the importance of his position and, after a few months, he developed a routine that was settled and safe.

To Danes' surprise, Ron was more of an asset than a liability for the business. Since he was Jim's only son and tagged along with his dad to a variety of business and social functions, he was a known commodity in the good-old-boy network. For those who did business with the old man, having Ron around was a good thing, sort of a quiet testament to a family business surviving in an age of hostile takeovers and corporate restructuring. Their trucking business prospered in an age where a man's word was his bond and the only signature needed to square a deal was a firm handshake and a confident look in the eye.

It was a good compromise, a win-win situation the old man orchestrated to honor his son, keep his business afloat, and help his son-in-law Dane get established in a good business. Through the years Dane learned the fine art of keeping Moore close enough to stay out of trouble but far enough to keep him from doing harm.

Moore was safe to bring on trips like this; trips for relaxation and not for politics. Fishing trips with dignitaries were never relaxing although productive. Whether it was in business or politics, it never mattered which because the basis of both were the same- money and power - Dane mastered the art of losing without taking a dive, victory without a victim, and compromise without violating one's dignity.

Dane replayed the scene in his mind of catching the big trout. He drifted a midge earlier in the morning and saw the water swirl and the big flash from the side of the rainbow. He was sure the fish took the midge and promptly spit it back out so he left the big boy alone and went back later. Fishing for the big trout was no different than landing a big contract in business. One can't be in a hurry in such matters and must use every ounce of skill and cunning to get them to bite. Sometimes you have to walk away for a little bit then come at them with a new presentation. He landed many business contracts like he landed a big trout.

Dane chuckled as the image of Moore splashing around in the water screaming like he was drowning. Chris kept hollering at him just to stand up and he'd be okay but between the noise of the river and Moore's own yelling, he hadn't heard him and consequently thrashed around worse than the little twelve-inch rainbow that he caught.

At the end of the day, Dane slid into the rustic lodge-pole pine rocking chair that creaked near the edge of the stone hearth of his room. The cane seat moaned softly as he unfolded his athletic six-foot-four-inch frame. Running his hands through his coal-black, wavy hair, he let out a sigh that echoed from the empty chambers of his soul. Leaning his head against the back of the rocker, his deep blue eyes reflected the shimmering flames of the pinion pine as he wandered, lost in the mesmerizing blaze. It was a good day on the river; especially watching Moore fall in. Again.

He was hungry; Jenny's breakfast worn away by the cold of the river. No biscuits tasted better than Jennifer Conroy's. Though Dane usually ate a light breakfast, he lost all resolve in the Lodge of the Whispering Pines. Although he asked for the recipe, she insisted it was a secret family recipe and her Aunt Flo would come back to haunt her if she ever divulged the ingredients. Fresh out of the wood-stove oven, Jennifer served them with cinnamon butter that melted one's taste buds into a quivering heap.

As the fire cracked, Dane chuckled remembering that early that day as he put his waders on he swore never to eat that much breakfast again. But he knew that as disciplined as he was, he was certain to repeat this performance again the following morning. He wondered if standing in a mountain stream all day assisted one's metabolism because Chris seemed as fit as a fiddle, yet Dane heard him grunting when he put his waders on, too.

Learning long ago that some memories disappear as quickly as a snowflake on the water if not captured, Dane deliberately relived the memories of this day. Etching in his mind these moments of pleasure, he would later, when surrounded by the frantic pressure of politics and instantaneous decisions that made or destroyed entire careers, recall these memories of a simpler life. These were the photos hung in the halls of his mind.

Suddenly, his mood changed. "Oh, no, here it comes again," Dane moaned.

Like a storm brewing over the ocean and bursting onto the land, the overwhelming waves of grief came as gale-force winds of sadness emptied him of any joy. Try as he could to subdue the torrent of tears, his body trembled and shivered as he reached out into the darkness to feel the touch of Debbie's hand once again.

"Just another minute," he cried in the emptiness of the night. "I would give anything for just another minute with her."

It was almost two years since his wife, Debbie, died but in the darkness he could hear her voice again and see her sitting there in the yellow glow of the fire with her crimson tresses falling over a white robe. For ten of the best years of his life he traveled down the twisting trail of life with the fiery redhead by his side. She was not only his better half; she was the melodic harmony that made his life make sense.

They met at the scene of an accident in college. Walking out of restaurant with some of his buddies, they heard the loud sound of metal crunching and turned around to see a young woman jump out of her car yelling at a driver that smashed the side of her red Mustang. Although he didn't know her yet, Dane was impressed with this fiery beauty giving the other driver a piece of her mind. She suddenly looked at Dane.

"Did you see this? It was his fault, wasn't it? He ran a red light! And they say women drivers are bad! Call the cops! Stay around, you were a witness," she spouted like a Gatling gun.

Dane told her that he hadn't actually seen, but rather heard the accident, but she would have none of him leaving. When the officer finally arrived and asked Dane to fill out a report, he looked at him rather puzzled.

"Well, that won't do us any good!" the officer retorted. "No sense wasting my time and paperwork. I need eyewitnesses!"

Dane wasn't sure why he stuck around but most likely it was because he felt like she needed him to be there even though he was a stranger. He was worried because the other man in the accident seemed to get angrier and started mouthing off to Debbie. The man calmed down, though, and backed away as soon as Dane walked over beside her. As he drew near her, he could see beneath her tough exterior that she was softly shaking inside.

A knock at the door interrupted Dane's thoughts and grief.

"Just a minute," he called. "I'll be right there."

"That's okay, Governor," Chris spoke through the pine door. "I just wanted to see if you still needed a ride to the airport in the morning. Do you want me to pick you up at six?"

"Sure," Dane replied. "Six is great. See you then."

"Good night, Governor. Jenny left a plate on the stove for you whenever you're ready to eat. See you in the morning."

Sleep hid from Dane that night like a slippery shadow in the darkness; always out of reach. When slumber did fall, Dane twisted the sheets in an unconscious cry for the way things used to be.

He wakened long before the alarm sounded at five. He showered and packed his bags, careful to make sure his fly rod was dry from the day before. The man who made the split bamboo rod gave explicit instructions to never pack the rod in its case while it was still wet.

Moore, as usual, stumbled out excuses for being late. Dane's Dad passed on to him the philosophy that if you're not at least twenty minutes early, you're late, and so Dane was always punctual. Moore, however, was late to everything. Dane tired of his lame excuses through the years and raised his hand when Moore started, as if to say, *I've heard them all.*

As the lights of the Jeep bounced against the tamaracks, Dane looked across the meadow still resting in time between the shadow of night and the pale dawn of the morning. A gentle mist rose off the serpentine Cascade Creek winding lazily through the meadow. A bull elk grazing in the tall grasses pierced the morning with a shrill whistle; months away from the time of rut when that same whistle would seek a cow for mating or another bull for fighting.

Dane made a mental clicking sound as if he was a photographer snapping the shutter of a camera to record this fleeting moment in time. Dane stored this memory in his archives, like the one from the day before of catching the big rainbow, to be retrieved and relived at a later time when any slice of heaven seemed so different from the hell that sometimes surrounded him in life. Like an artist who freezes a moment in time and captures the essence of a feeling, Dane stored this in the gallery of his soul for those meditative retreats among dizzying distractions of day-to-day life.

"Heaven must look a lot like this," Dane spoke as they sputtered out of the canyon. "Or at least that's what I want my heaven to look like." Chris and Moore nodded in agreement, both at a loss for words to describe the beauty.

Winding slowly up the switchbacks, Dane lost himself in thought as the others talked about fishing and hunting. Dane felt the stress rise with each mile they climbed out of the peaceful valley. Within a day he would be back in front of the public answering questions about school financing or meeting behind closed doors with heads of industry or deflecting criticism of his views on the environment. Debbie warned him that the political arena was like the herd of wildebeests on Wild Kingdom in which the predators stalked the weak and vultures feasted upon the dying. But he had today yet to enjoy, before the onslaught of the unknown tomorrow.

Chris pulled the Jeep beside the classy red and white Cessna 182 that was parked in the grass along the field. An orange windsock dangling from a rusty pipe floated softly in the breeze – wind out of the north/northwest – and the cerulean sky was dotted with cotton ball clouds shimmering brightly in the morning sun; a fine day for flying.

Dane loved to fly almost as much as he loved to fish. After he and Debbie married, her father decided it was cheaper for Dane to fly rather than pay commercial prices. Dane learned from one of the best pilots around; a retired pilot that flew commercial for years. Not only had Dane studied under a master, but he also developed a deep friendship with the old pilot. In fact, there was no man's company he enjoyed more than his old pilot friend.

"There's old pilots, and there's bold pilots," Jim would say before the start of each session. "But there ain't no old, bold pilots so son, don't get me kilt."

Jim Cunningham was the funniest man Dane knew. Once you crawled in the cockpit, there was none better than Jim. But sitting around a dinner table with him made you think he was as a comedian.

"Don't be funny when we're flying," Dane told Jim several times. "I can't laugh, cry, and fly all at the same time."

"Fly your airplane, son," Jim said. "I ain't ready to meet my Maker because of some dumb Kansas plowboy what don't know the difference between the rudder and propeller!"

"Ron, do you mind grabbing my stuff too?" Dane asked Moore as they were getting out of the Jeep. "I need to run in and check the FBO before we go."

Once inside, Dane found the Fixed Base Operative to check the weather. His brow tightened and eyebrows furrowed as he saw Marginal VFR warning on the screen along with the icing level at 8,000 feet. Pushing the chair away from the table, he consoled himself that where he was going in Kansas was only 1,200 feet so he would, in essence, descend the entire way and fly below 8,000 feet. Nevertheless, it wasn't as clear of a weather report as he wanted.

Dane looked at his checklist as Moore put the last of their stuff in the airplane. Jim drilled in to him the importance of deliberately going over the checklist, one item at a time, so it took Dane longer than some. He was glad it was just the two of them now – not as much gear and a little roomier than if they brought others. Dane reached for the ignition and the familiar sound of the Lycoming I0-540 and all of its 230 horsepower roared to life.

Taxiing to the open runway, Dane spoke into his headset, "Tower, Niner-one-eight-eight-six-November requesting permission to take off."

"Niner-one-eight-eight-six-November, this is tower," a voice squeaked through the ear piece. "You are clear to take off."

Pushing the throttle forward, the sleek Cessna 182 dashed down the runway and lifted into a destiny no prophet could foretell.

Chapter Four

The sleek Cessna 182 rose flawlessly in the brilliant morning sun kissing the dew off the grassy slopes of the eastern slope of the Rockies; a nice grass strip on the front side of the Continental Divide. Taking off from that plateau and drifting out over the leveled high plains was a lot easier than trying to deal with the wind, the upslope fog, and low visibility those massive mountain ranges seemed to create. Almost like their own little world, the Rockies had weather patterns, up-drafts, downdrafts, and a host of other tricks up its sleeve to make a novice pilot, like Jim said, *get sweaty palms.*

The noise of the engine made conversation difficult so Dane didn't have to worry about visiting with Moore. Moore had motion sickness anyway and took medicine to fall sleep quickly. As they flew over the plains, he mused to himself how nice it would be to be away from the public life of politics. He daydreamed of a career flying people into remote areas for fishing expeditions.

But, for now, his life as a politician was all consuming. His father-in-law encouraged him to run for office and the preliminary polls indicated the people were quite disgusted with the incumbent and were ready for a more reputable leader. Dane dealt with huge contracts involving millions of dollars in negotiations with other companies in the business sector, but he was surprised at the amount of money involved in politics.

He was surprised that Debbie was so excited about politics. He kidded her that she liked politics so she could dress up for fancy banquets. While she did look stunning in an evening gown and turned the eye of every man as she danced, there was a fire in her eyes when it came to shrewd political maneuvering. She played the game with keen awareness of nuances and connotations that Dane often missed. He paid attention to her opinions of issues and people. More than once she warned him to be cautious of a certain person and, within time, her suspicions were warranted.

Dane missed that about Debbie. There was such an outpouring of support after she died. Perhaps it was her Irish fire mixed with a little mid-western charm that caused even her enemies to respect her, but no one questioned where they stood with her. The governor of Oklahoma's wife, who was considered one of the more unpleasant women in the tight circle of governors, was so kind as to say of Debbie that, "She could be trusted as a friend, feared as an foe, and somehow convince you of her point-of-view no matter how mightily you disagreed with her."

"Fly your plane, son," Dane heard Jim's advice run through his mind.

Dane looked at the controls and everything seemed to be fine. Although there was hardly a cloud in the sky and the wheat fields, still green before harvest, laid out on the ground in their symmetrical square grids of Jeffersonian surveying tactics, Dane knew that trouble was brewing along the plains. The Midwest had been socked in with a warm, humid spell in which temperatures were unseasonably warm. Although this was good for the wheat crop to turn gold, it made for bad weather whenever a blast of Canadian air ripped down from the north. Dane knew that mixing a cold front with warm, moist air moving inland from the Gulf of Mexico was like tossing a coon on top of a coon-dog treading water; all hell could break loose and you didn't know whether to run away or jump in after them.

But the sky was clear and their groundspeed was better than the forecasted winds so Dane picked a course heading south/southeast to fly over his land. Often, just to get away from the dizzying distractions of phones and meetings, Dane climbed into his airplane and flew south of the capitol to check on various land holdings that he held with his father-in-law.

His latest acquisition was the old Clatterbuck homestead in the Flint Hills. He chuckled to himself remembering the dealings; an unusual family whose great-grandpa homesteaded the land over a hundred years before, they were the quintessential Kansas rancher. Fiercely independent and sentimentally simple, they were more concerned with who got the land instead of how much they could sell it for.

Josiah Clatterbuck was in his nineties when his wife of seventy years, Ethel, passed away and left him on the ranch alone. Josiah and Ethel lived in the house for over fifty years and hadn't done a thing to it; it was already fifty years old when they moved in. Heating with only a wood stove in the winter and sleeping with the windows open in the summer, the Clatterbucks raised eight kids in the old farmhouse. The old oak floors were worn and the screens on the windows were tattered, but it was home. When Dane negotiated with them, Charlie, the oldest son, recalled going to bed in winter fully dressed and waking up with snow an inch deep on the inside of the window sills.

But Josiah needed to move to town for the doctor. The ranch was so big that none of the kids could afford it and they all decided the best thing to do was to sell it outright and have Josiah live out the rest of his life in as much ease as possible. That seemed the fairest solution to them, one that would keep the family from splitting over squabbles about who got more than the other. Little did they know that old Josiah would die not more than six weeks after leaving the ranch; he just drifted off to sleep and never woke up. He left the ranch willingly, but his heart stayed out in the old two-story clapboard house where he and Ethel hammered out seventy years of marriage.

Dane recognized a good investment in the vast holding of pasture was a great tax shelter as well as a way to keep a heritage of Kansas alive. For over a century, cattle grazed these pasture lands and would for centuries to come. Dane had no intention of interrupting the rhythm of the prairie; he knew that working with local agricultural experts they could maintain the ecosystem. There would not over-graze on his property and each parcel would be carefully monitored. This was a great, vast, natural resource that Dane intended to maintain, not profit from.

He heard about Ethel Clatterbuck finding the adobe oven exposed on the flood swept bank of the creek She told a couple of locals about it and by the time it was over, there was almost a community war over the university restricting the site and all the locals who felt a right to trespass on private land to see local heritage. Josiah rode up and down the creek with a shotgun just to warn people not to traipse on his land. If the archaeologists hadn't been so arrogant and controlling, it might have been a good thing for the community, but by the time it was over, it left a bad taste in everyone's mouth, even the archaeologists who didn't find what they were looking for. Whether or not Ethel actually showed them where she found it or, like some, assumed Josiah directed them to another place where he knew the diggers wouldn't find much, no one really knew and neither Josiah nor Ethel were forthcoming with the truth.

Suddenly, Dane felt the bottom of his seat drop out from under him as the plane lurched sideways. Gripping the controls, Dane braced himself for the next invisible force to jolt his airplane. He flew in turbulence before and it never bothered him much, but he was startled by this suddenness. Moore groaned awake.

"Oh, just a little rough air," Dane assured. "Go back to sleep. It will be all right."

Moore readjusted his pillow that he was drooling on against the side window of the plane and drifted back to sleep.

Dane looked out his window to the left and saw on the northern horizon the faint dark of clouds. Along that line, he knew, would be the leading edge of that cold front. The forecaster said the weather would be great until late afternoon and since it was mid-morning, he should make it in plenty of time.

His father, Johnson Richards, would be waiting for him at the airport, along with the Lieutenant Governor Greg Simms. He would park his airplane in the hangar then be whisked to a meeting with the State Board of Education. School financing was always an issue and even though schools received almost three-quarters of each state dollar in taxes, they were always struggling for funding. While this was an issue that many states struggled with, he approached the process with an attitude that he could help foster communication between all the entities involved and eventually they would come up with a workable solution. As long as there was healthy dialogue, then solutions could be found.

He found much wisdom in the counsel of his father. His father said there were two kinds of people in life, either problem makers or problem solvers. Any idiot, his father would say, can identify a problem, but a good leader helps folks find a solution. Dane chuckled to himself knowing that simple, homespun advice from those who weathered the Great Depression and the Dust-Bowl in Kansas was far better than high-paid consultants whose advice was based on the latest polls rather than common sense and what was good for the people.

Dane pondered the strategies to facilitate positive discussion. It annoyed him that what they discussed in the meetings was reported in the papers the next day with an entirely different twist. He read the newspaper and wondered if the reporter was at the same meeting. But that was politics and journalism.

Another jolt of turbulence rocked Dane. The dark line to the north was advancing rapidly so he drifted south a little further. Banking his airplane, he looked back to the southwest and saw clouds coming together with the unmistakable beginnings of a thunderstorm. Some storms, like the one coming in from the north, already built up it's powerful, dark, brooding punch and would barrel across the country like a freight train with it's weight pushing forward. Others, like the one to the southwest, erupted out of nowhere with the punching power of a brawling boxer.

Dane got nervous. The storm from the north he could avoid by flying to Oklahoma. But this new storm to the southwest now blocked that path.

"Flight Watch," Dane radioed ahead. "Niner-one-eight-eight-six-November requesting flight advisory, over."

"Niner-one-eight-eight-six-November," a calm woman's voice cackled over the radio. "This is Flight Watch. What is your position, altitude, and direction of flight, over?"

"Flight Watch, I am currently at seven thousand feet heading south-southeast and see thunderstorms off to the south-southwest. Please advise of current weather conditions, over," Dane said.

"Current weather conditions," the soothing voice betrayed the impending report, "show a series of thunderstorms forming a squall-line moving north/northeast zero six five degrees at fifteen to eighteen knots, over."

An overwhelming panic gripped Dane. That was the worst possible news that he could get. The popcorn-size hail from the thunderstorms forming in the squall line had the ferocity of a shark feeding frenzy on a single-engine plane bouncing through the sky. With almost hurricane force winds and invisible wind shears, his small airplane would bounce around like a lotto ball in the squirrel cage.

"Fly your airplane, son," Dane heard the familiar voice of Jim in his mind. Jim warned Dane that when pilots started getting in trouble it became like a snowball tumbling down a hill with increasing momentum until one simple error proved fatal. Taking a deep breath to steel his nerves, he slowly considered his options.

To go back would be pointless; he was too far to return to the airport and the storm could easily overtake the course he just traveled. Although he had adequate fuel to make it home, it was a long way back if he turned around. He considered the possibility of finding a level field below but he couldn't tie the airplane down to anything secure. His tiny airplane alone on the prairie, although worth a half million dollars, would be tossed about like a plastic model with wind gusts up to a hundred miles per hour.

Dane's best bet would be to try to squeeze between the storms, a task that might prove as impossible as leading a camel through the eye of a needle. Once again he heard Jim's advice, *Head for the light spot!* Dane scanned the horizon in front of him for the lightest part, that eye of the needle he needed to thread.

The storm to the south was building with beautiful ferocity and billowing thunderheads that seemed to boil up out of the checkerboard fields below. Clouds collided and clashed doubling then tripling in size; arcs of concentrated lighting shot from cloud to cloud then ground to cloud. It was a terrorizing combustion of nature that crashed with dazzling white clouds set starkly against the cerulean sky.

Suddenly an updraft like an invisible rush of an ocean current of air lifted the plane in startled ascent. Fear crawled over Dane as he watched his altimeter spin wildly. He was cruising along at six thousand feet but uncontrollably the plane lifted to seven thousand then eight thousand feet. Drops of rain mixed with ice began to pelt against the windshield.

"What's going on?" Moore wakened.

"Nothing," Dane replied. "Just ran into a bit of weather here, but we'll be okay." Dane had his own concerns and he didn't want the burden of comforting the frightened Moore's inner child.

"Are we going to make it?" Moore peered against the pelting rain. "Where are we anyway?"

"Fly your plane, son," Jim whispered to him again. Moore's question brought him back to reality of flying the airplane instead of watching the chaos outside. Fortunately, Jim trained Dane to fly the airplane watching only the instruments, completely oblivious and unable to see the world outside the windshield. Dane checked his instruments as the plane lifted by an invisible hand.

He worried about the rain mixed with sleet that meant they were high enough for the airplane to ice. Hail formed as raindrops went through a cycle of falling then climbing high enough to freeze then falling again only to be caught by another updraft. Icing not only made the aircraft heavier, it began to ice over the air breather causing induction icing which would restrict or even cut off the air flow of the engine causing. No air; no engine.

The plane, which seemed to have a mind of its own with the updraft, now felt sluggish against the turbulence. Moore fidgeted nervously.

Like jumping free-fall from a hundred-story building, Dane's stomach climbed into his mouth as a sudden down draft cut the support from under the plane; the invisible hand forced the plane back down into the coming storm.

"Fly your plane, son," Dane spoke out above the din of rain pelting against the plane.

"What'd you say?" Moore shouted back at Dane. Dane glanced over at Moore and saw the sheer terror in his eyes.

"We're doing fine!" Dane shouted. "Just fine!" Years of public speaking taught Dane how to control his emotions with measured speech and deliberation. "Nothing much different that riding a roller coaster!" Dane forced a laugh.

Dane watched the altimeter spin backwards as the plane descended. He controlled the plane well enough to point it to the light spot on the horizon, but he was helpless to control the rate of descent. He felt the invisible hand level out around seven thousand feet. The outside air temperature was forty-five degrees, not near as warm as Dane would have liked it but certainly better than freezing.

"I've got to go to the bathroom," Moore blurted. Dane found his anger rising towards Moore, something he was usually able to keep under control but this was life-and-death and he didn't really care to hear of Moore's bladder problem. Dane warned him that morning not to drink so much coffee but Moore, as usual, made a braggadocios comment about being able to hold it longer than anyone. He better hope that was true.

Dane's knuckles turned white as the plane lurched side-ways hit by another invisible force. Often the challenge of flying is reacting to things you can't see.

Dane watched his altimeter slowly start to climb again. Another updraft. Eight thousand, then nine thousand feet and now the rain was ice as Dane watched the rpm start to slow; the air breather was icing over. Still rising, the plane's engine sputtered then stopped. Dane restarted it again in only a couple of seconds but seemed, with temporal distortion, to last ten minutes.

"Are we out of fuel?" Moore screamed and grabbed the controls on his side.

"Get your hands off the controls!" Dane shouted at Moore. "I'm the one flying this airplane, not you! I mean it, get your hands off NOW!"

Moore pulled his hands off the controls and twisted nervously in his seat. Dane peered through the freezing glass but to no avail. The light spot disappeared but he kept the plane headed due east. Sputtering again, the engine stopped completely. However, the altimeter slowly climbed as the updraft lifted the plane. With only the sound of the rain and ice pelting against the plane, Dane, for the first time, accepted the reality that he might possibly die. The words he penned after a long walk on the prairie years before came to mind:

A place where no one dies
A place where no one cries
And my heart finds its healing rest
In my Father's house this journey ends
And the winding road no longer bends
And my heart finds its healing rest
From the winding road.

He tried in vain to start the engine.

"At least I'll get to see Debbie," he thought to himself. "It will be good to see her again."

"We're going to die!" Moore shrieked.

"Shut up, Ron!" Dane screamed back.

The altimeter stopped and Dane watched with bated breath as it slowly began to reverse in decent. He hoped another down draft would slowly lower them rather than leave a vacuum; the iced over plane would fall like an ice cube dropped from a four story house.

Moore vomited into a large plastic baggy and Dane felt himself getting light headed. He never had motion sickness but this ride was unlike anything he had ever been on with abrupt sideway shifts and sudden rising and falling. "Focus," he kept telling himself, "Fly your plane. Fly your plane."

An ear splitting scream pierced the cab as Moore shrieked, "God you've got to save us!" He grabbed at the controls again and Dane slammed his elbow into Moore's chest, "Keep your hands off!"

Dane tried again to start the engine but the outside temperature was below freezing; he would wait until they got back to lower altitude and warmer conditions. The eerie silence of the engine but the thunderous roar of the weather outside was suffocating. The plane twisted and shuddered against the wind and rain. Lower, lower, lower, it descended. Moore was thrashing about in his seat and reached for the door handle.

"You'll get us both killed if you open that door!" Dane shouted at Moore. Dane wished he could get one hand free and knock Moore out.

"God, you've got to save us!" Moore sobbed in the enveloping gloom. "I promise if you get us out of here alive I will never be unfaithful to my wife again. Please don't kill us God!"

Although Dane was consumed with flying the plane, he was surprised at this confession. He was as close to Moore as anyone but never imagined that he was unfaithful. Dane never did understand how any woman could be attracted to Moore and Debbie often joked that the only way Moore got a girl was because of a rich daddy.

The plane trembled again as Dane tried to start it to no avail. Slowly they shuddered through the storm. Seven thousand feet; six thousand; five thousand. Finally, the temperature warmed up and ice melted off the windshield. Dane tried to start the engine. It sputtered to a start, ran for a few seconds, then sputtered silent. Moore screamed again and the plane shook. Dane was suddenly inundated with the strong stench of urine; Moore wet himself.

Four thousand; three thousand. Dane found the light spot now widening out and visibility much better. He tried the ignition and the engine sputtered to life. A wave of relief washed over Dane and he expelled the breath he was holding.

But as soon as the plane started, it sputtered again and stopped. Two thousand. Dane scanned the horizon to find a place to land. This was familiar country to him; he spied a place in the distance flat enough to land. If he could just get the engine to run for a little bit he might make it. He tried again and, again, the engine sputtered to life.

Dane sighed as the plane's engine engaged and the plane leveled out. He made it between the storms and the path to the light spot led him out of harm's way. Moore slumped against the side with the vomit from his baggie all over his lap and down his legs. The stench was pungent.

The engine died again. Dane gripped the controls as the plane descended again. This was no down draft this time, this was just a plane falling out of the sky and even though it had wings, it wasn't built for gliding. Dane tried the engine again. It sputtered then stopped. One thousand.

In the distance, Dane could see an open, undulating, pasture that was lined on both sides by a hedgerow of trees. Although not as flat as he would have preferred, by this time he had no choice. The engine started.

Eleven hundred. Twelve hundred. The engine died again.

One thousand. Nine hundred. The ground was rushing at them. Moore screamed and covered his face with his hands. The engine sputtered to life and they leveled out again. They flew a few minutes then the engine died. Eight hundred. Seven. Six. Five. Four. Three.

Dane started the engine again and he could control plane, but they were headed down too fast for him to pull out.

Two hundred. One hundred. Dane saw the tall grass below waving in the wind. He hoped there would be no big rocks hidden in the grass where he was going to land.

Fifty. Twenty-five. Moore's screams nearly burst his eardrums.

Ten feet. Five feet. Dane felt the grass clipping the main landing gear and the nose dip. The grass was too tall to land in; it would bind the landing gear and entangle the propeller. The plane shook violently and Dane found it impossible to maintain grip on the controls.

Rising up out of nowhere, Dane saw the barbwire fence snaking across as the plane rushed at break-neck speed. The propellers shattered as it hit a fence post and Dane felt the back of the plane rise and stand them on end. The engine groaned and metal shrieked as the airplane twisted into a pretzel. Dane felt a searing stab in his right leg as he covered his face with his hands; the twisting metal screamed at the snarling engine. A solid "thunk" against his head exploded a thousand stars screaming in the night sky.

The light spot he was flying towards was brighter and Dane was so dazzled by its brilliance that he lifted his hand to shield his eyes. It was a sweet, warm light that coaxed him into a place he had never been before. He heard his name being called, no, whispered gently against the prairie, as he suspended above it with weightlessness. He looked down and saw the twisted red and white metal pieces of an airplane mangled in wire and tall grass. Suddenly, a woman's face appeared right before his face. Her skin glistened and her eyes flashed with thunderheads and lightning. He saw his reflection in the storm.

Chapter Five

Sunny's heart froze as the plane bobbed in its rapid descent against the darkening sky. Starbuck pointed his ears sharply to the odd noise and shifted uneasily ready to run but not sure where or why. Starbuck leaped forward when Sunny, unknowingly, let out a yelp when the plane's landing gear dragged in the tall grasses.

"They are going to hit the fence!" Sunny shouted to no one, but Starbuck leaped again. As soon as the words left her mouth, she saw the tail section flip up and the nose entangle itself in the wire.

Although a half a mile away, the sound of the grinding metal and the growl of the engine shivered her soul. Twisting, turning, flipping, the carnage of metal and sound crumpled in the deep prairie grass. She expected it to burst into flames at any minute. She was paralyzed momentarily with fear. Should she go to the plane? What happened if it exploded? Should she ride to the house and get help? It was almost a mile back to the house and precious time could be lost either way.

She squeezed her legs against Starbuck and raced toward the crash. Along the fence the grass wasn't as tall so they scrambled up the hill as the wind started picking up. The storm advanced fast across the prairie and soon the rain would be upon them. The smell of rain in the air was usually sweet, but as they drew closer to the site, Starbuck threw his head in protest at the unfamiliar smell of fuel.

Cresting the hill, Starbuck stopped immediately and began to shy away from the metal alien. Sunny nudged him on but he danced sideways and threw his head. Even a well-trained horse like Starbuck could not resist the self-preservation instinct. Sunny dismounted and ran fearfully towards the wreckage. A gumdrop sized raindrop splashed against her bare arm as she stumbled amongst the rocks and grasses.

"Oh my gosh!" Sunny shrieked in horror as she parted the last section of grass and saw the crumpled heap. Gas dripped out of the wing, which was disconnected and twisted onto a rock, and Sunny spied a pool of blood near the cockpit. The plane flipped over and the wing lodged in the twisted landing gear. Sunny climbed over the wing trying to reach the cockpit. A large boulder on the other side wedged the door of the plane and the only way in was under the wing. She wondered how many were in there and if they were alive or dead.

She could not reach the cockpit so she tried to lift the wing. Someone groaned inside the airplane as she tried in vain to move the wing. How was she going to get it off? Should she race back to the house and call the sheriff?

Starbuck whinnied in the background and she remembered her rope. The rain increased as the thunder grew closer. Lightning danced across the darkening sky as she scrambled back to get Starbuck. She grabbed her rope from the side of the saddle.

"Come on, Starbuck," Sunny grabbed his bridle. "I need your help. There are people hurt and they need us."

Starbuck reluctantly moved forward overcoming his fear and desire to flee. He trusted Sunny and knew she would never lead him to a place of harm.

Looping the lasso end of the rope around the end of the wing, the rain fell harder; pea-sized hail slapped her forearm. Sunny took the other end of the rope back to Starbuck and quickly jumped into the saddle.

Dallying the rope around the saddle horn, Sunny turned Starbuck sideways and clicked her heels against his side. Starbuck lunged against and the rope tightened. Sunny knew Starbuck was strongest if she could get him to pull more directly from behind but she was afraid to get caught between the rope and the saddle. The wing barely moved as Starbuck strained.

Suddenly the loop shot off the wing and Sunny almost fell of Starbuck as the sudden release sent him stumbling into the grass. Hail pelted them harder as Sunny tried to get the loop around the wing again. To pull directly with the tapered wing was going to be impossible so they would have to pull it to the side.

"Come on, boy," Sunny coaxed Starbuck. "Let's try that again."

Climbing back on Starbuck, her leather gloves were so slick she had a hard time hanging on to the rope as she tied it off around the saddle horn. Squeezing her legs against him, Starbuck lurched forward and the wing began to move. Creaking and groaning against the strain, Starbuck finally pulled the wing off the plane.

"Good boy," Sunny patted his soaking wet neck. "You done good, Starbuck!"

Dismounting again, Sunny coiled her rope as she ran back to the plane. She shivered against the pouring rain and gripped her hat as the wind raged.

Kneeling down by the plane, she found the handle of the door and tried to open it. The wreckage was twisted enough that the door was jarred shut. Her wet gloves provided little gripping power as she grabbed the edge of the door and tried to open it.

"God help me," she shouted against the storm.

Bracing her feet against the plane she strained until it felt like her back would break. Finally, she felt the door open just a little bit. She relaxed for a few seconds, found a better grip, and began to pull again. Blood spilled into the rain and mud as she peered in. The sudden stench of vomit mixed with urine and blood caused Sunny's stomach to convulse; she stifled a desire to retch.

Sunny saw the two men twisted in their seatbelts in the wreckage, both either unconscious or dead as they hung upside down. Should she just leave them there or cut them down? If she cut them down, she would have to drag them outside and with the storm raging that might not be good either. But if they stayed upside down and they were alive, that might be worse.

Taking her gloves off her hands, she reached inside the cockpit and found the hand of the pilot. It was still warm as she placed her finger on his wrist. He had a pulse! Racing back to Starbuck, she reached inside her saddlebags for the knife. Tying the rope on hard and fast around the horn, she began to uncoil it as she stumbled through the mud back to the plane. The pilot was a big man and she would not be able to pull him out by herself.

Back at the plane, she cut the pilot free. He collapsed in a heap with his arms flailing to the side. Sunny lifted his head matted with blood and mud and slipped the lasso around his chest and arms. She noticed a deep gash in the skull through his dark, wavy hair.

"Back!" Sunny barked at Starbuck through rain. She felt the rope tighten as Starbuck pulled against the body. Starbuck sensed he must be gentle and slowly backed up. Sunny twisted the pilot's arms and made sure his legs weren't trapped as Starbuck continued to pull.

"Whoa!" she shouted as she saw the leg wedged under the dash. Starbuck stopped.

Reaching under the dash to get at the knee, Sunny felt the huge gash in his leg. Blood rushed down her arm as she moved the leg.

"Back!" the rope tightened again. The man began to groan. Sunny saw the bone that pierced the skin.

Slowly, Sunny guided the pilot through the wreckage and mud as Starbuck backed away. He moaned as the horse gently dragged him.

"Whoa!" she shouted.

Unwinding the lasso from around his chest, Sunny inspected his wounds. Rain washed the blood into a puddle underneath the man's head and leg. Untying her bandana from her neck, she pressed hard on the head wound to stop the bleeding.

She had to stop the bleeding in the leg with some sort of

tourniquet, but the leg was too thick and muscular for her bandana. Running the saddlebag inventory through her mind, she suddenly thought of baling wire. She always carried baling wire, the rancher's universal fix-all, so she raced back to find a strip of wire as well as a rain slicker. The man was wearing shorts and she hated to wrap the wire against his skin, but if she didn't stop the bleeding he would die. Twisting the wire tighter with the pliers, she the blood slowed to a trickle. She cut the bottom half of a leg off her jeans and used it to wrap around the bloodied leg.

The rain eased a little. Like most thunderstorms, they travel quickly across the land. Sunny prayed this one would hurry. The man moaned as she wrapped his legs and his eyes fluttered open. The deep blue eyes gazed up at Sunny's with a desperate yet silent plea for help. "Thank you," the man grimaced as she cinched down the wrap. "Is my friend okay?"

"You just hush," Sunny shielded his face against the rain with her hat. He drifted unconscious again.

She covered him with the slicker and moved to the plane. A bolt of lightning hit so close the ball of fire almost blinded her. Immediately a deafening roar of thunder clapped and startled both her and Starbuck. Being on top of a hill in a thunderstorm was asking for trouble, especially with all the metal lying around.

Peering inside, she found the other man. She felt his wrist for a pulse and he was alive too. Grabbing the stiff webbing of the seatbelt, she quickly cut through. She was thankful her dad made her buy good knives and taught her how to keep them sharp. Her brothers would be proud of her, too. She wished they could see her now.

The passenger crumpled in a heap in a puddle of water, mud, and blood. "Come!" she hollered at Starbuck. She was going to have to move Starbuck to the other side of the airplane to pull the passenger out. She moved Starbuck around the plane, careful to step between the wreckage. Although the rain made it difficult, at least it kept the plane from bursting into flames.

"Whoa!" she said when she had enough rope. He didn't seem as wounded as the other man, but she was repulsed by the vomit on his clothing and the strong stench of urine.

"Back!" she commanded Starbuck and he slowly eased back. The rain drizzled and the passenger's body slid easily through the mud and grass. "Easy. Back. Back." Starbuck never performed better, almost as if he knew he was saving a human's life.

"Whoa!" she said as Starbuck dragged him close to a rock. "That's a good boy, Starbuck. Come! Whoa!" As Starbuck moved forward, the tension on the rope released allowing her to undo the rope. She looked but couldn't find any major cuts or wounds, but could see a bump on his head that seemed quite large and some scratches on his face. He would be all right, but she better get the other one help.

Racing around the airplane, she found that the bandana stopped the flow from his head wound and the makeshift tourniquet of baling wire stopped most of the bleeding from the leg. The man's eyes fluttered as he moaned to sit up. Even though severely injured, she could feel the strong, muscular chest flex as she pressed her hands against him to gently push him back down. She heard him whisper, "Who are you? Where am I?"

"I'm Sunny and you're in the Flint Hills. You're going to be okay but you need to be still. I've got to go get help." He drifted off again before she could finish.

"Come!" Starbuck snaked his way through the wreckage. She swung in the saddle and squeezed her knees; they raced to the house.

"Whoa, Starbuck, Whoa!" Sunny pulled back on the reins. Setting his haunches almost down in the ground, Starbuck planted his front feet and slid to a stop. *Why didn't I think of that?* Sunny wheeled Starbuck around and raced back to the wreckage. Jumping off the horse before he was completely stopped, she raced to the most wounded man and reached beneath him and found the pocket with his wallet. She found his driver's license and squinted at the name: Quinton D. Richards.

She recognized the photo on the license; he was the Governor of Kansas.

Chapter Six

Starbuck sliced through the prairie grass. The saddle was sopping wet and Sunny's jeans were soaked to the skin, but she barely noticed as they sped across the prairie with her tight in the saddle. It was a long way for the ambulance and nothing but a four-wheel drive could cross the soaked prairie.

Starbuck rounded the corner corral and instead of heading for the barn, he knew to get Sunny to the house. Sunny dismounted before he stopped and threw open the screen door on the back porch. Her boots were so wet she almost fell on the linoleum floor. Grabbing the phone on the wall, she quickly dialed 9-1-1.

"This is 9-1-1 dispatch, may I help you?" a woman said.

"Yes, my name is Sunny Morgan," she said. "And there's been a plane crash in my pasture!"

"Could you tell us the location, Ma'am", the dispatcher asked.

"Yes, we are on the Lonesome Star Ranch on 19647 North West Satchel Creek Road. The crash happened in the northwest corner of the section."

"How many people were in the plane?"

"Two. They are both unconscious but one of them is badly hurt."

"We'll send an ambulance right out."

"Ma'am," Sunny said. "It has been raining and there is no way an ambulance can get out there. Can you send a helicopter?"

"Ma'am, I will have to send the Sheriff first and he will have to authorize a Life-Flight helicopter."

"Ma'am," Sunny was getting frustrated. "There is no way that one man will make it if we have to wait on the Sheriff to get here. It's forty miles out here and another fifteen minute drive if the pasture is dry, but we've been hammered with an inch of rain in the last hour and an ambulance just won't make it."

"I'm sorry, Ma'am", the dispatcher droned. "Only an officer at the scene can authorize a helicopter."

"But it's the Governor!" Sunny shouted. "I read his drivers' license and it is Governor Richards!"

"Ma'am," the dispatcher questioned. "Are you sure that's Governor Richards?"

"The name on his license was Quinton D. Richards and I recognized his photo!" Sunny burst into the phone.

Sunny heard the dispatcher ask someone else in the room what the Governors real name was but the other person didn't know. A pregnant pause ensued.

"Ma'am, I'm going to have to put you on hold while I check this out."

"On hold! A man is dying on the prairie and some bureaucratic nonsense puts a caller on hold!" Sunny shouted at the phone.

"Ma'am," the dispatcher came back on the phone. "We are sending a helicopter out there. You do realize, ma'am, that if you are calling in a false report it is a criminal offense, don't you?"

"Ma'am," Sunny said. "If it takes me going to jail to save a man's life, then have the Sheriff arrest me on the way out. Tell your pilot to be looking in the northwest section of the Lonesome Star Ranch for a horse and a red blanket laying on the ground."

Sunny slammed the phone down. What a ridiculous waste of time. She needed help now! Her friend Shauna could help; she took several classes in sports medicine. As she picked up the phone to call, she felt herself start to get dizzy. *Not now*, she thought, *this is not the time to pass out.*

She dialed again.

"Hello?" A groggy female voice answered.

"Hey Shauna, I need your help," Sunny said. "There's been a plane crash out by the knoll. Come as quick as you can!"

As Sunny raced upstairs, she thought to herself, *I can always depend on Shauna. It's good to have a friend who sticks by you no matter what happens.*

Rummaging through the cedar chest, she found the blankets. Although the red one had sentimental value – her grandmother gave it to her because it matched the school colors – it would be the most visible. Rushing to the medicine cabinet in the bathroom, she grabbed boxes of gauze and tape. She glanced in the mirror and saw blood on her face and in her hair.

Going down the stairs too fast, she stumbled and almost fell. *Slow down! You don't need the ambulance coming to get you.*

The wooden screen door slammed shut behind her as she sped to Starbuck. She stuffed the blankets and gauze inside the saddlebags, slipped her foot in the stirrup and raced off.

The thundering hooves on the prairie echoed. *Will they still be alive?* She hadn't checked the other man's wallet and wondered if he was some kind of aide or maybe the Lieutenant Governor. She wasn't into politics and didn't even bother voting, but Governor Richards was well liked in the state, especially by the agricultural people. However, she didn't like him because he was always trying to buy the Lonesome Star from her daddy.

Cresting the hill, Sunny was astonished to see a person standing. *That can't be the Governor, it must be the other man. Maybe he can help.*

Starbuck slowed as he neared the wreckage and Sunny, used to calf roping and jumping off the horse before it stopped, landed on a run. The other man walked towards them. Sunny noticed he was shirtless.

"I need help!" he cried. "I think I cracked my skull."

Sunny looked beyond him to the Governor. "Is he okay?"

"No, I think he's dead. But I'm alive and I need help!"

Sunny rushed beside Dane. She felt his wrist; no pulse. She pushed her finger near the carotid artery in his neck and found a faint pulse.

"Go grab the blankets and gauze out of my saddle bags! He's still alive!" she shouted. "My name is Sunny, what's yours?"

"Moore. Ron Moore!" Moore stared stupidly at Sunny. "Are you sure he's alive? That's Governor Dane Richards you're tending to."

"Yes, there's a faint pulse! Please, get the blankets. We have to keep him warm."

Moore stumbled through the grass over to where Starbuck was standing. Starbuck sidestepped and threw his head up in the air; horses can smell stupidity and fear.

"Starbuck!" Sunny shouted. "Stand!" Starbuck stood motionless as Moore began to fumble around with the saddlebags.

"I can't get them open," Moore complained. "I can't get the buckles undone."

"Good grief." Sunny ran to the bags. She handed the red one to Moore. "Here, lay this out on the top of that grass over there. A helicopter is on the way out and is looking for the red blanket."

Moore moved to where Sunny pointed as she knelt down by Governor Richards. The wire on his leg was doing the trick to stop the blood flow, but the leg below was turning awful colors. She hoped he wouldn't lose it, but he could live without the leg; the blood he couldn't. He moaned as she laid the blanket over him.

Sunny glanced at her watch: forty-six minutes since she got on Starbuck to head to the house. She wondered how long it would be before help arrived.

She heard the slight whoop-whoop of the helicopter and looked up to see a black pickup bouncing across the prairie. She could count on Shauna.

"Do you have that blanket laid out?" she yelled over at Moore. "Here comes the helicopter!"

"Yes, I got it!" Moore hollered back. "Could you look at my arm when you're done? I think it's broken."

Sunny turned back to Dane and inspected the bandana she put on his head earlier. The mixture of mud, blood, hair, and gas was putrid. Even through the deathly pale from the loss of blood and the trauma, she noticed his handsome chiseled features. A piece of grass stuck at the corner of his mouth; she picked it away.

Sunny stood and began waving her arms as the helicopter approached. The pilot signaled in recognition; the wind and the noise was deafening as it landed close. A paramedic jumped and rushed across the prairie with bag in hand.

"Hello, miss," the man shouted. "Who is hurt the most?" Sunny pointed to Governor Richards. "Do you know his name?" the man asked.

"It's Governor Richards!" Sunny shouted back. "And that one over there," she pointed at Moore, "is Ron Moore."

"Governor Richards?" the man asked. "What's he doing clear out here?"

"Sunny!" Shauna's shriek from behind Sunny startled her, even though she knew she was coming, "Are you okay?"

"Yeah," Sunny said, ready to collapse. "I'm okay. Thanks for coming!"

A flicker of light off a windshield caught Sunny's eye and she looked up to see the familiar gray and blue four-wheel drive Sheriff's pickup ambling across the prairie. She heard the sirens about the time she saw the truck and was glad that she convinced dispatch to send out the helicopter. Right now two men were working on Governor Richards while Moore was trying to get someone to pay attention to him. If they waited on the Sheriff, it would have been thirty more minutes. The Governor would never have made it.

Sunny looked around for Starbuck who wandered far enough away to clear the helicopter; he stood like a soldier at attention watching her every move.

The Sheriff finally turned off his siren and slammed his truck to a stop. He swung open the door and stumbled tripping on a big rock hidden in the grass. Hitching up his pants to hide his water-balloon-belly drooping over his belt, he swaggered over.

"What happened here?" he barked at Sunny. "Are you the one that called and said the Governor crashed out here?"

"Yes, sir," Sunny replied politely. "The Governor is the one they are loading on the stretcher."

"Well, it's a darn good thing," Sheriff Alvin Mitchell said hitching up his pants again and spitting a brown stream of tobacco juice in the grass, "that's the governor or you'd be in a heap a' trouble young lady. I heard you got pretty sassy with my dispatcher."

Sunny dated Sheriff Mitchell's son in High School and discovered he was not the kind of man she wanted. They hadn't dated long, but he took it pretty hard when they broke up and Sheriff Mitchell held a grudge longer than the Hatfields and McCoys. Although she never had any problems with him, her brothers blamed her for all the tickets they got. When he saw a Morgan vehicle, his lights and siren went on and the cuffs came out. Even a speeding ticket got them shoved to the ground and cuffed.

The Sheriff walked to where the paramedics were tending to Governor Richards. "How's he doin'?" he drawled. "Is he gonna make it?"

"It doesn't look good, Sheriff," one replied. "That lady over there did a fine job of taking care of him, but he's in pretty bad shape. He's lost a lot of blood and has a pretty severe head trauma"

"Well, be a good Republican and do what you can to save his hide. What about the other one?" Mitchell asked.

"He's going to be fine," the paramedic responded. "We've got him in the helicopter already. He has a head injury and should be okay. But if you ask him, he thinks he's dying. And if you get a whiff of him, you might think he already did."

Sunny stumbled but caught herself against Shauna. "Are you okay?"

Shauna asked. "You look white as a ghost."

"I suddenly feel kind of sick to my stomach." Sunny replied. "Maybe it's just too much excitement."

"Weren't you scared?" Shauna asked.

"Well, now I am, but I didn't have too much time to be scared. One minute I'm checking fences and the next a plane crashes right in front of me. That was a horrible, helpless feeling. I still can't believe they're alive. I just hope the Governor makes it."

Chapter Seven

"I will NOT have that existential idiot ruining yet another gallery showing!" Marian Satterfield sat on the edge of her chair with her back becoming more rigid with the further discussion, "The last time that Peter Radcliff showed up he was obnoxious, arrogant, intoxicated, and rude. I swear, if you vote to allow him to show, you will be looking for a new Chair for the Center for the Arts. I don't care how handsome he is!"

Norma Riseling wearied of the endless discussion by the board concerning their upcoming competition for regional artists. Thanks to a grant by the State Arts Commission and the backing of some wealthy patrons, the Tenth Annual Art of the Prairie competition drew national and even a modicum of international attention. What started as a dream of a couple of local artists morphed into a competition with prestige and substantial cash prizes. The Governor specifically requested his sister, Norma, be a part of the Arts Commission. He trusted her judgment; she practically raised him after their mother became ill.

Peter Radcliff either won or placed in several of the last competitions and became a regional favorite for art collectors. Many artists entered these competitions to get their works noticed by patrons. Naturally, the winning piece would sell well, but the other pieces were assured of being purchased by patrons hoping that anyone showing was an up-and-coming artist. No one wanted to overlook a potential Van Gogh.

Radcliff was exactly what Marian said: handsome, obdurate, obnoxious, rude, condescending, and arrogant. Radcliff won the previous year and insisted on being present when they hung his work in the gallery. Most artists trusted the curator, but not Radcliff.

Norma was the curator for the Norman L. Chandler Museum of Fine Art and was accustomed to precocious artists. While she thought some eccentric, she never felt uneasy except around Radcliff. Last year, as she was hanging the pieces with one of the volunteers, Ted Vintner, they ran out of wire. After Ted left for more, Radcliff entered the back door of the gallery.

"Well, there's the beautiful and artistic Norma Reisling," Radcliff oozed. Norma felt the hair rise on the back of her neck, but stifled the emotion so as to appear professional.

"Good morning, Mr. Radcliff," Norma replied. "How are you today?"

Within an instant, Radcliff was beside her peering at a work that Norma hung. As he brushed up against her side, she again stifled the feeling of repulsion. She felt his hand rest on her shoulder then slowly move down her spine.

"It looks like something a first grader painted," Radcliff spewed as Norma moved away to adjust the corners of the painting.

"Well, Mr. Radcliff," Norma said while gazing at the painting she favored above the others, "the beauty of art is that it truly does end up being very subjective and the final judging is done by the person who admires it for reasons unknown to even the trained eye."

"Ha!" Radcliff spouted. "Spoken like a true Midwesterner who loves the cliché and is happier with a Norman Rockwell rather than a Pollack."

His arrogance she could ignore, but the unsettled feeling whenever she was near him like an internal mariner's bell warning of danger rocks. She put distance between them and walked over to get another painting. As she reached inside the crate, she felt his cold thin fingers reach on top of hers and felt his breath against her neck.

"Here, Norma, let me help you," his cigarette smoke breath nauseated her.

"That's quite all right, Mr. Radcliff. I appreciate your help, but our gallery's policy dictates that only trained staff handle these works," Norma said.

The familiar tones of the front door sounded sweetly in Norma's ear as Ted entered.

"Hello, Mr. Radcliff," Ted said. "Can we be of assistance to you?"

"Hi, Ted" Radcliff moved from Norma. "Has your wife entered one of her photographs this year?"

Ted's wife, Billie, was considered one of the finest landscape photographers in a five-state region and could sell her works in galleries all across the Midwest, but many in the world of art don't consider photographers to be artist.

"No," Ted replied. "She's on a book tour across the U.S. now autographing her latest book, *Images of the Wind*. In fact, she just won the National Landscape Photographer's Guild Award and flies to San Francisco tomorrow to get the prize and pick up her check. Did you know she even has a gallery in Sante Fe now?"

Norma stifled a laugh under her breath. Sante Fe was considered to be the Mecca of artists and, if you could get a gallery to show your work, let alone own your own gallery, you had made it in the art world. Ted might look like a retired construction superintendent, but he was no dummy in the art world.

"Actually, Ted," Radcliff parried the insult with another thrust. "I came in ensure that my soon-to-be winning piece is hung properly. I was in a preposterous gallery recently and not only had they put my piece too high, they were using a dreaded fluorescent light to illuminate it. I never know if you people have any training in this matter."

Ted turned to walk away. His dad said that wrestling with a pig was always a bad idea because even if you won, you still end up smelling like a pig.

Norma was jolted back to the meeting by Marian pounding her first against the table.

"Then we need different jurors!" Marian said. "Why don't we hire someone from a Midwestern university rather than some high-falutin' easterner that thinks elephant paintings are art!"

Marian was right in some ways. Much of the flavor of Mid-Western art came from the likes of Fredrick Remington, a Yale trained illustrator that moved to the West and used the artistic styles of French Impressionists to capture manufactured scenes of the Wild West. Most people walking through galleries would not notice the influence of Monet or Van Gogh in the works of Remington. Rather, they saw the wild-eyed broncobuster or the multicolored headbands of the Native American Chiefs.

Thomas Moran, who, in the late 1800's painted massive majestic landscapes of Yellowstone, the Grand Canyon, and Mountain of the Holy Cross, influenced other artists. Teddy Roosevelt, President of the United States at the time, was so inspired by Moran's images of the West he set aside these geographic treasures as national parks.

"Isn't Chicago considered the Midwest?" Anne Jenkins interjected. "The jurors for our show last year were both from the University of Chicago."

"Yes," Marian retorted. "But they selected a painting a pig could have done as 'honorable mention.' My four year-old can paint better than Radcliffe!"

"But they said the same thing about Van Gogh," Gertrude Osborne, a long-standing member of the community, squeaked. "And look at how famous he became!"

"But at least you could tell what it was!" Marian shouted at the octogenarian whose appreciation for fine art was uncommon in one of her age. "The painting that Radcliffe did last year looked like a bunch of black stars on an orange plate. And then to title it, 'Ad astra per aspra' which everyone knows is the state motto of Kansas was a mockery of our state."

"Actually," Anne spoke quietly. "What Mr. Radcliffe was trying to do was play with opposite colors in the spectrum. You see, if you would have stared at those stars on that plate for a while, then turned off the lights, you would have seen those stars as white and the plate as blue. Only someone familiar with art and the phenomenon of the human mind would recognize that.

"I don't care," pouted Marian. "It still looked like crap to me and I want my stars white!"

Norma sat through yet another meeting with heated debate about the questions of what constitutes art, is there really such a thing as universal beauty, and is it all determined subjectively or objectively. She smiled to herself knowing that most artists would be pleased at such controversial views being aired. No artist displays their work expecting a "ho-hum" attitude. The conversation in this room is one that fills the classrooms and studios of aspiring and accomplished artists all over the world. Is beauty in the eye of the beholder or are there universal principles that define beauty? What is art?

"And if we allow Mr. Radcliffe to make a mockery of our state," Marian threatened. "Then I know some very influential patrons that will seriously review their support of such art."

That's typical. Every Satterfield threatens to take their toys and go home when things don't go their way, Norma muttered to herself.

Norma watched Gertrude Osborne put her things in her purse – a sign the meeting was over for her. Norma knew Gertrude would engage in battle, but on her own terms. An open meeting with a Satterfield behind the bully pulpit was not a place for Gertrude to fight. Not that she was afraid of confrontation, in fact, Norma learned much from watching Gertrude completely humiliate someone in an argument in such a way that her quarry never knew what hit them. But Gertrude also learned to pick her battles well. Another time; another place; a different strategy.

Norma quickly rose to her feet and asked Marian if she could address the august committee. Marian looked relieved knowing her temper had backed her into a corner again.

"I can remember a time," Norma began, "when I sat beside my dad on the porch swing watching yet another glorious Kansas sunrise. He quoted poetry written three thousand years ago by a shepherd who said, 'The sun rising was like a groom on his wedding day rushing out of his chamber to meet his bride, or a like a strong man ready to run a race.'"

"I was only ten at the time," Norma continued. "But I remember looking at those myriad hues of purples, orange, yellow and red and thinking that I wanted to paint a Kansas sunrise. It wasn't until my second year of art in college and many, many frustrated attempts at sunrises that I realized that an artist isn't painting a memory, they're painting an emotion and they use colors and light and design as a carpenter uses hammer and nails and wood."

"I understand," she agreed. "What it is like to look at something and think my child can paint better than that. But I realize now that every visual image, if we concentrate on it long enough, will speak to our souls like watching puffy clouds in the sky and imaging what animals they represent. An artist wants to stir our imagination and if everything painted looks like real life, then there's no stirring of our imagination. I think we can find a balance between the wonderful representational artists who capture an emotion in realistic likeness and the artist that pushes our imagination and creativity to interpret their work with our own frames of reference."

Norma noticed Gertrude had quit putting away her things and that Marian had graciously sat down while Norma was talking.

"But I still don't like him!" Marian blurted.

"We completely understand," Gertrude said. "I wouldn't be too surprised if Mr. Radcliffe shows up at our gallery sometime missing an ear!"

As the group laughed, Norma thought to herself, *and if he ever touches me again, there'll be more missing than his ear.*

Suddenly, a knock came at the door of the conference room. "Hi, John," Marian greeted Norma's husband. "Come on in, we were about to finish up."

As the door opened up, Norma could tell by the look on John's face he was not carrying good news. Her stomach knotted.

"Norma," John said. "Can you come out here a minute?"

She slipped around the table and stepped into the hallway.

"What's the matter?" she asked. "What's wrong?"

"I just got a call from the Lieutenant Governor. They've Life-Watched Dane to Mercy General."

Chapter Eight

"We'll be praying for you!" Marian grabbed Norma and hugged her as she was leaving the meeting. "Let us know as soon as you know."

"What happened?" Norma asked her husband. "When did you hear about this? Is he going to be okay? Where was the crash? Wasn't Ron with him? Is Ron alive? Who got a hold of you?"

"Easy, honey," John reassured her as they got in the car. "One question at a time. Don't forget to buckle up. Here, I brought you some coffee."

John eased the car out of the parking lot and started the one-hour trip to Mercy General. "I was in a meeting with the Director of Public works when Greg called. He thought of calling you first, but thought it would be better if I was the one that told you."

"The Sheriff's Department called the Capitol," John continued. "They said that Dane's plane went down in the Flint Hills. As close as I could figure, it must have been pretty close to that property out there he owns. Apparently he got caught between two of those thunderstorms and the plane went down. Some cowgirl out checking fences found them and called 9-1-1. He's in bad shape but Ron was unhurt. Greg said he'd call me as soon as they found more out."

"I never did like him flying," Norma began to weep. "I thought he would stop after he lost Debbie, but he seemed to do more of it. I worry about him every time he goes up and I know a lot of times he doesn't bother telling me when he's going. He's as stubborn as Daddy."

Norma and Dane had always been close. Although she was eighteen when he was born, their mother's illness required that she take care of him. After she got married and began raising her own kids, Dane always had a special place in her heart. Although she often felt like a mother to him, the transition to being a friend happened without notice when Dane was in his twenties.

She was the first person he called when Debbie died. She hardly recognized him on the phone that night. There were a lot of dark, lonely days that she walked with Dane through that valley of the shadow of death. He lived such a public life that he had to be careful about the way he grieved. Although the press had been kind at first, within a few months their visceral attacks on Dane resumed and one reporter even went so far as to suggest his grief was affecting his role as governor. Fortunately, the public outrage towards the journalist was severe enough that any other compassionless journalists were put on notice. Dane remained popular in the polls.

"Do you think Dane will ever get married again?" Norma asked John.

"I don't know," John replied. "It's been almost four years and he doesn't seem interested though God knows there's plenty of birds preening for him. It won't be from lack of effort on the ladies part, that's for sure. I always figure he will get married after he gets out of office. He knows how vicious the press can be and I think he wants someone to love him for who he is, not for what he is. He and Debbie had something rare and Dane knows it."

"What about Governor Littleton of New Mexico? She's divorced and drop-dead gorgeous."

"No, Dane would never get hooked up with her," John replied. "She is one of those women who use their beauty and appeal to charm men into doing what they want and, although Dane might be just as charming in return, he secretly loathes women like that. No, it will take a woman who doesn't know she's beautiful with an independent streak a mile wide to turn his head."

"I just hope he makes it." Norma began to sob. "I can't bear the thought of losing him."

"He'll make it, honey. Like you say, he's too hard headed not too."

Norma stared out the window at the passing hills. She tried to imagine his plane crashing into a hillside and shivered at the thought of him being hurt. He was tough, all right, and in great shape so if anyone could make it, he would. But she trembled at the thought of him lying in the twisted carnage of steel. *Who was this angel of mercy was that had found them?* Out in the Flint Hills, they could have been missing for hours before anyone found them. *Thank you, God, that you had someone there to help him; thank you for the cowgirl angel.*

Lt. Governor Greg Simms met them at the emergency room entrance with a pale look on his face. Norma stiffened with fear when she saw him.

"How is he, Greg?" she asked.

"Well, they just took him into surgery and we won't know anything for a while. The doctor said he would send a nurse out as soon as he could to tell us what was going on. The paramedics wouldn't say much other than he had head trauma and a pretty severe broken leg. He lost a lot of blood by the time they got there."

"How's Ron?" John asked.

"Oh, you know Moore," Greg rolled his eyes. "He managed to get out with just a slight concussion but I heard him a while ago yelling at the nurses that he was not getting enough attention. I asked the paramedics how he was and they just smiled at each other and said he'd be okay. His wife is supposed to be here anytime. Maybe she can calm him down. He'll milk this one for all it's worth."

"So who found him?" Norma asked.

"Apparently the lady that owns the ranch was out checking fences and she saw it all happen right in front of her," Greg said. "She was on horseback out in the middle of nowhere and was able to use her horse to get the wing off that had them trapped. Then she used her horse to get both of them out at the same time a thunderstorm was hammering them. The paramedics say she used a piece of baling wire as a tourniquet on his leg to stop the bleeding. They had seen a lot of things used for tourniquets, but never baling wire. Then she cut off the bottom of her jeans to wrap around his leg wound. She also stuck her bandana in the deep gash on his head and stopped the bleeding. She saved his life; without her there, he would certainly have died."

"Do you know her name?" John asked.

"Oh, no, here it comes." Greg saw the local press pouring into the parking lot. A reporter with a cameraman burst through the sliding doors and thrust a microphone into Greg's face.

"Lieutenant Governor Simms," the dainty blond with a short skirt said. "We understand that Governor Richards has been killed in a plane crash. Can you give us any details of his death and can you tell us when you will be sworn in as governor."

Greg had been in front of the camera too many times to be rattled with the question so, with measured speech, he replied, "Governor Richards and Ron Moore are alive and currently under the care of the best trauma physicians. We will receive an update on their condition as soon as it comes available. Until then, we have nothing further to say."

Greg grabbed Norma and John by the arm and led them down the hall to a private room for families. At least they would be safe from the glaring lights and rude, probing questions. Greg put a call in to the Press Secretary, Stephanie Riddell, who could handle the press better than anyone he had ever seen. She had been a journalist and knew all the tricks of the trade. No one could ruffle her feathers.

Once inside the safe environs, Norma began to ask more questions. "So do you know the name of the lady that rescued him? You know it's a miracle that she was out there at the right place at the right time. Things like that just don't happen by chance, you know."

"No, the Sheriff didn't give me her name," Greg said. "He just gave out enough information to know what she had done, but wasn't forthcoming with too many more details. He had called the FAA who was already aware. They received a May Day call from the Governor's airplane before he crashed so they were already garrisoned to go inspect the crash."

"Why did the plane crash to begin with?" Norma asked. "Did it get hit by lightning? Or did a tornado get it? Did the engine just stop?"

"We really don't know any of the particulars, other than it crashed and this mystery woman saved his life," Greg replied. "I'm sure once the investigation is over we will find out. Better yet, why don't we just ask Dane when he wakes up?"

Greg's optimism made Norma feel better, but the foreboding sense of losing her brother was overwhelming. Soon, Ron's wife would be there and she would be a whole other issue they would have to deal with. Loud and abrasive, Cheryl Moore could offend almost everyone she met. With a paranoid chip on her shoulder, she thought everyone was out to get her and her family. She went from a little hole-in-the-wall ghost town in Oklahoma to living in a half-million dollar house and driving a Lexus. She claimed she had fought her way to the top, but everyone knew it was her husband's inheritance from his Daddy that funded their lavish lifestyle.

A knock on the door interrupted their thoughts. Greg opened the door just a little in case it was a reporter, but suddenly the door flew open and in charged Cheryl like a western Kansas dust devil.

"What's going on?" She blurted. "Is my husband dead? Is Dane dead?

"No, Cheryl," Greg replied. "Ron is doing fine and Dane is in surgery. They both survived but Dane is in bad shape. Here, I'll take you to Ron. He's in one of the rooms in the Trauma section."

Norma breathed a sigh of relief when they left the room. Although not directly related to her - she was Dane's sister-in-law through marriage to Debbie – she still had to be around her entirely too much. Cheryl never shut her mouth. Like Norma's dad said of some people, *They have a tongue that's hinged in the middle and flappin' on both ends.*

Family get-togethers with Ron and Cheryl almost always ended up with the two of them arguing over something then storming away mad. They started driving separate vehicles to family functions in anticipation of leaving at different times.

Even with the door closed, they heard Cheryl ranting to the charge nurse. "I demand to see my husband. His name is Ron Moore and he was in that plane crash with the Governor. He is the Governor's best friend!" Cheryl knew that the nurse would let her go back, but with an audience not far away, it seemed as good a place as any for melodrama.

Another knock and Greg opened the door to Johnson and Meredith Richards. After they received the news, Johnson rushed home to get his wife knowing that she was too fragile to make the trip to the hospital herself. Although a woman of great dignity, the Parkinson's disease was getting noticeably worse and operating a vehicle was too dangerous.

"Oh, Mother," Norma wept as her mother embraced her. "He's going to be okay, isn't he?"

"I didn't raise any child of mine to be killed in the middle of a cow pasture in a plane crash," Meredith quavered. "He comes from too strong a stock to let something like this do him in."

Johnson and Meredith Richards weathered a lot of difficult times through the Great Depression, the Dust Bowl, polio, World War II, and a host of other travails that plagued a nation. Norma admired her Mother's pioneering spirit and intestinal fortitude. It was men and women like her parents that made this nation so great. And Meredith was right; they raised their children to be tough and hopeful even in the darkest times.

Greg came back in. "Well," he said with as much diplomacy as possible. "If one were to measure Mr. Moore's health by the amount of shouting going on in his room, then we can expect a full and immediate recovery." They all learned to avoid Ron and Cheryl in highly stressful situations that exacerbated the worst in both of them. "The doctors say that Ron suffered a concussion and they want to keep him over night for observation. " Greg continued. "Naturally, Cheryl wanted to make a full explanation to the press so she's in front of the lights already. I told her that Stephanie would do it when she got here, but Cheryl insisted. I gave her strict instructions not to mention a word about Dane."

"What is Dane's condition?" Meredith asked. "Did you get to talk to anyone?"

"I did ask the charge nurse if she had heard anything and she had not." Greg replied. "She did say an update would happen within the hour. They should know something by then."

"He will be fine," Johnson said. "I have a good feeling about all of this."

Johnson was known to be right about most things he had a good feeling about. Trusting instinct more than education, he had become a successful businessman based on the way he felt rather than what numbers or studies showed him. He learned to trust his "gut feeling" while in the trenches in World War II. He lost a lot of good friends on the battlefield and believed that his instincts were what kept him alive. His instincts combined with hope helped him endure almost two years as a prisoner of war. Poor Meredith was told he was a P.O.W. and for two years stopped everything that she was doing at seven different times of the day to pray for his release. She was not surprised when he called her and told her he was free.

"So who was the young lady that rescued him?" Meredith asked Greg. "Does anyone know anything about her?"

"No," Greg responded. "Only that she was on horseback and saw it all happen. She had been out checking fence and managed to take care of them then rushed back to the house to call for help. It seems like angels even ride horses!"

"I would like to meet this young lady sometime," Johnson said. "I know lots of young men who survived the war because of Florence Nightingale's like her. We want her to know how much we appreciate what she's done."

"I'm sure that Dane will want to meet her too," Norma responded. "Maybe when he gets better, we can bring her up her to meet us."

"Better yet," Meredith injected. "Why don't we go down to meet her?"

"In time, Merry," Johnson patted his wife's arm. "We have plenty of time."

Another knock on the door came. "Maybe it's the O.R. nurse," Greg replied as he opened the door. The doctor was standing in blue scrubs with a cap still covering his wavy hair and a mask dangling around his neck. Norma gasped.

"Hi, I'm Dr. Silvan," he introduced himself to first Greg then the others. "We usually send a nurse out but considering it is the Governor, I wanted to be able to answer all your questions. Why don't you folks go ahead and have a seat?"

Chapter Nine

"Girl, we got to get some clean dry clothes on you! And what happened to your pant leg?" Shauna grabbed Sunny by the arm and headed towards her truck. "Deputy Dog can take care of this place now."

Sunny looked in Sheriff Mitchell's direction hoping he had not overheard Shauna's caustic remark. Shauna dated the Sheriff's son for a while, too, and came to loathe both the son and the father. She coined the nickname for him off a dopey dog in a cartoon and now almost everyone called him Deputy Dog behind his back. However, if he ever heard you say it, you witnessed police harassment in an entirely new light.

Bouncing across the pasture in the pickup with Starbuck trotting dutifully behind, Shauna asked Sunny, "So tell me what happened? Did you see the crash? Did you know it was the Governor? Did you get to talk to him at all?"

"Whoa!" Sunny said. "Slow the truck and slow the questions. They're both making me dizzy."

Sunny recounted the story to Shauna and as she told it, even she found it hard to believe. She might wake up at any moment to find this all too absurd to be true.

"You tied your rope around the wing and Starbuck dragged it off?"

Shauna exclaimed. "Girl, you're a real, live, cowgirl hero. Why, John Wayne's got nothin' on you! You and Starbuck are going to be famous! You're going to be on *Dateline USA!*"

It all came so natural that Sunny never thought for one minute that she might be a heroine. She wished her two brothers could see her now. Growing up the youngest, she wanted to be as tough and smart as them, but they always teased her about being weaker because she was a girl. They left for bigger jobs in the city and she had been stuck on the ranch trying to make ends meet. Granted, that's where she wanted to be, but she still yearned to hear their compliments.

As they drew near the house, Sunny noticed a van coming down the long drive. "Woo-hoo, cowgirl!" Shauna laughed. "Here comes the TV crews now. We better get to the house and get your makeup on, girl. You're going to be on TV!"

Sunny recoiled in horror at the thought of being interviewed. She had hated speech classes in school and even dropped out of 4-H because it required public speaking. "No," Sunny almost burst into tears. "I can't talk to a reporter! I won't know what to say and I'll just look stupid."

"Oh, good grief," Shauna chided her. "Just flash that pretty smile of yours and toss in a little of that cowgirl drawl and tell 'em how you and your mighty steed came to the rescue! You'll have cowboys from as far south as Texas driving all the way up here with marriage proposals."

Sunny wanted to hide. The late afternoon sun would soon give purchase to a rising moon and she and Starbuck could easily find retreat out on the prairie. They knew every trail that would lead under the starry sky where no reporter could find them.

"Sunny," Shauna said knowing of her tendency to isolate herself, "you know you're going to have to tell the story sooner or later so you might was well get ready for it."

"But I did what anyone else would do and it's no big deal."

"It was the GOVERNOR!" Shauna shouted. "You rescued the most famous man in Kansas! People are going to want to know who you are."

With that, Sunny wept as they pulled up near the barn. "But I don't want people to know who I am. I want to be left alone. That's why I live on the ranch so people will leave me alone." She jumped out of the still-moving pickup and slammed the door. Starbuck whinnied and came to her side as they both walked into the barn.

"Sunny!" Shauna shouted across the truck's hood. "You can't keep running from people just because you got hurt once. This isn't about you and Shane. This is about you and your horse rescuing the most famous man in Kansas!"

Sunny wheeled and pointed her finger at Shauna, "I told you NEVER to mention Shane's name to me again. How dare you bring him into this!"

"How can I not?" Shauna retorted. "You are going to stay out on this ranch and shrivel up like an old tumbleweed all because he hurt you. You know, you're not the only person that's ever been hurt. You are too bright, too beautiful, and too much fun to be stuck out in the middle of the prairie with only a horse to talk to."

"Well," Sunny shot back. "At least the horse doesn't go chasing after some other filly when I'm not looking then start calling me names when he gets caught."

"Sunny," Shauna softened. "I'm sorry I brought Shane into this. You are too good of a woman for him and all your friends are afraid you're going to dry up out here on the prairie. You just have so much to offer someone. So much to give. You're so beautiful."

"Yeah," Sunny said. "They're lined up for miles trying to get a date with me. It's getting so bad I have to beat them off with a stick."

Sunny heard the slamming of car doors as she entered the barn. She cringed at the footsteps and mumbling voices, "I wonder if the people in here can tell us where it is."

Sunny noticed the clean-cut young man with a blazer was wearing make-up. She chuckled under her breath as she slowly unsaddled Starbuck, "Well, Starbuck, he wears more make up than I put on in a year."

"Miss," the young reporter asked Shauna who was standing closer. "We heard the report that the Governor's plane crashed on this property. Could you tell us how to get there?"

"This is private property, Mister," Sunny growled from behind Starbuck. "Did you not notice the 'No Trespassing' sign at the gate? You're more than welcome to leave the same way you came in."

"Is this your property, Ma'am?" the reporter turned on his youthful charm.

Sunny suddenly thought of Nellie Clatterbuck and the adobe oven and chills went down her spine. She heard another vehicle coming down the drive. She imagined the prairie being over-run with reporters and officers and ambulance chasers and God-knows-who-else would traipse across private property.

"Actually," Shauna intervened, "what you need to do is go back out the gate you came in and go about two miles south then turn back left. If you keep following that road it will take you right out to where the plane crashed."

Shauna wasn't exactly lying – that old road that turned into a cow-path would get you there in dry weather – but it was a long way around and, after the rain, they were sure to get stuck. The low water bridge about halfway back would be flooded and while it looked like there was concrete all the way through, they would sink up to their axles.

"Thank you, Ma'am", the reporter said with some skepticism. "Would you mind going with us to show us the way?"

"No, thanks," Shauna said. "We have to get the horse unsaddled and this girl some dry clothes."

"Why are her clothes wet?" the reported asked. "Was she out in the rain this afternoon? Did she see the plane crash? What happened to the leg of her jeans?"

Shauna grabbed the reporter, "I'll tell you what. I'm leaving - gotta go home and take care of the kids - why don't you follow me out? I'll show you a short cut down by the windmill. Bye Sunny, I'll call you later."

Sunny chuckled to herself. They were certain to get stuck now. Yes, the road by the windmill was shorter, but a lot worse. Her anger at Shauna subsided as she realized that, once again, her good friend came to her defense. She supposed Shauna was right; she would have a lot of people in the news wanting to hear her story, but not now. In her time. She didn't have to answer any questions she didn't want to right now, or ever for that matter. This was her life and although there wasn't much she felt she could control, this was one of those things.

As she brushed the currycomb across Starbuck, she wondered what she would say. Although she had never been on TV, she knew people interviewed when something tragic happened often ended up looking like idiots. If she was going to be on TV, it would be on her terms and she would rehearse what to say. Shane might be watching and it would show him what a fool he had been for leaving her.

Tossing grain in the feed bunk, Starbuck whinnied as Sunny patted him on his haunches. She closed the latch to the stall and walked towards the barn door. As she stepped outside, she gasped in horror. In the early hours of the evening, the car-lights coming down her driveway glimmered like the yellow eyes of coyotes lurking around a campfire.

One by one, cars, trucks and vans bearing logos of various news organizations drove up the driveway. Sunny ran into the house before the first one stopped. Slamming the door shut and locking it, she scrambled to the front door to make sure it was locked too. Racing from room to room, she quickly pulled the blinds down. Hopefully no one saw her but to be safe, she made sure not to turn on any lights. She would rather sit in the dark all night than go outside and face a reporter.

As she walked up the stairs, she heard the first knock on the door. *They can knock all night long as far as I care*, she said to herself, *I'm taking a shower and going to bed.*

She could hear the knocking even above the roar of the shower.

Would they ever give up? When finished, she walked out in the dark to sit on the edge of the bed where she could look out the windows. With the windows open, she could hear the voices from below.

"I know I saw someone run in there when I drove up," a woman spoke. "It looked like a woman running across the drive."

"Well, it doesn't seem like they want to let us in," a man laughed in the encroaching darkness. "Just keep knocking and maybe they'll give up and answer. After all, we're getting paid time-and-a-half anyway so I'm in no hurry."

"I'll wait them out." Sunny thought to herself. "This is my home; they have to leave some time."

Sunny watched as a pickup passed by the other cars sitting in the drive. This one had red lights flashing on top and, as it drove under the mercury vapor light on the pole in the front yard, she could see an official seal on the side but couldn't make out what department it was with. As it veered off into the pasture headed straight for the wreckage, the others raced to their vehicles and jumped in. Like race-day at Kansas Speedway, each vehicle quickly jostled to fall in line behind the pickup. Sunny trembled with a mixture of anger and fear. These interlopers were violating her precious prairie and there was nothing she could do about it.

Sunny walked to the window and watched the vehicles form an erratic line behind the pickup with the flashing lights. *I hope they all get stuck.*

Car lights flashed against the bedroom wall and Sunny looked outside to see red lights flashing from another official looking pickup stopping in the driveway. The driver and passenger got out wearing blue jackets with the white, iridescent high-visibility letters "NTSB" on the back. *This is the National Transportation Safety Board official and they want to talk to me.*

Slipping into clean clothes, Sunny went downstairs to answer the knock at the door.

Chapter Ten

"Governor Richards suffered a lot of trauma." Dr. Sylvan spoke to the somber crowd in the family waiting room. He was getting ready to go into more detail when another knock came at the door.

"Can I come in?" Stephanie Riddell asked Greg as he opened the door.

Greg looked at Norma who nodded. "Yes, she needs to hear what the doctor has to say."

The Richards family had known Stephanie since she was a little girl. Johnson and Meredith practically raised her since they lived next door to her parents who were gone much of the time. Although ten years younger than Dane, you would have thought they were brother and sister. Norma was enough older that she never developed the close ties with Stephanie like Dane did, but she loved her nonetheless. Stephanie's dad died when she was fifteen and she asked Johnson to walk her down the aisle when she got married.

They were glad that Stephanie left a high-paying journalism job at the Tribune to become Dane's Press Secretary. Johnson joked that she could describe a pigpen and make it smell like a rose garden. She didn't twist the truth or delude people with false information; it was her optimistic outlook on life that turned political disasters into themed triumphs for the Governor.

She was foxlike when it came to the media. Pouring over words and speeches, she diligently communicated the Governor's thoughts in ways to disarm even the harshest critics. She had the rare combination of inward beauty that matched her outward beauty. Even the fiercest amongst the journalists were often charmed by her wholesome innocence.

She sat down by Meredith who leaned into her embrace.

"As I was saying," the doctor continued, "the Governor suffered a lot of trauma and it will take much time to heal. He had lacerations all over his arms and face and we think we can save his leg, but the tourniquet that helped save him also cut off a lot of blood flow. He lost a lot of blood and we had to give him several units of blood. Lying out in the rain didn't help much, but whoever took care of him before the paramedics got there saved his life."

"Do you know who that was?" Meredith asked.

"No, all I know is that the paramedics who brought him in said it was a sopping wet cowgirl with half a pant leg missing. Apparently she was able to drag the Governor out of the plane using her horse and a rope," Dr. Sylvan responded. "He also suffered a concussion and a pretty severe laceration on the front of the skull. She used a bandana to stop the blood flow and the tourniquet she used was made of baling wire."

"Most farmers live with the motto, 'Baling wire can fix anything'," Johnson chuckled. "I've seen it fix a lot of things but never dreamed it would save my son's life."

"How soon can we see him?" Norma asked.

"Well," Dr. Sylvan replied. "He will be in Post-Op for a while and after that we will have him in Intensive Care for several days. As soon as we get him in ICU two at a time can go in to see him. But, I must warn you; you won't recognize him when you first see him. He's pretty banged up with internal damage and bleeding that concerns us. We think we took care of it, but we're going to watch him carefully. I'm going to go back in and check on him. The charge nurse will let you know when he's in ICU."

"Thank you, Dr. Sylvan." Greg closed the door behind the doctor and turned to Stephanie. "Well, are you ready to meet the press?"

"Looks like Cheryl already has," Stephanie smiled. "I heard her on the radio on the way over. I've got to give her credit, she didn't bite any of the bait they were tempting her with to make comments about Dane."

"So she did okay?" Greg asked.

"Well, okay if you are talking about Dane. But if you're asking about Ron, then she made him sound like he was the hero in all of this. But what is this about a cowgirl rescuing him?" Briefly they shared with her what they knew.

"I just want to see him and hold his hand," Norma wept.

"I know, dear," Meredith spoke. "We can see him a little bit. Right now we must remain strong and pray that he heals."

Stephanie stopped writing and said, "Let me read you what I've got and tell me if it's okay. If a security guard had not have brought me in the back way, I would never have made it past the press outside. If I don't get out there quickly, someone is going to start speculation about the Governor and that won't do anything more than start rumors. Here's what I have:

Governor Dane Richards and Ron Moore both survived a single-engine plane crash earlier today. Mr. Moore is doing well and will be kept in the hospital overnight for observation. Governor Richards underwent surgery to repair a broken leg as well as receiving numerous stitches to his scalp as the result of head trauma. Dr. Sylvan reported that he made it through the surgery and will be taken to the Intensive Care Unit.

On behalf of the Governor's family and the great state of Kansas, we ask that you pray for Governor Richards, Mr. Moore and their families. Until we have more information, we will not offer any further comments.

"Short and sweet." Johnson said. "But you know you're going to be blasted with questions about the mystery cowgirl."

"No further comments means no further comments," Stephanie

smiled. "They can ask all they want, they aren't going to get any answers from me."

Another knock on the door came as the charge nurse informed them that Dane was in the ICU and two of them could go in for ten minutes to see him.

"Is it true that people can still hear you even when you're unconscious?" Norma asked.

"That's what I've heard but I don't know how they know that," John responded.

"Mom, Dad, you guys want to go in first?"

"Why don't you and John go in first," Meredith said. "I know how close you and Dane are and it would be good if your voice is the first one he hears. We'll go in right after."

"Are you sure?" Norma asked but already knew the answer. She admired her mother's ability to sense what was best in a situation, not just what made her happy. That kind of sacrificial love was demonstrated over and over especially now with her illness. Norma knew there were many rough days that her mom went through that no one, especially Johnson, would ever know about. Norma refused to let her illness adversely affect others around her, even to the point of being too independent and not allowing others to help her.

"Let's go." Norma grasped John's hand and followed the nurse down the long, tiled corridor. The nurse pushed a large button on the side of the hall and two large doors swung open.

"Put a little of this on your hands," the nurse spoke reaching for germicide foam beside the door.

Norma started feeling light-headed as they walked further into the room. As they passed by room after room of critically ill people, the smells and sounds began to overwhelm her. Taking a deep breath and resolving to be strong, she held her head up as they found Dane's room.

Norma stopped abruptly as they walked into the room, then turned and ran back out. That man lying in the bed could not be her brother;

he was too grotesque. She expected a little head bandage and a cast on his leg, but she was not prepared for the swollen face and black eyes hidden behind the gauze. His usually rugged tan muscular body was placid and tiny lying between huge machines that monitored his vitals or dripped medicine in his veins.

John caught her as she began to faint. A nurse, noticing Norma's reaction, helped John ease her into a chair. Norma began to shake and weep, leaning into the arms and chest of John.

"He looks so bad," she sobbed. "What if he doesn't make it?" Images of their childhood flashed through her mind. Being old enough to be his mother, she had changed as many of his diapers as Meredith. She stayed home and attended the local college so she could help her parents as much as she could. Although it took years for them to diagnose Meredith's condition, it had affected their family long before a doctor ever put a name on it.

Norma first noticed Meredith struggling when she was doing things that required fine motor skills like chopping vegetables with a knife or trying to fasten a diaper pin. She hid this from her family for years and would make up excuses about having spent too much time in the garden or just getting clumsy in her old age. When she slurred her speech, which was rare at first, she would say she was tired and needed a nap. Although there was no cure for it and it hit Meredith earlier than most, she fought a tremendous fight against the disease.

Norma rocked Dane to sleep many a lonely night while she was in college. He was four when she graduated and he wore her blue mortarboard around the house at her graduation party. He had problems with pronouncing the letter "r" and "l" so he marched around saying he was "gwaduwating." He crawled up on her lap with cake and ice cream and promptly dumped it on her graduation dress. "I'm sowwy, sis!" he cried.

He was the ring bearer when John and Norma got married. He marched around in his little tux with chest out and head held high telling folks he was going to someday be "Prethident of the NewNited

Sthath." Even at six years old, he loved the pomp and ceremony of large events.

He was stunning in his tuxedo standing at the top of the stairs at his inauguration party. Debbie and he made a striking couple with her blazing red hair and sequined black evening dress. Norma gave him a congratulatory kiss on the cheek and told him he looked like the "Prethident of the NewNited Sthateth,", he laughed. He was one of the finest orators the state had ever known with a command of the language that made even his detractors admire his eloquence. But, there was nothing like an older sister to keep a man humble.

"Norma," John spoke. "Our time is about up, Honey. Do you want to go in and see him or let your mom and dad?"

"No," Norma braced herself, "I need to go see him. I'll be fine." She walked back into the room, careful not to touch any of the machines. She found his hand sticking out from under the blanket with an IV attached to it and gently caressed it. She was surprised by how cold and clammy it felt. He always had such strong hands.

I hope he doesn't lose his leg. If he can't run and climb rocks and fly-fish and golf, he will go stir crazy. But he would adjust to anything with a positive attitude and all the gumption he could muster. Gumption. Norma wondered if that was a real word or one their Dad made up that described everything from courage to conviction. But that's one thing all the Richards family had – gumption. If anyone could beat the odds, it would be Dane.

"Dane," Norma spoke. "It's Norma, Dane. John's on the other side of the bed. We love you, Dane."

Norma fought back the tears as the drain tube coming out of Dane's mouth gurgled a brownish-yellow liquid from his stomach. "You're going to be fine, Dane. We need you to fight through this and we'll help you. I hear a cowgirl and her horse rescued you on the prairie. Was she pretty? You always managed to have a pretty girl bail you out of trouble."

The whir of a foreign machine sent chills down Norma's spine.

Feeling nauseous again, she leaned away from the strong sterilized smells coming from Dane's skin. "We've got to go so Mom and Daddy can come in. We love you, Dane. We'll be back as soon as they let us in again." Norma leaned over and kissed him. She was sure she felt his hand tighten around her fingers.

"We need to go," John touched her back. "Johnson and Meredith are anxious to come in."

Norma followed John out the door of the ICU. She looked at the clock on the wall and spoke to John, "You know, it was only a short time ago that I was caught up in heated discussion over art. Standing in there holding on to life or death with my brothers' hand kind of makes that other stuff ridiculously trivial, don't you think? We were arguing over who makes decisions about art and people were threatening to pick up their toys and go home, yet in one quick moment of time, fighting over something like that seems so childish."

Chapter Eleven

"Hello, Ma'am," the man in the blue windbreaker said through the screen door to Sunny. "I'm Agent Ross Scanlon with the National Transportation Safety Board and this is Agent Alex Rodriguez. May we ask you a few questions?"

"Sure, I'm Sunny Morgan. Nice to meet you gentlemen." Sunny opened the door to let them in. "Come on in. Here, lets sit at the kitchen table. Would you like anything to drink?"

"No, thank you, Ma'am," Agent Scanlon replied. "We know it's late and we won't be here too long. We have a few questions to ask you then we will leave a report we would like you to fill out in the next few days, if you would be so kind."

"We heard that from Sheriff Mitchell that you saw the crash happen," Agent Rodriquez spoke. "Would you tell us as much as you can? And would it be okay if we recorded this, too? We've learned that people's memories tend to wane over time and this will give us something to reference."

"Sure, no problem," Sunny responded. Burying her head in her hands, she tried to figure out where to begin. Taking a drink of water, she began to tell the story with as much detail as possible clear to the point where she rushed up to the plane. She figured they only wanted to hear about the accident, not the rescue.

"Ma'am," Agent Scanlon spoke. "We also were told that you were the one that rescued Governor Richards and Mr. Moore. Could you tell us about that, please?"

"Have you heard how the Governor is doing? Did he make it?" Sunny asked. "And what about that other man that was with him. Is he doing okay?

"The last we heard was that the Governor was hurt badly and was going to need extensive surgery. We also heard that the other man, Ron Moore, was going to be just fine," Agent Scanlon said. "He only had a concussion. They are both at Mercy General Hospital."

"That's good," Sunny said. "The Governor seems like a strong man. Hopefully, he will make it."

As Sunny told the story, it seemed almost unbelievable even to her. Holding the water glass with both hands, she stared vacantly at the water as she concentrated on telling the story. She didn't want to make herself out to be some super heroine so was careful not to exaggerate any part, but as she told it, she found it almost too surreal to have transpired. She was amazed at how well Starbuck worked with her.

Occasionally, one of the agents would stop to ask about the direction the plane was pointing, certain smells that she noticed, or anything else that seemed odd even in the middle of the crash site.

Finally, Agent Scanlon looked down at his watch. "Well, Miss Morgan, it's almost midnight and I'm sure you've had a long, exhausting day. We really appreciate you taking the time to tell us this story." Reaching in his briefcase, he grabbed a couple of pieces of paper and slid them across the table to Sunny. "It would help us tremendously if you could fill out this report, though. There is no big hurry on this, but the sooner you could do it, the better your memory will be."

"Okay," Sunny replied. "But would it be okay if I just typed it out on paper instead of writing it all out by hand? That would take forever."

"Sure, no problem," Agent Scanlon said. "Ma'am, Agent Rodriguez and I also want to convey to you how much we admire you for what you did in this situation. We heard bits and pieces of what you did and found it almost unbelievable how quick you were to respond. Now that you've told us the rest, it is borderline miraculous!"

"Thank you, that's very nice," Sunny blushed. "I appreciate your kind words but what I did was what anyone else would do in the same situation."

"Maybe, Miss Morgan," Agent Rodriguez said. "And maybe not. You might not be aware of it, Ma'am, but all the talk out at the crash site is about how you and your horse rescued the governor. There are a lot of reporters who want to talk to you. Some of them asked us when we were leaving if we were going to talk to you tonight, but we just told them we were going back to town."

"Oh, yeah, Ma'am," Agent Rodriguez continued, "we thought you should know that there is a big satellite truck stuck somewhere south of here. The reporter said that a friend of yours showed them a short cut and they got stuck. They were covered with mud!"

Sunny laughed. Shauna would be tickled pink to hear about this. "Good night, gentlemen. I'll let you know when I have my report finished."

Sunny stood under the mercury vapor light as the men drove off. A thousand bugs fluttered around the humming light. It had been a long day and she felt the exhaustion creeping into her bones. The bed would feel good tonight.

"Jasmine," Sunny spoke to the cat lounging on the top step, "Sorry, girl, but you're going to have to move your lazy body so I can open the door." The cat meowed in complaint for being disturbed. "I'm sure there's mice in the barn that need chased." Sunny reached down and scratched the cat behind the ears. She thought of Shauna's remark about being left out on the prairie with only the animals to talk to. Stooped over, Sunny realized that most of her conversation lately was with the cat, Starbuck, or a variety of cows and creatures on the prairie. Pretty sad to be twenty eight years old and spend most of your time talking to animals.

Jasmine jumped up as the screen door began to creak. Sunny walked inside and around the house to open up the blinds. It was a pleasant spring evening and the cool breeze on the prairie had a cleansing effect on the house. It would be a good night to crawl under the quilt her grandmother made.

Making it upstairs, Sunny flipped on the lamp beside her bed and opened up the nightstand. Words moved her like nothing else in this world. Although she loved a Kansas sunrise or sunset, she would rather have it described in words for she found they engaged her soul and stirred her imagination.

She discovered as a little girl that what she read about right before bedtime, she often dreamed about that night. She was deliberate about the books that she read before she went to bed. If she read an action book, she would find herself engaged in some swashbuckling adventure. If she read something scary, she had nightmares.

She was careful not to read too much romance. Sometimes she dreamt of magical places and valiant princes with hope of true love. But often she slept fitfully aware of the loneliness and awoke with despair that followed her like a cloud blocking out the sun.

She opened the recently published collection of poems. Several works by an anonymous author mesmerized her since it concerned the prairie and nature.

She was memorizing her favorites. She had the first part, but she wanted the rest. The more she would read it, the easier it was to commit to memory. Laying her head against the pillow, she propped the book up on her chest and began to read.

The wind lays soft against the prairie
And gives it breath to the new day
This winding road I'm traveling on's a memory
Of a place I've been and a place I'd like to stay
But a Voice in the distant hills is calling

From the shadows, He whispers my name
And the winding road I'm traveling on will take me
To a place I'll never leave again.
A place where no one dies
A place where no one cries
And my heart finds its healing rest
In my Father's house, this journey ends
And the winding road no longer bends
And my heart finds its healing rest
From the winding road.

The winding road leads to a sun-kissed stream
And I drink in the waters cool flow
As I plunge my soul deep in its healing powers
And waves of mercy like a river roll
But a Voice in the distant hills is calling
To green pastures just over the hill
And this winding road I'm traveling on will take me
To a place where the water's deep and still.
A place where no one dies
A place where no one cries
And my heart finds its healing rest
In my Father's house, this journey ends
And the winding road no longer bends
And my heart finds its healing rest . . .

She fell asleep before the poem's end.

While asleep, Sunny was transported to a dark, green, lush part of the prairie where she could look over a vast valley. She was sitting in what seemed to be a patio out in the middle of nowhere. She looked down at her sandaled feet and found them resting on exquisite flagstone that had been skillfully quarried and expertly laid. Surrounding her was a fence of pearl white lattice work that reached about eight feet in height and resting on top of finely turned wooden poles was an open air roof made of boards that were crossed in a square pattern. A late spring breeze drifted across her skin that was warmed by the overhead sun. Suddenly, she heard her name being called by a deep male voice. Her heart raced with passion, as she knew that it was voice of her lover, her friend. Her mind didn't recognize the voice, but her heart did. This was her man! This was her lover calling her. This was her friend! She turned to peer out the lattice at the direction the voice came from, but all she saw was a shadow fleeting across the prairie with a limp.

The alarm brought Sunny straight up in bed. Startled by its suddenness – she only fell asleep what seemed like five minutes ago – she saw the light from the sun slowly cast a shadow across the west wall. She quickly fell back into bed and pulled the covers up over her eyes.

"Oh," she groaned. "I feel like I've been run over by a truck." Her mind began to race with all the memories of the day before. Could it really be true? Did that plane crash really happen? Would she get up and look outside and find it was all a dream, or nightmare?

The ache in her shoulders and arms reminded her that it was true, that the plane crash had happened, and the tranquil life on the prairie interrupted by something far beyond her ability to prevent. She wondered how the Governor was doing.

She threw the covers back and forced herself to get out of bed. She heard a vehicle coming up the drive so she walked over to the window for a better view. *It had better not be a reporter this early in the morning.* She was relieved when she recognized the rusty old red Ford pickup of Spook Masterson scissoring up the drive. Spook worked for the Clatterbucks most of his life and only retired because Josiah had passed away.

The old pickup clanged to a halt as Sunny stumbled downs the stairs. Her legs ached. A cup of coffee would feel good to wrap her fingers around.

"Git!" Sunny spoke to the cat. "I can't open the door with your lazy body laying here." Sunny looked across the yard at the welcome sight of the bow-legged old cowboy and his dusty black Stetson.

"Howdy Miss Sunshine," Spook drawled. "How are you this fine mornin'?"

"I'm great, Spook," Sunny spoke. "What brings you out to the Lonesome Star this early in the morning?"

"I was down at the café this mornin'," Spook spit a stream of tobacco juice between his teeth, "and I heered the talk about the plane crash out chere and figured that, by golly, that little heifer out chere ain't got no one to help her out so's I just saddled up ol' Bertha and drove on out chere to lend you a hand."

Spook had a nickname for everything he owned, like his old red Ford, and even things he didn't own, like people. If he liked you, you got a good nickname like Sunny's –Miss Sunshine. If he didn't, you got a bad one like the town gossip, Irene Jones, - Telephone Jones. Spook said there were three quick ways to get rumors around town: Telegraph, Telephone, and Tell-a-Irene. Spook was the object of one of her rumors and he nicknamed her Telephone Jones because, he allowed, all she did all day was talk on the phone.

Some folks thought that Spook nicknamed everyone because he couldn't remember anyone's name. Others thought it was because he figured if no one called him by his real name, Alvin, then he didn't have to call them by their real name either.

He had all kinds of names for people: Flower, for the lady that did the belly dancing at the annual town party with a flower tucked behind her ear. Not your typical belly dancer, she was rather large and unattractive. Spook said the only thing worth looking at on her was her flower. The name stuck and soon everyone in town called her Flower, but no one told her why. She assumed it was because folks thought she was pretty and everyone was nice enough to let her think that.

He got his nickname because he jumped about two feet high and let out a little scream whenever he got startled. It was purely an involuntary reaction because he was the most fearless man Sunny had ever met. In his younger years, he was one of the best bull-riders and bronc-riders in the state and even made a living on the national circuit.

"Thanks, Spook," Sunny smiled at the old cowboy. "Come on in and have a cup of coffee with me. I slept in kind of late this morning. Usually, I'm up and out of the house before the sun even comes up, but I guess my body was kind of tired."

"A cup of old joe sounds purty good, Miss Sunshine," Spook said. "I reckon I'd be mighty happy to have somethin' better than that rotten cook that lives with me could ever make."

Sunny chuckled to herself. Spook talked about the rotten cook he lived with. Strangers that didn't know him thought he was talking about his wife, but he was talking about himself.

"So I heer you're a real-live, cowgirl hero, Miss Sunshine, and that fine gelding of yorn is going to be a movie star!" Spook traipsed up the stairs.

"Oh, Spook," Sunny chided him. "I'm just little Miss Sunshine that you helped raise and you know I ain't nothing of the sorts. I just did what anyone else would do in the same predicament."

"Yeah, Miss Sunshine, that might be, but no one else but you was in the predickyment and you're the one theys all talking about saving the Guvner. Wouldn't s'prise us none if you get to be rich and famous!"

"Oh, Spook," Sunny got on him again. "You just hush that kind of talk and drink your coffee. I'll saddle up Starbuck and that old Palomino mare, Clipper, and we'll ride out and check out the crash site after breakfast. Now you just sit down and have a cup of coffee while I fix us something to eat."

Sunny poured a cup of coffee for Spook and walked back over to the stove to fix some breakfast when the phone rang. "Spook," Sunny said with her back to him. "Would you be a dear and grab that phone for me. I wonder who's calling at six thirty in the morning?"

"Sure, Miss Sunshine," Spook moved the chair away from the table and got up to answer the phone. "Howdy!" Spook almost yelled into the phone. "What's that? You're looking for who? Sunny? She's right here, I'll get her for you." Turning to Sunny he said, "It's for you, Miss Sunshine."

"Hello?" Sunny spoke.

"Hi, Sunny!" Sunny recognized the voice of her brother, Cal. "I hear there was a plane crash on the ranch yesterday. I turned on CNN this morning and heard that the Governor's plane crashed on the Lonesome Star. What happened? Do you need me to come home?"

Cal was older than her by four years and moved to Philadelphia right out of college to work as a computer programmer. Married twice, divorced twice and a kid from each, he often joked that between his ex-wives and Uncle Sam, he made as much money as the fry-boys at Burger Central.

She was never close to Cal. He was a jock in school and, standing almost six feet six, was a bully. He had all kinds of honors as a High School football, basketball, and track star in their little school out in the middle of a cow pasture, but once he went off to college on an athletic scholarship for football, he found guys a lot bigger and a lot tougher. She felt guilty for taking a secret delight in him failing, but he had always been so arrogant and demeaning. Philadelphia was a good place for him to live; it was a good place for him to stay. He was the kind of person that put himself in charge of everything. Josiah Clatterbuck said that if you have to go around saying you're in charge of something, most likely you're not.

"No," Sunny said. "There's no need to come home. Spook came out to check on me this morning and we're going to saddle up the horses and ride out to see what's going on. Most of the people left last night and the guys from the government said the crash investigators would be out there for another day or so. They talked like tomorrow or the next day they would haul the wreckage away." She told the story as briefly as possible.

"So have you been on TV yet?" Cal asked with a tinge of jealousy in his voice.

"No, and you know me well enough to know I don't want to," Sunny retorted.

"Well, you better get ready because the way the news made you look this morning you're quite the little cowgirl hero," Cal teased her. "They even had your high school picture on the news!"

Sunny shrieked, "Oh, no! Not *that* picture!"

"Yep," Cal laughed. "The one where you still have your braces and your face was all broke out from getting into that poison ivy."

"Oh, no," Sunny groaned. "Of all the pictures ever taken of me, that one was the worst. But if the reporters had shown me the way I looked last night, I didn't look much better."

"The reporter said that they couldn't get an on-air comment from the mystery cowgirl that rescued the Governor and the picture was from a school yearbook. But they did get a shot of the house briefly. It sure made me miss the old home place."

"Good grief," Sunny said. "I wonder how they got that picture of me? It had to be late last night when they did that. If I find out who did it, I'm going to rope 'em and drag them by their heels through the cattle pens."

"Yeah, I hope they get a better picture of you sometime today," Cal laughed again. "If all the people I work with are going to find out my sister was the mystery cowgirl, I don't want them to see some dorky picture of you from high school."

"Gee, thanks Cal," Sunny said. "I'd hate to make you look bad for all your friends." The sting of his remark touched old wounds that she thought covered over with scars. He said she was nothing but an ugly little tomboy and nobody would want her. She smirked inside at the old childhood rhyme, *Sticks and stones can break my bones but words will never hurt me.* Sunny would rather have been beat with a stick than to have had some of the names she was called as a kid. Words hurt. Words last a long time. Unfortunately, those demeaning words spoken over her in her life were unwelcome voices on the prairie that occasionally turned from whispers into shouts creating a deeper sense of worthlessness.

"I'm just kidding," Cal apologized. "You still can't take a joke, can you? What if I told you that I was proud of you and I'm going to brag about how you rescued the Governor of the State of Kansas?"

"Thanks," Sunny said. "I think." She hated apologies where people apologize to you for you being a jerk. She knew Cal would take the credit for raising her to be a heroine. Cal was handsome, but Cal was all about Cal and no one else. "I gotta go. Spook's got the horses saddled and is waiting outside. You know how impatient he is."

"Bye, Sunny," Cal said. "Don't be surprised if I come home this weekend. I'm going to check for cheap flights."

"Bye, Cal," Sunny said. She didn't want his arrogance on the prairie.

"You okay, Miss Sunshine?" Spook knew her well. "You sorter look like a horse kicked you in the gut."

"I'm fine, Spook." Sunny said, stroking Jasmine. "Let's go out to see what's happening on the prairie."

Chapter Twelve

"Norma," John touched her shoulder to awaken her. "It's time again we can go back in to see Dane."

Norma unfolded her stiffening body from the love seat in the family waiting room. She rubbed the back of her neck to work out the kink.

They could see Dane every two hours but only for ten minutes. Johnson and Meredith got a motel room near. Meredith's condition exacerbated under stress and regardless of how resolute a woman of courage, it was incredibly taxing on her to see her son lying there helpless.

Wiping the sleep from her eyes, Norma slipped her shoes on and glanced at her watch. It seemed impossible that within the last twenty-four hours she went from heated discussions about things painted on canvas to wondering whether or not her brother was going to live. Suddenly, arguments over Peter Radcliffe's art seemed pretty inconsequential in the scheme of things. She wondered how many people in hospitals across the nation sat through a similar vigil. Yesterday she was waist-deep in an argument over things that will someday rot; today she didn't care.

Beyond the doors, down the tiled hallway, and into the sterile environs of the ICU, she confronted life and death. There, in the theatre of mortality the helpless spectators watch the un-rehearsed drama with anticipation of successive acts. The audience applauds the tiniest glimmer of hope and cheers on the actors who must, by the nature of the performance, ad-lib all scenes. The audience recoils in horror at the slightest decrescendo of the orchestra or gasps in terror when the curtains are drawn as they wonder if it is for intermission or the final act.

"John," she slipped her arm into his, "thank you for being here – for staying through the night with me. Times like this make a person realize what the important things in life are, don't they? I don't know what I would do if I lost you, John, or one of the kids." She began to cry.

"We need not borrow trouble, Norma," John said. "I wonder the same things myself. I don't know how people make it through these things without a good family, and we have a great family."

"We sure do," Norma agreed. "One of the ladies on the Arts Council lost her brother not long ago and when the family, many who hadn't talked to each other in years, got together for the funeral, they started fighting again. She hoped that death would draw them together and they would realize how trivial their differences were. Instead, it seemed to make it all worse."

"Death and sorrow bring out raw emotions in a lot of people."

"I don't want to go see him, John," Norma stopped before the doors to the ICU opened. "If he dies, I don't want that image of him to be with me the rest of my life."

"I understand," John replied. "But Dane's not going to die and he needs to hear your voice."

As they walked through the doors near the nurse's station, they saw two nurses rush in to Dane's room.

"What's going on?" Norma glanced fearfully at the charge nurse who had come out to meet them? "Is Dane okay?"

"Ma'am," the nurse replied. "I'm sorry but we can't have you in here right now. Mr. Richards is going to be okay, but we are working on him. I know this must be frightening, but if you will go back to the waiting room, I will come out and give you information as soon as I know something. We have called Dr. Sylvan who is on his way."

"Come on, Norma," John led her back to the waiting room. "Dane is in the best care there is. Let's just go back and say a prayer for him."

Norma stared at the floor. A million vignettes of her and Dane raced through her mind.

Once inside the room, she collapsed on the sofa in a heap of tears.

"Why? Why? Why?" she sobbed. "Why Dane?" Her anger resurfaced again as she looked across the room at John who was started a fresh pot of coffee. "Why would God allow such a bad thing to happen to a good man?"

"Dane is one of the best people I know," Norma said. "From the time he was just a little kid he is one of the kindest and most truthful people I've ever been around. The newspapers take their shots at him and try to trip him up, but if the people of Kansas knew that they finally do have an honest politician in their Capitol, they would make those journalists leave him alone!"

"Dane is a good man," John agreed. "He's got the courage of a grizzly bear, but the heart of a teddy bear."

"Then why did God let this happen?" Norma pleaded again.

"Boy, Norma, I don't know. Maybe you ought to ask the Reverend that the next time you see him. I'm just a CPA, I don't know those things."

"I'm sorry, John," Norma apologized. "It's not fair for me to take out my frustration on you. It's just that if I was God and I was big enough to make the universe, then I wouldn't let bad things happen to good people. I would only let good things happen to good people and bad things to bad people.

"Come here and sit by me. It's too late at night and our feelings are too raw to have this discussion." He said as she snuggled. "We have each other, we have our family, and we have Dane. He needs us to be strong and pray for him."

"It's Dr. Sylvan," the voice through the door spoke. "Can I come in?

"Hello, Doctor" John said. "Thanks for coming down in the middle of the night."

"I thought I should let you know that we are going to have to take Dane in for surgery," Dr. Sylvan said. "I don't want to and I know he's been through a lot, but there are indications that there is further internal hemorrhaging and we must do an exploratory surgery on him to find the cause."

"Is he going to be okay?" Norma asked. "Will he be able to survive another surgery?"

"Ma'am," the doctor responded. "We don't have any other option. At the rate he is bleeding, if we don't do surgery we will lose him. It is our only option."

"Yes, Dr. Sylvan," Norma leaned on Johns' shoulder, "we understand. How long do you think it will take?"

"I have no idea." Dr. Sylvan said. "If the hemorrhaging is where we suspect, then it will be a quick surgery. If not, then we will have to explore and there is no telling how long that will take."

"Thank you, Doctor." John shook his hand. "We know he's in good hands with you."

"I suppose I ought to call your parents and let them know they are taking Dane back in." John reached for the phone. "Do you have the hotel's number?"

"Do you think we ought to let them know?" Norma asked. "It's the middle of the night and they just got to sleep a couple of hours ago."

John hung up the phone. "You're right." He agreed, "They need their rest and if I called them they would rush right over here and there's not a dadgum thing they can do about it. It would be best to let them sleep and tell them in the morning."

"John," Norma asked. "Would you get married again if I died?"

"Whoa, where did that come from?" John asked. "Haven't we talked about this before?"

"I know we joked about it several times, but we've never been this close to death and I was just wondering if you would remarry."

"Would you?" John rebutted. He hated *what if* conversations. The Army taught him to prepare for *worst-case-scenarios*, but *what if* scenarios usually ended with one person questioning whether the other one was telling the truth.

"I've always thought Dane would one day find another wife and I've told you that I would want you to remarry after I'm gone. But now that I'm this close to someone dying, I don't think I would want you to get remarried."

John felt trapped. First he had to try to answer the *Why does God allow bad things to happen to good people?* question, and now he has to answer the *Will you get remarried when I die?* question. Both were like walking through mine fields – one wrong step and all hell would break loose. "Honey, I love you completely and this is not the time or the place to have this conversation. We must focus on getting Dane well."

"I know, I'm sorry," Norma said. "I've never been this afraid of anything before in my life. I try to sleep but I just dream of Dane. I wish Debbie were here. But another thing that frightens me is that if Debbie is somehow trying to get Dane to go over to the other side with her right now, he won't want to come back here."

John pulled Norma closer. He felt guilty since he had spent most of the night worrying about practical things like shifting the power over to the Lieutenant Governor and wondering about the press lingering around outside. He wanted to watch the news, but was afraid to turn on the television in fear that Norma would get upset. They were the ones that knew the true status of Dane and what they would see on the news was mere speculation. He knew Norma's proclivity to worry and if some half-baked reported claimed to have inside information, it would cause her tremendous stress.

John did admire Dane. When he started dating Norma in their senior year of college, he hadn't always been happy that Norma wanted to take Dane everywhere. He joked that had Norma had her way, they would have taken Dane on their honeymoon. But it was her love and care for Dane that helped John fall in love with Norma. He admired the mothering qualities of Norma and Dane was such a good kid. He was enjoyable and she was the credit for much of his personal development.

Dane was not only a good brother-in-law, but also a good friend. He never quite understood the relationship between Dane and Ron Moore, but Dane was better to Moore than most would have been.

Dane taught John to risk. Being a number cruncher and watching people take big risks lose it all, John's own father played his cards close to his vest and took little, if any, risks. Any investment was secure and any hobby was safe.

But Dane coaxed him into a variety of outdoor pursuits that John never thought he would like. However, once he did it, he found it more exhilarating than he imagined. He chuckled thinking about the sheer terror he had felt while looking out the airplane with a parachute strapped to his back. The look on Dane's face was priceless as he yelled, "Geronimo!" and jumped out.

John remembered the first few seconds of falling and how, even though a man raised in a strict Christian home and never one himself to curse, shouted one expletive for a good thirty seconds while hurling towards the earth.

"If anyone can make it," John whispered to Norma, "it will be Dane."

Chapter Thirteen

"Now, who do you reckon that big fancy truck yonder is coming acrost the prairie?" Spook asked Sunny. "Want me to fire off a couple of rounds out of ol' May-Belle to scare 'em off?"

Sunny chuckled. "No, Spook, better not do that. Sheriff Mitchell is lookin' for a good reason to give me trouble anyway, I don't want to give him one."

She knew Spook wouldn't do it – he only carried that pistol, Maybelle, for "rat'lers" as he called them. Spook's old friend, Charlie Calhoun whom Spook called "Chuckwagon" since he was so portly, told the story about he and Spook stumbling along a stony creek bank years ago looking for a stray calf when a big old diamondback rat'ler started hissing at Spook. Being spooky anyway, Chuckwagon claims Spook jumped two feet straight up in the air when the rat'ler lunged at him causing the big snake to miss. When he came back down he crushed the snake's head, by accident, with the heel of his boot. That snakeskin is still wrapped in a band around Spook's black Stetson.

But to hear Spook tell it, he had gone into mortal combat with the snake catching it in mid-air and wrestling it down with his bare hands and even skinning him alive while he was still hissing. He would tell the young cowboys, "Take a poke at me, boys, and I'll be wearin' yore hide around my Stetson!"

The thought of trying to keep people away was pretty appealing to Sunny. Already the prairie had a path worn into a road as repeated vehicles ran down the grass. And making it worse, there were multiple paths across the prairie. They rode into one valley where a big vehicle had been stuck and there were deep ruts. Sunny got angrier. None of these people had a right to trespass on private property let alone tear the prairie up while they were at it. It wasn't her fault and it wasn't the prairie's fault that the Governor crashed out here. By gosh, the Governor's office better pay for the mess they made!

They crested the hill to where the crash site was cordoned off with bright yellow tape. She recognized Agents Scanlon and Rodriquez in their blue jackets with the NTSB letters on the back. They looked up as Starbuck whinnied and waved.

The big cobalt blue pickup roared across the prairie towards them, startling both of their horses. Starbuck laid his ears back and danced away from the roar of the big diesel engine as the truck slid to a stop on the early morning dew. One by one, the doors of the club cab flew open and out from one jumped a short, bearded man with a T.V. camera. He was busy hooking something on his belt when a tall blond, a reporter that Sunny had seen on the local evening news, came striding around the corner like a model straight out of a western clothing catalog. "City slickers." She mumbled to Spook.

"Hi, Ma'am," the blond spoke. "I'm Mackenzie Foster with KDTV from Topeka. Are you the mystery cowgirl that rescued the Governor?"

Sunny moaned. Now it begins. She hadn't even thought about being interviewed today and threw on her favorite old gingham shirt that morning. She felt like a rube and already the bearded man was scaring the horses with his camera trying to get various angles.

"Well," Sunny replied. "I don't know what you mean by being the mystery cowgirl or rescuing the Governor, I just did what anyone would do. And my name is Sunny Morgan and this here is my good friend, Spook Masterson."

"Would you mind stepping down from your horse so I could ask a few questions?" Mackenzie asked Sunny. "You are quite a heroine young lady and there is an admiring audience that wants to meet you."

Sunny grudgingly swung a leg over her saddle to dismount and no sooner had she got the other foot out of the stirrup and the bearded man ran around the back of Starbuck. "Mister," Sunny said. "Sneaking around the backside of a horse that's nervous is a good way to end up with your butt between your ears."

Mackenzie burst out in laughter and spoke to the man, "Al, why don't we come out here away from the horse. Maybe Mr. Masterson would be so kind to hold the horse and we could get a shot of Sunny out in the grass with the horses and Mr. Masterson in the background."

Sunny glanced up at Spook and saw him puffing up like a toad eating June bugs. He was a sucker for a pretty lady and was preening himself like an old cock pheasant strutting down a cornrow. "I'd be right happy, Miss Foster, to hep you'uns out any way I can." He adjusted his black Stetson and fixed the red bandana around his neck. Sunny wondered what kind of nickname he would come up with for Mackenzie.

"Has anyone else interviewed you yet?" Mackenzie asked Sunny. Once Sunny got closer to her she realized that Mackenzie was older than what she appeared on T.V. Although her face seemed flawless with the deep blue eyes and perfect complexion, Sunny noticed Mackenzie's hands sticking out from the long sleeved shirt. Those were definitely not the hands of a young woman.

"No," Sunny replied liking her more than she thought she would. "There was a guy last night that came to the barn but my friend kind of led him the other direction."

Mackenzie laughed. "Oh, that must be Rob! We heard that he and his cameraman got stuck in a low water bridge somewhere around here. They didn't get out until four this morning."

"Serves them right!" Sunny exclaimed. "They were being rude and wouldn't take no for an answer!"

"Well," Mackenzie laughed again. "I hope you don't think we're being rude and please forgive my cameraman. He is the best in the state but sometimes forgets to ask permission." Sunny relaxed.

"Sunny, this is how this will work today, if it is okay with you," Mackenzie began. "I'm going to clip this little microphone on you and it will just hang on the lapel of your shirt. That way you don't have a big microphone stuck in your face. Then I'm going to ask you a few questions and you just say whatever you feel comfortable saying. Just look at me when you talk that way the camera won't make you nervous."

"Al," Mackenzie turned and found the cameraman scurrying back from the truck. "Why don't you give us a little space while you're filming?" Sunny could tell that Al didn't want to give them space, but Mackenzie sensed that Sunny would retreat into a shell faster than a box turtle.

"Have you heard how the Governor is doing?" Sunny asked.

"The latest report was that he had had surgery and was recovering but had a long road to recovery ahead of him. Didn't you watch any news?"

"Oh, by the time I got cleaned up last night the news would have been over and what little I heard this morning was what Spook picked up down at the Wrangler Café so I don't know much. Was the other fellow okay?"

"Ron Moore?" Mackenzie asked. "Yes, his wife was interviewed last night and she said he was doing very well. Now, enough of them; let's talk about you."

After the first few questions, it didn't feel like an interview at all to Sunny but a conversation instead. Occasionally, she would notice the cameraman working for different angles and watched him creep closer, but she was more engaged in conversation with Mackenzie who seemed genuinely interested. For the most part, she just recounted the story as it happened with just a few questions from Mackenzie. Mackenzie was impressed.

"Sunny," Mackenzie said when they were finished. "I'm going to have Al take your microphone away and you and I are just going to visit for a while – sort of off the record.

"Oh, okay," Sunny said. "Can I go get Starbuck though, I'm sure he's getting pretty nervous by now."

"I'll tell you what," Mackenzie said. "Why don't I follow you back there and that way Mr. Masterson can hear what I have to say to you. Do you trust him?"

Trust him? Sunny almost laughed out loud. Spook Masterson was the most trust worthy person she had ever known outside of her Dad. In fact, in all of the rough times of her life with her Mom dying of cancer when she was twelve then her Dad taking his life, Spook was the only thing that kept her sane. If he had not have stepped in like he did, she would have lost the ranch.

She often teased Spook that he needed to have a son her age just like him so she could marry him. Or, if he were thirty years younger, she'd calf-rope him and make him marry her. That was about the only thing that could make old Spook blush. "Why, shucks," he said, "a purty little filly like you can find the finest stallion in the pasture."

"Yeah, but!" she retorted, "the problem with most stallions is they like to breed a lot of mares!" As he turned to walk away, she could see the red traveling up his neck above the bandana. She did it just to watch him blush, but she also knew that she made the old bachelor feel pretty good.

"Oh, Mackenzie," Sunny replied. "I'd trust Spook with my life."

Mackenzie admired Sunny's grace as she vaulted into the saddle. "You were probably born on a horse weren't you?" she asked not expecting an answer. "Sunny, I really like you and I have some things to say to you that you can either take or leave, but I want you to seriously think them over."

She continued, "I don't know if you're really aware of what you have done in rescuing the Governor. You might think just anyone else would have done the same things under the same circumstances, but the fact is, no one else was out here but you and your horse. Most everyone is saying that if it had not been for you, the Governor would not have survived."

Sunny blushed, "Thanks, Miss Foster, but I just did what anyone would do."

"Well, be that as it may, the fact is that you did it and you, whether you want to or not, are going to become famous," Mackenzie explained. "I've been in this business a long time and I can tell when a story is so unusual that it has staying power and this one does. The kind of thing you did, Sunny, is so unique and so inspirational that people are going to want to know everything there is to know about you and what happened."

"There's nothing to be afraid of," Mackenzie noticed the fear in Sunny's eyes. "As long as you have someone that you can trust to help you. Sunny, I want you to listen very carefully to what I am saying: There are going to be offers for you to appear on national television with some of the biggest names in the news. There are going to be writers who want to tell your story for you and will offer you what seems like a large amount of money. You most likely will be approached by someone wanting to make a movie." Mackenzie wanted to go further but backed away when she saw how nervous Sunny was becoming.

"I'm telling you this, Sunny, so you will be protected," Mackenzie warned. "You love this ranch and this prairie don't you?"

"More than anyone will ever know." Sunny said.

"Well, I don't know how you sit financially," Mackenzie went on, "but I grew up on a farm in western Kansas and know that most farmers and ranchers struggle to keep their head above water and you will most likely have the opportunity to make a lot of money. I know you didn't rescue the Governor with this in mind, but I'll guarantee you that the offers will be coming. But you have to be careful, Sunny, there are some folks out there that aren't very nice and you could end up sorry you ever got involved with them."

"So what should I do?" Sunny asked, "I don't know anything about any of this?"

"I'm sure you don't," Mackenzie replied. "Sunny, I really like you and admire you. You have innocence about you that I remember once having. I'd like to protect that if you'd let me."

"Well," Sunny said. "I'd have to think about it?"

"Of course you do." Mackenzie backed away. She admired Sunny and knew there were pariahs that would leave her penniless. Sunny's story could be told with purity or vulgarity; it depended on the writer.

"I'll tell you what," Mackenzie offered. "I'll give you my card and you think about it. If you need me, give me a call. Ask others that you trust for advice and get back with me if you're so inclined."

"Thanks," Sunny said, "I'll let you know."

Mackenzie turned to walk back to the truck but stopped. "Sunny, in our business we see a lot of bad things happen and meet a lot of bad people and show a lot of bad stories. When we get together in a newsroom and talk about stories that we have to tell and how depressing they become to even us, we often talk about how we need more good stories to tell. Sunny, you have a great story to tell and of all the work I've done through the years, I think your story is the best because of you."

Sunny felt the red creeping up her neck as she ducked her head struggling for words to say. "Thank you, that's really nice, Ma'am."

"No, thank you, Sunny, for just being you," Mackenzie replied. "Oh yeah," she said as almost an afterthought, "there are going to be more cowboys come out of the wood work than you've seen in ten years. You be careful about them. Some of them just want a trophy to show off and won't care a lick about the real you underneath. You protect yourself just like you want to protect this ranch. Okay?"

"Okay." Sunny agreed. The few attempts at a relationship after Shane had been awkward. Even though she knew it was silly, the little girl in her longed for the handsome prince charming to come rushing in on a gallant steed and sweep her off her feet. Instead, she got Spook on a swayback Palomino mare.

"I'll make sure Miss Sunshine behaves herself real well." Spook interrupted reaching into his saddlebags to pull out his pistol. "I got my trusty old friends here, Mr. Smith and Mr. Wesson and betwixt the three of us companeros, ain't no wild-eyed stallion gonna git next to our filly, I don't care how pedigreed he is."

"Thanks, Spook." Sunny patted the old man on the leg and spoke to Mackenzie, "You don't have to worry, ol' Spook here's been keeping me out of trouble for most of my life."

"Good!" Mackenzie smiled; that old man at his age was twice the man of men half his age. She wished she had a Spook Masterson in her life. "Well, you two take care of each other. Oh, yeah, if you watch the news tonight at six and at ten, you'll be on! Goodbye for now. Don't forget to call if you need anything."

"Goodbye." Sunny turned Starbuck in the direction of the crash site. She recognized Agent Scanlon and Rodriguez and waved to them as they drew near the bright yellow tape that cordoned off the area.

"Good morning, Miss Morgan," Agent Scanlon spoke first. "How are you this morning?"

"Oh," Sunny said, "just wishing everyone would leave my property alone."

"I'm sure you would, Ma'am. We'll only be here another day or two and will get the wreckage cleaned up. Sorry, but we have to try to do our job."

"I know," Sunny softened. "It's just that folks are already helping themselves to the gate that's closed and has a *No Trespassing* sign on it. I suggested to Spook we just lock it but he remembers years ago our neighbors found some Indian artifacts and some folks just cut right through good fence to get out there. I don't want to have to fix any more fence than I have to."

"Hopefully," Agent Rodriguez chimed in. "Once we get out of here, the curiosity- seekers will go somewhere else. By the way, while you're out here could you show us how that wing was laying on the plane?"

Sunny dismounted and walked over to the plane. She felt her skin start to tingle like static electricity and her stomach tie up in knots. As she got closer, she smelled the combination of blood, mud, urine, and vomit; it made her nauseous. Agent Scanlon noticed her stumble.

"You can come back later, if you'd like, Ma'am," Agent Scanlon said. "We don't have to do this right now."

"No," Sunny replied, "I'm just fine. That smell was worse than I remember."

"Well, you probably had a lot of adrenaline pumping yesterday and didn't notice it," Agent Rodriquez replied.

"Oh, I noticed it all right!" Sunny exclaimed. "The first time I stuck my head in that plane I thought I was going to lose it. I've smelled some bad things out on the farm, but that was one of the worst."

Changing the subject, Sunny asked, "So do you know why they crashed?"

"Although we have a lot of tests to run, it is most likely that he got caught in those thunderstorms and the plane started icing up," Scanlon said.

"Icing up when it's 70 degrees outside?" Sunny asked.

"Yeah, it's easy to forget he was flying maybe as high as eight to ten thousand feet and, like going up in the mountains in the summer, it's a lot colder up there than down here."

"But why would he fly in a storm. I'm not a pilot and I even know better than that."

"Well, Ma'am, sometimes those storms build so fast and go in directions you don't quite anticipate and pretty soon you're trapped."

Sunny nodded in acknowledgement. There were many times she had been out on the prairie and thought she had plenty of time to get back to the house only to get caught in a deluge by a storm. They were ferocious and unpredictable.

"About here," Sunny motioned. "It was lying at an angle but sort of twisted too."

"And how did you get it off again?" Agent Scanlon asked.

"Well, I grabbed the lasso off of Starbuck and looped it around the end, then I jumped in the saddle and dallied the other end since I didn't know how much weight was on there," Sunny explained.

"What do you mean, you *dallied* it?" Rodriguez queried.

"Well, there's basically two ways to wrap a rope around a saddle horn," Sunny explained. "You can *dally* it, which means you wrap it around the horn and hold on to the end. That way, you can turn loose of it real quick if you need to, like if you got a mad cow on the other end that wants to perforate you with a couple of holes with its horns and you and the horse need to get out of the way real quick like. Or, you can tie it around the horn with a little clip that lets it stay there and most likely the saddle would get dragged off the horse before that rope turned loose."

"Oh," Agent Scanlon replied. "We're from the city and aren't familiar with cowboy terminology."

"Why don't you come plop yoreself astride this old mare heer and I'll l'arn ya a thing or two about bein' a cowpoke."

Scanlon laughed but politely declined. "There'd be another wreck out here to clean up if I got on that horse."

Chapter Fourteen

"Chris! Chri-is!" Jennifer Conroy shouted out the door of the lodge for her husband who was walking up from the river. "Hurry, there's something you've got to see on the news!"

Chris was fishing by himself that day, something he rarely got to do since he spent most of his time guiding. He hit his own "honey-holes" up the river that he kept entirely for himself. It wasn't that the fish were any bigger; it was more secluded and the fish, although smaller, were more beautiful.

"What is it?" Chris shouted back.

"It's Governor Richards! He went down in an airplane crash and they're interviewing the lady that rescued him." Jennifer shouted back.

Chris lengthened his stride and rushed into the lodge. Usually, Jennifer would get on him about wet waders, but not today. As Chris rounded the corner of the study he was startled to see the television footage of the tangled heap of the Governor's airplane.

"What happened?" he asked Jennifer. "Is he okay?"

Jennifer filled him in on the details but stopped when the interview with Sunny came on again.

"That's Sunny Morgan!" Chris shouted. "I know her! She went to school with my little sister!"

"Wow, he was just here! That is incredible! Who would have

113

thought that Sunny Morgan would rescue the Governor? She was always such a tom-boy, though, so if anyone could do it, it would be her."

"Why don't you call your sister? She still lives out there doesn't she?" Jennifer suggested.

"Yeah, but I haven't talked to her since last Thanksgiving. I feel bad just calling her up for gossip." Chris felt guilty for not calling her, then remembered she hadn't called him either.

"Shauna?" Chris spoke into the phone. "Is that you?"

"Hey, Chris!" Shauna said. "Great to hear from you. Sorry, but I had my mouth full when you called. What's up?"

"Jennifer and I just saw the news about the plane crash. Have you been out there yet?"

"Yeah, Sunny called me up as soon as she got back from the house so I was out there when the Life Flight people were there. She did a heck of a job and is already quite the heroine around here. I went into the Wrangler for lunch today and she was the topic of conversation."

"I'll bet!" Chris said. "Are there a lot of people in town?"

"Of course! The Wrangler was full and there were car tags from Oklahoma and Nebraska sitting in the lot. I reckon they'll be more from other states as time goes by."

"Is Sunny married? Didn't she date Shane Hollowell for a while?"

"No, she's not married. He treated her pretty badly and she hasn't had a whole lot to do with men since. I keep expecting him to show back up in town, though, just to try to horn in on all the publicity. He was a pretty boy that wanted to be the star of any show. But ol' Spook Masterson is out there now taking care of her. She's been like a daughter to him for years so it's good someone's watching out after her. Anybody that goes after Sunny is going to have to get through Spook first."

"Spook Masterson!" Chris laughed. "Is that old coot still around? He has to be one of the orneriest old cowboy's I've ever met. I remember working cattle with him when I was a kid one summer and

114

he slipped while cutting mountain oysters off a calf and ruined my brand new pair of boots. That scalpel cut clear through the leather for four inches but never drew a drop of blood. When I started complaining he told me to go start nursing on one of them old milk cows."

They both laughed. Spook was a fixture in the community that all had a story about. He was well liked, but never got close to anyone, except Sunny, and he was known to dote on her.

"Did you know the Governor had just been fishing with me before all this happened?" Chris asked.

"No!" Shauna exclaimed. "He was with you? In Colorado?"

"Yes, he and his brother-in-law, Ron Moore, were out here fly-fishing with me for a couple of days and they must have crashed on their way back."

"That other guy was his brother-in-law? Sunny didn't care for him very much. Said he was a whiner and she was pretty sure he wet himself and threw up everywhere."

"That sounds like Moore," Chris said. "Governor Richards is so nice to him but most of the time I just want to hold his head under the water until the bubbles stop. He fell in the river the last day they were here and I'm sure I heard the Governor laughing."

"Well, you must be doing pretty well with yourself," Shauna said. "Fly-fishing with the almighty Governor of the great state of Kansas."

"I've been pretty fortunate, Shauna," Chris said "It was just divine appointment that I got this lodge out here anyway. I could never have afforded it myself, but I had been guiding Dane before he became Governor and he asked me one day what my dreams were. I told him I wanted to own my own fishing lodge and he asked me if I had any spotted that I liked. I told him of one I knew might come up for sale. He asked me why I didn't go after it and I told him we just didn't have the money."

Chris continued, "After he got back home from his trip, he called me up and told me that his wife had a dream while he was gone and in that dream, he was helping a young man start a business. So he told me to write a business plan, get all my ducks in a row, and he would help me out by partnering with me."

"Wow, Chris," Shauna said. "I never knew that. We always just thought you got all your money from Jennifer's family since ours was so broke we couldn't afford to pay attention."

"No, we have purposed to make it on our own without tapping into Jennifer's family fortune. We figured we would be a lot better off than some of her siblings spending their fortunes on all kind of things yet end up miserable. Her Dad offered to give us the money, but we decided to partner with Dane and borrow what we needed. He co-signed for us, but this is a pure business deal and we intend to make him money with it, too."

"Didn't Sunny have a couple of brothers?" Chris asked.

"Yeah, she had two - Cal and Daniel - both are jerks. Cal lives back east and Sunny mentioned he might come in this weekend, but I'll guarantee you she ain't looking forward to it. We're hoping he figures out there isn't anything he can do and just stay home."

"What about her other brother? Whatever became of him?" Chris asked.

"Daniel? He's actually out in California now and that's a good place for him to be too. One on the east coast and one on the west is best for Sunny. Sunny doesn't hear from him much other than when he calls her up telling her of his latest promotions. He's a graphic artist at one of the studios and will call her up and brag about his work. She made the mistake of asking for some money to help pay the taxes on the land and he let her know real quick-like that the ranch could go back to the bank. He hated growing up there and never wanted to go back."

"So Sunny runs it by herself?" Chris asked disbelieving.

"For the most part. She hires seasonal help with the haying and Spook's out there a lot of time to help her so they manage to get by, but I know it's a struggle."

"How long has it been since her father killed himself?" Chris asked.

"Gosh, I'll have to think about that. Let's see, it was my sophomore year of college. Wow, it doesn't seem like it was that long ago."

"I was gone when that happened. Why did he do it? I can't remember?"

"He'd been fighting depression for years and after having lost his wife to cancer a few years earlier, guess he just got tired of trying."

"But what a horrible thing to do to your kids." Chris said, "I imagine they all wonder every day what they could have done differently to make things better."

"Sunny and I have had a lot of long talks about this and she gets pretty angry at her dad, which just makes her feel bad about herself. I know it hurts her a lot every day."

"Well, the kids are being awfully quiet and I've learned to become very suspicious when that happens. Hey, don't wait for another plane crash to call me again sometime!"

"Wait a minute, little sister," Chris laughed. "The phone line goes both ways, you know."

"I know," Shauna chuckled. "I was just kidding. It really was good to talk to you Chris. Tell Jennifer *Hi* for me. I love you big brother."

"I love you too, little sister."

Chapter Fifteen

"Mackenzie?" Sunny asked through the telephone. "This is Sunny Morgan, the lady that had the plane crash on her land. Do you have a minute?"

"Of course!" Mackenzie answered. "How are you anyway? It's so good to hear your voice again. And how is our good friend, Spook?"

"Oh, Spook's just fine. He's feeling pretty important right about now. He managed to get a new chain and padlock on the gate down the end of the driveway so we don't have near as much problem with *furiners* as he calls them. He caught someone trying to cut through a fence down on the south section line and fired his pistol in the air to warn them. He said *'dem city slickers piled in that car like a bunch of treed 'coons running from a blood hound.'* But it must have worked. Haven't had any problems since then."

"He's quite a guy," Mackenzie said. "All the folks on my crew said that he was a pure American cowboy, the last of a dying breed. So what can I do for you?"

"I've been getting phone calls on the answering machine from different radio and television stations wanting to interview me and I don't know what to do. One of them was even from an assistant to that big talk show host Candace Cox. There must have been fifty messages yesterday and if I talk to all of them, I'll never get anything done."

Mackenzie was surprised that Sunny called her so quickly. It had only been a couple of days since the crash and she knew the media would swarm in like a flies on a cow-pie. Even the short bit that their station ran sparked a tremendous amount of response from the viewers. Sunny had a great story and the nation would clamor to hear it.

"Sunny, I told you that you have a great story on your hands and there are going to be a lot of people that want to hear it," Mackenzie responded. She knew if Sunny understood the magnitude of the audience that would want to hear this, it would probably make her too nervous to ever interview with anyone. "I'm glad you called me though, I think I can help you through this." Mackenzie received a few calls herself from folks wanting her to help set up a meeting with Sunny.

Mackenzie talked with the station manager, Gordon Chapman. Gordon had the reputation in the media industry as being a tough old curmudgeon, but fair. He should have retired years ago, so most said, but it was all he knew. He joked to Mackenzie once that if he retired, he'd die within the month. Although considered a relic from a different era of journalism by some, he was still respected for his business savvy as well as his ability to know what the public did and didn't like, even before it got to the polls. It was a sixth-sense of sorts, one that was learned by intuition rather than an institution.

Mackenzie felt a special bond with Sunny when she first met her and developed a mothering inclination to protect her. She talked to Gordon about the story and they both agreed that this was the type of story that would someday end up in a movie. Like Mackenzie, Gordon saw his fair share of innocent people picked apart like carrion by the vultures of media and entertainment. Sunny was a Kansas girl, born and bred, and they needed to make sure no one took advantage of her.

Both Gordon and Mackenzie knew they needed a plan for the best way to help Sunny. Of course, an attorney would have be put on retainer since Sunny was going to be offered contract after contract, but if this was handled ethically and ran like a business, then Sunny would stand to profit. A good public relations person would need to be hired, too, which would help Sunny navigate the often-murky world of media and entertainment. The more they discussed, the more determined they were to protect her innocence as well as helping her to take care of the ranch.

"Sunny," Mackenzie began, "I know you don't know me very well but I do appreciate you calling me. I visited with my boss, Gordon Chapman, who is the station manager here and everyone agrees that this is a great story and you are likely to become somewhat famous."

"Oh, I'm not wanting to become famous," Sunny said. "I just want to know whether or not to return any of these calls."

"The last time we visited, Sunny, I told you that a story like this could become something that could help you take care of the ranch financially. I know this was all an accident and you just happened to be in the right spot at the right time, but it is a wonderful story and people in the news and entertainment business know a great story when they see it."

Mackenzie continued, "Sunny, people in the news and entertainment business are still in a business and businesses have to make money. So while they know this is a great story, they are discussing ways to make money off this story. The more people they get to watch their show, the more sponsors are willing to pay for advertising, the more people shop the advertisers, and on, and on, and on, until everyone in the loop makes money, preferably lots of money. Sunny, they don't do it just to be nice people, although many of them are. They have to make money."

"But I'm not really interested in making money off this," Sunny replied.

"I know you're not, Sunny, that's what makes you so special," Mackenzie said. Could there be someone this innocent left in the world? "But there are a lot of people who want to make money with this story and you have all the right in the world to make money too.

Who knows, maybe this was just God's nice little gift to you to help you keep the ranch?"

"So what do I do?" Sunny asked, frightened by the staggering concept of it all.

"Well," Mackenzie explained, "the first thing you have to do is to get an attorney."

"What?" Sunny interrupted, "I can't hardly afford to pay taxes on this place, let alone pay for an attorney!"

"I know, Sunny, but there is such a thing as an attorney who will work for you and agree to a certain percentage of the profit you make if that ever materializes."

"Oh," Sunny softened a little. "You mean like Spook wont' let me pay him for helping me work all the cattle until he makes sure we have a good sale."

"Precisely," Mackenzie agreed. "They know they are going to get paid sooner or later and the harder they work now, the more money they're likely to make later."

"Spook says he would work for free, but I told him that no one works for me for free or they can just go back home."

Mackenzie laughed. "And I bet Spook probably takes all that money you give him and buys you Christmas presents with it."

"No, he tried that one year and I purt near ran him off the property. Now he takes it and buys the poor children in town Christmas presents."

Mackenzie was flabbergasted. In her crazy world of journalism and the constant barrage of corruption, competition, crime, and heartache, could it be that there was someone else as kind as Sunny and Spook in this world?

"Gordon and I know an attorney we both know and trust. He is a good man and considered to be as honest as the day is long. I don't mean to jump ahead of you, Sunny, and we have not contacted this man, I wanted to make sure I had good information in case you ever called," Mackenzie explained.

"I do appreciate that," Sunny replied. "It would be nice to be able to make sure I don't lose the farm. Cattle prices aren't the best and hay and grain just get higher each year. If you think this is that important, I'll trust you to help me out.

Mackenzie's spine tingled. Trust? She decided a long time ago not to trust anyone. She had been burned too many times in business and in love to ever to give away to someone something so valuable as her trust. And yet, this beautiful young cowgirl in the middle of nowhere surrounded by tall grasses and fat cattle told Mackenzie that she trusted her. Mackenzie swore an oath under her breath that she would never, ever, violate this special gift of trust this innocent beauty was handing her. She would guard it as one of the most precious gifts in life.

"Will you be able to make money off of this, too?" Sunny interrupted her thoughts. "I would want you to make money from this story if that ever happens. But I've got to tell you, I feel really odd talking about money. I didn't do any of this to make money."

"Sunny," Mackenzie said. "It might be that you don't make a dime off of this at all. It just might be that no one is really interested and that no one will try to make a dime off of this story. I know it feels odd talking about money when that was the last thing in your mind when you dragged the Governor out of the plane, but from my side of the fence and all my years' experience, I can tell you that this story has the potential to become a money-maker."

Mackenzie admitted to herself that a few appropriately placed phone calls to the right people and she would make a fat little finder's fee. But she also knew that they would wreak havoc on Sunny's life.

"I will be candid with you, Sunny," Mackenzie said. "Gordon and I both agree you need a public relations person to help you navigate some of the other aspects of this that are not legal, but still very important. But here is the deal I'll make with you. If you want me to be that person, then I will be happy to do it just like the attorney or when Spook works for you. If you make money, then you pay me for my time. If I'm wrong about this, then you're not out anything and I will be a better person for having taken a risk on something so admirable. But if you want to talk to Spook, and find someone else, then I will help you find the right person. It's your call."

Sunny began shyly, "Uh, I've already talked to Spook about this and he said he thought you were a *real fine filly and he'd been around the herd of hooman bein's long enough to spot a jackass trying to act like a thoroughbred.* He trusts you too, that maybe the Maker happened to send you along first seein's how I could get confused about which trail to follow."

Mackenzie had goose bumps. No one ever told her that she was the result of a Divine appointment. She laughed, "Well, you tell Spook I appreciate him calling me a filly and not an old pasture mare. I'll tell you what we need to do to get started. First, I want to make a few phone calls about The Candace Cox Show. Her ratings are the highest and you would by-pass kissing a lot of toads if you got straight in with her show. But, she's in it to make money and can be the right connection for a book or movie."

Mackenzie continued, "I know you're hard to reach, Sunny, so I'll give you my direct line and whenever you get back to the house through-out the day, you give me a call and I'll keep you up-to-date on where we're at. And if anyone else calls, just give them my number and have them talk to me. In the meantime, you need to figure out what day you might be free to come to the city next week. I'll need you to sit down with Gordon and the attorney plus me for an hour or so to discuss all of this. I'll warn you, Sunny, you'll need to sign a contract or two so be prepared. If you meet this attorney and decide you don't like her, then we will find someone else."

"Is it okay if I bring Spook with me?" Sunny asked.

"Absolutely!" Mackenzie said. "You bring that bow-legged cowboy to the big city and we'll take the both of you out for the finest steak dinner you've had in years."

Sunny got off the phone and sat down in a chair at the kitchen table dizzy by the thought of all of it. Attorneys, public relations people, books, movies, The Candace Cox Show. What happened to her world? Three days ago she was checking fences to make sure the cattle wouldn't get out and looking forward to the weekend and the Annual Prairie Festival Rodeo.

She won the calf roping last year and hoped to win it again this year. The purse had jumped up this year with some new sponsors, but that meant the competition would too. Last year, she took the $500 for first place and finished paying the taxes on land, but this year she needed to win the $1,000 first place money to make that happen. Spook worked with her on roping and she improved, but roping a calf in front of a grandstand full of people was a lot different than just chasing them across a bare arena with Spook perched on that calf-chute.

She hoped Shane wouldn't be there, or at least if he was, she wouldn't know it before she had to rope. He missed it last year and she was relieved he wasn't there. But she would like to win it with him watching her. She wondered if he ever missed her or was ever sorry. But from what she had heard in the rumor mill, he seemed to be getting along fine in his life and had been through a few other women since her, so apparently he didn't miss her too much. She dreaded the answering machine at the end of the day since he would occasionally leave messages. But those messages coincided with the times broke up with other girls. She never called him back.

She expected him to call now that she had been on the news. When she had played back the other messages, she kept waiting to hear his voice. It would be just like him to call now, but she knew that, like her bother Cal, he just wanted in on the glory.

"Cal! Oh, no, he might come home this weekend!" she groaned. She hadn't thought about Cal since the phone call, but suddenly remembered he threatened to come home this weekend. The last thing she needed was him nosing around in her business and trying to be the big shot. He would be particularly obnoxious at the rodeo trying to woo anything that wore a skirt. He had a drinking problem before he left and that explained his failed marriages. Him showing up and getting drunk at a rodeo would be too much for her to handle. Spook would keep him in check the best he could. Spook would protect her, even if it were from her own brother.

Would she go to the dance? She had gone to more rodeo dances than she could count when she was younger, but it seemed a little more awkward with each passing year. She had met Shane at a dance and he had to ask her several times before she said yes and she only agreed then because he was a good dancer. Most of the cowboys fancied themselves good dancers but, like Spook said, they looked like bulls trying to do cross-stitch: clumsy, frustrated, and way out of their element.

But at her age now, most of the cowboys were spoken for and the ones that were free had usually busted the gates of another holding pen for greener pastures and weren't to be trusted. And if she went to the dance and Shane was there with his newest flame, then it would be too awkward. No, she wouldn't even go to the dance. She would rope and be done. Spook didn't like dances any more than she did, even though he was light on his feet and could dance with the best of them.

Another reason Spook didn't like to go to dances was because of Mildred Van Arsdale, a woman that simply could not leave her hands off of him. She was quite a gad-a-bout anyway and when she saw Spook at a dance, she made it a point to be within arm's reach of him all night long. Spook commented that he was glad she lived another county away and it was long distance or she'd be calling him up more than Telephone Jones.

Old Millie wore more make-up than most and enough perfume that, as Spook said, "You could smell 'er in a litter of freshly sprayed skunks!" She made no bones that she would be happy to be Mrs. Spook Masterson, but Spook allowed, "Having her as a missus would be like livin' in a cave with a grizzly b'ar and a pole cat. Ifn' a feller ever did get cut loose, you'd be jumpy and smelly the rest of yore life!"

But Sunny loved to dance and remembered her bare feet on top of her Daddy's cowboy boots as they whirled on the dance floor. He taught her the Two-Step and a host of other dances. When he was in college, he took a few dance classes and when he and her Momma danced, folks sat down and watched. They mixed up the Tango and the Two-Step that was particular to them and no one else. Watching them dance, you could tell they were in love and two-of-a-kind.

Sunny had yet to find a cowboy that was as good a dancer as she was. There were a couple of good ones, but they had wives now so she had lost them as dance partners. Gosh, how she would love to dance with her Daddy again. She closed her eyes and felt the slick wood floor of the haymow slippery beneath her boots as she glided across the spattering of straw tracked loosely on the floor. The country-western band in the corner belted out an old honky-tonk two-step as she felt the strong, leathery hand of her Daddy's gripping hers. She could smell a whiff of Old Spice lingering in the air, mixing with the sweet clover of alfalfa hay freshly spread out in the feeding troughs below in the horses stall. Old bare light bulbs sparsely spotted against the rafters held together by old knob-and-tube wiring strung between porcelain sockets. Fresh apple pie and homemade ice cream topped off a dinner of barbecued burgers and beans. This was as good as it got on a Saturday night at the Lonesome Star Ranch.

Sunny felt a tear stream down her face as she got up from the table and walked over to the sink. She looked out the window at the windmill creaking in the horse pens. She took a deep breath and tried to calm herself. She was doing so good, was so much stronger, and was able to push away haunting memories like this. But like a torrent of floodwater roaring through a ravine unstoppable and uncontrollable, she found herself immobile against the memories. A voice came from somewhere in the past and cried, *Why, Daddy, did you have to leave me?* The tears dripped in the sink, *I need you so much. Wasn't it worth it to stay? What did I do wrong? Daddy, what did I do wrong?*

Sunny stumbled to the living room and collapsed on the sofa, sobbing into a pillow. Pain hidden behind the veneer of a toughened cowgirl façade ripped through her heart like a broken, jagged-edged bottle mutilating as it tore muscle and nerves. The gloomy darkness of horror descended upon her soul quenching out any light of hope that glimmered. She felt as if she were dying, as if she could not take another breath, as if there would never be healing from the awful pain, as if the sun would never shine upon her soul and give her rest again. Her body racked so violently that her stomach churned with nausea amidst the convulsions of breath. She did not care to live. She did not care if she died. Who would miss her? Who would care? Her body contorted in a fetal position as she writhed in the agony of abandonment.

"I don't want to be on TV!" She shrieked against the encroaching darkness. "I don't want a book! I don't want a million dollars! I don't want to be famous!" She moaned to no one there. "I just want someone to love me and hold me."

Chapter Sixteen

"So I hear they're going to make a movie about our own homegrown cowgirl, Miss Sunny Morgan?" Irene Jones shouted to Shauna above the din of noise in the Wrangler. The early Saturday morning crowd lingered over biscuits and gravy longer than normal and Theta Sharp, the grizzled old waitress who poured enough gallons of coffee in her lifetime to fill a lake, allowed that it was because of the slight drizzle outside.

But the talk of the town was about the plane crash and the resulting rescue. Even folks that usually didn't bother stopping at the Wrangler popped in this morning for a cup of coffee, much to Theta's chagrin. *Tightwad farmers* she muttered under her breath, *won't spend nuthin' on a meal and try to get ten cups of coffee for seventy five cents.*

Shauna knew that she had to answer Irene's question or she would not quit shouting above everyone else. As she sidled over to the table, Irene asked again, "I hear they're making a movie about that Morgan girl. You two are still good friends aren't you? Didn't she stand up for you at your wedding? Have you talked to her lately? Are her brothers coming back? That's a shame what her Daddy did to that family. How come that girl never comes to church no more? Did she ever get another boyfriend?"

There is a reason why they call this woman Telephone Jones. When

Irene Jones started asking questions, she didn't care about what happened to people, she wanted new things to gossip about. Shauna knew that anything she said would be broadcast all over town by the time the day was over so she was cautious about her answer. Irene could rattle questions like a machine gun; Shauna answered the only ones she wanted to answer.

"Yes, Sunny and I are great friends," Shauna responded. "But I know nothing about any movie." The less information, the better; keep answers short and to the point.

"I still don't know why she don't come to church, though." Irene turned to Eudene Solomon, another lady known to circulate the town news with as great a frequency as Irene. "We got us that new preacher that them younger folks seem to like and a girl like her with all those problems needs to be in church gettin' herself back on the straight-and-narrow."

Shauna felt the red starting to rise in her neck. It was precisely women like Irene and Eudene that kept Sunny from going to church. They had been around so long that they either ran everything in the church or ran folks off with their criticisms.

"Shauna!" turning in the direction of the voice shouting her name, she saw the friendly faces of Kevin and his wife, Susan. "Come join us, we have some extra room here!"

Relieved, Shauna excused herself from the interrogation and walked across the restaurant to where they were sitting. "Can I get you anything, hon?" Theta said as she started to sit down. "A cup of coffee? Do you need a menu or do you know what you want? I see you ain't sittin' with them busybodies over there. I swear, what they don't know about folks they just make up. Where's that husband and them young'uns of yours?"

Shauna laughed, "Thanks, Theta, I'll have coffee and the special. Roy told me he was taking care of the kids today and I was to come down to the Wrangler for a good breakfast and a little socializing. He travels so much and loves to spend as much time with the kids as he can, but he also knows I need a little break, so here I am!"

"And it's good to have you here," Susan said. "Grandma and grandpa wanted the kids today to take to the zoo so we got the morning free too! We love our kids, but it sure is nice to have a decent adult conversation."

"Gosh," Shauna apologized, "I don't mean to interrupt you two. I can go sit with someone else."

"Oh, don't be silly," Susan giggled. "We could see you needed rescuing and besides, we would love to visit with you."

Shauna laughed, "I like those old ladies, but when they start questioning me I feel like I'm in one of those movies where a person's tied to a chair in a dark dungeon with a dangling light-bulb right above my head and Guido and his men are going to hurt me if I don't start spilling my guts."

Kevin laughed maybe a little too hard at this comment. "They mean well. Every town has them and everyone loves them but are just a little nervous around them. So how are Roy and the kids?"

"Oh, they're all doing great," Shauna replied. "We don't like it that Roy has to travel so much – he's such a homebody anyway – but it's a good job and it helps me to be able to stay at home and raise the kids. They're so small that it would cost an arm and a leg to have to pay for daycare for them. We keep hoping something else materializes so he doesn't have to travel as much."

"I'm sorry I'm not in church as much as I should," Shauna apologized. "It's just that a lot of time Sunday mornings are the only time Roy and I get to see much of each other."

"Shauna," Kevin said, "there is no need to apologize or feel badly about not being regular. We think that the most important thing in the world is your family and you need to take care of that first. You come when you can and if you can. Unlike some folks, God doesn't keep attendance."

Leaning over towards Shauna, Susan whispered, "Want to know the truth? There are times I don't want to go very much either. I love to hear Kevin preach, but getting the kids ready is like pulling teeth sometimes." There was something sincere in both Kevin and Susan that she found refreshing.

"So have you been out to see Sunny?" Kevin asked. "That was quite an event out at her place."

"Yes, she's doing well." Shauna responded. "She also told me you had called and offered to help her in any way. That was really nice and I know she appreciated it. Sunny is one of the most independent women you'll ever meet and she might never tell you she needs help, but if you go out to help her, she won't turn you down. She gets mighty lonely out there."

"Is it true about her father? That he took his life?" Susan asked.

"Yes, it was a horrible thing. He wrestled with depression and it got a lot worse after Sunny's mom died with cancer. Sunny was pretty young then and took that pretty hard when her mom died, but I don't think she'll ever get over her Daddy going the way he did. He was such a handsome man and so well liked in the community. He apparently kept it pretty well hid from everyone except his family. No one saw it coming."

"That is horrible," Kevin agreed, "something like that leaves a lot of guilt for those left behind. People have a hard enough time trying to cope with death but when it is done voluntarily by someone, it just makes the coping so much more difficult."

"Sunny's pretty strong, though." Shauna said. "I think she's done as well with it as anyone can."

"Does she have someone in her life now?" Susan asked.

"Spook Masterson, he's an old bow-legged cowpoke that's been a friend of the family for many years and he treats her like his own daughter."

"Oh, yes," Kevin smiled sitting his coffee down, "we've met Mr. Masterson and if there was ever the quintessential cowboy, it is Spook. I hear he has a nickname for everyone and apparently mine is 'Preach.' I'll see him at the gas station and he'll say, 'Hey, Preach, how's them sinners doin' today? They outscoring the saints again?' I invited him to church a couple of times but he said that I'd be having funerals for half-a-dozen gossipy old women ifn' he ever darkened the church door."

"It's good that Spook looks after her," Susan agreed. "Everybody needs someone like Spook in their life to keep an eye on things, especially a young lady out in the middle of a prairie trying to run a ranch. My goodness, that has to be difficult."

"Yes," Shauna admitted. "But if anyone can do it, it is Sunny. She's one of the strongest people I've ever met."

"You really admire her, don't you?" Kevin asked. "It's really great that she has someone that cares for her like you."

"Sunny is the kind of friend that everyone ought to have." Shauna explained. "She's trustworthy and loyal and would never say a bad word about you behind your back. I've watched her through the years and she keeps being positive, bouncing back from one disaster after another, and focusing on the future. Her mom died when she was young, her dad died in a horrible way, her brothers ran off and left her to take care of the ranch and the only man she ever cared about dumped her pretty much at the alter."

"Oh, my" Susan said sadly. "She's had her run of misfortune in life, hasn't she?"

"Yes, far more than most. In fact, I have to admit sometimes I wonder why someone as good as Sunny is with a heart of gold has to suffer so much heartache. It's not like she was a drug-addict, or promiscuous, or an alcoholic. She's a hardworking, loyal friend who wouldn't harm a flea yet one tragedy after another breaks her heart."

"Mmmm," Kevin said, sipping his coffee, "that's too bad. I'll never understand that about life, either. Didn't she used to go to church?"

"She used to go with me when I was in High School. We went to all the youth groups and such, but she didn't like to go on Sunday morning much. She didn't care much for the preacher that was here at the time - Hank Carmichael. But Sunny has a lot more faith than I think most folks would give her credit for. I know she says she talks to God a lot when she's out checking fences and working cattle. But some folks don't think she likes God," Shauna said looking back towards the table of Irene Jones, "'cause she doesn't go to church."

"Shauna," Kevin leaned towards her, "I've been in church all my life and I'll guarantee you that just because you show up on Sunday morning doesn't mean you're any closer to God than if you're sitting on a saddle out in the middle of the prairie. The way I understand it, the church isn't about showing up on Sunday morning in your Sunday-go-to-meetin' clothes as much as it is about how we treat one another."

Hank Carmichael would blow a gasket and have a stroke if he heard such thing coming from the guy that followed him at the Community Church. In fact, Hank would readily admit that Mondays were his day to go find the lost sheep that didn't show up on Sunday morning. No one in the church answered the phone or the door on Monday so they wouldn't have to listen to Hank's haranguing. Shauna felt a wave of relief come over her as she listened to Kevin talk.

"Shauna," Susan added, "the church is supposed to be a people, not a building, not a program, not a show on Sunday morning. The most important thing is how we treat one another. Kevin and I have both seen a lot of bad things happen in church by folks that thought they were better than everyone else. There are many times we've wanted to walk away from it too, but we want to do what we can to create a community of people who can trust each other, support each other, depend on each other, and care for each other. That's what it is supposed to be about."

"And we want to help Sunny any way we can," Kevin continued, "we know that when folks see us coming, the first thing they think we are going to ask them is to go to church or why they haven't been in church. But we would really like to be able to serve Sunny in some way. Is there any way you can think of we can do that?"

"I know that Sunny gets pretty tired of having to cook for herself all the time." Shauna answered. "She doesn't like to come in town and eat much because it costs too much and she's pretty tight with her money. But if you were to invite her for supper, she might get a little nervous about that. Better yet, you know what might be really good is if you called her up and asked her if there was a good place to picnic on the ranch and invite her to go with you and the kids. She loves kids! I know there are some beautiful streams out there that no one else ever sees except Sunny and a few of us. She would love to take you and your kids out there and picnic. Just meet her in her element, though."

"Then a picnic it is," Susan exclaimed. "I'll call her up next week and make arrangements."

"That would be great!" Shauna said. "Sunny needs some good friends who just want to be her friend. But I need to warn you, Sunny closes off pretty quickly if you try to talk to her about any of the troubles she's had and she'll be even less likely to talk about God to you. Just ask her about her dreams for the Lonesome Star and you might not get her to shut up!"

"I'd better get going and rescue Roy from the kids or the kids from Roy!" Shauna said, excusing herself from the table. "I really enjoyed visiting with you both. Maybe Roy and I can make it tomorrow."

"And if not," Kevin smiled at her, "it's okay. No one's taking attendance."

Chapter Seventeen

"Hello there, handsome." Meredith's voice quavered as Dane squeezed her hand. "You sure are a fine looking boy." She had been saying that to him from the day she first laid eyes on all eight pounds and twelve ounces of pure boy. They had had Norma years earlier and without question she was the apple of her Daddy's eye, but Meredith wished she could give Johnson a son of his own. She smiled thinking about how happy Johnson was when the doctor told him he was the father of a little boy.

Johnson, whose own father had died at an early age, purposed to be the best possible father he could be to Dane. He saw other fathers consumed with climbing a corporate ladder at the expense of their family and resolved not to fall into the same trap. Johnson and his "little man" were nearly inseparable, forging a bond that grew stronger through the years. Whether it was putting a worm on a hook while sitting on the dock of Wildhorse Lake, or building a picnic table in the garage, Johnson imparted to Dane the life-long love of learning and experimentation.

Dane sensed the uniqueness of his relationship to his father. Whereas some children would go through a rebellious period in challenging the authority, Dane never seemed to do that. Even as a child, it would break his heart to disappoint his father. He was not afraid of his father being angry; rather, he was concerned that he would let him down. Johnson was perfectly clear to both his children that he would never forsake them. Of course, he wanted them to make wise choices, but if they didn't, it would not diminish his great love for them.

Meredith had laughed when Johnson told her about his talk with Dane about the birds and the bees. He took Dane to a park in a town about an hours' drive away, a place where they could spend some quiet time. Dane was about ten years old and as they leaned against the tree munching on ham and cheese sandwiches, Johnson explained the facts of life. Quite nervous about it – his father never explained such things to him – he stumbled around with as little detail as possible. Dane soaked it all in and only asked a couple of questions, much to Johnson's relief.

Later, as they were leaving the city and headed on their one-hour trip back home, Dane looked up at Johnson from across the pickup and asked, "So how long does it take, Dad?" Johnson stumbled around trying to find the right words to explain sometimes it takes a little bit and sometimes it takes a while. Wanting a little more clarity, Johnson asked Dane, "How long does what take?"

"Getting home from here," Dane said to the much-relieved Johnson.

"Oh, about an hour." Johnson breathed a sigh of relief. When he told Meredith of the day, she had laughed uncontrollably at the thought of her World War II hero being afraid of anything.

Johnson took Debbie's death as hard as anyone. He believed it was his job to raise a son to be a good husband and father and was pleased when Dane brought Debbie home the first time. He liked her fiery personality and blazing red hair and told Meredith as soon as they left, "That's the girl for our son!" Meredith thought he was a little premature, but Johnson was great judge of character.

They were not surprised that the romance blossomed and even did what they could to encourage it. Johnson often told Dane, "You got a tiger by the tail there, son." To which Dane would reply, "Yeah, but I don't know whether to turn it loose or hang on for the ride." Johnson was careful not to try to influence his son's choice for a wife, but taught him what it meant to be a good husband.

"Son," Johnson counseled, "a good marriage isn't so much about finding a right spouse as it is being the right spouse."

Johnson took Dane on a fishing trip up to the Boundary Waters in Minnesota the summer before he was to get married. Just the two of them floating down a river doing what they loved seemed like heaven to Johnson. Debbie told him he had better enjoy it because if they were going next year, she was going with them whether they liked it or not. She hated to miss an adventure.

They did take her with them the next summer. Johnson growled a little bit in the evenings because he had to sleep by himself – Meredith just couldn't stand the rigor of these trips – but liked it that Debbie helped with the cooking and cleaning. She was a pleasant addition and they laughed more on that trip than previous ones. She made everything enjoyable with her sense of adventure and humor. Johnson remarked when Debbie died, "Dane won't have anyone to laugh with anymore."

Dane's eyes fluttered as he tried to speak but Meredith said, "You let us do all the talking, young man. You just sit there and listen." She felt his tense muscles start to relax. "The doctor told us that you were not to talk, but we were to talk to you because you would have more questions than Carter has pills." Dane smiled at the corner of his mouth and squeezed her hand again.

"Hi Dane," Norma said. "It sure is good to see you smiling. You're doing a lot better. You've had a few pretty rough days. Do you remember being in a plane crash?" Dane's eyebrows furrowed together and his muscles tightened as he nodded. "You relax, we'll tell you all about it."

Slowly Norma began to tell the story, as far as they knew it, about the plane crash. Dane nodded as the memories came back to him.

"Apparently you were rescued by a cowgirl who watched it all happen from her horse. Although we don't have all the details yet, it sounds like you wouldn't have made it if she hadn't shown up to help you. Do you remember her?"

Dane lay motionless retrieving memories from the damaged archives of his mind. He remembered the cold rain pelting against his face and pressure around his chest and feeling like he was being dragged by something much stronger than a human. He had looked up into the face of someone hovering over him with a hat helping to shield the rain. His eyes were not focusing very well and he didn't know if it was from the blood and rain in his eyes or the jar to his head.

Slowly, he nodded and whispered, "Eyes like a doe."

"Did you say, 'Eyes like a doe'?" Norma asked. "So you do remember her?" Dane nodded and a slight smile turned up the corner of his eyes.

"From what all we've heard, and we got some of this information from some pretty reliable sources," Norma continued, "is that you crashed near where some of your land is and this cowgirl just happened to be out there and watched it all. Apparently the storm was still going on when she got there because it was real rainy but your plane was upside down and you and Ron were hanging there still strapped in by your seatbelt."

"How's Ron?" Dane rasped.

"Oh, he's fine. They observed him overnight then released him the next morning. He's been on television a couple of times already and there is a big article about you guys today in the paper and they quoted him a lot."

"He's loving that," Dane said.

"Yeah, a little too much," Norma laughed. "But anyway, back to you and the cowgirl angel. You and Ron were both unconscious and hanging upside down but there was a wing lying on top of the plane and she had to hook on to it with a rope and dragged it off using her horse!"

"Really?" Dane couldn't believe it.

"Really." Norma exclaimed. "Then after she got the wing off, she cut you loose from the seatbelts then tied the rope around your chest and had the horse drag you out! Can you believe that?"

"A horse?" Dane questioned. "I was rescued by a horse?"

"Yes, Starbuck pulled first you then Ron out, then she tied a tourniquet on your leg with baling wire, then raced back to the house to call the ambulance. They came out and got you with a helicopter and brought you here to Mercy General."

"Baling wire?" Dane again couldn't believe what he was hearing. "I was saved by baling wire and a horse."

"And a quite beautiful young cowgirl!" Norma teased. "You always did have a way of getting the women to chase you! Only this time they rescued you instead of them trying to get you to rescue them!"

As Dane lay there, the memories scattered like a jigsaw puzzle. He did remember the rain and looking up at the woman that was holding his head. He did remember the tug around the chest and feeling like he was being dragged somewhere. But a lot of it was still fuzzy.

"What is her name?" Dane asked.

"Sunny Morgan," Norma said. "And she was on the news the other night and seems like a really nice person. Very beautiful; very plain. In fact, Mackenzie Foster is the only one that has had an interview on television with her so far but everyone is calling her the *Cowgirl Angel*, thanks to Mackenzie calling her that."

"Has anyone from the office called her?"

"Yes, several times," Johnson injected. "Stephanie left numerous messages, but none of them have been returned. She was going to drive back down there in a couple of days and see if she could go out on the ranch and find her. They would like for her to be able to meet you once you got better so you could personally thank her."

"That'd be nice. Sounds like she saved my life," Dane said,

"Yes, it does." Norma replied. "When you think about it, Dane, the mere fact that you crashed out in the middle of nowhere in the middle of a Kansas thunderstorm, you could have been in serious trouble in a hurry. It does sound like someone sent you an angel, even if she was dressed in a gingham shirt and blue jeans with a cowgirl hat."

"I knew you were tough, Son," Johnson said. "I'm sure glad to see you pull through this like you are. It's probably a good thing I didn't go on this trip with you. I'm not sure I could have survived that crash. The bad thing about getting my age is you get asked to be a pall bearer at a lot of funerals and I guess the timing of old Bud's funeral worked out just right so I wouldn't be there in the crash with you."

"But you owe me one," Johnson continued, "By the way, how was the fishing anyway."

Dane stretched out his hands to show Johnson how big the trout were then grimaced as he started to laugh. He was disappointed when he found out that Johnson couldn't go on the trip. Naturally, that gave Ron Moore the opportunity he was looking for to butt in on the action. He really didn't want to take Moore, but after his Daddy had cancelled on him, he had a hard time telling Moore he couldn't go. If he would have had more time, he would have asked someone else, but Moore heard about Johnson's cancellation and called Dane before he could have a chance to ask anyone else.

"That figures," Johnson complained. "The best fishing trip of the year and I'm stuck at a funeral for a guy that pickled himself in booze. Ain't that the darn luck? Next time we go, I'll be lucky to catch a six-incher."

"May I come in?" Dr. Sylvan peeked his head in the door then came in to the room. "Well, Governor Richards, I have some splendid news for you today. The results of the latest CAT scan shows the swelling in your head is diminishing more rapidly than we expected. We were a little worried for a bit, but you're going to be just fine. And furthermore, it looks like the circulation in that leg is better than we expected. It's a good thing you were in good health when this happened. That is making your recovery a lot better than we anticipated."

"Thanks, Doc," Dane mumbled. "Great news. How much longer?"

"Well, if we can get you up and walking today, then it might be as soon as two to three days. Just depends on how fast you heal."

"How soon can I go fishing?" Dane joke.

"Well, if I heard right, you like to stand in those cold, fast mountain streams fishing for trout and that's going to be a while before you're ready to do that. Maybe if you can find an old dock somewhere and put a lawn chair on it, you'd be okay in a week or so," Dr. Sylvan joked back.

"I have lots of places like that," Johnson interjected, "it won't hurt you none to do a little catfishing for a while son. I know that's a lot more boring just sitting there waiting on them to bite than standing in a river going after trophy trout, but fishin' is fishin' and we did our share of that when you were younger."

Dane chuckled at the memory. When his Daddy got off work in the evening, they'd traipse through the pasture the half-mile to old Hobson's Pond which never had anything of size in it, but it was close. Johnson made an old makeshift dock and they would sit on it and dangle their feet in the water. Dane's first pole was an old cane pole with a piece of string and a red and white bobber. A rusty Sir Walter Raleigh tobacco tin served as their worm can full of feisty earthworms from the corral. They weren't as big as night crawlers, but they squirmed and fought more.

The first fish Dane ever caught was a bullhead, a small catfish that usually swallowed the whole hook and trying to get the hook out was both scary and hard. They had very sharp, pointed fins on the side like little barbs and if they happened to twist and poke you, it hurt worse than a thorn. Dane was swimming in Hobson's Pond once with his buddies and Luther Twitchell had a baggy pair of jean shorts. A little bullhead swam up inside of and starting poking Luther in the soft part of the inner thigh. Luther shot straight up out of the water screaming like he'd been stabbed by a red-hot branding iron. He didn't go swimming with them for the rest of the summer.

"As long as they're not bull-heads," Dane strained to answer.

"No, I'll take you to Murphy's Lake, I hear the channel cat are biting. They're a lot more fun."

"I'm not sure anyone is going anywhere for a while," Meredith said. "First things first. We have to get you up and walking today before you start worrying about a bunch of fish."

"Oh, Meri," Johnson said. "We're just planning for the future."

Dr. Sylvan interrupted, "You're right, Mrs. Richards, "It is important that Governor Richards is able to walk today." Turning to Dane he said, "I need you to get some rest for right now, but this afternoon, when you wake up, I have instructions for the nurse to take you for a walk. Do you think you're up to that?"

"Sure, Doc," Dane replied. "I'm ready to get out of here."

"I'll bet you are," Dr. Sylvan responded. "Is there anything we can get for you?"

Turning to Norma, Dane spoke, "Can you get a tape of that interview with that cowgirl? I'd like to see that."

"Oh, sure," Norma said. "I'll call Stephanie and have her bring it over while you rest. This TV has a tape player so we'll show it to you this afternoon."

"Good," Dane said. "I want to see the angel to whom I owe my life."

Chapter Eighteen

"Hi Mackenzie, this is Miles Applegate from *The Candace Cox Show*. I'm calling about the Governor's plane crash on the Kansas prairie and, in particular, about Sunny Morgan. We called Miss Morgan to set up an interview and she gave us your number and told us you were her agent. I must confess, I was a little surprised she found an agent so fast."

"I'm more her friend than her agent, Miles," Mackenzie said. "This is a sweet young girl that a few of us in the business want to make sure she's treated right, if you know what I mean."

"Sure," Miles responded. "I understand completely. I don't mean to put you on the defensive it's just usually that when I make these calls, I visit with the person involved and they are clueless about what's going on. It will be actually easier for us to do this knowing someone in the industry can help her along."

"That's okay," Mackenzie offered. "We both know this is a great story and I've met this girl and know she's the real McCoy. She mentioned someone from the 'Candace Cox' showed called, but I'm sure you know her answering machine gets filled up every day with someone wanting to write an article or do an interview. The poor girl just didn't know which way to turn. Gordon, our station manager, and I visited and decided we would do what we could to help her."

"Gordon Chapman?" Miles asked incredulously. "That old curmudgeon is still around?"

"Still alive and kickin'," Mackenzie replied. "He's got us with the best ratings we've had in three years and most folks were going to put him out to pasture. How do you know him?"

"Wow," Miles chuckled, "when I was a freshman in college and taking my first course in communications, he was the guest speaker at one of our classes. I just fell in love with him. In fact, I think he made more sense than any of the other people I've studied since. I keep thinking of different *Gordonisms* that I hear pop up in the industry and I know they came from him."

Mackenzie liked Miles more and more as she talked. She was very influenced by Gordon in her career and found him to be exceptionally honest and kind, not always an automatic combination in their industry.

"I saw your piece on Miss Morgan," Miles began, "that was done very well. I could tell it was hard for you to get her to talk much but it was easy to see that she felt comfortable talking to you and not to the camera. And by the way, tell that cameraman of yours that he got some great shots in there. That one with that old cowboy on the horse in the background was about as western a shot as you could get nowadays."

"That old cowboy's name is Spook Masterson," Mackenzie replied. "If there was ever a true-blue cowboy, that guy would be it. He's not any relation to Sunny, but he sure looks after her. You'd have to go through him before you ever got to her."

"Well, maybe we can just arrange for Mr. Spook Masterson to come to New York along with you and Sunny for the show. That is, if you think Sunny would be interested. Has she ever traveled much? Coming from Kansas to New York City could be a little daunting."

"Honestly, I don't think Sunny is very interested at all. I'm not kidding, Miles, this girl is as humble a girl as you'll ever be around. I've told her that folks are going to want to hear about this and that someone might end up even writing a book about it, but she couldn't care less. She'd just as soon saddle her horse and check the cattle as to load up in a plane and fly to New York City."

"So do you think we can get her back here?" Miles asked.

"I'll be right up front with you Miles. You and I both know this is a great story and it has all the makings of being a book or movie. But you and I also know there are a lot of folks out there that could sleaze this up with trash journalism and take advantage of her. Have you guys thought about this?"

"We've talked about this with quite a bit of detail," Miles said. "In fact, Candace is very excited about getting her on the show and has said herself that this could be the right connection to some very big deals for her."

"But what kind of connections? Do you guys have people that are trustworthy that we can get hooked up with?" Mackenzie asked.

"Candace makes it a point to have the classiest show possible." Miles explained. "She works hard to carve out a reputation for integrity and excellence. We have many people we could help get connected with Sunny if they think there is a story that can be told. Do you think she could handle being on national television?"

"I'm not sure," Mackenzie answered. "She was pretty nervous in front of the camera but as long as she was talking to me, that seemed to settle her down. I would think we could bring her into our station just to get her familiar with the way a studio is set up and how everything works."

"That would be a great idea and if she was able to bring you and this other fellow you were talking about, that might ease her a little bit more. Candace is very good at making people feel comfortable. Could you give her my number and have her call me sometime soon so we can establish some kind of rapport? I completely respect your position and would basically just ask her to tell me her story. I think the more she tells it, the more comfortable she will be in front of the camera."

"Sure, Miles. How soon are you thinking about doing this?"

"As soon as possible. This is a hot story and we want to get it on the air as soon as possible. We've already seen some interviews with the other guy in the airplane, Moore or something like that was his name, and we all agree he's not the best communicator of this story. All he knows is what he experienced in the crash and he just doesn't come across as a likable person. We know that the real story lies in the rescue, not the crash. The buzz is about this cowgirl angel and who she is."

Miles continued, "If you would call Sunny and get the okay from her, we would like to bring you out here within the week. Do you think you can get them all out here that fast?"

"I think so. I'm sure Sunny's going to have to make arrangements on the ranch and if Spook comes with us, then she'll have to find someone else. I just can't imagine Spook Masterson in New York City!" Mackenzie chuckled. "That poor guy will be like a newly weaned calf bawling for its momma."

"Well, it's your call whether or not you bring him. We spare no expenses in taking care of our guests and if you think Miss Morgan needs Spook to come along, then bring him back. But I need to know as quickly as possible. You clear this with Sunny and Spook and then call me back so we can get our travel agent to make arrangements."

"Sounds good, Miles." Mackenzie said. She was concerned about who might call and what show they would be on. Miles seemed genuine. "I'll get back with you sometime today."

Mackenzie hung up the phone and stared out her window across the parking lot in the general distance of the Lonesome Star. She remembered how beautiful the dew on the grass was the first time she had gone out there. As they drove towards the ranch that morning with her crew, they passed field after field of wheat still green and pastures thick with bluegrass. The heavy dew of the early morning sun christened it to look like frost. Oh how she missed the wide-open spaces and the dazzling array of colors at sunrises and sunsets! As a little girl growing up on a farm in western Kansas, she sat with her Dad on the porch swing watching the sun dip down over the horizon.

He said a Kansas sunset was God's way of showing you one more time that day how beautiful He is so you would go to sleep with good dreams.

New York City would be a huge culture shock for Sunny and Spook. She remembered what Spook said about her being sent by the Maker to help Sunny figure out which trail to take. There was a certain peace that settled on Mackenzie's heart as she thought about the idea of helping Sunny. For so long she had been driven by the ratings of television and each story she went after was fueled by the desire to increase the ratings. Many stories made her feel dirty and used over the course of her career, but there was something pure in this that was refreshing.

Trust. Mackenzie said it out loud. After a career of reporting on corrupt politicians, increasingly vicious criminals, and heart-breaking stories of people's lives being ruined by various tragedies, it felt good, even pure, to be involved in a story like this. Sunny trusted her. Mackenzie had no one tell her that in a long, long time. Most folks were suspicious of journalists and she learned to accept it as just part of the job. But here was a young lady in the middle of the prairie whose life would be forever changed by a plane crash and she handed Mackenzie perhaps the most valuable possession any person could ever give away – trust.

I'll do you good, Sunny. Mackenzie whispered out the window. *I'll take that trust and treat is as if it were sacred. I'll protect it with everything I have.*

Reaching for the phone, she called Sunny's number. She began to leave an answer on the machine.

"Hi Mackenzie," Sunny picked up the phone. "I just came in for lunch and heard you on the machine. How are you?"

"Oh, I'm fine," Mackenzie said. "How are things at the Lonesome Star?"

"The investigators finally left and they took all the pieces of the plane so there's not much activity out here now. But they sure left a mess with all their tire tracks." Sunny said, "I don't mean to complain, but I never did like tire tracks across the prairie. They don't belong there, but some of these will be around a long time since they got stuck in the mud."

"Maybe you can get the Governor to help take care of them!" Mackenzie joked. "It's his fault they made the mess so when you talk to him, tell him to clean it up."

"I plan on doing that very thing!" Sunny responded. "It's bad enough I got my life interrupted, but the prairie didn't do anything to deserve getting so messed up. Spook and I traveled down the ruts the other day and we saw several prairie chicken and pheasant nests that were destroyed. Folks don't realize when they look across the prairie that there are all kinds of animals that call it home. Oh, well, no use ranting. Thanks for letting me vent."

"Not a problem," Mackenzie said. "How's Spook doing?"

"As ornery as ever," Sunny chuckled. "Some reporter was in town the other day and started asking Spook a bunch of questions about me. Spook didn't like him much to begin with - called him a 'dandy with purty britches and made up like a gol' durn woman.' Anyway, he started asking questions about me and asked Spook to take him out to meet me. Spook had his spurs on and told the reporter, 'Young feller, ifn' I catch you within spittin' distance of either the ranch or Miss Sunshine, I'm gonna sink these here spurs in a place where every time you walk your butt jingles ifn' you get my drift.' Apparently, the guy got the drift 'cause we haven't seen him since."

"Everyone needs a Spook Masterson in their life," Mackenzie laughed. She could imagine the reporter wondering if the ornery old cuss would make good on his promise. It wouldn't take too much smarts to size Spook up and take him at his word. "Sunny, the reason I called was because I got a call from a man with *The Candace Cox Show*. He said he called you but you gave him my number."

"I really like the man, Sunny," Mackenzie went on, "and they are interested in getting you on the show as soon as possible. I know it's busy with cows calving this time of year, but do you think you could turn loose in the next few days to fly back to New York City?"

"New York City?" Sunny asked. "By myself?"

"Oh, heavens no!" Mackenzie realized she hadn't set her up very well. "If you wanted, I would go along with you and, if you think he would like to go, they will even pay for Spook."

"Spook in New York City?" Sunny laughed. "I'm not sure New York City's ready for Spook. Shoot, Teterville doesn't know what to do with him half the time. That would be great to take him though, if he'd go. He doesn't like to travel much. Said he saw plenty of the world when he was in the Army and they took the sense of adventure plumb out of him. He's supposed to be out here this afternoon sometime and I'll ask him."

"Are you interested in going, Sunny?"

"I – I – I guess," Sunny stammered. "I've never been to any place that big either. I wouldn't know where to go or what to do. Do you think this is a good idea?"

"Yes, I do," Mackenzie affirmed. "I really think this is a good step for you to take and I will be right there with you the whole way. In fact, we want you to come to our studio sometime so we can let you see how this works."

"Gosh," Sunny said, "This is all so sudden. I've only seen bits and pieces of that show a time or two – we don't get very good reception on the antenna out here on the ranch – but I know it's pretty big. What happens if I get on there and get so petrified I can't talk?"

"That's where I come in, Sunny," Mackenzie said. "I will help coach you through all of that and besides, Candace is a professional and knows exactly how to make people comfortable on her show. You will do great. I'm not worried about you at all. But if you are interested in going, Sunny, I'll need an answer from Spook pretty quickly. Do you think you can call him and ask him?"

"Sure. I know he likes to hang out down at the Farmers Grain feed store in the mornings and gossip with the other ranchers so I'll call down there. He's going to be strutting around like a peacock with them old boys. He'll be glad I called him down there. Them old coots are trying to one-up each other all the time anyway and this will be a perfect way ole Spook can get a good lick in. But he's going to want to know what kind of clothes to wear. Do you have any suggestions?" Sunny asked.

"You tell him to wear the same clothes he wears all the time. He doesn't need to go buy anything fancy. New York City needs to meet Spook Masterson just like he is." Mackenzie insisted.

"Well, that'll make it a whole lot easier," Sunny laughed. "I got him to wear a suit and tie for Josiah Clatterbucks funeral and he squealed like a scalded pig. Sitting by him in church that day was worse than sitting by a little kid with poison ivy. I told him it wouldn't kill him to dress up in a suit but he told me his life flashed before his eyes. He made me swear when he died I'd let them bury him in blue jeans, checkered shirt, a red bandana around his neck, and his boots and spurs on. I'm not sure that old cuss will ever die. He says he hopes to be dead and in heaven two days before the devil knows he's missin'."

"Sunny," Mackenzie said, "you are going to be just wonderful in all of this. I know you might be nervous, and that's quite okay, but remember, all you have to do is tell the story of what you did. That's what Candace is going to ask you about, and that's all you have to concentrate on. It's a piece of cake."

"Thanks, Mackenzie," Sunny said. "I'll call Spook and let you know as soon as I find out."

Chapter Nineteen

"Good morning, Governor," Stephanie Riddell greeted Dane as he was sitting on the edge of the hospital bed. "Are you ready to go meet the world?"

"You bet!" Dane replied. "As ready as I'll ever be. They have treated me so well here, but it will sure be nice to sleep in my own bed for a change and not be waked up every two hours by someone wanting to stick something in me."

"The press is outside and waiting for an interview with you, so be warned," Stephanie explained. "It got out that you were being released today and, frankly, they're tired of talking to me and are anxious to see how you are doing. I have a little speech ready for you if you'd like to look over it."

"Sure, Stephanie," Dane agreed. "I jotted a few things down myself. I saw the satellite trucks pull into the parking lot this morning and figured they would be outside."

"Just don't let them hurt you," Meredith interrupted. "You still aren't a well man and I've seen how pushy they can get."

"Oh, Mother," Dane chuckled. "I have my cane and if any of them get too close, I can just rap them upside the head with it. Don't worry, I'll be fine."

"So did you get a chance to look at the interview with Miss

Morgan?" Stephanie asked. "What did you think of her?"

"It was simply a miracle that she was out in the middle of that pasture," Dane mused. "You know, I'm sure I've seen her before sitting on horseback when I've flown over the land I have out there, but I had never met her. I tried waving at her a couple of times when I got the plane low enough, but she wouldn't ever wave back. I talked to her dad a few times about buying up some of his land, but she never came up the house when I was there – always hung out in the barn. I'd heard he died – committed suicide I believe – and I never did go out there again. I just felt like that would be way too inappropriate and unkind to ask her if she wanted to sell her Dad's ranch."

"I guess the thing that struck me the most in the interview were her eyes," Dane went on. "I remember waking up at one point with the rain in my face and she was holding my head apparently. My vision was kind of blurry, but she wiped away the rain and blood from my eyes and once I focused, I just remember thinking her eyes look like a doe."

"Well, that might not be something you want to say to the reporters outside," Stephanie smirked. "They would have a hey-day with a statement like that."

"Oh, Stephanie," Dane laughed. "You don't have to worry about me. I'm not going to get starry eyed over some girl that rescued me. If you and half the other people on my staff would quit worrying about me falling in love, we would all get a lot more work done. I've told you all before, as long as I'm in office, I will not pursue anyone or allow anyone to pursue me. I live in a fishbowl with every move being scrutinized, photographed, and written about. For crying out loud, I even have people writing articles about what kind of food I like to eat, like anyone really cares."

"Governor," Stephanie apologized. "We just want to protect you. Your approval ratings are the best any governor of the state of Kansas has seen for decades and your ability to work with the lawmakers is unprecedented. But we all know your enemies out are waiting for the slightest little mistake to discredit you."

"Thanks, Stephanie," Dane smiled. "I know you and the rest of my staff deserve the credit for our success."

"Thank you, Governor," Stephanie nodded. "You will be asked a lot of questions about that cowgirl from the press. She's a pretty hot item and we have been informed that she is going to be on *The Candace Cox show*. We talked about it at staff meeting this morning and think it would be a great idea if you could meet her before she goes on television."

"And a good photo-op, I'm assuming," Dane replied. "I can see the headlines now: 'Reckless Richards Meets Cowgirl Angel and Horse.' She and the horse will definitely be the shining stars in that picture."

"Politics being what they are, I think you are poised to make a few points on this one too," Stephanie retorted. "Folks are going to want to know what you are going to do to repay the woman that saved your life. This is a great opportunity to raise your approval ratings to an unprecedented mark."

"Oh, Stephanie, not everything has to be about photo-ops and approval ratings!"

"I know, but you did hire me to put the best side to the camera, so to speak, and it's my job to make you look good." Stephanie shook her finger at him. "And remember, the higher your approval ratings, the more you can get accomplished with your goals as Governor. So it's not a bad thing to put a good spin on everything that happens!"

"Okay, okay, let's go meet the press," Dane said. "I'm not sure I'm ready for this, but I want out of here and I have to run that gauntlet to do it so let's get it done."

As the nurse pushed Dane's wheel chair out the door, Dane felt the loving squeeze of his mother's hand on his shoulder. "Honey, I know Johnson keeps saying that everything in politics is about politics, but this girl saved your life. So when you look at that camera, you talk to her, not to your constituency. This isn't about politics; this is about a girl that was miraculously put in the right place at the right time to save your life. You tell her thanks."

Dane had a natural charm that endeared him to even some of the most unpleasant in the press. He liked people and it showed. He cared about what people thought, was cautious not to hurt the feelings of anyone even to the point of staying out of the normal mudslinging during the elections, and was considered one of the finest statesmen the state had ever known. He had a genuine smile - one that lingered long after it broadened his face - and an ability to empathize with people that made folks feel like he was their best friend. As they wheeled down the tiled corridor to the sliding glass doors that opened up into the parking area where his limo was waiting, he quickly re-thought what he was going to say.

As soon as the doors slid open, a dozen reporters started shouting questions at Dane. Although accustomed to this type of badgering and invasion, he found himself more distracted than normal. This time the questions, the lights, the microphones, the pushy journalists, were different. He wasn't just answering a question about school financing, or the environment, or health care issues, or a host of other political questions. This time he was answering questions about life and death, about destiny and divine appointments, and about courage and fear. He slowly raised his hands to stop the barrage of questions. "Please," he said with a smile splashing across his face, "one at a time."

"The Governor is quite weak and apologizes for not having the energy to answer all your questions," Stephanie chimed in. "He has a prepared statement that he would like to read, then we will be loading him in the car to take him to the Governor's Mansion at Cedar Manor for his recuperation. Governor Richards."

Dane took out the brief release that Stephanie wrote as well as a few notes he jotted down. His hands were shaking as he began, "I would like to thank all of the wonderful people who have been a part of my recuperation. I owe a debt of gratitude to all of the EMS people who brought me safely to the hospital, to Dr. Sylvan and all the staff of Mercy General for their excellent care which has made this recuperation far more successful than what anyone expected, to my loving family who has kept vigil by my bed day and night, and to all of you that have offered up prayers on my behalf. Without your prayers and support, I am sure that this story would have ended far differently."

Dane continued, "Last, but certainly not least, I would like to thank Miss Sunny Morgan of the Lonesome Star Ranch and her horse, Starbuck, who rescued Mr. Moore and myself from the wreckage. Without her miraculous intervention, I . . ." Dane felt the emotion surge up within his soul and tears quiver right below the surface. He took a deep breath and folded the paper in his lap.

"Miss Morgan," Dane spoke directly into the camera and the jostling crowd of reporters grew very still, all wanting to hear every word he softly spoke. Stephanie's grip on his shoulder tightened, concerned with him deviating from the script.

"Miss Morgan," Dane began again without the notes, "as our plane was plummeting to the ground and I wondered if we would survive, I knew that only a miracle would save our lives. So with a death grip on the controls, the plane lurching violently, the rain and hail beating ferociously and the ground rushing at us, I prayed for a miracle, for angels to rescue us. On behalf of my family, and especially myself, I would like to thank you for being that miracle and for being that angel. Although I have yet to meet you, I want you to know that each morning as I awake, many times throughout the day, and each night before I go to sleep, I thank God you were sent to be our cowgirl angel. And by the way, tell your horse, Starbuck, that we know he's a miracle and an angel, too."

Stephanie released her grip to wipe a tear from the corner of her eyes then spoke to the unusually silent press, "Ladies and gentlemen, Governor Richards has been through an extremely difficult ordeal and needs to have his rest and recuperation. As soon as he is strong enough, we will visit with you all again."

Dane weakly climbed out of the wheel chair into the waiting car.

Stephanie, Meredith, and Johnson climbed into the other side and as soon as the door was shut, Stephanie spoke, "Dane, you did it again. You have always known how to get to the heart of a matter and although I wouldn't have advised you saying that, it was perfect. Your adoring public will weep just like I did."

"I didn't do it for the public, Stephanie," Dane winced as the car moved forward. "I wanted Miss Morgan to know that she was an answer to a prayer. It's not often in life we are told we are an answer to someone's prayer. I did pray for a miracle. I did pray for an angel. She was that miracle. She was that angel. Wouldn't the world be a better place if we all could be a miracle and an angel in someone else's life?"

"I was thinking, Dane, that we could invite her to the Cedar Manor and have a banquet in her honor some time," Johnson said.

"That's a great idea, Honey," Meredith agreed. "But it seems like this cowgirl is kind of shy and bashful. That might be pretty intimidating to her. How about we just go for a ride one of these days and take Dane out to meet her, then he can see where he crashed?"

"Yes," Stephanie added. "I think it would be a perfect opportunity to let the public see the Governor going out to the scene of the crash and meeting her on her own ranch. I could schedule it to where we had even some national coverage in the news while we were there."

"Do I get a say in this?" Dane asked. "It seems that if it is my accident and I'm meeting the person that saved my life, I would have some kind of say in this. While a banquet in her honor at the Cedar Manor would be nice, that's in the distance somewhat. I like the idea of going out there – I'd like to see where I went down and, frankly, I'd like to meet her horse which I'm sure won't come to the banquet. But as far as press, I'd just as soon not have anyone around then. Maybe at the banquet, but not at the ranch. This isn't about politics, it isn't about state issues, it isn't about public relations or photo opps; it's about me meeting the person that directly saved my life." Dane was getting more emotional than anyone had seen him in a long time. "And the horse," he added, making everyone chuckle.

"While the plane was falling through the sky, I just kept thinking of Debbie and wondering if I was going to see her again soon. I wondered what heaven is like and what our bodies are like. I wondered if I'd recognize her or if she would recognize me, if we would love each other all over again. I wanted to live, I wanted to survive the crash, but I also knew that if I didn't, I'd be okay, that I'd be with Debbie again. But I knew that if I did live, that it was going to be a second chance of sorts, a new way of living. I've enjoyed my life, but I felt like if I made it, things would be very different."

Dane went on, "As I laid in the hospital bed in the middle of the night when the only thing keeping me company was a fluorescent light and an I.V. bag, I became aware of the impact of being rescued. Don't get me wrong, I've loved my life and other than losing Debbie, it has been a good life. But something happened that I can't find words to describe, something unexplainable, something unsettling yet, paradoxically, peaceful. It's as if a part of me did die on the prairie but also that a new part of me was given birth. This might sound like a man on too much pain medicine, but I'm believing that something very sacred and special took place on that prairie and that the person I'm destined to be is yet to be discovered, but has been given eyes to see more clearly."

"I guess what I'm saying," he struggled to articulate emotions and feelings yet defined, "is that something special happened to me on that prairie and I want it to remain special. No offense, Stephanie, and I know you're looking out for my best interest, but I just want it to be us and our family out there, not a crowd of reporters. We can have them at her banquet, if she will come to that."

"No offense taken, Governor," Stephanie wiped a tear from the corner of her eye, "I just wasn't aware that this accident impacted you so deeply. I'm just looking out for your best interest, you know that."

"Of course, I know that and am very glad. You have done an exceptional job and I wouldn't be where I am today if it weren't for your work. But just this once, I want this to be about what I want and not what the public or the press wants. But I would like you to be there Stephanie, along with my family. Would you do that?"

"I'd be honored, Governor," Stephanie replied.

"Good. Then let me rest a few days then you sneak me out of the Cedar Manor early some morning and we'll head south to the Flint Hills."

Dane leaned back against the seat, exhausted from the excitement of the day. He had been in great shape, but found his energy used up quickly. He looked forward to being in his own bed. It had taken a long time to feel at home in the Cedar Manor and never quite did completely, but it was getting better. Debbie died in the first year he was in office and the memories of her were as fresh as this morning's sunrise. However, it was not as difficult as going to their real home, the one they lived in before he became governor. He knew that when this term ended, it would be very difficult to return there and feel at home again. But he would take those things as they came.

For right now, he had to determine what happened to him on the prairie. Although he lay awake many nights reliving the crash in his mind and running through the list of "what-ifs", he knew something happened that forever changed his life. It felt as if his internal operating system was now rewired and there would be subtle changes. He would discover things about himself that he never dreamed possible.

And a tranquil sensation that he would not be alone on the journey.

Chapter Twenty

"Hi Shauna," Sunny said as she opened the door. "Thanks for coming out."

"Sure," Shauna said. "It's always good to get out of the house for a little bit. Out here, I can let the kids run wild, but in town I'm always wondering if their going to get ran over in the street. Roy keeps talking about fencing the yard, but he's so worn out on the weekends that he just wants to spend time with the kids and me. The worst that could happen to them out here is that they would fall down in a cow pie."

"Cal called again last night. I was so happy he didn't come home like he said he was, but I told him about the Candace Cox show and he got really nasty with me."

"What?" Shauna asked. She never liked Cal, not after that summer at the swimming hole by the Arched Bridge. One of the few remnants of beautiful limestone bridges build by German prisoners of war during WWII that had been shipped over here to America, it spanned Diamond Creek, a spring-fed creek that traversed in serpentine fashion across the prairie. During the spring when rains added to the creek's level, the top of the bridge was seventeen feet from the water that was about eight feet deep. The bravest of the crew liked to dive, but for the most part it was cannonballs and can-openers that most people did.

One summer, the water snakes got so bad that most of the girls refused to go. The boys made it their project to eliminate the snakes so they perched on top of the bridge with .22 rifles and proceeded to pick off twenty-eight snakes one weekend. It didn't take long for the crowd to build back up

One of the fathers had climbed out over the creek on the branch of an old cottonwood tree and tied a cable with a handle that dangled above the water so the kids could go catapulting out from the bank with all kinds of country-kids acrobatics. More clumsy than graceful, most of the attempts ended up as belly-busters or face-plants.

Like all teenagers, especially those with hormones raging, the swimming hole became a place for rituals of courtship. Guys would show off with jumps off the bridge or acrobatics off the cable-swing and the girls would lie out on the bank covered in suntan lotion. Occasionally, the guys would get the girls to ride on their shoulders as games of chicken were played in the water.

Cal was undoubtedly the strongest and most well-built and, most agreed, the best looking of the boys. Shauna climbed up on his shoulders one day at the swimming hole for a game of chicken with several other couples. Amongst all the squealing and splashing, they had all collapsed in a pile in the middle of the creek. While in the melee of bodies, she had felt someone's hands go places on her body that was more than just an accidental touch.

When she emerged from the water, she was angry but uncertain of who had done it. She felt a scratch like from a class ring and looked at all the boys and Cal was the only one wearing one. She pointed at his face and screamed, "Don't you ever touch me there again!" Cal feigned innocence, but they both knew what he had done. Even though she was a best friend with Sunny, she was cool to Cal from then on. She purposed never to be alone with him again.

"Why would he be nasty about you being on television? Shoot, the rest of us think it's wonderful and that you're going to put Teterville on the map!" Shauna exclaimed, echoing the sentiment of the talk around

160

town. "Calling Spook at the feed store was the best thing that ever happened to him. My dad was there and he said Spook repeated everything you said loud enough that everyone could hear. He's still strutting around like a banty rooster. Gosh, even Kevin mentioned it in church on Sunday and told folks they could learn a good lesson about ordinary people being used by God to do extraordinary things."

"Oh, you know Cal," Sunny said. "If it's not about him, then it's not worth paying attention to. He told me that as bashful as I am that I'm liable to get on television and not be able to talk. I don't think he was trying to be mean or anything, but it just kind of hurt."

"Sunny," Shauna said, "he was trying to be mean and hurt you. Don't you listen to a word he says. He's just jealous and, you're right, if it's not about him, it's not worth paying attention to."

"Sunny," Shauna went on, still seething inside but careful to make this a time to encourage Sunny and not just express her disgust for Cal, "all the folks in town are as happy for you as they can be. In fact, I even heard Irene Jones talk about what an inspiration you've been to her and how it just proved that you can never judge a book by its cover. She always thought you were real timid and shy and had no idea you would be brave enough to do what you did."

"And Sunny, the folks in town are also real glad that something good is finally happened to you. You might not know it, but when folks talk about you, it is always in an admiring tone. They admire you for your strength and bravery. Most folks are amazed that you could run the ranch and stay out there by yourself. While they might not say it Sunny, people have a great deal of respect for you and they are glad to see a good thing happen to you."

"I don't know how a plane wreck on my ranch is a good thing," Sunny said with a certain amount of revulsion in her voice. "I don't want to be on television. I don't want people traipsing all over my property and ruining it. I don't want people asking me about it every time I see them. I just want to be left alone with my cattle and horses."

"I know you don't, Sunny, but what has happened has happened and you can't escape the fact that it was a wonderful thing you did. I remember a poet I read in college that said, 'Most men lead lives of quiet desperation.' Sunny, in the regular world of the mundane, what you did causes folks like me to be hopeful that, in the same circumstance, we could do the same thing. You remind us that there is greatness in everyone waiting for an opportunity to come out. My days are consumed with changing diapers, keeping siblings from fighting, reading books, taking naps, fixing meals, and doing laundry. Day after day after day. But your story brings light to that drudgery because I secretly hope that in the same circumstance, plain old ordinary me could do something extraordinary."

"Thanks, Shauna," Sunny said wiping a tear from the corner of her eye. "That's why I wanted you to come out here. You always know the right words to say to help me feel better about myself. I've grown up being told by my brothers that I was pretty much useless and it doesn't take much of a comment from Cal or Daniel to make me want to curl up and hide somewhere."

"Did you see Shane at the rodeo?" Shauna asked. Usually when Sunny got in a funk like this, she had either talked to her brothers or had seen Shane somewhere.

"No, thank God he wasn't there," Sunny said, "I wasted my entry fee on that rodeo anyway. I was so bad that night that I couldn't even rope a post standing still. I didn't feel like hanging around for the dance. I'd already told the story so many times my voice was wearing out and I just wanted to go home and be alone."

"Well, that's good." Shauna breathed a sigh of relief. "That's the last thing you need is him showing back up."

"What is it in me that men don't like?" Sunny surprised her with the question. "Am I ugly? Does my breath stink? Am I that repulsive that they just don't want to be around me?"

"Whoa, whoa, whoa, whoa, girl!" Shauna said. "What do you mean that men don't like you? Just because you've got a couple of idiot brothers that treat you like dirt and you had a bad experience with one guy, doesn't mean that men don't like you."

"Bad experience with one guy?" Sunny cried angrily, "He cheated on me the night of his bachelor party! How could he run off with some hussy the night before we were to get married? That's more than just a bad experience in my books!"

"I'm sorry, Sunny, it was an awful experience, maybe the worst thing a person can ever go through is to be rejected and cheated on. I can't imagine how awful it must have been for you to have him cheat on you."

"And what about my Dad?" Sunny wept. "Why couldn't he stay around? Wasn't I worth it to him? He promised me that he would always be there for me and to protect me, but then he takes his own life? What did I do wrong? What makes me so unlikable that men that I'm close to would rather die or cheat on me than to stay faithful? Am I like my brother said, *a cur that needs culled from the herd?*"

Shauna walked through a lot of Sunny's dark times with her and shed many tears with her, but as time went on, the discussions surrounding Shane or her Dad's death diminished and Sunny seemed quite content with being alone on the ranch. She had companionship with Spook, but that was more like a father/daughter relationship or just plain friends.

Shauna realized that the pain never went away in Sunny's life, just buried. She spent all the time on the ranch taking care of the cattle and the horses and arranged her world in such a fashion that no one except the closest people, ones that she trusted, would be allowed in. It was for self-protection, an increasing isolationism that Sunny was cocooning herself in. Regardless of how many padlocks they had on the gates, this recent event opened her up to the outside world in a way she didn't want to deal with.

Shauna saw the wounds were still fresh, the cuts still deep, and scar tissue not grown over. Like a festering, infected wound, the past betrayals in Sunny's life were cut open. Like any wound that's been injured again, the pain seems more intense the second time around.

"Sunny, none of these things were your fault. I know you don't believe it, but that's okay. There are voices in your past that are coming in and telling you that it is your fault. I don't know how many voices there are or whose they are, but you have to stop believing them. I know that is easier said than done, but you have to stop those voices somehow and start believing other voices."

But Shauna wondered to herself: who would those voices be? Sunny didn't have really anyone except her and Spook. Shauna was so consumed with her marriage and raising children, that she didn't often speak words of encouragement to Sunny – she just assumed she was doing okay since she never talked about those things any more.

"You know, Sunny," Shauna went on, "Kevin's sermon on Sunday was from a Proverb that says that the power of life or of death is in the tongue. He said that the words we speak either give life or cause death inside the person who hears them. When you think about it, that makes so much sense. That's why I avoid Irene Jones as much as I can because I can still remember what she said to me when I turned up pregnant. She said it didn't surprise her any since I'd always seemed like a whore anyway. You know, I still haven't gotten over that. Her voice rings in my ears to this day."

"You are not a tramp!" Sunny said. "I know better than that."

"I know I'm not either," Shauna said. "But that one comment is a negative voice that causes death in me. There's not a good thing that a comment like that can do for a person. It's mean and hateful and causes death. So like Kevin said, we ought to purpose to cause life with our words. What he said is so true. I remember when I got pregnant that Grandma, who I was petrified would scold me, told me that Roy and I would have the most beautiful babies in the world. And you know what, Sunny? Each night when I tuck them in, I remember that and tell them they are the most beautiful babies in the world."

"Sunny, you need to start believing the other voices, those who are going to say good things about you."

"Like who? Spook?" Sunny chuckled.

164

"You bet," Shauna agreed. "Spook is one of the most respected people in our town. He's as honest as the day is long and when he offers an opinion about something, he's always right. He might look like a used cowboy and drive that beat up old red Ford he calls Bertha, but folks around here consider him to be a legend, the last of a vanishing breed. He thinks you're about the most wonderful thing since sliced bread. I'd rather have the respect of someone like Spook Masterson than I would someone like old Telephone Jones!"

Sunny laughed, "Yep, me too!"

"Sunny," Shauna realized that Sunny's problem was she didn't hear many good voices in her life and she could help pass on the good things she heard people say, "I was at the Mercantile the other day and Ralph Parker was talking about what you had done and he said, 'I never had any daughters, but I think a man would be right proud if he had one as good as Sunny Morgan.'"

"Really?" Sunny said. "Ralph said that? I've been in that store a zillion times and I never thought he liked me much."

"And Dad was telling me that at the feed store, every one of those old geezers in there said they wished they were thirty or forty years younger and single so they could hitch up with you. They also said you raised some of the finest looking cattle in the Flint Hills and that buyers from as far south as Texas talked about that purty young filly out on the prairie that raises cattle better than most men they know."

"Folks say that about me? I think you're making this all up."

"No, Sunny, I'm not," Shauna said. "The bad thing about it is that all these folks saying good things about you say it to one another and you don't get to hear it all. See, don't you feel a little bit better about yourself now that you've heard these things? That's what Kevin meant when he talked about words either causing life or death. The words you hear, the voices that rattle around in your mind and whisper across the prairie seems like they're just causing you death. Make a deal with me, Sunny."

"What kind of deal?" Sunny asked.

"The next time you hear one of those voices from the past criticize you or you start to criticize yourself, you just put your hand up like you're trying to stop someone and say, 'I'm not going to listen to words of death anymore. I only want to hear words of life.' Will you try that?"

"Well, I guess I'll try it," Sunny said. "But there's not many words I hear that have life."

"Okay, then, start looking for them." Shauna spoke as much to herself as she did to Sunny. "We both need to replace words of death with words of life.

"So tell me about the big trip to New York City." Shauna could tell that it had eased Sunny's mind to hear these things, but she made a mental note to jot down things she heard people say about Sunny so she could repeat them to her.

"Whew. Where do I begin?" Sunny breathed. "Mackenzie and Spook and I are flying back there next week. We get in one afternoon then go to the show the next day. I'm supposed to go in to Mackenzie's studio sometime before the week is up to get a feel for it. Then after the show, they're going to let us stay an extra couple of days so we can see the sights of New York City. I'm excited about going and seeing the Empire State building and the Statue of Liberty, but I am not a bit excited about being on the show. I don't have a clue what I am going to wear."

"Have they told you what kind of clothes to wear?" Shauna asked.

"Mackenzie said she'd take me shopping next week at Riley's Western Store. She says that they're talking about me being a *cowgirl angel* so I need some new boots and maybe a pretty western skirt and blouse. I haven't had a dress on since I went to Josiah's funeral and even then it felt funny. I made Spook wear a suit that day and he wouldn't have been any unhappier than if I'd told him his old red Ford was stolen. He said that since he was wearing a suit, he was pretty sure the undertaker was sizing him up for a pine box. He also told me that me sitting next to him looked like a rose sitting by a thorn."

Suddenly the dream that Shauna had the day that Shauna had

called her to come to the ranch after the accident came flooding back to her. A lily among thorns. "Sunny," Shauna began, "You might think this is really odd, but the day that you called me to come out to the plane crash, I was actually having a dream. In fact, I've had the dream before."

"In this dream," Shauna continued, "there were winding, gnarling braches that wove together in web-like trap and spun around me almost like I was in a vortex of a tornado. Whirling and swirling, I became almost dizzy. But slowly the swirling subsided and I saw the branches scattered and strewn about on the land almost like a carpet. I spied something small and white lying amidst the branches and began to walk out to see but found that sharp thorns in the branches poked through the soles of my shoes."

Sunny listened intently. "Gingerly finding my way past the thorns, I came upon a snow white lily lying among the thorns. As I reached to pick it up, suddenly the swirling began again and the lily was whisked away. Looking down, I found myself surrounded by shiny white pieces of thin metal scattered about randomly. Reaching down to pick one up, it suddenly disappeared and I found my hand covered with blood. Then you called and the dream was over."

"So do you think it means something?" Sunny asked.

"Absolutely!" Shauna cried, "Don't you see? It was a dream about the plane crash! That's what those shiny pieces of metal and the blood was about. That blood was from the men you rescued. And the lily: that lily that was in there amongst the thorns that got whisked away was you. You're the lily. Not just a rose, but a pure white lily. And those thorns are all the stuff that entangles you around here like your brothers and Shane and all those bad voices that condemn you!"

"But I don't want to leave here." Sunny contested.

"It doesn't mean that you are going to leave here, but it does mean that you are going to be rescued from the thorns that have trapped you. I know that this sounds kind of goofy, but we've talked about my dreams before and you know that I've learned to pay attention to them," Shauna explained with passion.

Sunny had to agree. Ever since Shauna was a little girl, she had dreams rich in symbolism and meaning and, they would discover, later those dreams would help explain something that happened. Never foreboding or frightening, but often unexplainable at the time, they had learned that quite often those dreams made things make sense.

"So, Miss Sunny Morgan," Shauna teased, "your brother is wrong. You're not a cur that needs culled from the herd. You are a pure white lily among thorns."

Chapter Twenty-One

"Are you sure you're ready for this?" Johnson asked Dane as they pulled out onto the highway. "It's a two hour trip down there and some of those roads aren't the best in the world."

"Sure, Dad," Dane replied with a smile. "I'm just fine and would like to get out of the house for a while."

They had a difficult time reaching Sunny. Many messages were left before she ever returned the call. Dane wanted to visit with her personally but the Stephanie had ended up scheduling the meeting. They were sure that no one would follow them all the way down there but to be certain, they had loaded up in Johnson's big Chrysler so it wouldn't look too official. They made his security personnel follow at a distance in an unassuming vehicle. And somewhere behind them would be Ron and Cheryl Moore who insisted on going. Dane was glad that there wasn't enough room in the Chrysler for the Moores to ride with them.

Dane healed more rapidly than anyone anticipated but he knew that much of that was because he took good care of himself. The walks around the halls of Cedar Manor moved outside so he could walk around the grounds. He missed his morning runs, but his leg had that lumbering cast on it yet so that would be some time before he would be able to do that.

Dane was glad for the time away from the dizzying distractions of his office. Although he had been so busy for so long from early in the morning until late at night, those brief vacations to Colorado were wonderful, but they seemed hurried as well. It was almost as if he was as busy trying to relax with activities on his vacations that he came back more exhausted than when he left.

But this recuperation was as good for his soul as it was for his body. Books he never opened he now read. He listened to entire music collections instead of just a sporadic song on the radio. Norma came to see him each day and they sat on the veranda chatting about life while tasting the latest coffee Norma found. Johnson and Meredith stopped by and they would re-tell family stories Dane hadn't heard in years.

Reflection. Dane hadn't paused to reflect on his life much in the last few years. He kept busy to keep the loss of Debbie minimized, but this forced slow-down of time combined with the fact that he had almost died caused him to inventory his life and where he wanted it to go.

Because of his popularity and success as Governor, it had been suggested – and he had given it much thought – that he would be a perfect candidate to run for President of the United States. While the thought of going down in history as one of the most powerful men on earth was appealing, he also had developed enough of a distaste for the acrimony of politics that he wasn't sure he wanted to swim in shark-infested waters.

What did he want? Dane asked himself that question many times since the crash. The crash forever changed his life in ways that he would yet discover, but he discovered that some of the things that seemed important – like amassing political power and wealth – just didn't seem to matter that much anymore. He asked himself repeatedly, *What do I want to do with the rest of my life that I could enjoy each day?* There had to be something more fulfilling than what he had known.

"Dane," Meredith interrupted his thoughts, "have you thought what you are going to say to Miss Morgan?"

"Sure," Dane smiled at his mother. "But each time I prepare a little speech, I feel like I'm starting to be the Governor and not just some incredibly grateful person whose life has been saved. I don't want to intimidate her and I certainly don't want to offend her by coming off as a politician so I'll just ad-lib and see where the conversation takes us. More than anything, I want to hear her story. I want to know what all she went through in rescuing us."

Dane gazed out the window. It was a clear, peaceful morning with a slight breeze blowing the green wheat back and forth in gentle waves. It wouldn't be long and the spring sun would turn to summer and the wheat would turn to amber waves of grain and the annual harvest would begin with combines and grain trucks dancing across the fields.

"Let's just hope Moore doesn't do all the talking," Norma injected.

"Now, Norma," Meredith chided. "Ron almost lost his life too and we shouldn't say bad things about him."

"I'm not saying bad things," Norma chuckled. "He just never knows when to shut up. He gets to rambling and this poor girl's going to want all of us to head home."

"I've already talked to him about it," Dane said. "I told him that we did not want to intimidate her and all we are going to do is thank her and let her tell her story. I think he'll listen to me."

"As long as you're near him, he will listen to you, Dane," Norma agreed. "I just never have liked him very much."

Dane often wondered how Debbie and Ron could be brother and sister. Debbie was sweet, deferring, caring, and completely trustworthy, but Ron was arrogant, rude, selfish and shifty. Although he had promised Debbie's father that he would look out after Ron, there were many times he regretted it. He gave Jim his word, but it was really in honor of Debbie that he befriended Ron. There were certain mannerisms, phrases, and looks of Moore that would remind Dane of Debbie, but when it came to personality, they were polar opposites.

Dane stared out the window oblivious to the chatter in the car. Debbie said that there was no place on earth more beautiful than

Kansas in spring. After long, hard winters with howling winds, piling snow, and skeletal trees stretched naked against the sky, the welcome warmth of sunshine brought healing to the land. Early rays of warmth coaxed the jonquils out of the ground first teased the red-bud trees into blossoming with their violet hues splashed in contrast amidst the greening foliage of the sycamore, oak, walnut, and hackberry trees which lined the creeks like stately sentinels guarding their travel across the hills and valleys.

They were traveling the Scenic By-Way, one of the many things Dane pushed through the legislature to encourage both tourists and natives to explore the glorious places often hidden and neglected. The two-lane highway wound through the Flint Hills hugging the banks of the Cottonwood River for much of the way. In open fields of alfalfa near bends in the river, magnificent tom turkeys with fanning tail-feathers strutted for admiring hens as whitetail deer grazed cautiously, always ready to flee. They made a good combination since what the turkey perfected in vision and hearing but lacked in smell the deer made up with keen olfactory senses thereby forming a protective alliance against predators.

Before he became Governor, Debbie and Dane would take off early on Saturday mornings and find remote areas to hike. Loading up Clancy, their golden Lab, they hiked wandering creeks and crested rolling hills. They slowly walked freshly plowed fields looking for the gleam of an upturned piece of flint, which might be an arrowhead or spear-point that was hundreds, maybe, thousands, of years old. They had a collection of tomahawk heads, drills, knives, and arrowheads all knapped from the native flint for which the hills were named.

A wave of loneliness washed over Dane. *Oh, to don a pair of hiking boots, load up Debbie and Clancy, and head out on a hike.* They went on a hike the day after Debbie found out she had cancer. Debbie had her suspicions about it but kept it from Dane so as not to alarm him, but together they discovered the horrifying news.

That was their last hike together. They performed surgery on

Debbie the following Monday and found the cancer far more invasive than they realized. They removed what they could, but Dane could tell by the look on the doctor's face when he walked into the room it wasn't good. Intensive chemo might give her a year or she could leave it alone and have six months.

Debbie chose to take the chemo although, because of the severity of her reaction to it, they often wondered if they had made the right decision. It did prolong her life but she often commented that six more months of hair and appetite was better than a year of baldness and vomiting. She was valiant. Even Johnson told her she deserved the Silver Star for bravery in the face of death.

"Dane?" Norma interrupted his thoughts. "Are you okay? You look very sad."

"Oh, just thinking about hiking through the hills with Debbie again. Sorry, but just kind of got lost in the past," Dane apologized.

"I was thinking about her, too," Meredith said. "Debbie loved spring time in Kansas, didn't she?"

"Debbie loved life!" Dane agreed. "That girl was always a good time looking for a place to happen. She could make anything you did turn out to be a lot of fun."

"I hate to interrupt your conversation," Stephanie said. "But according to these directions, we must be getting close to the ranch. It shows that after you make that last bend in the road that it's about two miles further."

"I've been out there before and it's pretty easy to find that driveway because there's a big iron star on a gate and a brand emblem of an LS right beside it."

"You didn't tell me you had been on the ranch before," Stephanie seemed startled. "What were you doing out here?"

"Well, I own some pasture land that is adjacent to the Lonesome Star and I'd been up to the ranch to visit with Mr. Morgan about buying some of his."

"So have you met Sunny then?" Stephanie asked.

"No, I saw her out in the corral messing with the horses, but she never came up to talk to us. But I knew she had a lot of influence in the decision making because Mr. Morgan seemed interested but said he had to talk to his daughter first. When I called him later, it was a pretty firm 'no' that I got from him. He said she wanted to keep the land and she wasn't selling out to some rich guy that didn't know a horse from a heifer. I think he would have sold me the whole thing, but she didn't want to. Then he died and she must have got it all, but I never did ask her about it. Dad, you need to be slowing down, the gates are right where the red pickup's parked."

Spook Masterson had gone down to the gate to unlock it for the Governor. With his cowboy hat cocked back slightly, he spit a stream of tobacco juice on the ground as the big Chrysler pulled in. Johnson rolled down his window, "Is this the Lonesome Star Ranch?"

"I reckon it is." Spook stooped over to look in the car at the rest of the passengers. "And you must be the Guv'ner. Howdy, my name's Spook Masterson." Spook reached in the window to shake Johnson's hand, then across to shake Dane's. "Welcome to the Lonesome Star. Let me open this 'chere gate for you'uns and we can go on up to the house. Got to keep this gate locked to keep all the vermin out. Are those other vehicles with you?" Spook motioned to the other two cars. "Ifn' they're not, I ain't lettin' 'em in."

"They're with us," Johnson nodded.

As they drove up the mile and a half long driveway, Dane thought back to his last few minutes in the plane before he crashed. He saw the house and hoped that someone from there might notice their plight but had no idea that Sunny was out on horseback watching it all unfold. Once again, he breathed a sigh of gratefulness for her being in the right place at the right time.

The old red Ford lurched to a stop under the light pole and the other cars followed suit. Sunny opened the screen door of the back porch and started down the steps. Dane was surprised at how nervous he was as he got out of the car. He had met movie stars, national and foreign dignitaries of great importance, and some of the most famous people in the world, but he was never nervous in meeting them. Like Johnson said, *they put their pants on one leg at a time just like you,* so Dane purposed never to be intimidated in the presence of another, no matter their status. Yet he was suddenly overwhelmed with a mixture of fear and anticipation.

Sunny heard the cars coming up the drive and nervously made her way to the living room window and pulled the drapes back a little so she could see. Oh, how she wished the plane had never gone down on her prairie. She should be out taking care of newborn calves today, not wasting time meeting some dignitary that didn't bother making the phone call himself to set up this appointment. Ever since that lady, Stephanie, had called her from the Governor's office to set this meeting up, she had been nervous, like Spook would say, *as a preacher in a cussin' contest.*

She liked the normalcy of her life. The day-to-day routine of mending fences, checking the cattle, watching the markets, and worrying about weather were familiar. Rhythms. But the confusion since the plane crash was like an unwelcome interloper trespassing on her land. *No trespassing* signs were posted around the perimeter of her land but trespassers that drop out of the sky? How could she post a sign for that?

She didn't want to meet the Governor. Although she felt compassion for him the day of the plane crash even before she realized who he was, she still held the prejudices against him that many life-long inhabitants of the prairie felt towards those big city folks with all the money to buy up our land but not enough sense to take care of it. Rich sportsmen whose only desire was to hunt game or fish the ponds for bass and channel cat purchased much of the land. There was a lingering resentment in those who had worked from sun-up 'till sundown with backbreaking work taking care of animals, fighting with the weather over crops, and trying to navigate the endless maze of governmental subsidies and programs.

The Governor was another rich city boy who looked at the land as a hobby, not a livelihood. Sunny remembered the first time he visited her Daddy about selling the ranch. She was trimming the hooves on Starbuck when he pulled up. She didn't know who he was at the time – he wasn't even Governor yet – but he looked like a city slicker and she didn't have much use for them.

Sunny couldn't believe her Dad would sell what their ancestors homesteaded. It wasn't just a piece of land that they lived on; it was over a century of family memories. Almost every photo in their scrap books were taken on that ranch, whether it was of Great-Great-Grandpa Isaac Morgan with his team of oxen hooked up to a single-bottom plow breaking land or the aerial shot of a cattle round-up when Sunny was ten.

But now she had to deal with this man driving up her driveway. And, in just a few days, she would be going to New York to be on a television show. She wished she could saddle up Starbuck and meander through the hills checking calves and maybe take a dip in the Rock Bluff pool, the most pristine place she had ever seen in Kansas.

Shauna urged Sunny to get new jeans and a shirt for when the Governor showed up, but Sunny refused. "I'm not spiffying myself up for someone I don't even like."

"You don't even know what he's like," Shauna argued.

"He's just another rich city slicker that wants to buy up our land so he and his other rich city slicker friends can have a place to play. You know what they say about the only thing different between men and boys is the price of their toys. Well, all he wants to do is buy a big new playground and until the bank takes it away, I'm not selling."

So Sunny deliberately put on an old pair of jeans with a little tear in the knees from a barbed-wire fence and her old Tony Lama boots that had been repaired twice. She didn't even bother cleaning the dried cow manure off them. She also found the rattiest shirt she owned, one faded by the sun and frayed around the cuffs. He might think he's someone special, but she didn't. For all she knew, he would offer to buy the ranch again and she just might have to sic Spook and his revolver after him.

"Well, you look like a cowgirl," Shauna rolled her eyes as Sunny walked through the kitchen. "The Governor of the state of Kansas is pulling up the driveway and you look like you're going out to work cattle. Sunny, you're the most beautiful girl on the prairie but in those clothes you look like an old cow hand."

"Shauna, we've had this discussion before and I'm NOT going to try to impress someone I don't like. I don't even want them out here."

"Oh, you wouldn't know a gift if it slapped you upside the head. Now get out there and meet the Governor!"

"Get, Jasmine!" Sunny moved the cat lounging in the sun. The old wooden screen door, rusty brown and torn in a few places, creaked as she went out. Shauna followed closely behind. Sunny was glad Spook and Shauna were there. Mackenzie had offered but when Sunny told her that the Governor's office said it was to be private and they weren't bringing any press, Mackenzie thought it best to stay away too. Sunny would be okay with Spook and Shauna there.

"Howdy, Miss Sunshine," Spook drawled as the ambled towards the porch. "Look what the cat dragged in. I done found the Guvner of the State of Kansas and he wants to meet 'cha."

Sunny felt a cold shiver through her body and her hands turned clammy. As the people in the cars slowly filtered out, she noticed the Governor was limping across the driveway with a smile on his face.

"Miss Morgan?" Dane asked. He noticed that Sunny walked with her head down, watching the ground as if she didn't want to look up. "I'm Dane Richards."

Sunny looked up and politely smiled, "Hello, Governor, I'm Sunny Morgan. You don't have to call me 'Miss', you can just call me Sunny." She was taken back by the smell of his cologne. The last time she smelled that was with a mixture of blood. Even though she washed that shirt from that day, she finally had to throw it away because the blood stain never left, nor did the lingering smell of his cologne. She came to like that smell.

"And please don't call me 'Governor,'" Dane replied. "You can just call me Dane."

Dane was not ready for the reaction in his soul as his eyes met Sunny's. He had long wondered if that brief vision he had when injured was a figment of his imagination or if she really did have the innocent and soulful eyes of a doe. But as their eyes met, the dark brown eyes gazing back at his immediately captivated him. That was her that he saw. He wanted to tell her that, to let her know that in that moment in time at the crash scene, he looked into those same eyes and drew strength and courage and hope and peace, all from one single gaze.

Quickly he caught himself in the awkward moment of staring into her eyes, mesmerized by the mystery, intrigued by the innocence, and drawn into their depth.

"I hope you don't mind," Dane caught his breath. "I brought along some family and some very close friends. I'd like to introduce you to Ron Moore, the other man you rescued that day, and his wife Cheryl."

Sunny turned to meet them and her stomach knotted up. She recalled reaching in with her knife to cut him free from the safety belts and he smelled awful, like the mixture of urine, blood and vomit.

"A handshakes not good enough for me," Moore said lunging towards Sunny and, throwing his arms around her, picked her up off the ground.

Startled, Sunny felt a cringe of disgust start to wash over her as Moore hugged too long and made her uncomfortable. She could tell that Moore's wife wasn't too thrilled about it either, but once Moore let her go, Cheryl was quite nice to Sunny and thanked her profusely for saving her husband's life.

Dane was embarrassed as Moore rambled through a canned speech that seemed more for the press than it did for Sunny. Dane watched Sunny as Moore rambled on and could tell she was being polite, but not particularly impressed. Finally, Moore came to a close and Dane was able to start introducing the rest of his family.

Sunny immediately liked Johnson and Meredith. Sunny got along with older folks better than those of her generation and she found herself drawn into the handshake and smile of them both. There was something a little distant about Norma and her husband that Sunny couldn't quite describe, but they were very pleasant nonetheless.

"Sunny," Dane began, "would it be alright if you took us out to the crash site and told us about everything that happened that day? Can we drive our vehicles out there or do we need to walk?"

"Oh, you can drive your vehicles alright," Sunny disgusted. "Between the folks from the press, rescue vehicles, and inspectors, they cut several new roads going out there."

"I'm sorry," Dane apologized. "The prairie is so beautiful yet fragile and new roads cut through it do a lot of damage. If you don't mind, I would like to do what I can to repair that. I know a lot of experts in prairie ecology and they would love to come out here and restore that for you. And don't worry about the cost – it's my fault that this happened and it's my responsibility to take care of it."

"That would be nice, Governor, it really did upset me that it got tore up. This ranch has been in our family for several generations and we've always been cautious about where we drive and where we make paths. We know that once we do, the erosion worsens and we like it to be as much like it was a thousand years ago as we can." Sunny was relieved he brought it up.

"Young man," Johnson told Dane as they crawled back in car, "that is one fine young lady that rescued you. Judging by the looks of the peeling paint on her house and the flapping shutters on that old barn, I think you ought to figure out a way to help this girl with more than just fixing her prairie."

"I agree with you, Johnson," Meredith said. "but I suspect this young lady is too independent to accept any kind of help that she didn't have to work for. Her family has had to be pretty tough to make a go of it out on this prairie for so many years."

"Dane, are you okay?" Norma seemed to sense Dane's moods better than anyone. "You seemed a little, well, not quite yourself back there."

"Oh, I'm fine," Dane said. "I was just surprised at how I felt back there. I can't remember being that nervous meeting someone in a long time."

"So, did she have eyes like a doe?" Norma teased.

"Oh, quit that, she seems like a very nice person."

Those eyes sweetly haunted him. He learned the virtue in public relations of making and holding eye contact with people and had, on occasion, used a fixed gaze at adversaries to intimidate them. He learned to read the eyes of people, those windows to the soul that could tell you more about the person than their words. "Look 'em in the eye, son," Johnson told him.

He was startled, though, by what he saw in her eyes. It was if he was looking through a portal into a rich heritage of previous generations who, by reason of necessity, developed a keen awareness of the ebb and flow of nature and living off the land with a pioneer spirit. There was a blissful innocence of hope in those eyes in the face of agonizing adversities that gave a flicker of light through the darkest of nights. The pain he saw hidden in the shadows of her eyes, deep and dark, a mystery that beckoned someone to discover yet warned invasive intruders to disappear also disquieted him.

Dane was surprised at how badly the vehicles damaged the prairie. Many felt at liberty to make a new road through the grass wherever they chose so the paths were a spider-web. He understood why Sunny was upset. He was upset his ignorance and inexperience caused such chaos.

The old red Ford shuddered to a stop and Spook, Sunny, and Shauna all bailed out of the truck and headed for the place on the knoll where stakes marked the site.

"So this is it?" Dane asked. "It sure looks different from down here than it did from up in the air as we were plummeting towards the ground. It's a miracle that we made it."

"I never had a bit of concern about making it," Moore boasted. "I knew the Governor would get us out of it."

"Where did you first see us?" Dane asked Sunny, trying to interrupt Moore from saying something else.

Sunny pointed over to the place she and Starbuck watched it unfold. Slowly, she told the story from the beginning.

Dane stared off into the western sky trying to imagine, from Sunny's perspective, his plane coming down. As the story unraveled, Dane become more aware of just how critical the situation was and the miracle of their survival. If just one thing had been different, they would not have made it out alive. Moore kept interrupting Sunny with what started as questions and ended as bragging. Cheryl was the only one impressed.

Sunny walked up to top of the knoll where the plane had come to rest and as they stumbled through the torn up ground and still damaged grasses, she explained how she found them, the plane upside down. Dane suddenly remembered that Moore vomited and wet his pants.

"Did it smell inside the cockpit?" Dane asked.

"Awful," Sunny replied. "I about lost it when I stuck my head in there."

Dane watched Sunny as she told the story about finding them hanging upside down then getting Starbuck to drag first the wing off the plane, then slowly drag Dane and Moore out to safety. He was amazed that any animal would respond that well to a human being.

"It's a wonder your horse just didn't kill us when he was dragging us out! I still have a hard time believing that horse did all you said he did," Moore shot off his mouth again.

Dane watched the sparks fly in Sunny's eyes as she wheeled to face Moore. Though Moore was several inches taller, he cowered as Sunny spoke. "Mr. Moore," she said, "if you've ever been on a horse, you'd find out real quick like that they're a whole lot smarter than most humans. I've raised Starbuck since he was a baby and I would trust him more than I would about any person I know. And I've never known a horse to be scared enough to wet himself."

Dane turned away so no one would see the smile that flitted across his face. This girl had spunk! Most folks usually just let Moore ramble and didn't pay much attention to him, but she put him in his place. Dane made a mental note to remember the affection she felt towards her horse.

"Where was it that I was laying?" Dane asked. Sunny pointed to the spot where the grass was matted and blotches of blood could still be seen in the grass. He admired the way Sunny told the story matter-of-fact without any kind of embellishment that made it look like she was a hero. Occasionally, Johnson, Meredith, or Norma would pause her to ask a question, but for the most part they stood on the knoll of the hill mesmerized by not only the narrative, but by the narrator. They were anxious to meet Sunny, but as they heard the story for the first time in complete detail, a deep, abiding respect for her grew.

"That is quite a horse you have, Miss Morgan," Moore apologized. "I'm sorry that what I said came across so disrespectful." Moore had been mulling over his comment and her retort and figured the best way to save face was to apologize. But Dane noticed that Moore, in typical fashion, didn't apologize for what he said so much as for the way it was taken, which put the responsibility for the offense on the hearer more than the speaker. Sunny ignored him and continued telling the story.

Dane looked wistfully across the prairie to the south, to the land that he owned, and wished that he too could spend his days on horseback checking cattle, mending fences, and worrying about the weather. What a serene, tranquil life it would be to spend one's efforts in such a primal fashion. The more the prairie enveloped him, the more he began to understand the enormous invasion his crash was on this land and Sunny. He heard that she refused invitations for interviews but reserved an agent to get her on national television. Smart girl. Or at least surrounded by some smart people to help her.

Dane took an immediate liking to Spook. Although the cowboy

was relatively quiet in all the conversations, one could tell he was protective towards Sunny. Quite often Dane noticed Spook positioning himself between Moore and Sunny. While most didn't notice, Dane got the message: you want to get to Sunny you'll have to go through Spook.

Sunny finished the story and they milled around, trying to absorb the impact of the event.

"Young lady," Johnson spoke, "I've lived a long time on this earth and have seen my fair share of heroes during the war, but I have to tell you that what you did out here on the prairie is nothing short of a miracle. When I think that the only thing between my son and death was the fact that you were here, it makes me and Meredith extremely grateful and beholdin' to you."

"I second that," Norma said. "My little brother is a stubborn and persistent man, but would not be alive today without you being here. We heard so many different accounts of the story, but being here today has made us aware of how incredible a person you really are. You really are an angel for our family."

Sunny ducked her head, unsure of how to take this adulation. "Oh, I was just doing what anyone else would have done in the same situation." Shauna moved beside Sunny and put her arm around her waist not only to support, but to affirm what was being said.

"Sunny, I don't know if you saw me on television thanking you, but I want to say it again. When we were eight thousand feet off the ground and in more trouble than I thought we would ever get out of alive, I started praying that God would somehow perform a miracle and send an angel to rescue us. The plane would run, then die, rise, then fall, and I just held on for dear life feeling like I was being controlled by some force way beyond my power. The last thing I remember was the feel of the grass catching the wheels on the plane and I really figured we were going to die."

Sunny kicked the ground with the toe of her boot, but Dane kept going. "I just want you to know that you were that angel, you were that miracle and I want you to know how incredibly grateful I am to you for saving my life. I remember bits and pieces, but after being out here today, I've come to understand that my life was not supposed to end, that I'm not finished here on this earth. And I have you to thank for it."

Dane could tell what he said made her extremely uncomfortable and decided not to go any further. Shauna squeezed Sunny a little more tightly and said, "See, cowgirl, I've been telling you all along you're something special. I'm not the only one who thinks that, now, am I?" Sunny leaned her head on Shauna's shoulder and quietly wiped away the tears from her eyes.

"Thank you, Dane," she said. "I'm just glad Starbuck and I could be of some help."

An awkward silence fell on the group that was interrupted by Johnson. "We need to be getting Dane back to the house so he can rest. Thanks, Miss Morgan, for letting us come out."

Slowly the crowd began to disperse.

"Guv'ner, kin I git a word with ya?" Spook motioned Dane to the side wanting a private conversation. Out of the range of hearing for the others, Spook met Dane's gaze as if there was a hidden meaning in his words. "Guv'ner, I've watched this chere filly grow up since she was nuthin' but a foal and I'm here to tell ya that there ain't no better lass to be found anywhere in the world. But she ain't special just because she rescued you and your buddy over there. She's special because of what's inside her that you don't find in too many people."

"You might think I'm a crazy old cowpoke whats been tossed off too many horses and landed on my head each time, but I get certain feelin's every now and then that I can't expain, but it starts somewhere in my gut and finally makes it's way to my mind and ifn' I don't let it out, it just simmers in there like fresh cowpie on a hot July day."

Spook went on, "I read 'nough papers to watch 'nough news to know that you're a widower. And I smelled a burnin' in the air today when you first laid eyes on Sunny that had a faint whiff of the smoke on the prairie when it first catches fa'r. Now, I don't reckon on tellin' anyone how to live their life, but I'm askin' that if what I done smelt was right, that you be real careful not to let it burn Miss Sunshine up. I'd hate to have to go to jail for stringin' up the Guv'ner of the state of Kansas."

Dane laughed nervously. Something strange happened when he first met Sunny, but he attributed it to the emotional circumstances of meeting the person that rescued him from death.

"Oh, I assure you, Mr. Masterson," Dane explained, "I have nothing but the utmost respect for Miss Morgan and can assure you that I have no amorous intent."

"Wa'll," Spook spit a stream of tobacco juice in the grass, "maybe I was smellin' the a'r wrong and readin' the signs wrong, but ifn' I did get 'em right, I just wanted to send a smoke signal yore way and let you know I'd be plumb happy to walk her down the aisle for you."

Chapter Twenty-Two

"I just don't think I can go through with this." Sunny sat down on the edge of the bed that had new clothes sprawled out over it. "I would just as soon go home as to stay here and go on television."

Mackenzie sat down on the edge of the bed beside Sunny and put her arm around her shoulder. "You don't have to Sunny. If you want to stay just go home, you can and we'll make sure every one leaves you alone. But if you can just endure this week, think about what it will do for the Lonesome Star. I talked with Miles Applegate and they are already lined up with a publisher to offer you a book deal. Sunny, you not only will be able to pay those taxes that are due, you'll be able to build a new barn for Starbuck, get you a new truck and horse trailer, and really won't have to worry about much for a long time if you play your cards right."

"I know," Sunny sighed. "The only reason that I'm doing this is because of the ranch. I really want to buy my brothers out. They left and never want to come back but once they know I've got money, they're going to want their share. We haven't made profit off this in years but I've got to send them the full books each year just to prove to them I'm not making money. Even then, they don't believe me. Maybe I can buy them out and the ranch will be mine."

"What do you dream about for the ranch, Sunny?" Mackenzie

asked.

"First, I'd like it if the Governor got that mess fixed all those people made. Fortunately, when he came out he offered to do it rather than me have to ask him. Folks sure made a mess of things."

Mackenzie found Sunny's love of the land refreshingly innocent. Most folks who were ready to come in to a lot of cash would be thinking of cars and houses and creature comforts, but a person liked Sunny had an affinity for the land, a love affair that transcended survey points and tract descriptions. She, too, experienced that as a little girl growing up on a farm where generations of her family made their life from the earth. But that was many winding roads ago for Mackenzie. She decided the glitz and glamour of a bigger city won out over the dark canopy of a summer evening with stars scattered like buckshot over the deepening sky or the breath of air that would coax the wheat into swaying rhythmically like an undulating sea of gold. But innocence once lost proves impossible to rediscover.

A knock came at the door and Mackenzie walked over to open it. As she opened it, a fragrant waft of rose gently floated through the door.

"Miss Sunny Morgan?" the concierge asked.

"No, I'm Mackenzie Foster. This is Sunny," she said, pointing to Sunny who was getting up off the bed.

"These are for you, Miss Morgan." The concierge said.

"Who would send me flowers?" Sunny asked. "Shauna is the only one that knows what hotel we're at and I know she doesn't have the money to send flowers."

Sunny walked over to the waiting man and took the vase of canary yellow sunflowers in a nest of deep red roses and gentle stalks of prairie grass. Opening the card, she read its contents, "Sunny, Best of luck to you. You make our state proud to call you our own. Governor Dane Richards."

"Wow," Sunny exclaimed. "That was nice of him."

"Git chore cotton-pickin' hands offn' my suitcase!" They heard

Spook challenging a bellhop as he walked down the aisle. "I'm fit as a fiddle and ifn' I needed someone to carry my gear I'd a brought me pack mule."

Mackenzie was still standing with the door open when Spook walked in, "G'mornin' Miss Sunshine. Whar'd you git them purty flowers? Done looks like someone snuck in to the widder Joneses flower bed and done helped themselves when no body was lookin'."

"The Governor sent these to me," Sunny replied as she handed him the card to read.

"W'all, ain't you just the queen of Prairie Chicken Festival!" Spook laughed. Sunny was coaxed by Spook into trying out for the annual Teterville Prairie Chicken Festival when she was sixteen and her grand prize for winning it was a new saddle. She argued with Spook vehemently about that but Spook knew she was the prettiest girl in town and was sure to win as long as Irene Jones hadn't tried to rig it for her niece who Spook said, *was so ugly as to make a pig run out in front of a train.* Irene was surrounded by a great deal of suspicion of rigging the contests when her daughters were in it. Although no one could prove it, it seemed rather than odd that the judges for the contests over the years when her daughters were in just happened to be Irene's closest friends.

Sunny couldn't sing or dance but she was the best trick roper around having learned from Spook and her dazzling display was the audience's favorite. Most of them sat through the hot and humid July evening swatting mosquitoes, sweating profusely, and listening to one wannabe queen after another warble with a poorly working speaker system about loves lost or dreams crushed. So when Sunny came out all decked out in a pair of new red boots and matching leather chaps and a new straw Stetson and started twirling that rope, the crowd went crazy. No amount of wrangling by Telephone Jones could sway the judge's vote when they saw the crowd go wild.

Sunny still had that saddle setting up in one of the extra bedrooms in the house where she kept all of her trophies from rodeos and horse shows that she had been in through the years. Although the saddle was pretty, it was a trophy and not a tool like she needed for the everyday work on the ranch.

Irene Jones was pretty rude to Spook after that accusing him of rigging the contest. Spook asked her if that wasn't like the pot calling the kettle black and Irene took a swipe at him with her umbrella but he was too quick. That was one of the few times Sunny had ever seen Spook angry as he clinched his teeth, lowered his voice, leaned towards Irene and said, "Miss Jones, any manure spreader that would stoop so low as to rig a contest ain't nothing' but the north end of a south bound mule." With a loud *harrumph*, Irene swung her head around, stuck her nose up in the air, and promptly tripped and fell off the edge of the sidewalk.

"Oh, Spook," Sunny chided him. "This ain't Teterville and this ain't the Prairie Queen festival, is it?"

"No it ain't," Spook responded, glaring at the bellhop loitering for a tip. "Folks in Kansas help others because it's a right good thing to do and only them fellers with beady eyes like a rattlesnake would want money for it." With that, the bellhop abruptly excused himself and left.

Mackenzie laughed at Spook. Bringing him was a brilliant idea of Miles since she could visibly see Sunny at rest in his presence. Obviously, she felt a degree of comfort from years of developing trust. She knew that if Spook got rattled – which Mackenzie not only had never seen but couldn't imagine anything rattling him – then Sunny would. If Spook stayed calm, then Sunny would.

Spook had never been on a plane before and did not like having to take his hat off while walking down the aisle. It was the first time, Mackenzie realized, that she had seen him without his hat on and was surprised at the full salt-and-pepper hair. His weathered face and hands betrayed his when she had first met him, assuming that he was a good twenty years older than her. But once she had been around him for a while, guessed him to be just a few years older. Unlike women, guys like Spook didn't have the ability to look younger because of make-up.

"Ifn' I were made to fly, God'd gave me a dadgum pair of wings and covered my hairy body with feathers," he complained as he boarded. Not only had he never been on a plane, but he never traveled more than one state beyond the border of Kansas. Mackenzie frequently watched him as they traveled, wondering what he was thinking. Her respect for him continued to grow as he watched him protect Sunny, always deliberate to put himself between her and anything that might harm her. Mackenzie understood why Sunny felt so at ease around him. Mackenzie realized that even she felt safer with him near. She had traveled to a lot of places and always was on guard but, with Spook near, it was as if there was someone watching her back instead of trying to stab it. That was a surprisingly good feeling.

Spook knew no stranger. On the hour-long trip in the taxi to the hotel, he struck up a conversation with the taxi driver who was a foreigner and difficult to understand. They learned the man grew up in the Middle East to a family of Bedouins that wandered nomadically with their sheep. They talked about the difference between horses and camel, sheep and cattle, deserts and prairie.

The man didn't get angry when Spook asked him if they wore towels on their heads and bathrobes when they rode their camels. Spook allowed a nice straw hat was cooler than a towel on the head. As they got out of the taxi, Spook and the driver made a deal that before they died, Spook would ride a camel with a towel around his head and the driver would ride a horse wearing a straw hat and chaps. Mackenzie noticed that the taxi-driver did not deliberately overcharge these obvious tourists.

"Spook," Sunny asked, "Which of these outfits should I wear tomorrow?"

"W'all, Miss Sunshine," Spook drawled, "I reckon you could w'ar a gunny sack and still be the purtiest filly in the corral."

"Oh, Spook, if I'm as purty as you say I am, how come thar ain't no cowboys a'chasin after me with their lassos?"

"Well, Miss Sunshine," Spook said, nodding to the huge vase of flowers he had followed in. "I'd say there's some galoot already starting to feed a little slack into the loop already. He's already perched atop his hoss and just waitin' for the chute to open."

"Oh, Spook," Sunny said genuinely surprised. "Not the Governor. Why you silly old cowboy, the Governor wouldn't have a thing to do with a plain old country girl like me and you know it. Now quit teasing me."

Spook turned and winked at Mackenzie. There was something knowing, something deep in his eyes that surprised Mackenzie. Mackenzie didn't know Spook that well, but couldn't imagine that Spook would tease with something as delicate to Sunny as her feelings about men. Was there something he sensed when the Governor was at the Lonesome Star that would make him believe something was in the offing? Surely not the Governor and Sunny! But, why not? Stranger things had happened.

Once again, Spook surprised her. Perhaps it was because so many of the farmers and ranchers she knew as a kid she considered to be, well, less than highly educated and socialized. She liked Spook and the more she was around him found a certain wisdom in his home-spun tales and takes on life. He might hide behind the drawl and the aw-shucks persona, but there was a deep river in him that she found intriguing, perhaps even inviting.

"I think ya need to ask Miss Foster here what looks best on ya," Spook deferred to Mackenzie. "I ain't no expert on the latest styles and Sunday-go-to-meetin' clothes."

"Well, neither am I!" Sunny shot back. "When's the last time you saw me in Sunday-go-to-meetin' clothes? The last time I got dressed up was for Josiah Clatterbucks funeral and you were too busy squirming like a kid in the principal's office. You thought the undertaker was measuring you for a coffin."

Mackenzie saw a little bit of crimson creeping up the back of Spook's neck.

191

"Sunny," Mackenzie walked over to the bed and started picking out clothes, "now, when we bought you these clothes, you remember I told you that they want to see the cowgirl from Kansas, not another frilly high-falutin' woman from New York. Spook is right, you would look drop-dead gorgeous in a feed sack, but we've got you some wonderful clothes that are just perfect for you. You will look absolutely smashing."

"Okay," Sunny said. "If you say so. I just don't want to look like a dork."

"Honey," Mackenzie said, "the last thing you will look like is a dork. By this time tomorrow evening, every single man in the country is going to want your number."

"Well, I ain't answering," Sunny said, holding up a shirt for Spook to look at. "I ain't settlin' for nobody until I find me another Spook Masterson about twenty five years younger."

Mackenzie looked over at Spook whose entire face turned crimson. He turned to leave.

"W'all, I've had just about enough of this chere nonsense. I think I'll saddle my cayuse and go see ifn' I can find me a waterin' hole." Spook tipped his hat, bowed slightly, and grabbed the door knob, "Ifn' y'all don't mind, this old cowpoke's going to mosey on down and whet my whistle with a shot of fa'rwater."

"Now, Spook, don't you be getting into trouble."

Mackenzie was not sure whether he heard Sunny or not and, if he did, whether he paid attention. Spook wouldn't look for trouble but trouble had its way of looking for him. Guys like Spook had the old gunslinger aura to them that some young buck felt like they had to draw out every once in a while. Spook might look a little saddle-worn, but Mackenzie noticed his lightning fast reflexes when the door of the taxi started to slam shut on her hand. And he handled their seventy-pound suitcases like they were light as a feather. He could handle himself just fine, Mackenzie surmised.

"Mackenzie," Sunny interrupted her thoughts. "I'm really glad you and Spook are here. I'm scared enough, but I can't imagine being here

192

without you."

"I wouldn't miss this for the world, Sunny," Mackenzie smiled. "I feel like this is the beginning of a whole new way of life for all of us and like Spook says, I'm just going to grab the saddle horn and hang on. I would like to .." the phone rang and interrupted her.

"Hello?" Mackenzie answered the phone. "Why yes, Governor Richards, she's standing right here. Hold on just a moment."

"Hello?" Sunny said. "How are you Governor Richards? Oh, sorry about that, I forgot I'm supposed to call you Dane. Yes, we made it just fine and thank you for the flowers. A little splash of Kansas here in New York is a welcome sight. Yes, we go out to supper tonight with a man from the show named Miles Applegate. He's going to walk us through the studio so I can get prepared for tomorrow. Mackenzie is here with me and Spook just left. What's that? Oh, I suppose I'm a little nervous, but having my friends here helps a lot. It's in the paper? Well, I'm sure it's the talk of Teterville at least. I just hope I don't embarrass them all."

Like a little girl on a phone, Mackenzie watched Sunny pace around the room twirling the cord up then unwinding it again. Occasionally she looked at Mackenzie and shrugged her shoulders, but they chatted for quite a while about the trip. Mackenzie thought it odd that the Governor would spend so much time in a casual chat, but, after all, this was the woman that saved his life.

"That was nice of him to call." Sunny said as she hung the phone up. "I keep wondering how he knows where we are but I suppose that is one of the perks of being the governor. I wonder what Spook is doing?"

"I'm sure Spook is just fine. It's New York City that's in trouble if anything, not Spook." Mackenzie could tell Sunny was ready to be alone for a while. "As a matter of fact, if you don't mind, Sunny, I think I'll mosey on down to the same waterin' hole and check on our old cowpoke. There are some mighty fast women in New York City and he wouldn't know what hit him. Maybe Spook needs a little protectin' of his own!"

Chapter Twenty-Three

Dane put down the phone and swiveled in his leather chair and looked out the window. Tiny puffs of cotton-like seeds falling from the cottonwood trees rode invisible air currents past his window and sunlight gleamed across the deeply oiled walnut paneling. It was good to be back to work, even if only for a few hours at a time. He gazed out the window towards the east, wondering how Sunny and her Kansas entourage were faring in the Big Apple. He had been there numerous times and knew it was a far cry from the Kansas prairie that Sunny was accustomed to roaming. But with Spook and Mackenzie along, she would be just fine.

He thought about flying back to New York to watch the airing of the show, but Stephanie told him that was not something Governors did. Now, if he had been invited to be on the show, then that was one thing, but just to show up in the audience was entirely different.

Entirely different. The last few weeks that phrase rattled around in Dane's mind like a pinball ricocheting back and forth in a pinball machine. His life was entirely different since the accident. Yes, he still slept in the same bed and sat in the same office answering the same kind of questions, but the passion for his work cooled. He found the maze of politics not only less challenging, but perhaps even boring. He knew it was a chess game and surrounded himself with fine strategists to help him win, but the flame that burned in him to conquer was now a mere flicker instead of a raging fury.

More money? Why? More power? Why? Maybe that Kansas thunderstorm splashing against his unconscious face began to put the fire out as he lay there on the prairie. For years he awakened each morning feeling like a jet sitting on the tarmac with engines starting to race with ambition and just waiting for the signal to go full throttle on the latest cause, the latest bill in the legislature, or the latest political battle to strategize over. He considered going to work like going to war and believed the greatest prizes in life were victories not only won, but won well and decisively with a great deal of strategy involved.

But the last few mornings he awakened to morning rays racing through his room like silent spies seeking to illuminate the darkest crevices and simply pulled the covers back over his head with weariness. Although the emptiness of their bed after Debbie's death took months to adjust to, that aching feeling of waking up alone had crept back in.

He walked around Cedar Manor that morning with dew soaking his tennis shoes and the squawking blue jay complaining of his intrusion and realized that he had a wonderful family, a few trusted friends, a million acquaintances, but no one with which to share his life. He had two more years left in his term and he vowed never to seek any kind of relationship while in office, so that meant two more years of waking up alone. He was not a person who wasted time wishing he were somewhere else for he had developed the discipline to live in the moment, but as he stared blankly out the window, his mind wandered through the tall native grasses of the prairie.

"Governor Richards," his secretary, Marjorie Marshall paged him on the speaker phone. "Your sister is here to see you. May I send her in?"

"Hi Dane," Norma hugged him as she came through the door. "My you're looking great! I can't get over how much better you look than when we saw you first after the crash. I never thought you'd look this good again. I just stopped by to talk to you about a banquet for Sunny. Have you thought any more about that yet?"

"As a matter-of-fact, I have." Dane sat down on the edge of the deeply oiled walnut desk. "I just got off the phone with Sunny and asked her about a few dates that might work. If we have it, I want to be sure she isn't off on some television show somewhere."

"You called Sunny?" Norma asked with a look of disbelief on her face. "Isn't she in New York filming that show?" Norma knew that Dane only called people of great importance and even she had a hard time getting him on the phone even though she was his sister. That was Marjorie's job to call and schedule appointments, not his.

"Yes," Dane replied. "I called to wish her well on the show tomorrow and to let her know that all the fine folks in Kansas are proud of her."

"That we are," Norma agreed. "I would imagine that almost every person in Kansas will be watching or taping that show tomorrow. When do they air that interview with you?"

"I'm not sure," Dane shrugged. "They are supposed to let me know. But after being interviewed, I could tell they really wanted to hear more about Sunny's story than mine. I don't blame them. My story was a result of being a novice and overconfident. Her story is about heroism and courage and quick thinking."

"She is a remarkable young woman," Norma agreed. "I find myself wanting to go back out to the ranch and spend time there just wandering around. It was so peaceful out there, so remote and removed from the hustle and bustle of our lives."

"Yes, I was just daydreaming about being out there when you came in," Dane said. "I imagine hiking through those hills and finding the crystal clear spring-fed streams, stumbling across that ancient Indian burial ground they say is out there somewhere, and maybe even finding a few arrowheads."

"Were you alone?" Norma asked with a slight smile turned up at the corner of her mouth and a slight twinkle in her eye.

"What do you mean, was I alone?" Dane appeared to be shocked at the question.

"Dane, I'm your sister. I was a docent at the Nelson-Atkins Art Museum in Kansas City one summer and there was a work by a seventeenth century Baroque painter Michelangelo Caravaggio that I completely fell in love with. In fact, if I could own any piece of art in the world, it would be that one. Although I can give language to the aesthetics of the piece and can give you the complete history of the artist and the era, there is something mysterious in that work that speaks to a deep part of me where there is no language to describe."

"I have shown it to hundreds of people, but I remember one day that a young lady, a complete stranger mind you, was in our group and when I finished, she asked, 'It's your favorite painting isn't it?' I was completely taken back when she said that, and I asked her how she knew and she said, 'Because your voice changed.' Dane, after we were out on the prairie to see Sunny, your voice changed. I think she somehow spoke to that deep part of you, too. As I listened to you talk about her on the long drive home that day, I sensed softness in your voice that I haven't heard in a long time. You like her, don't you?"

"Well of course I like her," Dane said. "She saved my life you know. Who wouldn't like someone that saved their life?"

"Now, don't get testy with me!" Norma laughed as she patted him on the leg. "You know what I mean. Dane, I have often wondered when, or if, you will find someone to love. I have watched you since Debbie died and I don't know of a man in this world that I admire and respect more than you. With your great looks and winsome charm, you could have any woman you want. I know you have vowed not to get involved with anyone until you're out of office, but John and I have talked about you and we both agree that someone, someday, is going to invade your world and you will fall in love almost immediately. I think you fell in love with Sunny that day on the ranch."

"Well, I'm certainly glad you and John have my life figured out for me." Dane rolled his eyes. "You know, Sis, you might be older than me but you're not always right about everything. Sunny is a fine young woman, but she's ten years younger than me and we live in two totally different worlds. Besides, I'm not getting involved with anyone until I'm out of office and I'm sure that Sunny Morgan has a ton of cowboys out there eating out of her hand just waiting to marry her and her ranch. She only knows me as the governor and I want someone to know me as Dane Richards first and that I was once a governor doesn't mean a thing to them."

"Oh, Dane," Norma chided. "When you were a little boy, I could tell when you liked a little girl in the neighborhood because if I said something to you about her, you started coming up with all the reasons in the world why you weren't interested, but in a couple of days you would come into my room and ask me whether or not you should call her. Well, the only difference now is that you didn't ask for my advice on whether or not to call her."

"Can't we talk about something else?" Dane threw his hands up. "I love you but you're starting to meddle. I'm not going to just fall in love with some lady at first sight. That's for teen-agers and romance writers. I'm thirty eight years old and am not a giggly little teenager that doesn't know the difference between raging hormones and romance."

"Okay, I'll leave it alone," Norma laughed. "I just thought I'd let you know that it's okay to fall in love again and, quite frankly, I hope that you fall in love so hard the next time that you can't even talk straight. Mark my words, Dane Richards, you are going to fall in love so hard and fast the next time that you will think that plane crash was the easiest ride of your life. There, I've said my piece and I'll leave it alone. Now, let's talk about other stuff. First of all, when is the banquet and what exactly do you have planned?"

"I really haven't thought through the planning of it, but my initial inclination is to have some of her family and friends along with other dignitaries from the state. I think some kind of an award for heroism might be a nice touch, don't you?" Dane asked.

"So you're treating her like a constituent or is this your first date?"

"Would you knock it off?" Dane scowled. "If I let you handle all of this it's going to be a first date, engagement announcement, and wedding ceremony all in one fell swoop."

"Okay, you just leave the details to Stephanie and I. Naturally, this will be a banquet that will attract a lot of press and while I know you want it to be low-key, that just isn't going to happen so you might was well get used to it." Norma knew that Dane had a private side that he longed to protect, yearned to engage more in, and found such solace there that he sometimes forgot that everything he did was a press release.

"And while we're planning banquets," Norma continued, "can the good Governor of the fine state of Kansas honor us with his presence at the Tenth Annual Art of the Prairie reception? We are gaining more and more national attention, and I might add, respect, with our competition and it is becoming quite popular. If the good Governor could come, I'm sure that Marian Satterfield would forget all about Peter Radcliff winning. I have never known anyone to loathe someone without personally knowing them like she does that artist. He's not my favorite either, but we do have independent jurors who judge this show and they have national credentials and respect so it's not like we picked some rube out of the cornfield to do this."

"Wasn't it Edvard Munch that said, 'There is a battle that goes on between men and women. Many people call it love." Dane mused.

"If this is love," Norma said matter-of-factly, "then I wouldn't want to see their hatred."

"So why doesn't she like him?"

"His arrogance. Although I wouldn't be left in a room alone with him, I don't find him that loathsome and I'm used to the eccentricities of some artists. I agree with Tolstoy who said that art should cause violence to be set aside. If people wrestled with the ideas of beauty as much as they did with territoriality, then this world would be a much better place. I can't imagine wars being started over whether or not one should varnish an oil painting with one coat or two."

"Wars start in the heart of man," Dane spoke, "not in things or ideas, but in a desire for power. Thank God we live in a civilized enough society that duels are not fought or I am sure in the course of my political career, I would have been challenged to more than just a few duels. It was just a couple of hundred years ago that Aaron Burr and Alexander Hamilton settled their long political battles with a gunshot. I have a lot of men that would love to take me out on the south lawn of the State Capitol and fire a couple of shots at me and it all has to do with a desire for power."

"Norma, every morning I write in my journal this simple phrase: This is war. For all of these years I have warred with people and ideas that I know are meant to profit a few at the expense of others. Edmund Burke said that all it takes for evil to triumph is for good men to do and say nothing. That fans the flames of my passion for public service; I know there are charlatans and hucksters and vultures out there ready to feed on the innocent carrion of the weak and poor. If someone doesn't stand up to them, then the evil of a powerful few will trample upon the rights and privileges of the weak. I don't do this just to be someone important in Kansas. I often think of how Dad went off to war to fight Hitler and the ideals that generation had which kept Hitler from invading the world. I might not put on a helmet and green fatigues, but each day that I wake I know that I am in an arena of warfare and must protect the innocent and weak irregardless of the fact that they might never know nor appreciate what I do on their behalf."

"My, my," Norma said. "You're getting rather philosophical. Having plenty of time to think about things lately?"

"Yes, I have," Dane said. "I'm thirty eight years old and have two years left as Governor. Although my party is pressing me to throw my hat in the ring as a presidential candidate, the more I consider it, the less I'm interested in it."

"You would make a great president Dane. You could help a lot of people."

"Perhaps, but you know what I miss the most? I miss relationships with people because of who I am, not what I am. In the political arena, you just never know who you can trust and someone always has an angle. While folks are sweet to you, you just know that if the right storm comes along, they are liable to find another vessel to sail on if they don't think the one you're captaining is good enough. That's just the nature of politics. I want to use my skills and resources to help people, but more in the context of one-on-one relationships than trying to lead the masses."

"I figure I've lived about half of my life and while I'm tremendously blessed, I have given more consideration to the next forty years of my life than ever before. I imagine myself when I'm sixty-five and the thought of retiring and playing golf or going fly-fishing sounds boring. I want to be engaged in something that gives me satisfaction to the day I die."

"What do you think that might be?" Norma asked, knowing that these moments with Dane were sacred as the fresh spring water gurgling up from a deep reservoir.

"I don't know, but it is exhilarating to think about. I keep thinking of Rockefeller when he was asked how much money was enough and he said, 'One dollar more.' I have more money than the vast majority of people in Kansas, I have an incredible amount of power at my disposal to use or abuse, but I drift off to sleep at night or wake up in the mornings lonely and unsatisfied."

Dane got up and moved to the window, staring outside. "I had a dream the other night that was as lucid as any dream I've ever had. I don't know where I was, but it certainly wasn't America; I was surrounded by faces of children. The smell was awful, like raw sewage and burning wet leaves and the heat was stifling. There were no bodies attached to the faces. Some were laughing, some were crying, and some had the most hollow eyes you have ever seen, full of desperation and pitiful beyond comparison. But when I would make eye contact with them they would smile and their eyes would light up. They had a variety of skin colors and you could tell they were from various nationalities, but my smile made them smile and their once gaunt faces lit up with fullness and life. Do you think that was some kind of omen or prophecy?" Dane asked.

"I don't know, Dane," Norma replied. "But it sounds like something is stirring deep within you that is going to be life-changing. No matter what you do, you will be great at it and you know you have our support. Was that all there was to the dream?"

Dane turned and walked back over to the edge of the desk and sat down on it. Looking thoughtfully into Norma's eyes, he said, "No, that wasn't all of it. Suddenly the children all got bodies attached to their faces and there were about twenty of them surrounding someone kneeling down about twenty feet away with their back to me. One of the children, obviously of Spanish descent, came running over to me and grabbed my hand and shouted, 'espousa, espousa!' which I know enough of Spanish to know it means 'spouse.' So I walked over to where the children were kneeling down around this woman on the ground and I waited for her to turn around."

"Did you recognize her?" Norma asked like a little girl waiting for the end of the fairy tale.

"Yes, I did," Dane responded.

"Well! Tell me who it was!" Norma almost shouted.

"It was Sunny Morgan."

Chapter Twenty-Four

"I look ridiculous!" Sunny blurted as she stood in front of the mirror looking at the white flowing skirt with the hem barely covering the tops of a brand new pair of white cowboy boots. She adjusted the collar on her pale yellow blouse.

"Sunny, you look anything but ridiculous," Mackenzie argued. "I wish I was twenty five years younger and had your figure and your complexion. I swear, girl, you are the prettiest woman I think I've ever met."

"Oh, you're just saying that to make me feel better. Thanks for trying, but it's not working. I wish we were headed to the airport instead of the studio. I just want to climb on Starbuck and ride out across the prairie."

"You ain't in Kansas anymore, Toto," Mackenzie joked. "You're in the Big Apple, now, girl, and today is the day the world gets to meet Miss Sunshine Morgan, the Cowgirl Angel."

"But I'm not ready to meet the world," Sunny said. "I thought I was okay until I did a tour of the studio last night. There are too many lights, too many people, too many instructions. What happens if I just pass out right in front of the camera right in the middle of the interview?"

"Sunny, you are not going to pass out. You will do just fine. In fact, by this time tomorrow, you will have it all behind you."

"But I'm so nervous! Hey Spook, what should I do for those butterflies in my stomach?"

"W'all," Spook intoned from the chair in the corner. "I was told oncet that if'n you got the butterflies, you just take an aspirin. But I tried it and all them butterflies did was play ping-pong with it. I get nervous, I just take a long-deep breath and double shot of Jack Daniels and I settle right down."

"Well that might work for you," Mackenzie put her hands on her hips and rifled off a sit-there-and-be-quiet look to Spook. "But a double shot of Jack Daniels for Sunny and she will pass out in front of the cameras." She turned to Sunny, "Now, we've talked about this before. You are not being interviewed; you're just having a conversation with Candace that just happens to be on television. She's not going to ask you anything embarrassing or any question you can't handle. She's really looking forward, like many others, to hear the real story unfold. Most folks have heard bits and pieces and this is the first time people will have access to the whole story. Just talk to her. Trust me, she's a professional at this and will make you feel at ease the whole time."

"I know. I just keep thinking about Cal and Daniel and Shane and I want to do so good they will be sorry they ever did anything bad to me."

"Miss Sunshine," Spook spoke up again, apparently ignoring Mackenzie's disdainful look earlier. "What them fellers did to you was no fault of your own. Remember that stallion I tried to break a few years back? That black one with the white socks? He just had a bad heart and wanted to hurt anything that he could hurt. He was the meanest, orneriest old galoot I ever throwed a saddle on, but each time I climbed on his back, I knew he meant trouble for me. Some folks like them brothers of yours and that no-account Shane are the same way. No matter how good you are to them, their dark hearts just like to hurt others."

"Kind of like that lady sidling up to you down at your 'watering hole' last night?" Mackenzie teased Spook. "I think she had a dark heart no matter how pretty her face looked."

"You mean Blondie? Now, don't go calf ropin' me for just bein' friendly. That poor ol' gal was here in New York all by her lonesome and just wanted to chat."

"Oh, Spook Masterson, she was warm for your form and you know it. I walked in there and you were grinning like a mule eating corn-on-the-cob," Mackenzie retorted. "That gal probably just lived down the street a couple of blocks and figured she met her a real live cowboy and wanted to corral him. Good thing I came along and rescued you."

"Maybe I didn't need a-rescuin'," Spook shot back. "I seemed to be doing fine all by my lonesome. She was a sure sight purtier than that first heifer that sat beside me. I swear, the last time I saw a set of lips like that, th'ar was a fish hook in 'em."

Sunny and Mackenzie burst out laughing. Mackenzie went down to the "waterin' hole" that Spook referred to, a little Irish pub just across the street called and found him holding court with several folks mesmerized by his cowboy charm. Most New Yorkers could easily spot the difference between a tourist and a traveler. The patrons in O'Clancy's found a jewel from the prairie and were tapping him for information about the Wild West they had only read about in travel guides or seen on television.

Mackenzie was surprised to find a small crowd gathered around Spook. Although she enjoyed his little quips and observations, she never heard him regale anyone with a story. Yet there he sat on a bar stool exuding his cowboy charm with a story about breaking horses to ride, something he made a living at for most of his life. She sat down on the perimeter of the group and was as enthralled as the others at Spook's mannerisms and country drawl. This endeared him to the small gathering who sensed the genuine product of the west.

Mackenzie spotted the hussy from a mile a way and the peroxide blonde inching closer to Spook was trouble. Mackenzie thought it odd that she felt like she needed to step in and protect Spook from a piranha. When Spook finished telling one story and started telling them about rodeo cowboys, Mackenzie intentionally crowded her way to Spook and let everyone, especially Blondie, know that her and Spook were best friends. Spook might be in his element on the back of a bucking bronco, but there were just some things men like him, Mackenzie thought, were just plain ignorant of.

"Can you believe the prices on that menu last night?" Sunny asked as she continued to get ready. "I could pay the ranch taxes with what they must have spent on us. I had a hard time eating the food knowing how much it cost. You could feed a hundred people at the Wrangler in Teterville for what that dinner cost."

"W'all, at least at the Wrangler they give you enough to eat," Spook complained. "When they brought me out my dinner, it looked like someone done helped themselves to the rest of my vittles. A feller would think ifn' you paid that much money, you oughter walk out with your suspenders ready to snap."

"That was a really nice man we met at the studio, too," Sunny said. "I couldn't believe how many people work there just to put on a show. That place was swarming with people and they all acted like they were going to a fire somewhere."

"Are you talking about that artist?" Mackenzie asked. "The one that was going to be on another show they were doing there? What was his name again?"

"Radisson? No, that doesn't sound right. Radmacher?" Sunny asked, trying to remember his name.

"Radcliff," Spook said matter-of-factly. "Peter Radcliff. That tall feller what looked like he got dressed by Chuckles the Clown?"

"That's not nice, Spook," Sunny chided him. "He was a real sweet man and very handsome. He was just dressed in the current fashions. Just 'cause we Kansans have been wearing the same pair of jeans all of our lives doesn't mean that some folks can't try new styles of clothing."

"Ifn' I showed up down at the Farmers Grain wearing my hair in a pony tail and had on a pink shirt and white britches like he was w'arin',

Mort and the boys would dunk my head in the molasses barrel until I got some sense back."

"Well, I for one thought he looked good in them," Sunny said. "I thought he was a nice man and he was real friendly. I studied art while I was in college and I don't run in to very many artists out on the ranch so it was nice to visit him. He invited us all to a showing that he has at a gallery in the Soho district. I'd like to go there while we're here."

Mackenzie was surprised by Sunny. She pegged Sunny as a country bumpkin of sorts, and forgot that she was an educated person and this new twist - a love for art- came as a bit of a surprise to her.

"W'all, Miss Sunshine, he might wear fancy britches and purty shirts and have his paintings in the Blowhole district, but I don't think anyone paints a purtier picture than you," Spook complimented her.

"You're an artist too?" Mackenzie asked. "I didn't know that."

"Oh, heavens no," Sunny blurted. "I just like to doodle and draw. I'm not a real artist; I just like to paint whenever I get the chance. But I get pretty frustrated with what I do since I think it looks like a paint-by-numbers painting, but I still like to set an easel up out on the prairie and try to capture a sunset."

"When I told him I was from Kansas, Mr. Radcliff got real excited and said he had won some kind of an award at an art show in Kansas and was going to be going there soon. He asked if he could come out to the ranch and do some painting. I think that would be neat, don't you? He said he would like to capture the emotion of what I felt with the crash. He said that what he wants to do as an artist is to paint the way I feel. I like that."

"I think that's a great idea. That ol' floppy barn needs painted real bad like," Spook mused. "I'd even help that city-slicker paint it ifn' he wanted my help. He looks like he could use a few hours out in the sun and dem white britches is just like dem britches that I've seen painters wear."

"No, silly, he wants to paint images of the Flint Hills. He said he would even teach me how he goes about it. Just think, a real artist coming to the Lonesome Star and giving me lessons. Wouldn't that be wonderful?" Sunny was excited at the prospect of learning from a professional the techniques and philosophy of their work.

"I don't think art lessons are what that feller has in mind to give you," Spook said. "Ifn' you want my opinion, I think . . ."

Sunny interrupted, "Oh, Spook, he was just being nice. How about when he shows up, I get him to paint an image of you and Starbuck. After all, you are the one that helped me raise him and break him and he's as much yours as he is mine."

"Ifn' that feller comes to the ranch dressed like he was last night, I'll be too busy doctoring the cows for conniption fits. I ain't never seen a cow laugh, but I reckon that they will when he shows up," Spook argued. "And Starbuck ain't never seen nothin' dressed up like that before. He's li'ble to turn around and leave a horseshoe-shaped bruise right on his behind."

Mackenzie found it odd that Sunny liked this man. When she met him, the first thing she noticed was his limp handshake. Although she tried not to pre-judge anyone, her daddy taught her you could tell a lot by a man's handshake. *Make it firm and make eye contact. Don't look at the ground and hand them a wet noodle*, he said. Shaking Radcliff's hand last night was like shaking a wet noodle. She recalled shaking Spook's hand the first time; now that was a man's handshake.

"All right, you two," Mackenzie interrupted them. "It's time to go. They said the limousine would be here at ten and we are to meet the driver in the lobby."

Sunny suddenly grabbed Mackenzie and hugged her. Mackenzie could feel her start to shake.

As Sunny cradled her head against Mackenzie's shoulder, Mackenzie glanced across the room at Spook who was getting out of his chair and coming towards them. Sunny released one arm from around Mackenzie and drew Spook close to her side, holding them both in an embrace.

"Miss Sunshine," Spook said. "Yore Daddy oncet told me ifn'

anything were ever to happen to him, that I was 'sposed to look out after you and raise you like you was my own daughter. I reckon I don't say it enough, but I can't imagine how dark my life would be ifn' it weren't for your sunshine in it. You're like the sun that rises each mornin' on the dark prairie and wakes up the prairie chickens and pheasants and makes the bluestem grow. Th'ar ain't nuttin' to be skeered of, Missy. You just need to get out there and let your sun shine on a lot more than just the prairie."

"Okay, Spook," Sunny replied. "But promise me one thing today. That you find that one spot last night like the guy showed you where you can stand so I can see you. I need to be able to see you standing here."

"Miss Sunshine," Spook placed a kiss on her cheek. "You oughter done learned by now that even if you can't see me, I ain't lettin' you outa my sight. I'll be there today. Just like I was yesterday. Just like I'll be tomorrow. I'll be there."

Chapter Twenty-Five

The crowd gathered at Cedar Manor to watch the show was larger than Dane wanted, but by the time he invited family, friends, and staff, it had taken on a different dimension.

Dane preferred to watch it with just his parents and sister, but Ron Moore, as usual, invited himself along with his whole family. He could also tell from the pouty look on Stephanie's face that he had better invite the staff so more than fifty people were crowded into the room ready to watch *The Candace Cox Show.* Dane looked across the room at Moore, who refused to make eye contact with him, and thought of the events of the previous week.

Stephanie had closed the door to Dane's office last week for privacy to inform Dane that she reliable sources told her Moore was working on a book deal about the crash with a sleazy outfit from California known for trash journalism. Stephanie stammered then finally burst out with her greatest concern; Moore would not only be the hero in the drama and take away the limelight from the real heroine –Sunny - but he would trash the governor.

"Just wanted you to know what might be going on behind your back, Governor." Stephanie confided then dropped the matter. She was good about that with Dane - would warn him of impending dangers - but then let him decide the best course of action.

Dane pondered it for a couple of days then called Moore into the office. He knew where there was smoke there was fire, so Moore was finagling behind his back. But Dane also wanted this story to be about Sunny and her heroism and he would do what he could to circumvent any shenanigans by Moore.

"Hi Ron," Dane motioned to Moore to sit across from his desk in the visitor chair. Dane understood that the imposing walnut desk between them was more than just an object, it was symbolic of their positions and Dane wanted to impose his resources on Moore.

"That was quite a ride we took out on the prairie, wasn't it?" Dane asked. "It seems like yesterday then it seems like it never happened. How are you feeling?"

"Oh, I'm doing better," Moore said. "And the doctor said I was good to get back to work, but I'm having a real hard time concentrating on anything. My head hurts a lot still and my left arm, which they said wasn't broken, still just wants to hang limp."

Dane knew Moore loved sympathy and while the arm must be working well enough for Moore to play golf several times a week, it would somehow develop a sudden limpness when the press was around.

"Yeah," Dane agreed. "I look forward to getting this bandage off my leg and for all of my hair to grow back. I'd love to start running again or at least doing something with some exercise that is more than just therapy. Oh, well, it will come in time. I'm just glad we're alive!"

Dane continued, "We're getting together at Cedar Manor next Tuesday to watch *The Candace Cox Show* with Sunny. Would love to have you and Cheryl come and watch it with us. It is going to be so good to have Sunny tell her story on national television. She's quite a lady.

"Oh, anyone would have done what she did." Moore said flippantly and began to diminish Sunny's role. He still stung from her attack on him at the ranch that day and did not like any woman getting the best of him, especially some no-account cowgirl out in the middle of the prairie. "I think the real story lies in the drama of what happened before the crash when we were in the air. Now, that's the story that needs to be told!"

Dane knew the answer to his question without even asking it. Dane wanted to play this hand out a little bit more to see what Moore was holding.

"That was pretty scary. I sometimes didn't think we were going to make it." Dane admitted.

"See! That's what I mean! That's the drama in this story is that time in the airplane from when we first started to see the storm until we actually crashed. That's the kind of thing that would make a great movie and have folks right on the edge of their seats! Can't you see some handsome actors like Pierce Brosnan playing you and maybe Brad Pitt playing me? They could show what courage we had to overcome all our fears. I can see it in my mind already! In fact, I've even started writing some things down that I remembered we said to each other when we were bouncing through the air. Don't you think that's the story?" Moore never was a good poker player.

So, Dane thought to himself, Stephanie was wrong; it's not a book deal he's after, it's a movie. Dane knew exactly how that would turn out if Moore had a hand in writing the story. Dane decided to play his ace up his sleeve.

"I suppose that would make a great story." He agreed with Moore. "There were a lot of things said in that plane while we were being bounced around the sky like a ping-pong ball. I've written down a few of them myself since the crash, just trying to relive and remember it all. It seems like as the days go by, I remember something else that was said." Dane hinted at Moore's marital infidelity admission but Moore was too daft to catch it.

"Great!" Moore said. "I think it would be a great idea if we took turns reading each other's notes sometimes. You can let me see what you remember and wrote down and then I can show you what I wrote down so we can get the whole picture!"

"I'm not sure you want to read all my notes," Dane replied, aware of Moore's angle. Like always, Moore was inept at the art of discreet nuance so Dane was going to have to be more blatant to get his point across. The ace up the sleeve came out. "There's some stuff in there that might make a good movie, but I'm not sure it would be good for your family, if you know what I mean."

"You wouldn't dare!" Moore blurted as he rose from the chair his balding head straining under the sudden realization of the threat being posed. "I have the opportunity to make millions of dollars off of this and you could too if we could just tell the story the way it ought to be told. We don't need to let some prairie tramp with nothing else better to do than to ride her horse around all day get all the glory for this."

Dane kept his emotions in check and, the angrier he became, the more deliberate and measured his words. While he wanted to grab Moore by the nap of the neck and throw him out of the office, he wondered how in the world Debbie could have such a selfish imbecile for a brother.

"Ron," Dane replied as he stood to tower his frame over Moore's miniscule physique. "Sunny Morgan is not a tramp. She is the person who saved our lives. If it were not for her, neither one of us would be here today. You've been on her ranch. You've seen the run down corrals and the weathered barns and the old beat up equipment. If anyone deserves to make millions off of this, it is her. You and I are both blessed beyond measure with enough wealth to feed a starving country, we don't need any more."

"Well, for your information," Moore hissed. "I've already got a contract lying on my desk for a book and a movie and no one, not even the fine Governor of the state of Kansas can stop me from signing it."

"You're right," Dane replied. "I cannot stop you from signing it. That is your choice. But let me make it abundantly clear, Ron, just so you don't misunderstand what I am saying or the gravity with which I say it. I have plenty of resources to find out who has offered you the contract and I will, without a moment's hesitation or the least bit of regret, tell them all that happened in that cockpit. And I'll guarantee you that admissions of infidelity and urinary incontinence are precisely the kind of things they would love to exacerbate. And the millions you think you will make will be the millions that Cheryl gets to spend after your divorce."

Dane trapped Moore and they both knew it. Dane, concerned that Moore would blunder ahead anyway, wanted to offer a compromise but knew there was none to offer. He, the master of political compromise, had no grace for any kind of a compromise with Moore. He almost regretted making the promise to Jim about taking care of Moore after he was gone, but whether or not Moore understood it, Dane was protecting him from his own stupidity.

Moore was shaking as he wheeled to leave the room. Making it half way to the door, Moore turned with a pinched face and shook his scrooge-like finger at Dane. "I have been in your shadows long enough! I am sick and tired of being known as "The Great Dane's" brother-in-law. Dad is dead. Debbie is dead. You are not my family anymore. I will show the world who the true hero in this family is!" With that, he slammed the door.

"Governor?" the voice of his assistant. "Is everything okay?"

"Sure, Marjorie, everything is just fine." Dane replied. "Do I have any more appointments for the rest of the day?"

"No, sir." Marjorie responded. "The last rattlesnake of the day just left."

"Marjorie!" Dane chided her. "That's not very nice to refer to Mr. Moore that way."

"I'm sorry, Sir. I just don't trust him, Sir."

"Neither do I, Marjorie, neither do I."

Someone turned the television up forcing Dane's thoughts back to the present. "Here it comes!" Stephanie cried.

"Hello, friends and welcome to *The Candace Cox Show*! We have a very special treat in store for you today, an exclusive that only *The Candace Cox Show* is privileged to air. We know you've all heard the buzz about the mysterious Cowgirl Angel that rescued the Governor of Kansas from a plane crash out in the middle of the prairie. Well, today, we are proud to bring you the exclusive interview with Sunny Morgan! Along with her now famous horse, Starbuck, she single-handedly rescued two men from a downed airplane and saved their lives. Ladies, and gentlemen, help me welcome Miss Sunny Morgan."

Dane chuckled softly as he watched Sunny walk out from behind a curtain to the warm embrace of Candace. Although he was sure that the clothes were new, she was simply dressed in a pair of red boots, a tight-fitting pair of Wranglers with a black leather belt with heart shaped silver buckle, a white denim western shirt with a some red piping on the pockets and sleeves, and a wheat colored straw cowboy hat with a simple black headband. She looked stunning.

"Hello, Sunny, it is so good to have you on our show!" Candace said. The camera zoomed in for a close up of Sunny and Dane once again felt a deep stirring as he looked into those doe-like eyes.

"Hi, Miss Cox." Sunny replied, tipping her head down ever so slightly as a slight tinge of crimson flushed her face betraying her fright. "Thanks for having me."

"Oh, please, just call me Candace." Candace patted her knee. "Sunny, we have all heard a variety of versions about the plane crash and Governor Richards, but we've brought you here today so we can get it, as they say on the ranch, straight from the horses mouth."

"Well, maybe you ought to have Starbuck tell it then, because he's the real hero. I couldn't have done anything without him," Sunny responded.

Candace laughed. "You know, we really tried to figure out a way to get Starbuck here, but we just didn't think he would travel in an airplane very well. We even visited with a veterinarian who advised against making him travel in a trailer that far. He said it would cause too much stress on Starbuck."

"Well, I can't imagine it causing any more stress on Starbuck than it did on my good friend, Spook Masterson. He volunteered to ride

Starbuck all the way here but he figured it would take six months one way." Candace met, and liked, Spook and instructed the camera operators to train a camera on him for occasional shots. The camera panned to Spook, standing off to the side of the stage in the shadows. With a slight blush and a charming grin, he tipped his hat in gentlemanly style to the camera. The studio audience burst in applause.

Sunny endeared herself to the audience. Her innocent charm and quick wit, combined with her heroism, was going to make her a public favorite. The camera panned back to Candace who was laughing.

"Now, Sunny, we are all dying to hear the story from you. Let's begin with what you were doing when you first noticed the plane in the sky." Candace coaxed her.

The camera panned across the audience and zoomed in occasionally on a mesmerized person as Sunny told her story. Surprisingly eloquent and able tell the story without digressions, Sunny told the story in journalistic fashion describing her actions in a matter-of-fact way that neither seemed arrogant nor self-aggrandizing. While most interviews were brief, Candace seemed to sense that Sunny's ability to tell the story well without intrusion was being well received by the audience. The only breaks she took were for necessary commercials and even then Candace apologized for interrupting the story.

"Did you ever think about just riding to the house when the plane crashed to call for help rather than to risk your life trying to save them?" Candace asked.

"It would have taken too long to ride to the house and to get an ambulance out there. It would have taken at least an hour to an hour and a half for help to arrive and I just didn't know if those men would make it. I had to do something."

"And let me get this straight." Candace said. "You used baling wire to make a tourniquet for the Governors leg? What exactly is baling wire?"

Dane wondered anew at the miracle of his survival and how it all hinged on Sunny's quick thinking. He so easily could have died on that prairie if it were not for her. He looked across the room at Moore, wondering if he would somehow absorb the gravity of her actions with gratitude instead of jealous hostility. He thought back to the confrontation between Sunny and Moore on the prairie when Moore disparaged Starbuck and Sunny's eyes flashed quickly when she alluded to the fact that horses never get frightened enough to wet themselves. She knew what had happened in that plane.

"Were you ever afraid?" Candace asked.

"No, not really." Sunny furrowed her brow. "I figured the rain would keep the gas that was spilling out of the wing from catching on fire. The only thing I wished is that I would have had some better first aid training."

"Well, it seems like you had enough to save their lives!" Candace affirmed. "Sunny, that is a great story and on behalf of those in our studio audience and those around the nation who are inspired by this story, thanks for being who you are and for showing the rest of us what we all would hope to do under the same circumstances. Now, I have one final question for you, Sunny. What's next for Sunny Morgan and Starbuck?"

The camera zoomed in on Sunny's face and Dane could tell she was suddenly very nervous. "Oh, I suppose I'll go back home to Kansas and check on the cows that are calving and get ready to start cutting alfalfa. Spook's already getting homesick and we've only been here a day but he says that *ifn' he can't see the sun come up or the stars shine at night, he gets as nervous as poodle in a Chinese restaurant.*" Candace burst into laughter as the camera zoomed in on Spook once again.

Candace turned to the camera and spoke, "Ladies and gentleman, today you and I have been in the presence of greatness. We hear stories and legends of brave people who have become heroes and, while we admire them, we wonder if we would ever have that bravery in the face of uncertain circumstances. Like myself, you have all fallen in love with Sunny Morgan today because we see in her something that we hope is in all of us. Wrapped in a simple package of denim jeans and a straw hat, this ordinary Kansas cowgirl has become the angel we all long for and all wish we were. Sunny, our Cowgirl Angel, thanks for making this world a much better place in which to live."

"Isn't she adorable?" Stephanie wiped away the tear that had cascaded down her eye. The group gathered at the Manor slowly rose and made their way to the table with hors d'oeuvres.

Norma slid over by Dane and wrapped her arms around his waist and squeezed him with a tight hug. She felt Dane's body began to convulse against her and she held him tighter. No words were spoken, but a thousand memories were relived and the inviolability of trust found refuge in the warmth of a siblings embrace. Finally peeling herself away, Norma looked into the softened tear-soaked face of Dane and spoke, "It's your turn to rescue her."

Chapter Twenty-Six

"Miss Sunny," Spook bowed and tipped his hat as he walked into her hotel room. "I reckon you done saddled up the hearts of everyone in America and rode off into the sunset with 'em. I'll bet them folks back home watching at the Wrangler or at the Feed Store is a hoopin' and a hollerin' and braggin' that they done raised you since you was a colt! And I'm a heap bit proud of you, too."

Sunny ran across the room and threw her arms around the old cowboy's neck. "Oh, Spook, I couldn't have done it without you. Did I do okay?"

"Did you do okay?" Mackenzie said. "You stole the show. I'll guarantee you The Candace Cox shows ratings shot through the roof today. That was the best interview I have ever seen and I have seen thousands of them in my career!" Mackenzie wanted to be a part of the embrace between Spook and Sunny. Spook, looking over Sunny's shoulder, winked at Mackenzie.

The phone rang interrupting their conversation and Mackenzie answered it. "Yes, Governor, she's right here." Mackenzie smiled as she handled it to Sunny. "It's for you. It's the Governor." Mackenzie turned to Spook and winked.

"W'all," Spook drawled. "He got on that phone faster'n a coon treed by coonhound." Mackenzie burst into laughter.

"Yes, Governor, I mean Dane," Sunny stammered. "I was pretty nervous. I can't imagine doing that without Spook and Mackenzie being right there. Miss Cox was real easy to talk to and all the folks were nice. What's that? Oh, we're supposed to come home in a couple of days. They want to take us on a tour of New York City and see the sights. They figured a couple of rubes like us don't make it to the big city very often so we might as well enjoy it while we can. Tonight we're supposed to go to the Soho district, wherever that is, to an art gallery. I met a man yesterday who was an artist that won some kind of an award not too long ago in Kansas and he has a gallery here that is showing some of his work so he invited us. What's that? Uh, his name was Peter Radcliff. What? Your sister is part of that competition that he won? She's on the board? Wow, that's neat. What a small world! I'll mention that to him tonight. He says he wants to come out to the ranch and do some painting sometime. I would love that!"

Mackenzie watched Spook get restless when she talked about the artist. The troubled look in his eye as he glanced at Mackenzie said it all: he was concerned with her fascination of this man. Spook caught her eye again and, though no words were spoken, they made a pact to use whatever influence they had to dampen Sunny's enthusiasm for Radcliff.

Mackenzie mused to herself. *Are there really men like this left in the world?* Here was this bowlegged, sun-leathered cowboy with no family ties to Sunny, yet he was always near to help and protect her. Mackenzie had been through a bad marriage and too many bad relationships to ever believe in the goodness of any man again, but Spook was slowly restoring her faith.

"Let's go!" Sunny smiled at them as she hung up the phone. "It's time to load 'em up and move 'em out."

"'Bout time!" Spook sputtered. "I'm a gittin' hungrier than a calf that's bein' weaned from his momma. Ifn' you don't get some grub down me purty soon, I'll be a bawlin' like a weanlin' calf."

Mackenzie pushed the button and the doors opened to an already crowded elevator. As they squeezed their way into the elevator, she found her self backed up against Spook who stood just a bit taller than her. Like always, Spook attracted the attention of the New York natives who knew the real deal. Spook did look extra sharp with what he called his Sunday-go-to-meetin' black Stetson and the red silk scarf knotted around his neck like a Kansas cowboy.

At the next floor, more crowded onto the elevator squeezing Mackenzie closer to Spook. She smelled the soft scent of his cologne and his breath upon her neck. She was surprised at how muscular chest pressed against her back in the crowded elevator. Oh, how she wanted to collapse into his chest and arms and be held! It seemed like the ride lasted both for an eternity and for a split second. Mackenzie bolted away from Spook once the doors opened. She was stunned by the stirrings in her soul. Confusion and excitement both coursed through like a rushing torrent through a prairie gully.

"W'all," Spook rambled, a slight bit of crimson crawling up his neck. "Now I know what 'dem cattle feel like when we squeeze 'em in the chute for doctorin'. Kind of a helpless feelin'. I kept expecting somebody to brand my britches with a hot iron and stick an ear tag in me."

Mackenzie laughed, but was a little disappointed. That wasn't how she felt while she was in there. "Oh, well," she muttered to herself. "Leave it up to a man to miss the moment."

"Do we take a taxi or the subway?" Sunny asked.

"I ain't takin' no subway!" Spook sputtered. "If God wanted to me live underground, he'd'a shut my eyes and made me a mole. If I had my way, we'd all load up in my old red Ford Bertha and scissor on down to Blowhole."

"Silly," Sunny corrected him. "We're going to the Soho, not the Blowhole."

"I wasn't talkin' 'bout where we was goin', I was talkin' about who we're gonna see." Spook retorted.

"Why don't you like Mr. Radcliff?" Sunny asked. "He seems like a real nice man and he is pretty good looking. So what that he wears white britches, as you call them, that's just part of the fashion here in New York."

"I'm sorry, Miss Sunshine," Spook apologized. "But ever time I'm near him, the hackles on the back of my neck raise like'n they do whenever the vultures on the prairie start a circlin' me."

"Well, he's not a vulture and we're not on the prairie so let's just go and have a good time ya silly old goose." Sunny punched him in the arm.

Mackenzie was surprised how quickly Sunny was recognized as they walked in the restaurant. Although Sunny and Spook both figured folks were looking at them because of their western attire, Mackenzie could tell by the whispers and turned heads that folks already recognized them from the show.

"Ma'am?" One young man got up from his table and stopped Sunny. "I hate to bother you, but are you that Cowgirl Angel that was on *The Candace Cox Show* today?"

Sunny was stunned. Mackenzie noticed Spook quickly sidling up beside Sunny as the man turned to him. "And are you the man they call 'Spook'?"

The rest of the patrons in the restaurant were watching and, before their dinner was done that evening, Sunny and Spook signed so many autographs they could not keep count. They crowded their way out the door and flagged down a taxi.

"Shoot," Spook complained as they crawled in the cab. "I ain't writ my name that many times in my life. Why would folks want my chicken scratches on their napkins? That don't make no sense to me."

"Get used to it," Mackenzie told Spook. "Whether you like it or not, you're a part of this story now, too. There's a lot of folks out there wondering if there are any real cowboys left in the west and, as you would say, 'I done reckon they found 'em one and slapped a brand on 'em.'"

Mackenzie laughed at Spooks obvious misery. "Why shoot, ifn' I'm somebody famous now, I'll never be able to escape old Millie's rope. She'll lasso me and try to hog-tie me quicker'n a fat kid on a Twinkie."

"She won't be the only one wantin' to hog tie you," Sunny patted him on the knee.

"We're about there!" Mackenzie said. "Now, Spook, you have to promise us you're going to behave yourself."

"Why shucks, Miss Mackenzie," Spook tipped his hat. "I'll be behave myself better'n hobbled gelding."

Sunny was excited to visit a gallery in arguably one of the premiere art bastions in America. She favored representational art and built close relationships with many local *en plein air* artists that set up easels on her land attempting to capture vast vistas and meandering panoramas. Yet, she understood the artist that pushed the edges with new interpretations to age-old dilemmas. For folks like Spook, they wanted their landscapes to look like photographs. And while she appreciated the artist skilled enough in *trompe l'oeil*, she had a visual language that understood artists whose abstraction of something concrete could stir the imagination and senses.

"Sunny!" Peter Radcliff briskly walked across the room as he spied them coming through the door. He quickly grabbed her and kissed her on each cheek. "Come, I have many people I want you to meet. We all watched your show today and, darling, everyone wants to meet you."

"I'll show her around, Peter!" a younger man interrupted them. "Hi, Sunny, my name is Patrick Dennehy - I'm Peter's publicist. Can I show you around?" Taking her by the arm, they wove through the crowd.

Sunny was unsure how to handle the newfound acclaim. Spook found himself being drawn away from Sunny's side, something he was reluctant to do. But these eastern folk watched John Wayne movies and had never met a bona fide cowboy so they hung on every word he said and encouraged him to tell one story after another.

"You must be her agent?" A lady in a slinky black evening gown walked up to Mackenzie with a drink in her hand. "My name is Olivia

Hutchings. I'm the owner of this gallery."

"Hi, I'm Mackenzie Foster and, yes, I am her agent, but also her friend."

"How quaint!" Olivia responded. "I didn't know there was such a thing as an agent and a friend."

"That's the way us simple folks in the Midwest like it." Mackenzie responded. "We still think a handshake is as good as a contract."

"Surely you jest!" Olivia cocked her head back and laughed. Through pinched lips she spouted, "We don't even put much stock in contracts around here! The person with the best attorney always gets their way, not what some silly contract or handshake says."

"How long have you had this gallery?" Mackenzie changed the subject.

"Oh, dreadfully long." Olivia whined. "It belonged to my father and he insisted that I keep the family tradition. It is the oldest, and, without question, the best gallery in New York City. Sotheby's is the only people we will allow to sell our works. We periodically have showings for artists like Radcliff who are gaining more national attention. While I personally detest his work and find it boringly cliché, there are enough undereducated imbeciles in this world that find it amusing enough to acquire."

"Howdy, Miss." Spook tipped his hat to Olivia as he walked up. "I reckon I don't know your name. Mine's Spook Masterson. Pleased to meet you, Ma'am."

"Well, hello Spook Masterson," Olivia curtsied. "My name is Olivia Hutchings and the pleasure is all mine. I have been dying to meet you but it looked like you were busy holding court. Tell me, Mr. Masterson, what does a real cowboy feel like in New York City? Come, walk with me now, and tell me stories of the wildwest." Olivia grabbed Spook by the arm and moved him away from Mackenzie.

Mackenzie's first instinct was to reach out and grab Miss Olivia Hussy by the long black hair on her nearly naked back. Spook Masterson was being led like a calf to the slaughter house and was too stupid to know it. For a man that could read the weather in the morning sky, or tell how much a horse weighed by the hoof print in the dirt, he was dumber than a post when it came to women. She turned to look at a painting of Radcliff's on the wall, an abstraction of a landscape done with monochromatic colors, and all she could see was Spook Masterson being led across the prairie with a hanging rope around his neck. She assumed he came to rescue her but instead, he got captured in the process. "Well, just let him hang!" Mackenzie fumed to herself.

"Quite the pair you're traveling with." A man walked up beside her, feigning gaze at the painting as well. "I don't think New York City will ever be the same. Allow me to introduce myself, my name is Pierre Dejanere. And you are?"

"Mackenzie Foster." She replied, thankful for the diversion. "Yes, they are quite a pair. There is no pretense with either one of them, that's for sure. I just hope that all this attention doesn't ruin them. And what do you do, Mr. Dejanere?"

"I'm an artist as well. But I prefer to work with ceramics and found art." Pierre replied. "Peter talked to me about a collection of artists perhaps traveling to Miss Morgan's ranch sometime and letting the Midwest inspire us. He said he talked with Miss Morgan about this and she thinks it's marvelous. I think it's a splendid idea, don't you?"

Mackenzie was startled that Sunny had agreed to this kind of commitment without first talking to her, or at least letting her know of the conversation. "Well, Sunny has inspired a lot of us." Mackenzie said with reservation.

"Peter talked with some travel agents and our biggest concern is where we would stay. There apparently aren't any hotels in Teterville, is that how you say it? I assume more than fifty artists are going to want to go. How romantic to go to a Kansas ranch and let nature inspire us! And Peter is talking about having our works juried and perhaps even have the New York Times send a journalist along. We're sure the major networks would give us a little coverage, too, especially if *The Crash* is our binding motivator."

Fifty artists? *The Crash?* Juried? New York Times? Mackenzie smelled the work of a marketer lurking behind the scenes of this developing idea. Sunny was still upset from the mess that the Governor's crash had made on her place and the influx of interlopers and ambulance chasers, Mackenzie couldn't imagine that Sunny would really want another slew of reporters and strangers traipsing across her prairie. Mackenzie would talk to Sunny about this later, but for right now, positioned herself to protect Sunny.

"I am sure that Mr. Radcliff's agent and I will be discussing all the particulars of such a venture." Mackenzie fired a shot across the bow. These artists didn't care about Sunny or the story. It was just a platform through which they could market their works. And if a book was written about the crash, and perhaps a movie, then these artists would have an immediate market.

"Ah," Pierre recognized the situation. "Yes, by all means, any such venture would require a great deal of collaboration from all parties involved. That would be a part of the artistic process as stroking a raw canvas with paint!" With a sparkle in his eyes, he demurely bowed and excused himself. "I am sure we will meet again, Miss Foster. And I must say that Miss Morgan has surrounded herself with wise counselors. The best of luck to you."

"There you are!" Sunny said, sliding up by Mackenzie. "Where's Spook?"

"Being dragged across the pasture by some heifer with a rope around his neck!" Mackenzie blurted. "For a man that can tell you how deep the snow's going to be by the thickness of the fuzz on a caterpillar in the fall, he doesn't have a lick of sense when it comes to women."

"Well," Sunny defended him. "You have to admit. There's not much selection of women out on the prairie and that's where Spook has spent most of his life. The nice thing about cattle and horses is that they never lie to you. They might try to fool you, but you know they are doing it when they start out. People are different. It's hard to tell when they're fooling you. I know Spook says he would never get married again, but that I see that lonesome look in his eyes when we're riding fence.

"By the way," Mackenzie changed the subject as she saw Spook and Olivia heading their way. "What's this I hear about a bunch of artists traveling to the Lonesome Star?"

"A bunch of artists?" Sunny asked. "I'm not sure what you're talking about. Peter said he would like to come out to the ranch sometime, but he never mentioned anything about other artists coming out."

"Oh," Mackenzie saw the worried look crossing Sunny's face at the thought of her privacy being invaded again by strangers. "You know how rumors are!" She waved her hand as if waving away the rumor.

"W'all," Spook interrupted them. "I don't know about you fillies, but this old hoss has done wore himself plumb out today and ifn' y'all don't mind, I think I'll hitch me a ride back to the corral and unsaddle myself for the night."

"But Mr. Masterson," Olivia pressed her body closer to Spook. "The night is still young and this city comes alive after dark! There's a wonderful place I would like to take you for a nightcap and I can show you the town!"

Mackenzie wanted to hit her. She remembered in fourth grade when she doubled up her first and hit the school bully, Leroy Hackler, right smack dab in the eye after he called her a sissy girl and pushed her down. Although she got in trouble, Leroy never picked on girls again after that. The teasing he got for the shiner was worth every five hundred lines of *It is not nice to hit people* she wrote on the chalkboard. Spook Masterson was old enough to be Olivia's father.

"Ahh, I think I'll just take a rain check on that, Miss Olivia. These old bones are starting to creak so loud I can't hear myself talk." Spook drawled. Miss Olivia would not be turned down.

"Then a rain check it is. I'll be by your hotel room at nine o'clock tomorrow morning and we'll spend the day seeing the sights of the city. You said you were here for at least another day, so why not spend it with little ol' me." Olivia batted her eyes.

"We actually have a very busy day already scheduled," Mackenzie interjected. "And Mr. Masterson needs to be with us."

"Then what about tomorrow night?" Olivia was undaunted. "I'll stay up as late as you need me to so we can spend some more time together."

Sunny later told Spook that he had that wild-eyed look like cows get when the vet pregnancy checks them – pure and absolute fear.

"I reckon I can give you a call." Spook answered. "They just saddle me up and point me in the direction they want me to ride so I guess I'll have to go where they tell me."

Mackenzie was furious as they crawled into the cab to go back to the hotel. "Go where they tell me!" she fumed. "I'll tell you where to go, Spook Masterson, and it won't be any place where the sun will shine for a long, long time."

"Gosh, Miss Foster, I didn't mean to put no burr under your saddle. I ain't rightly sure what I did to give you a saddle sore in there, but I sure aim to apologize for it," Spook said.

"Spook," Sunny interjected. "We were trying to protect you in there. While you might be the smartest cowpoke on the prairie when it comes to cows and horses, we don't think you're none too bright when it comes to women-folk. That Miss Olivia was trying to stick a bit in your mouth. We're just trying to keep you in the right pasture."

"She was just bein' friendly like," Spook defended himself. "Why, she was young enough to be my daughter and a purty woman like that with all the money she has wouldn't want nothing to do with a broken down old cowhand like me. She was just bein' nice."

"Okay, Spook," Sunny patted him on the leg. "But you just have to trust us on this one."

"Yes'm, Miss Sunny," Spook said. "If you'll trust me that that fancy-pants artist, Mr. Blowhole, ain't quite the nice feller you think he is. But you know, she is right, the night is young and I think I have enough fizz in my soda to go on top of the Empire State Building and see this here city. I've climbed enough windmills that I ain't afeared of no heights."

The night was warm and clear as they found their way to the top. As Mackenzie watched Spook's child-like fascination with the sights and sounds of the city at night, she found her irritation being replaced with admiration. Although he was a Kansas cowboy more comfortable under the stars on a saddle blanket than on top of the Empire State Building, his sense of adventure and awe at the majesty of the night were like a first grader on his first field trip to a museum.

"Miss Foster!" Spook cried to her as he was peering through the binoculars mounted on the post. "Look at that river over there. And that boat!"

Mackenzie looked through the glasses but could not concentrate. Spook was standing right beside het with his arm around her helping direct her vision.

"Miss Foster, I'm right glad you came along on this trip." Spook said to her as she pulled away from the binoculars and moved to the railing looking out over the city. "I don't reckon I'da been much help to Sunny all by my lonesome."

"I'm glad to be here, Spook." Mackenzie replied. "It's nice to know all my years of doing this kind of stuff is paying off and I can help someone like Sunny out."

"Miss Sunny deserves somethin' to go right fer a change," Spook agreed. "She's too good a woman to have one wreck after 'nother in her life. I just hope she finds a good man in all of this."

Spook continued, "Lookin' out over this here city reminds me that it's a great big world. For someone like me whats lived life in a small town on a big prairie, ya kinder get to thinkin' you're worlds always the same and ain't never gonna change. That ain't all bad, but it is kinder nice to travel to other pastures and see some new sights. Kinder makes a feller start dreamin' again. Makes a feller think things might turn out a little bit different if he just tried somethin' he was afraid of, but really wanted to."

Mackenzie was startled with this conversation. Spook Masterson being afraid of something never entered her mind. Being stupid about some things like the little trollop they just left was one thing, but, him, afraid?

"What is something you want to try but might just be a little bit afraid of?" Mackenzie pried the door open just a little.

Suddenly Mackenzie felt Spooks leathery hand grab her by the arm and swing her around to him. Staring into his eyes she saw the passion of a man who had long kept his feelings confined to a corral of complacency.

"Kissing you," Spook spoke firmly into her soul as Mackenzie collapsed in his embrace.

Chapter Twenty-Seven

Dane leaned the crutches by the armoire in the corner of the bedroom. Hobbling over to the bed, he pulled the downy comforter back and sat down and adjusted his stiff leg. He leaned over to pick up the picture of Debbie and him that was taken on a trip to Cozumel shortly after they were married. With feet mired in the white sands and their tanned, lean bodies still dripping from snorkeling in the cove, the azure water glistened like a mirror as a backdrop. It was his favorite picture and the last thing at night he looked at before he shut off the lamp by the bed. "Good night, my love," he whispered to the silver frame.

But tonight was different. As he picked up the photograph and stared into history, he felt a twinge of guilt and a need to justify himself to the memory of her.

He stared at the photo until he felt his eyes drying. Setting the silver frame on the nightstand, he switched the lamp off and groaned into bed. The pain of losing Debbie heightened when the day was over; that was when sleep beckoned them into a warm embrace. Life was good then. No matter what the day brought, whether tremendous triumphs or deafening defeats, the world somehow became right as Debbie snuggled into his arms.

Oh, they loved to talk in the dark! The dizzying distractions of phones and televisions and radios and secretaries and family all were silenced and it was the two of them, alone and in control of their world for at least the rest of the night. For as fiery and independent as Debbie was, the night purchased a need in her to be held in his strong arms, to feel the security of knowing that she was protected from all manner of ill.

Of all the feelings that Dane missed, that feeling of snuggling with Debbie and knowing that all was well between them was the one he missed the most. Holding her next to him and feeling her breathe deeper as sleep called her into the night was his refuge from the storms. Regardless of important decisions made that day or the trifling trivialities of the mundane, when the lamp by the bed was turned off and the sheets were drawn over their bodies as she backed into his chest and contoured her body to his, then their world was quieted like the first gentle snow covers the amber leaves of autumn.

He sat the photo down, turned off the light and collapsed on the pillow, hoisting his leg in to bed as he went. He thought again of Norma's comment after seeing Sunny on *The Candace Cox Show*. *Rescue Sunny? Rescue her from what?*

He was now in an unknown world. Fit and athletic before, he now experienced a humbling dependency on people. Always the giver and seldom the receiver, he experienced this weakness both alarming and sweet. After Debbie's death, he steeled his emotions through the task at hand of running the state. From the early dawn runs to finitely crafted meetings through the day and various banquets in the evenings, he had little time for reflection. His life was about making decisions and moving forward, but in the midst of recuperation he took inventory of his life as methodically as a clerk counting items on a shelf.

Imperceptible to others but stealing in quietly through vacant doors, he pondered his values and priorities aside from the urgent need of a daily schedule. His life did flash before his eyes before the crash, but now it caused him to answer questions he'd never considered. Is this issue really that important? Is this thing worth the purchase? Does all the stress and worry change anything except my attitude? What is my main reason for living?

His thoughts easily tumbled towards Sunny as if there was a mental gravitation like the moon pulling tides in the ocean.

What was it about this cowgirl that captured his thoughts? The governor of Arizona, Judith Rathbun, was clear of her intentions and affections toward him. Wouldn't it make sense to pursue her if he really wanted a relationship? After all, they lived and moved in the same circles, shared the commonalities of governorship, and she was stunning. But he told her, as well as himself and those amorous cupids around him, that he was not going to pursue any relationship until after he left office. The press waited for him to stumble, why in the world would he give them something else to go after him about?

Sunny's eyes; he was repeatedly drawn to her eyes. He wanted the camera to zoom in closer in the interview. The first time they met after the crash, he tried to coax her out of the demure tilt like a bashful child in the presence of an adult. When their eyes met, he was drawn into the corners of her soul but quickly turned away lest she discover his emerging feelings.

Restless, he threw the sheets off, turned on the lamp, and struggled to find his crutches. Thumping towards the den, he turned on the television. He played the tape of the show, only this time he muted the sound and watched her body language.

She was stunning. Her faded Wranglers and auburn hair cascading under her cowboy hat captured every man in America. She was not wearing make-up the day he went to the ranch and, as Norma later commented, did everything she could to cover her beauty. But it didn't work. Even with ratty jeans, a well-seasoned shirt, and cowboy boots with broken down heels, her beauty was simple as the vast prairie yet stunning as a Kansas sunset.

The make-up artist knew which features to accent on Sunny with her high cheekbones and the angular, mid-western jaw. Her lips were painted like sand-plums half-ripened lying on naturally tanned skin.

In the silent glow of the television, Dane commented to no one listening, *She has no idea how beautiful she is.* He paused the tape to freeze one particular angle when she seemed to be looking directly into the room at him. *Sunny Morgan,* Dane whispered in the darkness, *I...*

Dane clicked the television off and sat in the soft glow of light filtering in from a full moon.

He was a man of decision, not confusion. Leaders like him spend little, if any, time being confused. They are quick to assess a situation and make decisions. Good leaders make good decisions quickly. Bad leaders are plagued by analysis paralysis and can't make up their minds about anything. No one, ultimately, trusts them or follows them.

Dane could size a situation up and make good decisions. Well educated or at least well briefed, he knew the major points of each side of an argument, yet made a decision on which side to stand.

But now he felt confused. He didn't want a relationship to mar his judgment of running the state. Too many issues required his undivided attention for him to be daydreaming about riding his fine Appaloosa gelding, Stepper, through the tall, prairie grasses chasing after a cowgirl on a horse named Starbuck. Little boys or lonesome cowboys dream about those things, not the governor of Kansas.

His was a disciplined mind not easily distracted by the unnecessary. But his mind now wandered away from important issues facing the government and traipsing down trails of imagination. He imagined setting quietly astride Stepper on the knoll in the hills where they reputedly buried the Indian chiefs. This was the highest place in the hills, what some locals joking called, "Mount Sunflower." Of all the places in the Flint Hills, that place created a settled peace and oneness with nature and the product of human history.

You could see twenty miles in any direction on that knoll; it was his favorite physical and mental place to go. He sometimes timed it right so he could watch a full moon rise at the same time the sun was setting. Once, he sat astride Stepper on that knoll in the midst of waving tall grasses and watched as the earth eclipsed the rising full moon. Sweet memories like that is the place the soul wanders to looking for peace.

In this world somewhere between reality and desire, he watched below the hill as buckskin Quarter Horse ambled carrying a young woman wearing a billowy white dress blowing in the rising moonlight breeze. Her auburn tresses glimmered in the waning light of the setting sun. A bald eagle pierced the silent sky.

Dane flipped on the lamp by his chair and dug his journal out of the drawer. His Dad taught him to work his way out of confusion by writing so Dane picked up the pen and paper to settle his mind, to corral his thoughts running like wild horses in the refuge of the Flint Hills.

Tonight was a poem. Like a bull-dogger grabbing a 500-pound lunging steer by the horns and wrestling it to the ground, Dane wrestle reality into words. Slowly, his emotions scribbled their way onto the paper.

Come fly, fly with me my dove
To a secret place on the wings of love
Come fly, to the mountain high
Where the thunder roars and the rainbows hide
Come fly, come fly with me
Where the eagles soar so wild and free
Come fly!

Dane spoke into the darkness, *I am falling in love with her.* Dispatched for a moment in time from his emotions and applying analysis to settle on the *fundamental issue,* he came to this conclusion: he was falling in love with Sunny.

Was it because she saved his life? He barely knew her, how could he be in love with her? He didn't even know her real name. Was it Sunny? He recalled Spook's combination of threat and invitation both warning him and engaging him.

And what about Sunny? She didn't seem particularly fond of him when he was on the ranch. Rather, she seemed annoyed that he crashed on her land, interrupting her normalcy, invading her privacy and, worse in her estimation, violating the pristine virginity of the land.

She was pleasant but reserved when he visited with her on the phone. Like a Shakespearean dilemma, how does a king fall in love with a peasant girl? How does a governor romance a cowgirl? The press would go wild. He'd have to wait until his term ended before he could even consider making a move towards her.

But could he wait? He was a decisive man and in the soft glow of the lamp in the governor's mansion, he came to grip with the reality that one look from her eye had ravished his heart. He was not an adolescent boy with raging hormones unable to differentiate infatuation from love. He was a grown man who recognized that an ember was lit. He turned the page of journal and tossed together a few more words.

Just a glance from your eye
Sparks a fire's glow way down deep inside
With a ravished heart, on bended knee
I give my love for all eternity.
Come fly, fly with me my dove
To a secret place on the wings of love
Come fly, to the mountain high
Where the thunder roars and the rainbows hide
Come fly, come fly with me
Where the eagles soar so wild and free
Come fly.

He put the journal down.

This poem might take years to write. The words would birth with unpredictability. The poem could be tragedy or irony.

Or it could be a sonnet of wild-hearted romance.

Only the slowly turning pages of time could write this poem.

Chapter Twenty-Eight

"Shauna?" Chris spoke to the groggy answer on the phone. "Did I wake you up?"

"No, that's all right, I had to get up to answer the phone anyway," she retorted sleepily. "Rough night with the baby. Trying to catch up on sleep. What's up with the phone call? That makes twice this year already. That's a record."

"All right, enough with the sarcasm," Chris teased back. "It's just that I had real interesting conversation today with a client that I thought might interest you just a bit. I don't know much about this guy other than that he's from California and is into making movies for television. His name is Bernie Chapelle and he's been coming out here fishing a couple of times a year and always brings a different bimbo with him. I don't know what it is I don't like about him, but I just get the heebie-jeebies when I'm around him. I asked Jennifer if she knew of the movies that he made and she said she had watched one about half way through and turned it off because it was too trashy."

"Anyway," Chris continued. "He's always bragging about who he knows or how much he made on a movie or what big movie he's going to do next and he said that his next movie is about the governor's plane crash. Do you know anything about this?"

"No," Shauna said, suddenly very awake. "We've all talked about what a great movie it would make, but I haven't heard of anything like this and Sunny hasn't mentioned anyone talking to her about it. I know she's not too crazy about it, but I know she would have talked with me."

"Well," Chris admitted, "I kind of played dumb about it like I didn't know much about what happened or that I know the Governor personally, so I just started asking him some questions about it and it turns out it's really not going to be so much about Sunny rescuing the governor as much as it is about Ron Moore being the hero of it all, like he had something to do with the rescue."

"Ron Moore! The hero?" Shauna launched from her recliner. "You've got to be kidding me! Sunny told me he smelled like he had wet himself and had thrown up all over the airplane. She said he smelled worse than a feed lot in the spring."

"That's what I wondered. He's fished out here before and I never have cared much for him and could not imagine that he was the hero. I watched Sunny on TV the other day and it sounds like the Governor and Moore would have likely died out there if it hadn't been for her. She didn't paint herself as the heroine, but anyone reading between the lines would know that those two men, unconscious and hanging upside down, might not have made it long. Especially Governor Richards."

"Wow, wait 'till Sunny hears about this. I'll bet she knows nothing of this," Shauna grumbled into the phone.

"Well, you're really like this next part," Chris said sarcastically. "He said what actually happened is that Moore cut himself loose from the seatbelt first, then rescued Dane and Sunny just happened to come up on them when he was putting the tourniquet on Dane's leg. He said Sunny actually freaked out and went into hysterics but Moore had to calm her down and get her to ride the horse back to the house to get help."

"What!" Shauna shrieked at the phone. "That liar!"

"From the way that it sounds, they're either already producing it or are getting ready to. That blonde bimbo that was with him this time he says is going to play Sunny. Jennifer tried to talk to her a couple of times when she was back in the lodge waiting on Bernie. Jennifer said it was pretty tough to get any decent conversation out of her. The porch light was on, but no one was home inside. Can't imagine that she will be a very good Sunny. But then, again, from the way Bernie talked, they were going to make Sunny a pretty small part of the story. Apparently trying to cast her as some hillbilly blonde with no teeth and tobacco juice dripping off her chin, I guess."

"That would be horrible," Shauna began to realize. "If they get something like that out on TV in a hurry, it will make Sunny look like liar for all the things she said on the show. There's already enough people around here like Telephone Jones that are just jealous enough to start saying bad things about Sunny and whether she's telling the truth or not. Just last Sunday, that old battle-axe got up in church and asked for prayer for *fallen angels* and everyone knew she meant Sunny. Sunny didn't want any of this attention and it's just not fair. She's out minding her own business then a couple of idiots who ought to know better crash on her property so she saves their lives while people trash her prairies and invade her privacy and now they're trying to make her look like a liar."

"I knew this would upset you as it did Jennifer and I. I don't know what to do, though, and wondered if you could talk to Sunny and warn her?"

"Yeah, I could," Shauna said slowly. "But what good would that do? She wouldn't be able to do anything about it and it most likely would just upset her."

"Jennifer suggested that I call the Governor and tell him." Chris said more asking than telling. "Do you think that would help?"

"Well, I don't know if that would help anything either. I mean, what can he do about it? It sounds like the balls already rolling and you can't stop it."

"I know, but it just seems like there ought to be something that can be done. It's just not right letting them do this to Sunny. Now that I think about it, Bernie did mention that Moore was supposed to meet him out here fishing, but called and cancelled at the last minute. Which is odd, because we never booked him or Jennifer would have told me. She always lets me know when the knuckleheads come so I will be prepared. I wonder if they have a deal made on it yet."

"Now that we have talked about it for a while, I'm thinking you really need to call the Governor. After all, he is your business partner and I think he would really like to know. Who knows, maybe he can help."

"Yeah, you're right, I'll give him a call."

Chris hung up the phone and found the number for Dane's office.

"Governor Richards's office," Marjorie Marshall answered the phone. "May I help you?"

Chris had been told by Dane that to try to get past his secretary was harder than getting the legislature to vote unanimously on a bill so he had told Chris just remind her who he was and make the comment, "We all know the Governor would rather be fly fishing!" Marjorie chuckled.

"Hi Chris," Dane seemed pleased to speak to Chris. "How are the hatches?"

"Well, the mayflies are hatching just about the time the sun breaks over the canyon walls but the trout just lay around in their holes waiting for you to come back and try to catch them!"

"I'd love to be standing in the water right now dancing some line in the shadows," Dane said exuberantly. "Boy, how I'd love to be fishing for trout! But I'm guessing that you haven't called to talk about trout fishing so what can I do to help you?"

Dane listened with growing anger as Chris repeated to him the story of Bernie and the upcoming television movies. Apparently his previous conversation and veiled threat to Moore had fallen on deaf ears and Moore was making a deal after all.

"So did this guy mention when the show is coming out?" Dane asked.

"No," Chris replied. "I gather that they are trying to do it as quickly as possible so, as he put it, 'the truth can be told.'"

"Did he mention whether or not they had a deal signed?"

"No, but he did say that Moore was supposed to show up out here too, but had to cancel because of an important meeting with some lobbyists."

"An important meeting with some lobbyists?" Dane mused to himself. Moore's "important meeting" was probably a bad hangover.

"Did this Bernie person mention who he worked for?" Dane asked. His old school buddy, and a former U.S. Congressman from Kansas, now worked in the television industry. Mike would know this guy and the reputation of the company.

"As a matter of fact, I had Jennifer check the records and he works for 'Arcadia Enterprises.' It's out of Hollywood. Would you like his number?"

Dane took the number, exchanged a few pleasantries with Chris about how good the fly-fishing was and how successful the lodge was doing. Dane was glad that he had helped Chris and Jennifer buy the lodge and get them going. No one knew about it except for his accountant, Chris, and Jennifer, so it was a nice little secret Dane kept. And the financials that Chris had been sending his way showed more profit than either of them expected. And a side benefit was that Chris kept all the good holes in the river for Dane. Not a bad deal.

Dane leaned back in his chair and looked out the window across the lawn at the mottled sycamore tree with leaves glittering in the sun. He thought his threat to Moore would have kept him from pursuing a book or movie, but apparently not. He still wondered how Moore and Debbie could come from the same wonderful parents. They were polar opposites in social graces and people skills.

"Marjorie", Dane pushed the button on the intercom. "Would you please find Mike Spellman's number for me? I need to talk to him."

"Going to be a movie star, Governor?"

"Marjorie," Dane said mockingly stern. "Behave yourself."

"Well, if it isn't the honorable and highly esteemed Prince of the Prairie Governor

Dane Richards!" Mike responded affectionately into the phone. "What gives on old country bumpkin like me a phone call from the Governor of the great State of Kansas?"

"All right, Mike, you can knock it off any time. This is just little ol' me, your partner in shenanigans growing up. Want me to recall a few for old time's sake?" Dane joked.

"No, thanks, Dane," Mike exploded in laughter. "The statute of limitations has run out on all my delinquencies and you can not arrest me."

"Ahh, those were the days." Dane reminisced. "What I wouldn't give for another trip to the swimming hole doing a back flip off that old tire swing. I went by that old stone bridge the other day and that tree is gone, gravel has filled in the hole, and it doesn't look like anyone swims there anymore. Shoot, we must have spent half our lives in that hole."

"I was telling my kids about that swimming hole the other day and they looked at me like I was from outer space," Mike agreed. "Becky, my teenage daughter, wrinkled her nose when I told her the water was usually brown. They are too used to swimming pools and Caribbean beaches. But you didn't call to talk about swimming holes, so tell me what I can do for you. And by the way, congratulations on being alive. I watched that Sunny Morgan on *The Candace Cox Show*. I know a lot of those people who work for Candace and they all fell in love with her. And the ratings for that show went through the roof!"

"She did an amazing job of saving our lives, that's for sure. I still can't believe how close I came to dying and how incredible it was that she saved my life," Dane's voice trailed off with a soft sense of gratitude.

"And that's one of the reasons I called you, Mike. I'm hearing a pretty substantial rumor that someone's trying to cut a deal with my brother in law, Ron Moore, and get a T.V. movie out soon. The

242

company is 'Arcadia Enterprises' and the director's name is Bernie Chappelle. Do you know anything about him?"

Silence on the other end let Dane know the answer. Slowly Mike responded. "You know, Dane, we have talked about it in our studio, but have had a hard time getting through Sunny's agent, a Mackenzie Foster. Do you know her? We wanted to tell the story from her side and we've even talked about contacting you, but figured Sunny was our best bet. But if Chappelle is getting a hold of this, then we are going to have to get on it fast. They will not do it well. I'm sure Foster hasn't let them get through to her either."

"Would it help if I got a hold of Mackenzie for you?" Dane asked. "I don't think Sunny likes me very much, but I am the Governor and this Foster woman is a pretty well respected newsperson in Kansas so I'm sure I can get you in the door. I'll tell you what: I'll get a hold of Mackenzie immediately. I can assure you they will be interested in what you have to offer."

"That'd be great, Dane!" Mike responded. "I promise you, if they sign a deal with Spellman Enterprises, we'll do it up right. And who would you like to play your role?"

Dane laughed, "The handsomest star you have!"

"Well, it is Hollywood and we can write our own endings. You won't mind if we change the end of it a bit, do you?" Mike teased.

"Change the story?" Dane defended. "But why?"

"Well, when our writers were sitting around talking about it, one of them suggested that the real way to end this almost fairy tale story would be for you and Sunny to fall in love and live happily ever after."

"You know, Mike, if we were still at the swimming hole, I'd have to dunk you under water right now."

"Yeah, I know!" Mike laughed. "And by your simple reaction I would know that I was right in my hunch."

Chapter Twenty-Nine

Sunny breathed deep the morning sun stirring the sweet scent of freshly cut fescue. The distant drone grew softer as Spook jostled along on the old riding lawnmower by the bar ditch down the long, rocky driveway. He called that beat-up old mower "The Rock Crusher" and Sunny could hear the occasional bone-jarring grind of another rock crushed. Meadowlarks flashed their cadmium yellow chests pierced by a brown arrow as they flitted along the morning breeze. Jasmine purred against her leg then scampered off after a lurching cricket.

It was good to be home. The spring rains had been plentiful after the crash and the grass and wildflowers grew in abundance. She had saddled Starbuck the day before and sauntered across the prairie checking the cattle. The cattle seemed to be putting on weight quickly and the head count was right. It had been a spring with terrible thunderstorms and lighting often killed several head of cattle, but fortunately her herd had been spared. The ponds were full going into summer and the springs were dancing out of the hillsides and tumbling into crystal clear streams.

But she grimaced each time she saw the prairie violated by yet another vehicle that had rutted the virgin earth like a drunken farmer staggering around with a single-bottom plow. The rain helped to knock down the jutted edges, but water pooled in the tracks stagnated and became a cesspool of dung and a breeding ground for mosquitoes. The Governor promised to fix them but she hadn't heard any more. It would take thousands of dollars' worth of labor and soil to fix the ruts.

And the fences! Sunny felt her face flush with anger thinking about the morons that cut fences just to get on to her property. Fence wire had to be taut because cattle would lean against it so hard even the posts would bend over. So at each end of a long run of wire, big posts would be set deep in the ground and securely braced so wire could have a solid anchor. Little did those idiots know that cutting out a section of barbed-wire in the middle meant that you had to go clear back to the corner posts and re-string it if you wanted it to be tight again.

She had filed a complaint with the Sheriff Mitchell because she had been told who a couple of the people were, but he had never been any help to her and she didn't expect any now. Some people held grudges way too long.

As she looked over the waving grasses of the prairie, she could not begin to imagine ever trading the vast quietness of the prairie for the madness of Manhattan. Noisy traffic more dangerous that stampeding cattle, people being herded from one pen to the other in cattle cars called subways, and the unfriendliness of people reluctant to make even the slightest eye contact was like landing in outer-space to her and Spook. More than once whether in a subway, crammed in a taxi, crunched in an elevator, or standing in line at the airport, you could hear Spook softly moo like a calf, as he said, "Bein' wrangled up for the slaughter house!"

A smile crossed her face as she mused to herself and the cat, "How about that Spook, anyway! That sly fox! Jasmine, did you know that old coot kissed Miss Foster right on the lips!" Sunny laughed out loud. She was so happy for Spook. As she stared out over the prairie to the east, the annoyance of the tracks seemed to dissipate when she realized that if it hadn't been for the crash, Spook would never have met Mackenzie. Spook was right again: "There are wildflowers that grow where the cowpies drop!"

And it was like Spook was suddenly thirty years younger. Love does marvelous things to a person's complexion. And wardrobe! He had even gone to Baileys Western Wear and bought, as he said, "Some new britches and duds." And she was pretty sure, by the way he had complained about the fingertips on his left hand being sore, that he had taken to "plunkin' that dagnab gitfiddle again!" It had been a long time since she had heard Spook play, but he was known in his younger days was quite a country crooner in the local "Whiskey River Band." She had asked him a few years earlier why he didn't play anymore and he just shrugged his shoulders and said, "Aw, when my wife died, it plumb took the song right out of me."

The drone of the mower silenced and Sunny drifted back to the present. She turned to look down the driveway and saw the reason for the silence. Spook was visiting with someone in a fancy four-wheel drive. She knew it wasn't any of the local ranchers- this truck was too fancy with all sorts of chrome and, as Spook called them, "purty girls" accessories for it to be a local cowboy. They liked their trucks, but they liked them solid and manly, not decorated like a birthday cake.

Sunny could feel her brow furrow and forehead wrinkle as she squinted down the driveway. She wasn't expecting anyone and this was too expensive a truck to be driven by a local reporter. It didn't look like a government vehicle. Oh, well, she would soon find out.

Jasmine scattered as the big truck roared away from Spook. Sunny saw Spook turn the mower around; he was always her protector. The noisy diesel engine belched out black smoke as the driver, hidden behind darkened windows, gunned it around the circle drive. Whoever it was, she didn't like them already.

The truck lurched to a stop and the diesel quit invading the gentleness of the prairie. The door opened and out stepped Ron Moore. Sunny shivered.

"Hello, Sunny!" Moore shouted annoyingly. "How's the world famous Cowgirl Angel?" He walked towards her and quickly hugged her, much to her dismay. He held on too long. He held on too tight. She pushed herself away.

"It sure is good to see you again, Miss Sunshine!" Moore blurted. "I hope you don't mind me stopping by, but I was in the neighborhood and thought I'd pay you a visit. You country folk don't mind neighbors dropping in for a chat, do you?"

"No, that's fine, Mr. Moore." Sunny tried to be polite. "How is Mrs. Moore?"

"Oh, she's fine!" Moore replied. "She wanted to come with me, but she's busy planning a big party that the Governor wants to throw for you."

Sunny recoiled inside. She had heard from Mackenzie that Dane wanted to throw a party, but she had told Mackenzie that she was just too busy right now with the cattle needing watched and fence that needed fixed. She finally relented and let them set a date. But she had pushed it back in her mind to a place of insignificance. There were so many offers to go to parties and do interviews, but Sunny just wanted to be on the prairie.

"Well, we watched your show on the big screen at the Governor's mansion," Moore strutted. "We are all pretty impressed that a country girl from Kansas made it big on the Candace Cox show!"

Maybe he meant that as a compliment, but it seemed like more of an insult to Sunny. She didn't like Moore the first time she met him after the wreck and he demanded attention for his few lacerations while Dane was lying there bleeding to death. Then when she realized that he had wet himself as the plane was crashing, she lost any amount of respect for him. Even Starbuck didn't like Moore. Animals know people better than people, she had learned. She reached down to pet the cat.

"Sunny, one of the reasons I came out today was to thank you again and to apologize to you. I want you to know that I really do appreciate all that you did for Dane and I when the plane went down. When I think about that day and how we wouldn't have made it without you

247

being there, I really am grateful to you."

Sunny looked up from petting Jasmine. "Oh, sure," she said somewhat surprised by what seemed to be genuine. "Anyone would have done what I did. Thank God I just happened to be there."

"I also wanted to apologize for my rude behavior the last time I was out here." Moore continued. "I made a unflattering comment about your horse and I know how close you country girls are to your animals and it was just rude of me. From the way you told the story, if Stardust hadn't been there, you would not have been much help to us."

"Starbuck," Sunny corrected him. "And, you're right, us 'country' girls like our horses. They're a whole lot smarter and certainly a whole lot more loyal than most of the men we know."

"Well," Moore stammered. "Uh, well, it kind of looks like I did it again. My wife tells me that I ought to just say I'm sorry and keep my mouth shut because by the time I'm done apologizing, I've made someone mad all over again."

Sunny let her guard down and chuckled, "Really, that's okay, Mr. Moore, I do that sometimes, too."

"I, well, we also got something for you, too, as a token of our appreciation." With that Moore opened the door to the truck and grabbed a bag. Spook finally puttered up on the old mower.

"Oh, you didn't have to get me anything." Sunny said, feeling badly that she had not liked Moore. Her Mom had always told her to believe the best in everyone and she knew she should.

"Well, it certainly isn't much compared to the magnitude of what you did for us, but, like I said, it is a token of our appreciation. Go ahead, open it." Moore said as he handed her the purple bag.

"Hey, Miss Sunshine," Spook drawled as he got off the mower. "Everything okay here?"

"Just fine, Spook," Sunny mumbled as she opened the bag. Reaching past the paper, she recognized the cover of a book she had been wanting, *Voices on the Prairie – the Poets of Kansas*. It was freshly out, but with a price tag of nearly fifty bucks, she had decided to wait until the grazing season was over to see how she fared. All this promise of money and book deals and such had not materialized anything and she was feeling the pinch to pay taxes. Unnecessary purchases, like books, just waited until she saw how well the cattle market fared.

Drawing the book out of the bag, Sunny exclaimed, "Wow, Mr. Moore, thank you so much! How did you know that I would like something like this?"

"Well, in one of your interviews, you made a comment about liking poetry from Kansas writers so I decided that you might like this," Moore softened as he spoke to Sunny.

Spook had maneuvered himself between Moore and Sunny, as he often did with any man he didn't like, and looked suspiciously at the book. Turning to Moore's truck, Spook sputtered, "Mighty purty truck for a city slicker. That thing ever get any mud on dem tires? I reckon a feller like you what can afford a truck like that pro'bly ain't never had a real truck." He motioned to his old red Ford by the barn. "Well, ol' me and Bertha theres done everything from hauling hay to starving cattle in the winter to pullin' calves in the spring. But that get-up of yours ain't never done nothin' but look purty."

"Well," Moore said backing up. "Actually I brought it today thinking maybe I would need it. I have something else I'd like to do for Sunny if she wouldn't mind."

"Wal, young feller," Spook cornered him. "Me and Miss Sunny gots lots of work to get done today and ain't got time for ridin' around in some city slicker's truck tryin' to look purty."

"I'm sure you do, Mr. Masterson," Moore spoke respectfully. "But I would really like to go around and see the damage that was done to the land. I'd really like to do what I could to help fix it."

Sunny looked up from the book incredulously, "You want to do something about the ruts?"

"Yes, Miss Morgan," Moore explained. "I feel responsible for folks tearing it up and I have a lot of friends who are experts in grassland ecology who would like to help restore the land. That is, if you would let them."

"Let them?" Sunny almost shrieked. "I can't think of anything that would make me happier! I never figured that the Governor would do anything about it."

"Well, Sunny, this isn't exactly the Governor's deal. He's real busy trying to get back to business as normal and doesn't have much time for this kind of stuff. I mentioned it to him a while back and he said that he's too busy to mess with it and that the land has plenty of time to heal and he'll get to it when he has time.

Sunny suddenly felt betrayed. Dane had promised. She had made him promise to fix the land – it's the only thing she wanted. She didn't care about the shows and wild-blue-sky promises about book deals, she just wanted life to be like it was before the crash. And if she couldn't change her circumstances, at least they could try to fix the land. It wasn't the hill's fault they had been violated.

"Mr. Moore," Sunny blurted. "I'd be happy to show you all the damage. Do you have a camera or should I bring mine?"

"Oh, I have my own!" Moore said, turning to Spook. "And, Mr. Masterson, I'd sure appreciate it if you'd come along with us. In fact, I'd like it a lot if a real cowboy would actually drive my truck. Then maybe it would be a real man's truck after all." With that he threw the keys at a very surprised Spook.

"Wal, I guess that'd be alright, just hope ol' Bertha don't think I'm cheating on her," Spook muttered as he climbed in and fired up the truck.

"It doesn't matter how old they get," Sunny mused to herself. "Guys are suckers for pickup trucks."

Sunny couldn't remember the last time she had been in a pickup truck this nice. Trucks were badges of honor for cowboys and cowgirls. In fact, she knew a lot of them that owned trucks worth more than their home. A horse, their boots, a girl, and a truck were things cowboys would spend their whole paychecks on.

"You know I'm li'ble to smear a little cowpie goo on them purty little chrome mud-flaps." Spook looked in the rearview mirror at Moore who had deferentially let Sunny and Spook ride in the front.

"It'll be good for her." Moore laughed. "So if you're old truck is named Bertha, maybe I ought to come up with a good one for mine."

An awkward silence fell in the cab. Sunny turned to look out the window to hide the smile. Not only having a good truck was a badge of honor for a ranch hand, but nick-naming a truck was not something one considered lightly or without a great deal of reverence. There was a rite of passage involved in naming a truck. Nicknames for trucks had to be earned or maybe even divinely inspired. Bertha got her name for being able to wallow through mud up to her door handles. She was named, affectionately, after a big-bottomed woman who lived in town who was, as Spook said, *two axe-handles wide and tougher 'n a blacksmiths anvil.*

"Wal," Spook drawled. "Dem kind of names just get earned. Let me have this old cayuse for a year then maybe you can name her."

Sunny interrupted the testosterone and pointed out the first of the damage. Although some grass had grown up around it, you could still see the spider-web of six to eight inch deep tracks, some made by tandem trucks, that crisscrossed across the prairie.

"Oh, my!" Moore sighed. "They really did tear up the prairie, didn't they?"

"Yes!" Sunny cried. "This land has been unscathed by vehicles for thousands of years and in one week's time, damage has been done that is irreparable. Because with each rain that comes these tracks will soon turn into ravines which turn into gullies, which corrode the land and fill the crystal clear creeks with silt. If we wanted brown creeks out here, we would farm the land and let the rains take the topsoil into the river. But this is pastureland! Our creeks and rivers are some of the most pristine and untouched in the Midwest!

"I can see why you were so upset." Moore agreed. "To not try to fix this would be an insult not only to the land, but to all who have lived on it in the past and those who live on it now."

Sunny couldn't believe what she was hearing. Moore, of all people, was sympathetic to the land and was apparently in some position to do something about it. She had even avoided coming this way with Starbuck simply because it upset her so badly. Even though the Governor promised her, she was used to the empty glass of a man's promise so she had, as time went by, begun to believe that nothing would be done.

"So are you the one that flew over in the helicopter last week?" Sunny asked. "It hovered over for a while but I was back up at the barn so I couldn't tell who it was."

"Uh, yeah," Moore stammered. "We should have told you we were coming out, but I didn't have your number. We took pictures of the ruts. I guess I should have brought some of them with me."

Sunny thought to herself, *You only get disappointed when you expect something, Daddy used to say, so don't expect anything out of anyone and you won't get hurt.* Sunny had decided not to expect anything, but suddenly here was Moore who seemed like he could do something about it.

"I have lots of friends in high places," Moore bragged. "And all it will take is for me to bring them out here and we can get something done about it. Do you mind if I bring them back out here next week?"

"No, not at all!" Sunny got excited. "Bring them out whenever you would like. Just get something done, please!"

Spook jumbled the truck over the ruts to take Moore to what they considered to be the prettiest vista in miles. Not everyone got to see this, but Moore was changing their opinions about him so he deserved a special treatment.

"See that knoll up over yonder?" Spook pointed in the direction of the highest point on the land. "That's where they buried Indian chiefs, or, at least that's what legend says." Spook was revealing what he knew to be fact, but put it off as legend just in case Moore wanted to bring out treasure seekers. Through the years they had found all sorts of Indian artifacts around this area, but they didn't let folks know.

The talk turned to history as they ambled back toward the ranch. Sunny and Spook, like tag-team docents at a living museum, told Moore of the history of the land. Moore lapped it up like a puppy with a bowl full of milk.

"Would you like to have a sandwich with us for lunch?" Sunny asked as they all tumbled out of the truck. "It isn't much, but it's all we eat."

"Sure, I'd like that. Let me grab something out of my truck first." Moore replied.

Jasmine grudgingly moved from the weathered screen door hanging loosely on rusted hinges. The old linoleum on the kitchen floor was yellowed and cracked from too many taxes on cattle and poor markets. Just paying the government took any extra money. Fixing things up was not only low on the list, she had given up making a list. Empty promises don't remodel a drafty old farmhouse.

"Have a seat," Sunny pointed at Moore who was moving around behind Spook, already hunkered down at the table. "You have to fix your own around here. I have bread and bologna and some mayo, but other than chips, there's not much else."

"Bologna sounds great!" Moore said as he moved the saltshaker away so he could lay down his folder.

"Whatcha got in that folder?" Spook queried Moore suspiciously.

"Oh, just some paper work I thought we might go over about getting those ruts fixed up. You know, legal things and plans and stuff like that that make sure everyone ends up happy," Moore defended.

"Wal," Spook leaned back in his chair and crossed his arms. "I ain't no lawyer and, quite frankly, don't care much for 'em so if those papers are for your lawyers and a handshake ain't good enough, I reckon we don't want what's in 'em."

"Oh, Spook," Sunny chided him. "There's no need to get defensive. Paperwork is just paperwork and since the government's going to be involved, then you know some bureaucrat has to defend his salary by drafting up a bunch of paperwork. I'm sure it's all harmless."

"Actually," said Moore. "There isn't too much paperwork here. Some of the guys have already flown over and photographed the damage so they have a proposal here of what they think needs to be done. Of course, they want to come out and survey and assess the damage, but this is just a basic plan. But you know how they are, they have to have signatures before they can start. Really, all you need to do is just to put a quick John Hancock on them and my friends will be here next week."

Sunny was shocked. Next week? Too many betrayals had left her cynical so she figured she was bound to live out her years watching the continual erosion left after the crash. They were a continual reminder that unwelcome strangers had invaded her life. But now she felt truly excited, far more than she did about going to New York City.

"Sunny," Moore explained. "Basically what I have here are a few papers saying that these folks can come in on the land and fix it up. Another one here says that there will be no charge to you for any of this. Another one says is just a generic one saying that if someone gets hurt, they won't try to sue you. Just the usual."

"Sounds good to me!" Sunny set the sandwich fixings on the table and reached for the file folder. "Where do I sign?"

"Down at the bottom by the 'X' on each one that has that little yellow sticky note." Moore said nervously. "Boy, I just realized what time it is. I hate to eat and run, but we spent more time out there than what I allowed. Do you mind if I take a sandwich with me?" He hurriedly tossed one together.

"Oh, sure," Sunny said. "Here, let me sign these real quick so you can go."

"Wal, Miss Sunshine, don't you reckon maybe we oughter git a lawyer to look these over or spend a bit of time readin' 'em ourselves?" Spook asked cautiously.

"Well, I suppose that's fine, Mr. Masterson," Moore replied quickly. "But I really do have to run and my friends who are doing this work tell me they have a brief window of time they can do this before their next big project, so time is of the essence. They might not be able to make it out here next week if these aren't signed."

Flashing quickly through Sunny's mind was a mental image of quicksand and a girl with her back to her struggling in vain against the enveloping death. As Spook and Moore argued, she flipped through the pages.

"Uh, Mr. Moore," Sunny questioned. "I just noticed the company that is doing all the work is Arcadia Enterprises. Is this a government agency?"

"Well, uh," Moore stammered nervously. "No, not really. They are friends of mine who own a multi-dimensional company that does a little bit of everything. The do a variety of things, but they do have on staff these grassland specialists that they want to send out."

A line halfway through the last page caught Sunny's attention. "Furthermore, ownership of all copyrights will transfer to Arcadia Enterprises who will retain sole authority to distribute artistic properties."

"Mr. Moore," Sunny said guardedly. "Why would I sign over copyrights to this Arcadia Enterprises? They're fixing the land, right?"

"Well," Moore fidgeted with his sandwich, rising quickly to leave. "There will have to be reports filed and commentary written about the project for documentary, er, I meant documentation."

Sunny recognized the Freudian slip. She was on to him. Lunging to her feet she quickly moved around the table and stood face to face with Moore. Spook had positioned himself right behind Moore.

"You rattlesnake." Sunny said coldly, the anger rising in her neck so powerfully she could feel her carotids pulsing. "This isn't about fixing my land, you were trying to sweet-talk this dumb old country girl out of her rights to tell this story."

She pushed her index finger against his chest so hard he stepped back into the solid chest of Spook. Her voice dropped clear and low, like a distant thunder rumbling with intense ferocity. "You get off of this property right now and if Spook or I ever see that sissy truck on this land again, we'll load it just as full of buckshot as we will you. Now git!"

Moore's face was ashen as Spook grabbed him and hustled him to the door. He quickly turned back to Sunny but his countenance had changed. His face was the dark crimson of a prairie fire and his eyes blazed like streaks of devilish yellow lightning that kills the innocent.

"I'll get you for this, you stupid little cowgirl witch." Moore spewed. "By the time me and my friends are done with you, you little tramp, all the rotten things they say about you in this town will be known all over the world and the American public will see you ain't no angel. I don't need you – I talked to your brother, Cal, and he said whatever I wanted to do on the ranch was fine with him since he owns one third of it. He thinks you're getting way too big for your britches, too. You're nothing but a cowgirl whore!"

Moore landed on the floor with a thud.

"Wal," Spook said rubbing his hand. "I wish I'd boxed his ears a little closer to that sissy truck of his. Now I got to drag him out there and load him in it. Go git Starbuck, he'd pro'ly like to help. Git the rope, too. This time we'll tie it around his neck."

Chapter Thirty

"Have a seat, Stephanie." Dane spoke to his press secretary. "So what are the latest numbers?"

"Oh, Governor, if you were up for election for President of the United States today you would win in a landslide!" Stephanie almost shrieked. "Never before in the history of the State of Kansas has a Governor enjoyed such public approval. People like their heroes!"

"But I didn't do anything except make a mistake as a rookie pilot and got lucky enough to live," Dane argued. "I did nothing heroic at all. The only hero, or heroine, in the story was Sunny. And Starbuck! When you think about it, that horse was smarter than I was."

"I understand, Governor, but the public likes to believe what it likes to believe and you have been declared, by public opinion, a hero and a leader people want to follow." Stephanie countered. "I'm sure the other 49 Governors in the U.S. are wishing they could get rescued somehow and come out smelling like a rose."

"Okay, enough about me being a hero." Dane wearied of any talk elevating him in the story. "What's going on in my life you deem important enough to have a private meeting?"

"Well, Governor," Stephanie measured her words. "There are some conversations that have been going on that you need to be privy too. These are, perhaps, not matters of the Governor's Office and therefore require no official action, but they are matters that concern your friend Sunny and the ranch."

"Ahh, the ranch," a smile crossed Dane's face. "Did I tell you that the head of the Ag Department is going out with me next week to the ranch to look at those ruts. I've already had the lawyers draw up the contract to show that I am paying for all the repairs to the prairie out of my pocket. I sent a photographer out there last week in a helicopter to photograph the ruts and Dr. Ranwell has already put together a restoration plan to show Sunny. Sunny will be happy to see us show up."

"Well, Governor," Stephanie injected. "You know, if you wanted, the state could pay for that. After all, you are the Governor."

"Absolutely not! Dane said passionately. "I am not letting the state pay for my mistake. That was my fault, not the good taxpayers of the state of Kansas. Why should they be punished for my stupidity?"

"That's very noble, sir." Stephanie deferred. "You know that people are going to wonder so I suggest that we preemptively send out a release stating that you are going to do such. That would really vault your standings!"

"Stephanie," Dane chided in a lowered voice. "There are some things you do just because they're right, not because it makes you look good. I do not want a press release sent out about that. If someone asks, then we tell them. But until that moment arrives, I'd just as soon keep silent."

Stephanie marveled again at the depth of character of this man. She had known Dane for a long time and it seemed like he became a greater man with each passing day. It was a pleasure to serve someone so noble. If only half of the politicians were like Dane, the country wouldn't be in the mess that it is in.

"Very well, Governor, as you wish." Stephanie smiled. "Now on to the next subject. Your sister called me the other day and said that an artist that Sunny met in New York had called her. Some guy named Peter Radcliff."

"Oh, sure," Dane said. "I've heard of him. In fact, I think he won some kind of prize at an art thing in Kansas last year. I saw the exhibit and, if I remember his work right, was a little surprised that he won. His kind of art is not what is typically enjoyed by Kansans. But Norma said someone from Chicago juried it so that's not a surprise that they wouldn't have the sensitivities of a Kansan. So what did he want with my sister?"

"Well, apparently he and Sunny agreed to having a bunch of artists come out to the ranch for a week and spend time painting." Stephanie explained.

"Well, that old barn needs it, that's for sure," Dane laughed.

"I'm sure it does." Stephanie agreed. "But I don't think that's what they had in mind. They want to gather these artists on the ranch and do some *en plein air* type of work."

"*En plein air?*" Dane exploded in laughter. "Isn't that just an uppity French word for 'standing outside in front of an easel trying to paint'? Good luck with that in Kansas. They'll need cement blocks to hold their easels down if the wind decides to blow."

"Well, apparently this is getting more involved than just a few artists painting the Flint Hills." Stephanie went on. "They are wanting to make it a competition and have a theme that involves the crash and Sunny rescuing you."

"What?" The color in Dane's cheeks turned crimson. "Can they do that? That sounds like a sleaze-ball marketing ploy to me. Sounds to me like a bunch of artists that are riding on the coat-tails of Sunny."

"That's why he called your sister." Stephanie explained. "He knew she was on the Kansas Arts Commission and he wanted her to get them to endorse it, and maybe even have some grant money available to fund some of the expenses involved. Then, of course, have them jury the show."

"Unbelievable!" Dane muttered. "I wonder why Norma didn't say something?"

"Remember?" Stephanie replied. "She's in Aruba with John on

vacation. She took off the afternoon after her conversation with Radcliff. She tried to call you but you were busy, so she told me."

"Now, I recall," Dane looked out the window. "I wish I was in Aruba."

"With anybody in particular?" Stephanie teased.

"Stephanie," Dane chided. "Don't start with me. My sister is bad enough. Back to this artist thing: when are they wanting to do this and is Sunny okay with it?"

"Apparently Radcliff talked with Sunny while she was in New York and Sunny was very excited to see it all happen. Radcliff said she agreed to do it and was the first one to mention it to him. Seems it was all her idea. According to Radcliff, Sunny wants them to come to the crash site itself and be inspired to create."

"What about Mackenzie Foster? Is she okay with this?"

"I talked with Mackenzie this morning. That's one of the reasons I'm in here talking to you." Dane could see that Stephanie was worried. "She doesn't like it at all and thinks it is just a marketing ploy too, to take advantage of Sunny and you as well. But she said that Radcliff is a real schmoozer and Sunny seemed to warm up to him. Spook didn't like him a bit, Mackenzie said. Apparently Sunny had some art training in college so she's pretty enamored with the art scene and, as Mackenzie quoted Spook, 'That thar fancy pants artist feller is goin' after Sunny like a bull bustin' fences down chasin' heifers.' So they are concerned, too."

Dane looked out the window so Stephanie wouldn't see his face. Jealousy. He hadn't experienced that feeling in decades. Yet, within him he felt an ancient stirring that he could not hold back. He was surprised by this feeling. What had he been thinking? Of course men are going to be after Sunny. She's beautiful, courageous, and, now, famous. And certainly destined to be wealthy. Who wouldn't want her? Spook was right about Radcliff but there would be a lot more bulls bustin' fences. He suddenly felt a sense of urgency.

"What's the latest about the party in her honor?" Dane changed the subject.

"That was on my list, too! I cleared it with Mackenzie this morning - it's all set up and ready to go."

"So is she going to come?" Dane asked.

"Is who going to come?" Stephanie looked puzzled.

"Sunny." Dane responded. "Is she going to come to her own party?"

"I'm sorry, Governor," Stephanie was confused. "But why wouldn't you think she would come to her own party?"

Dane realized how childish he was acting. But the thought of a bunch of artists spending a week on her ranch stirred up uncertain emotions. He knew he had better get control of this and do it quickly.

"Oh, I'm sure she's going to be extremely busy with her new-found stardom and wonder if she even has time to come." Dane feebly explained. "It sounds like her plate is rather full."

"Back to this artist thing," Dane said, trying to compose his emotions. "I have a hard time believing Sunny would want a bunch of strangers interloping on her ranch. She's so protective of that and when the press gets a hold of this, she's just going to have more people invading the prairie. Do you think she realizes this?"

"First of all," Stephanie rationed. "I don't know Sunny as well as you do but she seems pretty innocent of people's intention. And I'm sure the thought of having artists out on her ranch, especially if she likes art herself, is really a pretty romantic idea- I certainly think it is. And secondly, you and I both know this isn't just about someone capturing the beauty of the prairie on canvas, it is a back-door marketing scheme meant to launch artists into national lime-light as they chase ambulances. Why haven't they offered before this?"

"So does Mackenzie think there is anything that can be done to stop this?"

"She's not sure. She's afraid that her and Spook can't dissuade her and this really isn't a marketing thing for Sunny since it's not a book or movie deal. It's really just about Sunny giving them permission to come out to the ranch. Mackenzie had done some research on this

Radcliff character and wasn't too impressed with him. She says he is an up-and-coming artist gaining some renown in the art world, but has a pretty questionable past. He's apparently even had a few domestic scuffles with a lady he lived with. There are reports about the police being called to their place, but never actually filed charges."

"Well," Dane said confidently. "Sunny is bright enough to see right through someone like that."

"Begging your pardon, sir," Stephanie said respectfully. "But I'm not too sure about that. Mackenzie said Radcliff is quite handsome and has a way with the ladies. She didn't care much for him, but some young girl that's lived on the ranch for years could be swept away in his charm."

"So what do you want me to do about this? It really isn't any of my business who Sunny lets on the property. And if she likes this Radcliff guy, why should I be concerned."

Stephanie stared at him with a smile creeping up the corners of her mouth.

"Why are you looking at me like that?" Dane spouted.

"I meant nothing by it, sir." Stephanie lied and changed the direction. "But it does concern you, Governor, because they will be using your crash as a way to market their idea. With your permission, I'll have your lawyer look into it and see what can be done to stop this."

"But that could get dicey, too." Dane realized. "If we keep them from going out there, Sunny might get upset."

"Wait a minute!" Dane pounded the desk. "I've got it. We might not be able to stop it, but we could get it delayed!"

"How's that?" Stephanie asked, her brow furrowing.

"Restore the prairie!" Dane smiled. "There is nothing more important to Sunny than getting the prairie restored. That's the only thing that brought a smile to her face and made her seem to forgive me when I was out there. And, if we start that project soon we'll have to do some tilling and dirt work, then there will come the re-seeding and that all takes a lot of time-a couple of years at least for the tender growth."

"And furthermore, the only other way to access the crash site is if you go through that lane on my land and that is all private land and I will not give anyone permission to trespass on my property."

"That sounds like a plan!" Stephanie rose to leave. "And as soon as Norma gets back from Aruba, we'll finalize the plans on the party."

"Thank you, Stephanie," Dane said. "I appreciate you filling me in with this information."

"May I have permission to speak freely, Sir?"

"Stephanie," Dane chuckled. "I've known you all your life since my folks practically raised you and can't ever remember a time when you haven't spoken freely so why would you ask me now?"

"Governor," Stephanie said. "Norma told me what she told you about rescuing Sunny. We women have a sense about us that you men just don't get. If I could step outside this office right now and it was just like we were growing up where you were like a big brother to me, I'd look you right in the eye, point my finger in your chest, and tell you to get out to the ranch before the day was over and start romancing this girl. She's vulnerable. There are vultures poised ready to prey on her innocence. Don't let the matters of the State of Kansas interfere with the matters of your heart."

"But how do I do that?" Dane asked. "I'm the Governor. Governors don't go romancing cowgirls!"

"Who do you see when you wake up in the morning?" Stephanie wisely asked. "Do you look in the mirror at Dane Richards or the Governor of the State of Kansas? One of you is forever, the other only for four years at a time."

"But I haven't romanced a girl since Debbie." Dane seemed confused. "This is so bizarre. How do I do it?"

"Let her know your heart." Stephanie offered. "Write her a letter. Drive to the ranch and tell her. But use words! You, of all people, the most eloquent orator in the state, should know how to romance her with your words."

"But what if she laughs at me?" Dane seemed like a teenage boy asking his first girl to a dance.

"Would you rather live the rest of your life with Sunny or without Sunny?" Stephanie asked. "What risk is greater? Getting laughed at or losing her?

Chapter Thirty-One

"I'm warning you," Sunny laughed into the phone. "You'd better bring concrete blocks to hold your easels down! Kansas means 'children of the south-wind' and when the wind howls, it's hard to pay attention. Spook says the best wind-gauge is a log chain tacked to a fence post."

"Well, I'm sure we can accommodate any weather conditions, Sunny!" The other voice on the line was Peter Radcliff. "After all, we are professional artists and have had to overcome enormous difficulties just to be where we are so a little ole' Kansas breeze won't bother us."

"Suit yourself," Sunny chuckled knowingly. "But you've been warned!"

"Did you know that one of the ladies on the Art Commission is the Governor's sister?" Radcliff asked.

"No! Really? Norma?" Sunny was surprised.

She met Norma when the Governor came to the see the place of the crash. She could tell they were close by the way they looked at each other with respect and gentleness. She liked Norma right away. In fact, she liked the rest of the family and felt immediately at ease. Johnson was a gentleman with a quiet strength about him that seemed dignified and daring, like many of the men of her father's generation. She wasn't sure what was wrong, physically, with Meredith, but Sunny could tell Johnson aided her in a way other than just being a gentleman. Too bad

Dane was a jerk.

"Yes," Radcliffe was enthusiastic. "And I personally called her the other day to talk about us artists visiting your ranch and she was thrilled that we were going to bring such prominence to the state of Kansas. She knew the Governor would be happy that artists would be capturing the essence of the prairie. She was sure the Kansas Arts Commission would want to help in any way they could."

"By the way, Mr. Radcliff," Sunny interrupted. "I forgot to thank you for the really nice flowers. There's a little old man that made the delivery and he didn't think he'd ever taken flowers to someplace as far from town as the ranch. They were beautiful."

It was nice to come in from a long day on the ranch and smell the roses wafting through the screen door. The kitchen table was so old the finish had started flaking and turning yellow and seeing the exquisite hand-thrown pottery vase - a gift from one of Peter's artist friends - with a cascade of roses and baby-breath was a splash of fresh air.

"Oh, a beautiful gift for the gift of one so beautiful," Radcliff charmed. "I'm sure that nothing on this earth that man could make would be as ravishingly beautiful as you, Sunny! All of us here in New York were mesmerized by your presence and all admit that we have been touched with a simple grace and elegance that will forever leave us profoundly changed."

"As you know, Sunny," Radcliff said. "We, in the art world, frequently discuss- no, the better word is disagree- over what constitutes beauty. But every last person that met you when you were here were finally in agreement over one thing they all considered beautiful – you! Perhaps you were not aware, Sunny, but the fragile and combustible personas of artists here in New York were taken back with the simple innocence and elegance of your beauty with which, we all agreed, emanates from within and manifests itself on the surface."

Sunny didn't know what to say. She hadn't heard a man speak words like this to her in a long time. Maybe never. In an ancient, sealed cave deep in her heart came a rumble of life yearning to have a breath of affection purge the darkness.

"So how soon are you wanting to do this?" Sunny deflected the praise. "It won't be long and the grasses will start changing. Now, it's pretty all year round, but it turns rather brown come late summer. Especially if the rain stops – it gets really dry then."

"Oh, we would want to do this as soon as possible. In fact, we were hoping to do it within the next month to six weeks if that were possible."

"Well, the prairie is the prairie and I know it doesn't have any appointments." Sunny reasoned. "So I really don't care when you do it. My calendar is pretty empty. I get calls to go on various shows, but I'm just happy to be here on the ranch so I turn them all down."

"How about I fly out there tomorrow and scout the ranch out?" Radcliff proposed. "I can catch an early morning flight to Kansas City and drive down to your ranch. Would that be okay so I could scout it out? I would bring my publicist with me to, if that is okay? We would only be there a couple of days."

"Sure," Sunny said quickly, knowing that a little company would be nice for the weekend.

"You'll have to give me directions, of course, and give me the name of the local motel," Radcliff seemed energized.

"Local motel?" Sunny laughed. "The local motel is 35 miles away. Mr. Radcliff, I live a long way from town!"

"Please, call me Peter," Radcliff insisted. "If it is 35 miles away, then that's where we'll stay!"

"Actually, you and your friend are really more than welcome to stay here at the ranch with me." Sunny offered. "It's just an old ranch house and it's not much – I live here by myself - but I have a couple of extra bedrooms and you're more than welcome to spend the nights here."

"Oh," Radcliff squealed. "That would be most delightful! What fun! We'll be able to spend a night in a real ranch house on a Kansas prairie! I'll be the envy of all the artists in SoHo!"

"So how many artists do you think will be here?" Sunny asked.

"Well, I'm thinking that it would be just artists from our circle of peers here in New York City," Radcliff explained. " We have a group of artists that have been like our own little community for years and they're all abuzz about the possibility. We've discussed this and know that if we open it up for the whole art world, there would be hundreds of artists that want to be a part."

Sunny recoiled at the horror of a crowd of people on her land again. The plane crash had been bad enough, but if the hills were swarming with people again, who knows what kinds of further damage would be inflicted on the prairie.

"Yeah," Sunny quickly agreed. "The smaller the better. How many do you think might come?"

"No more than twenty at the most," Radcliff sensed her reticence to a large influx of artists. "Norma agrees that an juried art show and the following exhibitions around the country would give more prominence to the professional artists and would keep the cliché and folk artists at bay. The last thing we need is a bunch of little old ladies from the Society of Cliché Watercolorists infusing their lack of vision into our world of creativity."

"Well, you are the professional artist. But I would appreciate a small group of people rather than a large one."

Sunny explained the directions to the ranch with rising excitement over Radcliff coming out the next day. It had been a long time since the old ranch house had any company other than Jasmine roaming the night. It would be good to have a couple of people here for the weekend. But the place was a fright. The spare bedrooms probably had dust on the comforters from last year.

Sunny thrilled at the thought of professional artists with their Julian easels dotted across the prairie. Although she would never dare let them see, or even know, that she had done a few paintings of her own of the prairie, perhaps she could be inspired from simple osmosis. Surely, since she was allowing them on her prairie, they could take some time to teach her a few things.

Sunny scurried to the first bedroom where some of her paintings hung on the wall. Quickly, she took them down and stuffed them back into the closet away from sight. She was right: the bed, the lamps, the bureau—everything was covered with a thick layer of dust. These rooms hadn't been slept in for years; she always left the door shut so as not to have to heat and cool the empty rooms. Or let the memories of a full house from yesteryear escape into her heart.

As she passed by the old oak dresser that belonged first to her grandmother, then to her mother, she wiped away the dust to look into the lonely eyes of herself staring back. Gently pulling back a wisp of hair that had fallen along her cheek, she glanced beside the mirror at the black and white picture of her parent's wedding day. She did favor her mother, as her Daddy always said. In fact, she would often catch her Dad looking at her with a deep forlorn after her mother died. He was quick to smile and turn away, but he often sighed, "Ah, Sunny, when the sun catches your hair just right I swear it is your Mom standing before me." While she knew he meant to compliment her, it was if he transferred his soul's sadness into hers.

Glancing back at the mirror, she leaned a little closer. "Jasmine?" she questioned the cat that had jumped on the dresser looking for affection. "What do you think of Mr. Radcliff? Do you think he might be interested in a plain ol' cowgirl like me or was he just sayin' all those purty things so I'd let him and his friends on the ranch?"

Sunny suddenly soured, "But you know, Jasmine, that old Spook Masterson ain't gonna like this one little bit. He don't like that fancy pants fellow anyway so I'm going to have to listen to him beller like a calf being branded about lettin' them artists out here. Maybe I can talk to Mackenzie first so she can talk to Spook. It seems that he'll listen to about anything she has to say these days. And boy did he give old Telephone Jones something to talk about when he showed that picture of the two of them with their arms around each other on top of the Empire State Building."

It had been a long time since Sunny had actually thought of a particular man she might be interested in. She'd had her fill of the cocky cowboys that ran in her circle of friends and she could think of no one that she knew with which she would ever be romantically involved. Radcliff was considerably older than her, but she wearied of the immaturity of the men, or boys rather, her age.

But she had to admit Radcliff was pretty handsome and, even though he was a little too effusive in his praise, it was still wonderful to hear words of beauty being spoken into her soul. Her Daddy always taught her that the mind is full of voices from the past and that they shape who we are. Good voices. Bad voices. It's all a matter of which voices you listen to. Apparently her Daddy listened to the wrong ones or else he would still be with her.

"Well, Jazzy," she stroked the purring cat. "Tomorrow night's going to look a lot different around here than anything we've seen in a while. And I hear it's supposed to be a full moon. Maybe Mr. Fancy Pants Artist from New York City himself will ask Miss Sunshine to go on a moonlight stroll across the prairie. And I reckon li'l ol' Miss Sunshine will just say, 'Yes!' Spook will never know the difference."

Chapter Thirty-Two

"You went and done what?" Spook spun around in almost a complete circle when he heard Sunny tell Mackenzie that Radcliff was coming out. "Wall, I'll be a monkeys uncle. In all my born'd days I ain't never heered of nut'in so dagblasted confound'n poke-you-right-in-the-dadgum-eye far fetched in my life! Tell me y'ur funnin' me! I'll be a gol-durned bucket calf. That riles me mor'n watchin' wider Johnson beat'n them kids o' hers."

Sunny hadn't seen Spook this upset in a long time. Not at least since he cornered Telephone Jones after the beauty pageant. She knew he would be surprised and maybe just a little upset, but that vein popping along his neck was an indication he was more than just a little riled. She glanced to Mackenzie for some help.

"Now, Spook," Mackenzie said trying to calm him down. "It's just for a couple of days and they'll be gone."

Spook never heard her. He was walking bow-legged as fast as he could across the pasture to the barn muttering the whole way. Every few feet he'd stop and turn around to look at Sunny and Mackenzie just standing there bewildered, then he'd shake his head and mutter something else and head back off again.

"Wow," Sunny said. "I knew he wouldn't like it, but I had no idea it would upset him that much."

"Spook's pretty protective of you, Sunny," Mackenzie defended her man. "If there is one thing I have learned about Spook Masterson is that he takes taking care of you pretty seriously. Why, he took me down to the feed store the other day and Buster Thomas smarted off something about Spook having two girlfriends now and faster than lightning Spook grabbed him by the collar and pinned him up against the wall. The look in Buster's eyes was pure terror and Buster had a good six inches and 75 pounds on Spook."

"You know, Sunny," Mackenzie went on, "I have only been around Spook a short period of time, but I can honestly say that I have never felt more protected in my life. There is a peace in just being around him that is good for my soul. I know he would never hurt me or let me be hurt."

"I know," Sunny agreed. "I don't know what I would have done without him all these years. It's really simple; I just wouldn't have made it. The ranch would have gone back to the bank and I would be working for someone else. But I think he's reading this one wrong. I don't feel threatened by Peter at all. By the way, Peter is supposed to be here around four this afternoon. Do you think you guys would stay for dinner?"

"So it's 'Peter' now, is it? Oh, I'm sure I'd like to stay for dinner but you know Spook. He doesn't keep his opinions of people to himself especially if he thinks they're going to hurt you," Mackenzie replied. "Are you sure you want us to stay?"

"Peter's not going to hurt me," Sunny surprised herself at that remark. "He just wants to bring a few friends out here to paint the prairie. I'm actually pretty excited about it."

"Well, I'll go out to the barn and ask him," Mackenzie said. She looked at the innocent eyes of Sunny and wondered, again, at the refreshing purity of the young lady. She had no idea how desperate some people were to make money off of her heroism.

She was surprised to get that phone call from the Governors' sister, Norma, about this art thing that Radcliff was trying to put together.

Norma was concerned that this was just a very clever marketing scheme meant to exploit Sunny and the Governor. Mackenzie had also found out from one of the producers at a local station in town that they had been contacted about this "Art on the Prairie" competition coming up in hopes that t.v. crews would be sent out to film the artists. Radcliff had his publicist working all the angles to make this a high profile event. She was sure Sunny had no idea the way this could turn into a media nightmare for her. Sure, the artists would love the notoriety, but Sunny would once again have trespassers all over her land.

Mackenzie found Spook in the barn furiously curry-combing Starbuck who seemed to enjoy the attention. "Hey cowboy," Mackenzie said affectionately. "Why don't you let me take a turn at that?"

"That gol durn fancy pants city slicker!" Spook fumed as he handed Mackenzie the comb, "He's done got his ears pointed at that li'l filly and she's got blinders on and can't see him comin'."

"I know," Mackenzie agreed as she gently stroked the mane of Starbuck who was enjoying all the attention. "It's just that she hasn't had a lot of suitors out here and loneliness can make a person think some pretty wild things sometimes."

"Wall, old fancy pants might be a dang sight y'unger 'n me, but there's still enough pepper left in this ol' shaker to plant his britches right 'twixt his ears," Spook fumed. "I done made a promise to her Daddy that I'd take care of her, but by golly, if she ain't got 'nuf smarts by now to spot a coyote trailin' the herd lookin' for stragglers, then maybe my job is done."

"Oh, Spook," Mackenzie said reassuringly. "You know you don't mean that. You have taken care of her and you will take care of her still, so don't be upset with her. Right now she's pretty confused. She didn't want any of this to happen and here she is again back on the prairie all alone. When we were flying back from N.Y. and flew over the prairie, she told me that day that she was anxious to get home, but hated more than anything to walk into that old lonesome house again."

"Spook," Mackenzie walked up to him and put her arms around his neck. "Don't you remember that lonely feeling way down deep in your soul that moans like an old farm house groaning in a bitter winter wind? I know I sure do. I thought I'd always be alone and just tried to get used to the pain, but now I have you it seems like I've forgotten all about what loneliness feels like."

"I reckon yur right," Spook softened. "I wouldn't never leave her. Shucks, she's just like she's my own girl. I guess I'm just an orn'ry ol' coot what likes to kick the side of the barn ev'ry now and agin. I just don't wanna see some city slicker that I ain't got good feelin's about to put a snaffle on her. And I been 'round enough livestock in my day to spot a renegade when I sees it."

Mackenzie had been impressed with Spooks' ability to figure people out in just a couple of seconds. She thought she had pretty good intuition about people until she got around Spook. At least with men anyway. She still bristled at the thought of that Olivia hussy in New York City. Were men really that gullible? Then she thought about a few of her choices and asked herself the same, *Are women that gullible?* What is it in the human heart that is so desperate to be loved that it becomes blind to the glaring reality that everyone else sees?

"Well, Mr. Spook Masterson," Mackenzie drew a little closer. "She's invited us to dinner tonight with Mr. Fancy Pants and I suggest that we show up and offer them a little Kansas hospitality."

"Yes'm, Miss Mac. I reckon I oughter be nice," Spook muttered. "But if he steps one foot outta the corral, I string him up so high he'll be singing soprano in the church choir." Mackenzie left Spook to tend Starbuck and headed back to the house. She loved hearing Spook call her Mac. He was the only person she would let call her that.

Sunny wasn't going to have anything too elaborate for dinner: grilled hamburgers and a fresh-from-her garden salad. She chuckled to herself wondering if Radcliff and his publicist were vegetarians. She knew Spook would go into great detail about butchering cattle and making hamburger just to see how strong their stomachs were. He was an ornery cuss.

Mackenzie was anxious to meet the publicist. She had received a call from Stephanie Riddell, the Governor's press secretary a few days before warning her that this Radcliff was trying to do an end-around to get out to the prairies with his little artists buddies. Normally, his publicist would have made contact with Mackenzie – since she was acting as her agent - but Radcliff was in too big of a hurry for things like contracts and negotiations. He was smart enough to know that if a movie deal or book deal was in the works, he'd have a lot harder time getting out to the ranch.

"Like shooting fish in a barrel. That's what they say." Her boss, Gordon, had warned her that the folks from New York considered anyone west of the Mississippi River country bumpkins and easy to fool. Being more cosmopolitan, or so they thought, they just assumed folks from the country would be so enamored with their money and prestige that they would bow down to any request. But what Gordon pointed out, after having lived in New York City for a while, was that many highbrow city folks seem to lack the just good old common sense that Kansans take for granted. She was sure she would hear one of them ask where Toto, Dorothy, and the Tin Man were and then laugh like they were the first ones that ever thought to ask that question. She chuckled surmising what Spook would say.

Stephanie told her that pretty substantial rumors had Moore was cutting a movie deal with a sleaze-ball tabloid journalism group out in California. Mackenzie was afraid of that and knew they really didn't have much control. Even though they might not have copyrights for Sunnys' story, they could sure tell it from Moore's vantage point and that would not be good. Gordon heard the same thing and, like they say in journalism, "Where there's smoke, there's fire." Only time would tell.

Stephanie told her about the Governor's conversation with Mike Spellman, an old buddy of his that ran a motion picture company in

California. She got in contact with Spellman Enterprises about a book and movie deal and felt good about it. They wanted to send an agent out to visit with Sunny, but it seemed like it was better that Mackenzie handle it. Mackenzie was kind of surprised how good things seemed to be falling in place. Not only was the Governor good life-long friends with Mike, but Mike had actually been in classes that Gordon taught while in college. Gordon still had contact with him and assured Sunny that he was trustworthy and would do Sunny right. It was nice to walk into a deal knowing there were years of trust and relationships established. This seemed to be certainly more providence than coincidence.

She had intended to show Sunny all the paper work today and the substantial offer they were willing to pay for the right to produce the movie and start a book. Sunny could buy her brothers out plus never have to worry each summer about whether there would be enough money to pay taxes. And if it took off, the royalties Sunny got would take care of her for the rest of her life.

She also needed to talk to Sunny about the Governor coming out. Stephanie had told her that the Governor had a plan all worked out to restore the damaged prairie. She knew that Sunny would like that news. Almost every time she talked to Sunny, she complained about the prairie and was really upset after Moore came out and pulled his shenanigan. Sunny would be relieved the Governor was going to get involved. Sunny had told her a few more details of the encounter with Moore. She'd noticed his hand was swollen and roughed up on the knuckles and when she asked him what happened, he just told her he'd "buggered his hand on the north end of a southbound mule."

But now she wasn't sure whether to talk to Sunny or not. Sunny seemed preoccupied with Radcliff and his publicist coming out and talking about a movie and a book deal might not be a good thing right now. Mackenzie didn't know why, but a check in her spirit just said that it wasn't the right time. Not today. Her heart whispered to her that something needed to happen to Sunny this weekend that can't happen if she's thinking about all the money she's going to make from a book and movie. Mackenzie had learned to trust those premonitions so she decided to wait.

"I wonder what's going to happen, Jazzy?" Mackenzie reached down to pet the cat which came running up to her in the yard. "Is she falling in love? Has Radcliff put on the charm too much already and Sunny's already gone?"

Jasmine purred and rubbed against her boot. "Then again," Mackenzie chuckled. "She might need all that money to settle a lawsuit 'cause I have a feeling that one Mr. Spook Masterson just might do the same thing to Mr. Fancy Pants that he did to Mr. Moore! He might just drag off one more unconscious galoot out to his truck by his ears."

Chapter Thirty-Three

Dane hung upside down in the cockpit with blood filling his mouth as it drained from his lungs. He knew he was slowly dying and had watched Sunny rescue Moore and help him on the back of her horse and ride off in the rain. Slowly the darkness surrounded him as he tried to breathe. Had she left him for dead? Did she not feel a pulse? Had she not heard him moan?

From where he was watching her, he could see them riding off in the rain into the enveloping gloom. It seemed as if they reached a certain point on the horizon and stayed the same size even though the horse seemed to be moving. He tried to holler but the blood clogged his throat. Is this what's it's like to die? Is there no bright light? Only darkness. Only intense pressure on his chest. He couldn't breathe. Slowly he felt himself suffocating.

Suddenly, Dane sat straight up in bed gasping for air. He could feel his heart beating wilding and sweat soaking his sheets. Moaning, he lay back down in bed and tried to regain his composure. Reaching over to flip on the lamp to chase away the dark shadows of night, he saw the clock: 2:56. He was wide-awake; there would be no sleep for him for a while. Slowly, he got out of bed and stumbled to the kitchen.

In the dark living room of the Governor's Mansion, he found the soft leather recliner and collapsed his frame into it. The moon was almost full tonight and the soft blue light trickled across the floor as his eyes slowly adjusted.

Staring into the nothingness, Dane felt as alone as he could ever remember. Debbie's death had been so hard and she had suffered so much that by the time she had died, he had grown accustomed to sleeping alone while she was in the hospital. He had sat in this chair many nights during her illness and after her passing mixed with myriad emotions. He admitted to no one, but was somewhat relieved when Debbie finally passed. He loved her so much but she had suffered so much pain he could not wish her here any longer.

He had gone to a counselor after Debbie's death and, while he found some encouragement in that, found his schedule was just too busy. Dane had lived such a wonderful life with great parents so never had deep issues to resolve, so he felt the trips became a waste of time. He knew their value to others, but knew that the grieving process of death –those five stages of denial, anger, bargaining, depression, and acceptance would just take time. So he gave himself time.

Another comfort was the Bible that had been his Grandfather Richards. An old army chaplain in WWI, his Bible was torn and tattered and had hand-scribbled notes written all over it. He cherished those notes. By Psalm 23, Grandpa had written, "Great comfort when Lydia and Sophia died." Lydia was Grandpa's wife and had died during childbirth of her only daughter. By the Psalm that said, "Whenever I am afraid, I will trust in Thee," were scribbled almost illegibly "Needed this at Battle of the Bulge."

This chair had been his friend, somehow comforting him in the middle of many other nights as the solitude ached his soul. Slowly, imperceptibly, he had found healing in writing. Poetry, prose, essays, mindless ramblings put to pen. Something special happened in the connection between his pen and his pain as they brought forth life and hope.

He had never considered himself a writer, and he didn't do it as an emotional release. Rather, life made sense to him when the pen was in his hand. Abstract thoughts that bounced in his head by the thousands each day somehow connected the endorphins in his brain to soothe the pain in his nerves. It wasn't done for anyone's benefit other than his own. He wrote because it healed him. He wrote because the random events of life connected like dots in a game. He wrote because he could not help but write.

He remembered the first time he sent a poem in for publication. He had intentionally done it anonymously because he wanted it to be published because of it's worth, not because he was the Governor of Kansas. No one knew those poems were his, except Norma who was sworn to absolute secrecy.

He flipped the light on, opened the drawer of the end table, and took out a pen and paper. The pen was a Mont Blanc that Norma had given him with a special blessing inscribed, "May the ink that flows bring healing and life."

Staring blankly at the paper, Dane waited for that almost mystical union between his hand, his mind, and his spirit. What was he supposed to write tonight? He had no agenda. He had not thought to put to paper that was prescribed. What was his first word? What did the deepest part of his soul want to say?

Sunny.

Sunny? Why Sunny? He wondered if he was supposed to write her a thank you letter. He listened to his heart speak to him.

Then began to write.

Dear Sunny,

I want to thank you again for your incredible act of heroism in the face of insurmountable odds. Had it not been for your valiant efforts in the face of danger, neither I, nor Ron Moore, would be alive today.

Dane reread it. "Good grief," he mumbled, "I sound like a politician." He wadded that one up and tossed it in the trash. He grabbed another piece. "Let the heart speak."

Dear Sunny,

I realize the great risk I take in writing this letter. You might toss it out onto the prairie the next time the pastures are burned, or you could show off my silliness to your friends for the sake of a good laugh. I heard someone once say that you have to risk the slap in the face for the pleasure of a kiss. While I'm certainly not asking you to kiss me, I do hope this letter is met with at least some small amount of favor on your part.

Even as I write this, I find it awkward to even explain to you why I'm writing. Perhaps the best thing I can do is to express it as a poet. So I'll begin to describe the mysterious machinations inside me using a few lines from a poem I wrote some time ago that was inspired by the Flint Hills.

"The wind lays soft against the prairie, and gives it breath to a new day

This winding road I'm traveling on's a memory of a place I've been and a place I'd like to stay

But a voice in the distant hill is calling, from the shadows it whispers my name

And the winding road I'm traveling on will take me to a place I'll never leave again."

I have always felt something in the Flint Hills call to the deep part of my spirit that even I don't understand and can't explain. And, since the accident, I find that draw on my spirit stronger than the thunderstorms that blast across the prairie in spring. And, for reasons inexplicable to me, I have discovered that another "voice" calling me. It is a voice that speaks to me in the hidden part of my heart that only the silence of the night can hear.

My first memory of you was from the haze of the accident. Knowing my predicament as we descended, I knew that I was very likely going to die. In the midst of the fog of my mind, my first lucid thought that I recall was seeing your face and, in particular, seeing into your eyes. I have seen those eyes many times since in my dreams. I gazed into your eyes as I teetered between life and death, I wondered if I was looking at a real person or into the eyes of the most wonderful creature God had ever made. I had never seen anything so beautiful in my life. I drew strength and hope from those eyes because I believed I was soon to die.

The next time I saw you was the day I came out to your ranch with my family to thank you. I had not forgotten the deep pools of intrigue and mystery that I had seen and I wondered if you would have that same affect on me again. Shortly after we stammered through our introductions, I managed to catch a glimpse again at your eyes and, while I might have appeared to be composed, I came undone inside. Something happened to me that I still don't understand. It was like some mysterious chain between my soul and yours was suddenly and irrevocably connected. One glance from your eye ravishes my heart.

I realize I am being very forward here, but I am willing to risk it all on this one chance I might have to tell you this. As I looked into your eyes, Sunny, I believe there are things that I see within you that you have allowed no one else to see. I know very little about you personally, other than what the media has portrayed and we all know that that is never the real person.

Can I tell you what I see when I look into your eyes? Can I tell you why I believe I can see these things? Can I tell you why I believe I am the one for you and you are the one for me?

When I look into your eyes, those unfathomable depths of intrigue and mystery, I find myself looking through the multi-layered colors of a prism without ease of definition but with irresistible beauty. You are, to me, at once mysterious and yet known.

I see within you a beauty of creation that has been destined to express delight in all that is around you with the magnificent poem of who you are. You have been captured on the prairie and by the prairie. When I think of you out there all alone on the prairie, I can't help but think of those spirited horses that are sometimes bound in a corral. You are meant to be free, not to go somewhere else, but to stay where you are yet without constraints. It is not that you would be happier somewhere else for you want to be right where you are. It is just that you want to be free where you are, not penned up in a corral of people's expectation or bound by the betrayal of friends. You just need someone to open the gate and let you out of the confinement. You are meant to stay where you are, but you are meant to be free and not corralled.

I see great bravery, but it is a bravery that has overcome incredible pain and suffering. It is the type of courage that people have when they have endured so much suffering alone that their faces become like flint, hardened and sharp. They have become brave because of necessity just to live through things forced upon them without their permission. You have such strength – a strength that has come at great cost to you and a strength you have developed all alone.

I also see your abandonment. Once past the dark brown eyes and the melt-your-heart smile, I see a young girl who has been betrayed by almost everyone in her life. I know nothing personally about your situation, Sunny, but I know you and I can see the years of pain that has made you suspicious, and rightly so, of anyone that would come close. You are willing to trust Spook – and who wouldn't! What a delight that man is to this world and how precious a gift he is to you. He has been sent to you by One who cares that you are not alone and I know you know that.

I also see a little girl who just wants to love. And be loved. But I believe you want to love more than just be loved. You have so much within you that bursts with energy to love. I would imagine that you have sat astride Starbuck and raced through the hills with pure joy just to express the love that you feel in your heart for all of creation. Your heart bursts with love and most often you only get to share it with Starbuck. Sunny, you are meant to share it with so many more. A heart like yours is rare- it would rather love than to be loved – and your happiness in life will come when you are given opportunity to fully express it. In fact, one of the dreams I have of you is that the faces of many children from all over the world surround you and you are making them laugh. I don't know what that looks like in your future, but I do know that you are meant to bring joy to so many more than you do. And I believe your newfound stardom is a launching pad through which you can bring hope and healing and laughter to thousands of children around the world.

I don't believe my crashing on your land and you watching was just an "accident." While I was responsible for making some bad decisions about flying, I believe there is Someone who over-rode my stupidity and orchestrated those events for a reason. And since I'm risking it all anyway, I will go ahead and tell you that I believe that I have been given the ability to see within your soul for a particular reason. I believe we are to be together.

I know that must stun you to read that last line. I confess it stuns me to finally write it even after I admitted it to myself some time ago. I know this is outside the box of the way romance happens in America. I should romance you with dinner and dance or a variety of other ways and, if given the chance, I will do so with great intensity. But I am not in a position to begin a courtship that might not turn into anything. With a man in my position with such public scrutiny, it would be a very distracting thing to "go out on a date" with you and play the game in such a way that I wine and dine you a few times and then tell you how I feel.

So I'm going to come right out of the chute: I'm telling you how I feel and hoping that you will allow me to wine and dine you. I promise you, if you give me the chance, I will romance you and build such trust between us that you will never doubt my affection and commitment to you. I am offering you the most sacred thing I can offer: my trust. And, I ask you for the most sacred thing you have to offer me: your trust. And I swear, by the moon and stars above, that I will cherish your trust and spend a lifetime proving to you that I am worth that risk.

I love you, Sunny. And while it might not seem that I know you well enough to say that, I would beg to differ. I believe that the fathomless part of my spirit which is not bound by reason is connected to your spirit in such a way that we are to be eternally joined.

I am not asking you to marry me. Yet. I will, in time. I promise that. But it will be much more of a surprise than just to write it in a letter. But I am asking for a chance to prove to you what I feel in my heart. I do intend to marry you if you will let me. But I intend, first, to romance you with every part of my being and get to know you in such a way that you would trust me with every facet of your being and I know that that takes time. Above all, I will become your friend.

I am not an adolescent schoolboy smitten with a girl because she's pretty and popular. I am a man that knows what he wants, knows that something mysterious has happened in his heart that he must act upon or live, eternally, to regret. My boldness in writing comes from a fear to miss this opportunity to love, and be loved, by such an incredible woman as you.

But I confess as I write this that I do feel somewhat like a schoolboy passing notes in hopes that the girl checks "yes" at the end. However, we are mature adults and so I will leave it up to you how and when to respond.

I also wrote another poem that I wished to be true at the time, but now fully makes sense. I'll close with it.

I hear your voice, and it's calling me
Across the wind, and it speaks to me
I run and hide, but you find me there
You speak to me and with a lover's care
You call out my name, you call out my name,
A gentle voice burning in the autumn trees
Or a thunders' roar racin' on the summer's breeze
A blazing star on a winter's night
A dew kissed rose in spring's dancing light
You call out my name
You call out my name
When I lose my way in this maze of life, your love will rescue me
You come to me in the shadows of my heart.
With a gentle voice to carry me to a place that knows no care
As you call out my name.
As you call out my name.
With love that lasts beyond death,
Dane

Chapter Thirty-Four

Mackenzie glanced over the top of Starbucks saddle to see Sunny standing by the house with her head thrown back in laughter. Peter and his publicist, Patrick, had arrived a bit early – much to Spooks chagrin – and bounded out of the rented four wheel drive truck giggling like a couple of school girls.

"Oh!" Peter squealed. "I've never driven a real cowboy truck before! I can see why the cowboys like them so much!"

"Yes!" Patrick shrieked. "Can you imagine driving up to a Broadway play in the city and being the envy of everyone in a limo?" Spook turned and walked to the barn.

"Gol-durn city slickers," Spook muttered as he backed the horses out of the trailer. He'd brought a couple over for Radcliff. "Ain't never been on a horse before and now I gots to drag their candy striped butts across the prairie. I hope the horses stampede and ..."

"Now, Spook," Mackenzie interrupted him. "It's only for a couple of hours. And we both know how hilarious it will be to watch them try to walk after they get off the horses."

"W'all, I don't have to like it!" Spook spit. "I think I'll pack some iron just in case I need to shoot me a varmint. And I'll get blood all over those purty new Wranglers of his. Those drugstore cowboys must have bought everything they had for sale at the western store. Never saw a fruitier pair of dudes in my life. That's it, I'm going after Maybelle."

"Spook!" Mackenzie chided. "You're not packing your pistol out on the prairie! The last thing we need is to see you get hauled off to jail for shooting an artist. Just go along for the ride and be nice and let things run their course. I have a feeling things will take care of themselves."

While Mackenzie tried to believe that, she was a little dismayed as she glanced again over at Sunny standing in the lawn talking to Peter and Patrick. She had to admit she hadn't seen Sunny that happy and animated in quite some time. It was not a good thing she was seeing, but she didn't want to alarm Spook.

Spook had finished saddling the last of the mares as Sunny made it to the corral with the two men. She was laughing and had one man on each arm. Spook turned away.

"Either one of you fellers ever seen a horse before?" Spook sneered. Sunny shot him a look but Spook turned too quickly. "This here part whats got the ears is the head and that bushy part back there is the hind end. These mares are kind of spooky critters kind of like me and don't like no one sneakin' around behind them so if'n you want keep partin' your hair with a comb instead of a hoof, I'd suggest you stay away from that bushy part back there. And if one of them starts to ra'r up on ya while you're in the saddle, just grab that horn and say yor prayers." Peter and Patrick suddenly grew quiet.

"Oh, guys," Sunny shot Spook another dagger. "Spook's just a funnin' you. These old mares are as gentle as kittens." She glanced at Mackenzie looking for help. Mackenzie just winked at her.

"Is there a stool that I can stand on?" Radcliff asked.

"A stool?" Spook almost shouted. "What are you tryin' to do? Give the horse conniption fits? I've never seen a horse die a laughin', but I figger every horse in this corral would if they saw you using a stool. If'n you hadn't got your britches so tight, maybe you could lift y'or leg up off the ground."

Mackenzie could see Sunny was getting pretty embarrassed by Spooks obvious disdain for these two. Quickly she walked over to Radcliff and reassured him. "Really, these are pretty docile horses. All you have to do is reach up and grab the saddle horn with one hand, the back of the saddle with the other, stick your foot in the stirrup, and in one fluid motion swing up and on." Sunny smiled approvingly at her.

It was a good thing these were old mares that would stand still while the two city slickers got on. Spook later described the ordeal down at the co-op: "Them two fellers tryin' to climb on them there horses looked like wider Jones trying to shimmy up the flag pole on Mayday greased like a pig for a race. If'n I'd been them horses, I'da branded them with a horse-shoe on each butt cheek."

The late summer sun was still bright and warm as a gentle breeze undulated the waning grasses of summer. They had pulled the cattle off just a few weeks earlier but it had been a good summer with plenty of rain and the grass was still surprisingly green. Sunny led the way with Peter and Patrick flanking her on both sides. Spook and Mackenzie followed far enough back so the guys couldn't hear Spooks social commentary.

"What are these ruts in the ground from?" Patrick asked. "Some of them are really deep and wide!"

"Oh, those are from all the vehicles that came out and tore up the land." Sunny answered. "The ground was wet when the crash happened and every guy with a four wheel drive and their dog came out here. The governor said he'd fix it, but I'm not holding my breath."

Once near the crash site, Sunny dismounted and invited the men to do the same. "Just leave the reins hang on the ground." Sunny explained. "They won't go anywhere. They are what we call 'ground-broke' which means they will stand still all day long with the reins hanging there."

"But what if a coyote comes up and runs one of our horse off?" Peter seemed quite concerned. Spook rolled his eyes and mumbled incoherently.

"Well, first of all we call them *kuyotes* out here, not *kuyotees*," Sunny chuckled. "And they won't bother us at all. They're mostly nocturnal and will probably keep you awake tonight when they start howling."

Spook and Mackenzie walked about twenty yards away from the site. Sunny had heard Spook mumbling the whole time and knew he had several opinions he wanted to share with the world, but she just wasn't in the mood to hear it.

"Wow," Peter seemed in awe. "This is where it all happened? I can feel the hair rise on the back of my head. The fact that two men could have died out here had it not been for the Cowgirl Angel really comes to life now that were here. Tell us again what happened that day!"

Sunny was tired of telling the story. She was finding more of her life being defined by one particular accident and her life was more than just a date on a calendar when a plane fell from the sky. She wanted to talk about the prairie, about the natives that had traversed these plains for thousands of years leaving tale-tale signs of their existence. She wanted to talk about cattle and free markets and how wrong it was for the government to subsidize already wealthy businessmen taking care of wild horses while they let the poor American rancher who raised cattle for consumption live and die by the fluctuations of the market. Generations of ranchers in these hills were being wiped out by businessmen who bought thousands of acres of pasture so they could get huge government contracts to take care of wild horses. It just didn't seem fair. But the animal rights activists had cost the taxpayer a lot of money to take care of the horses that were being relocated to pastures surrounding her.

It wasn't that she didn't like the wild horses. She loved looking out across the pastures and seeing the herds. Some were magnificent animals whose primal spirits were seen in their gaits and lofty manes flowing in the breeze. Others looked like 55 gallon drums on pop bottles- evidence of some crazy crossbreeding through the years.

What she didn't like is the way the government awarded millions of dollars each year to the businessmen who bought out her neighbors because of the volatility of the cattle market. These wannabe ranchers had federal funding to stretch mile after mile of brand new fences, rebuild roads and bridges, and install elaborate pipe corrals all to take care of the number of horses.

The animal rights activists had managed to shut down every slaughterhouse in America because it seemed inhumane to kill these wild horses. Much of the horse-meat had been sent over seas to cultures who eat horse meat, but nevertheless, horses are prettier than cows so it was decided by the pressure of the activists to spend millions to keep them alive. And a horse could live an easy 35 years. It just didn't seem fair. Not when there are millions of cattle slaughtered every day so Americans could eat beef.

The unintended consequences were now people had to wait on their horses to die of natural causes and it drove the prices down. Like Spook said, "If'n you got a horse trailer parked somewheres, you'd better keep it locked 'cause yous liable to come back and find a horse in it." Ranchers were finding strange horses dumped in their pastures now from former owners who no longer wanted to spend the money on feeding them.

"Sunny?" Peter interrupted her thoughts. "Would you mind telling us the story?"

Grudgingly, she recounted the detail of the day again and with each part revealed, found herself surprisingly reliving it in great emotion. As she gazed towards the west where she'd first spotted the plane in the terrible storm, the appreciation for the miracle of life deepened within her. Had she not been out mending fences that day, most likely the Governor and his brother-in-law would have died. Suddenly, the great weight of that surrounded her as the heavy realization that she had saved two lives came in to clearer focus. They not only could have died without her, they would have died without her. The crash, for the most part, had been an inconvenience at best to her. The fleeting popularity had yet to turn into anything tangible to pay the taxes for the year and the ruts left by the marauding ambulance chasers had yet to be leveled.

But she had saved two lives. Two men were able to draw breath today because of her. Two men had families who could look into their eyes at the dinner table, smell their breath as they drew close in conversation, hear the sound of their voices calling on the phone, and have the simple pleasure of a hug at each greeting. The Governor appreciated that gift far more than Moore did.

"Sunny?" Radcliffe queried. "You okay?"

Sunny had not realized she had stopped speaking. The overwhelming magnitude of all that had happened that day and each day since settled on her with a sublime sense of being chosen for a such a time as this. Granted, others could have done what she did, but some could not have. It was her that made the decision to rush to the site and not back to the house that would have surely been too long of a delay to keep them alive. It was her that had trained Starbuck to be calm as she lassoed the airplane wings and the resulting screeching of metal twisting against metal. It was her that applied the baling wire tourniquet to Dane's leg preventing fatal blood loss. It was her. No one else but Sunny.

And standing on the prairie in the late afternoon sun that curved red through the haze of the earth, Sunny was humbled by feelings of the divine leading that had orchestrated simple, seemingly mundane happenings, to save the lives of two men. Was this chance? Or was this the hand of God causing greatness to rise up in this prairie lass?

For the first time in years her thoughts were drawn in warm affection to God. She had not quit believing in Him- she was too afraid to do that. But she had certainly quit trusting Him. After all, if she were in charge of the world and possessed ultimate power, she would not allow any innocent person to suffer. Maybe she even hated him for allowing the heartache of death and betrayal she so deeply felt. And now, here on the prairie, she finally quit blaming Him for all the heartache she had endured. The feelings of aloneness dissipated quite mysteriously. The ache of abandonment slid away quietly while a sense of oneness filled her spirit.

And for some inexplicable reason, the feelings of worth and destiny and favor and purpose settled on her soul as gently and as powerfully as the night falls on the prairie. She was loved. She was worthy. She was secure. She felt a sense of destiny that she had never felt before. The joy that washed over her was unlike anything she had ever felt before. The exuberance of feeling loved, and being considered trustworthy enough to save the lives of two men melted the glacial covering of bitterness with which she had encased her heart. She had struggled to make sure her identity and self-worth were not tied to the rescue, but in this moment she realized that her worth predated the rescue. She rescued them because she was a woman of worth rather than becoming a woman of worth because she had rescued the dying men.

And she heard whispered into her spirit with language as crisp as the prairie air, "My favor is upon you. I trusted you with this. I will trust you with more. You are destined for greatness beyond your dreams and this will be revealed as you chase the mysteries of love."

Chapter Thirty-Five

Ambling back across the prairie, Sunny traveled deeper into the mystery of her experience. Did anyone else hear that voice? It sounded so real, but only in her spirit. Could it be God talking to her? Was it a memory triggered by the moment of history? Was that an epiphany? Where did that come from and why?

Sunny puzzled yet peaceful. Somewhat pensive but delighted. She had lived long enough to know that one of the most amazing experiences, almost romantic to her soul, had happened in the broad daylight in the presence of two people she barely knew and without any kind of precursor to trigger it. She felt alive for the first time in her memory. She was so excited about the promise in the voice that she felt like bursting but how do you tell someone that was standing beside you that you just had a mystical experience? Was it God? Did He talk to her? Did He make her feel that way?

What was her greatness? Some would think this notoriety of rescuing the Governor and the subsequent fame would be considered greatness. There was more coming? Destined? Is that the same as fate? Is it something I get to choose or something chosen for me? Mysteries of love? Isn't love just one big mystery anyway? Why mysteries? And what does it mean to chase the mysteries of love? How do you chase love? What does that look like on a daily basis played out in the mundane routine of life?

Lost in her thoughts, Radcliffe and Patrick talked incessantly about their plans for the artists coming to the prairie. Mackenzie had drawn Spook far enough away so as not to tempt his orneriness to bait the artists. He was just itching for a good tussle, verbal or physical. Spook often said, "We cowboys like to settle our scores out th'ar behind the woodshed instead of hidin' behind them sissy skirts of lawyers." Spook had the scars on his knuckles that came from the settling of a few scores like that.

Try as they might, Radcliffe and his publicist could not draw Sunny into any kind of a conversation as they rode back across the prairie. Not only had she not completed the story – Mackenzie came along and filled in the blanks - she seemed very disinterested in the suggestions Radcliffe was making about the artists coming out to the prairie. The chatty, ebullient, and animated Sunny on the way out had morphed into a quiet, serene, contemplative philosopher on the way back. They all sensed something happened on the prairie, but just what, they did not know.

"I don't think we're in Kansas anymore!" Patrick laughed. "So, Sunny, where did Dorothy and Toto live? And just where is the yellow brick road?"

Sunny could hear Spook groaning a deep, guttural objection. She smiled politely. Telling people you were from Kansas just triggered an automatic comment about Dorothy and Toto. And none of them were original. It was always the same. So she replied blandly, "Oh, wherever the Wizard of Oz is currently living."

Radcliffe sensed his opportunity slipping away from him. From the abrupt departure from the crash site to the ensuing quietness of Sunny on the ride back, he sensed something amiss. He was really confused. Sunny had seemed so enthusiastic about the idea and then at the crash site she was telling the story with great intensity, then it was like she turned into a completely different person. She stopped talking mid-sentence and looked very perplexed when he asked her to resume her story. She couldn't even finish it. Didn't seem a bit interested. It was like the person they went out with and the person they came back with were two entirely different people. Panicked, he tried to get Sunny to commit to his ideas.

"You know, Sunny, it would be really a great idea if we could nail a date down for this artistic gathering. We have some shows coming up in the late fall that we would like to have these works ready for and I know there are a lot of artists ready to book a plane ticket out here!"

Sunny was silent. It was as if she did not hear a word he said.

"Yes," chimed in Patrick. "It is the optimal time for us to galvanize the creative geniuses of New York to engage in this salubrious quest of bringing voice to the magnificence of our, er, your exploits!" His face turned ashen with the realization of his Freudian slip.

"What in tarnation is saw-lu-brius and why on God's green earth would we need you'n city slickers gallavantin' on our prairie shoutin' out about how purty you think you are!" Spook spouted even though Mackenzie smacked his leg with a quirt.

"I've done listened to all this h'ar high-falutin-mumbo-jumbo talk that I aim to listen to!" Spook protested. "I done kept my mouth shut for the last three hours and I'm a gonna open the floodgate and flush some of this bull hockey down the crick. We don't need a bunch of four-flushing fancy-pants that don't know how to git milk from a cow without opening a jug to come out her preenin' and struttin' like a banty rooster."

"Mr. Masterson," Radcliffe was getting desperate. "We don't mean to interfere here at all, but we would like you to reconsider this golden opportunity to make the prairie famous and bring a lot of notoriety to Sunny. We know you can talk her into this if you want and it would be of great benefit to her and to Kansas if this would happen."

"This prairie don't need you making it famous!" Spook shouted. "The last time this prairie got famous is when that idjut gov'ner crash landed his bird 'cause he didn't have the sense God gave a goose. Heck, I ain't no pilot but I got sense enough to crawl off my horse and git outta the rain when the thunder clouds gather!"

"Spook," Sunny spoke softly as she sidled up beside him. "It's okay, I'm not going to let the artists come out here."

"What!?" Radcliffe exclaimed. "Why not? Yesterday you were so excited and today you are telling me that you won't let us out here? Are you sure you won't reconsider? After all, we could make you that much more famous and with that fame comes a lot of money. And from the looks of your old house and the run down condition of the ranch, you could use all the money you could get. Gosh, Sunny, you could build you a brand new house and new barns and buy the best horses in the world!"

"Mr. Radcliffe," Sunny's jaw drew taught as she focused her steely gaze on him. "Let me tell you something about that old house and my run down barns. My great-grandfather homesteaded this land back when the Indians still migrated through. They built a sod hut just over the hill from where we were today, fending off brutal winters and a flu epidemic that took out five of their seven kids all in one year. That rock wall that you saw the ivy growing on was put there one rock at a time back in the day when rocks were a lot more plentiful than money and fence wire was too pricey."

She went on, "My grandparents built that old run down house with their bare hands and it took them nearly five years of buying a board or two at a time just to build it. In fact, that old floor creaks and the walls sometimes groan because it took so long to build that it was hard on the lumber. My Daddy was born in that house without a doctor or a nurse or anyone except a little Indian woman who was a midwife."

"My Daddy sat on that worn out old porch swing rocking me in the evenings when I had the measles and my fever soared to 105 and no one knew if I would live. I can still see him leaning against the rail of the porch holding my Momma close to his side when she started getting sick. My Momma died with cancer when I was five in the same room where I now sleep while the good folks from the church in town helped to feed us and take care of our chores because Daddy stayed by her bedside day and night, not wanting to leave the only woman he had ever loved. So it might be run down and dilapidated, but it's made me into the woman I am today and that woman is smart enough to know when she's being played like a two-dollar harmonica. It might not be much compared to your loft in New York City, but its home to me and its mine."

Nudging Starbuck gently with her knees, he broke into a gallop and distanced himself from the rest.

"W'all, young fellers," Spook looked pleased as spoke to the stunned New Yorkers. "I reckon you done went and run that thar little fox into a den you ain't gonna never get her out of now. Ifn' I was you, I'd climb down off them cayuses you're on and skeedaddle right over into that purty truck you rented and head back to the big city where you belong. Me and Mackenzie'll take care of your hosses and don't let the gate hit you in the butt on your way out."

Jasmine scrambled as Starbuck slid to a halt near the hitchin' post. Sunny jumped down and quickly tied the reins to the post and ran into the house. The wooden screen door slammed behind her as she shot past the kitchen into the living room where all the family photos hung silently on the wall like silent sentinels overlooking the passing of time, the making of memories, and the quiet remembrances of faith and family and mid-western values.

Grabbing the fading yellowish photo of her parents that was taken of them on their only vacation ever to the mountains of Colorado, Sunny finally burst into tears that racked her body. Only this time, the tears had a different source. Instead of erupting out of the bitter disappointment of losing them both, the tears came from a place of deep appreciation for all they stood for.

"Momma," she sobbed. "I miss you so much, but I want you to know how grateful I am for all you taught me. I was just a little girl but I can still remember you letting me crawl up beside you on the bed when you were sick and you would read to me and let me read to you.

You were sick for so long, Momma, and I never heard you complain at all."

"Daddy, I know it's been a long time coming, but I have something to say to you that I have never meant before, something I thought I'd never say to you. Daddy, I forgive you. I've been mad at you for a long time and did not know why you didn't love me enough to stay here with me. But you were sick too, Daddy, weren't you? Your mind convinced you of things that weren't true. I thought I hated you for a while, Daddy, and maybe I did. But I forgive you Daddy. And I thank you for loving me while you could while you were here. I won't be mad at you anymore Daddy. I love you and I know you loved me." She collapsed weeping tears of relief, tears of forgiveness, tears of appreciation, tears of history, tears of purpose yet requited.

The mysteries of love.

Chapter Thirty-Six

"Sunny?" Stephanie asked through the crackling telephone line. "Sunny, this is Stephanie Riddell with the Governor's Office. Do you remember me?"

Sunny remember her well. She liked Stephanie when she met her the first time as well as the rest of those around Dane. Just too bad he was such a jerk. She still broiled inside thinking about his empty promise to repair the land.

"Yes, Stephanie, what can I do for you?" Sunny asked.

"I am calling on behalf the Governor concerning the celebration that he and our staff would like to do for you in honor. You are okay with that, aren't you?"

"I'm not so sure." Sunny responded coldly. "I've got a pretty full schedule and am not sure I want to do that."

Stephanie was surprised. Almost every person in the state of Kansas or any other state for that matter would jump at the chance to have their Governor host a party in their honor.

"Well, I'm sure you do have a very full schedule," Stephanie agreed. "I am sure there are lots of media outlets wanting you to be on their shows. But I know the Governor would really like to throw a party in your honor."

"In my honor or his?" Sunny said. "I'm sorry, Stephanie, but I'm going to have to turn you down. I appreciate the offer, but I'm not really interested. Thanks for calling, though."

Stephanie slowly put down the phone and looked across the desk at Dane. "She stood you up!" she said in disbelief. "Can you imagine that? I have never heard of such a thing. I'm shocked."

Dane smiled and eased out of Stephanie's office. He knew better than to go in there, but Stephanie had invited him in and thought it would be great for him to hear the phone call. He had let his guard down. He had let her know that he was romantically interested in Sunny and it had all backfired. He knew better than to let some childhood friend like Stephanie play cupid in his life. He had a state to run and it needed his undivided attention. If she didn't want a party, then she would not get a party.

"Marge, hold all my calls, please," Dane said as the closed the big walnut doors to his office. He moved to the edge of the room and stared out the window at the giant cottonwood tree bustling in the late summer breeze. He felt like he was suddenly transported back to his junior high days when Missy Lamoyne turned him down for his first dance with a girl. A fellow just doesn't get over things like that for a while, especially when it has taken him all the nerve he can muster just to ask the question to begin with.

Well, Miss Sunny Morgan, Dane spoke. *I guess I know how you feel about me. I'm just glad I didn't send you that letter.*

Turning to his desk, Dane sat down and began to work. The proposal was laying on his desk for the restoration project on Sunny's ranch and Dane poured over the details. He had been so excited about sharing this masterful project with her and how they had developed a way to accelerate the restoration process. He had gone to extra lengths and spared no expense in producing a top-drawer plan with the best experts in the state of Kansas. But now to look at the proposal was a bittersweet dilemma. He genuinely wanted to restore the land to pristine condition because he, too, loved the prairie. But he secretly had hoped that it would score him some points with Sunny. He knew she didn't trust him at his word and hoped this would prove his worth.

But if she wouldn't come to a party at the Governor's Mansion in her honor, she most likely was not going to be impressed with anything else he had done. He felt strangely hurt. He was more excited about throwing a party to honor Sunny than he cared to admit.

Reaching for his fountain pen, he signed the work order for the restoration. Regardless of whether she came to a party in her honor or not, restoring the land was the right thing to do and, after all, he had given her his word. That meant a lot to him.

Setting the papers back neatly on his desk ready to be sent out, he unlocked the small drawer in his desk where he kept his most private papers. He was still reeling, like he had been punched in the gut and was still sucking for air. He opened the folder in his drawer to find the letter that he had written to Sunny as well as another writing that bounded out of his pen the night before as the sun set.

There's something about the water lapping gently at my feet
That stirs my soul with wonder and makes me feel complete
There's something about a sunset throwing violets on the lake
That sets my mind a-soaring and breathes my heart awake.
There's something about a summer wind that rustles in the trees
That calms my anxious spirit and drives me to my knees
There's something about the candle glow as the moon rises in the east
That quiets raging fears and gives me gentle peace.
For you're everywhere I've ever been and you're where I long to be.
For there's something about who you are that grows inside of me.
For if I just pause to look –you're already there
And if I just pause to hear –you'll whisper in my ear
You're the words that rhyme my heart as it sings a melody
And you're the something my spirit sighs in peaceful harmony.
There's something about the hungry touch of a hurting friends embrace
That takes an aching, broken heart to a spring of healing grace
There's something about forgiveness' kiss that melts a cold, cold heart

And wipes away the lonely years you've lived so far apart.
There's something about a newborn babe cradled snug against my chest
As the purest love I'll ever feel takes me to a place of rest.
And there's something about a child's smile that laughs away my fears
And reminds me of that sweet safe place I find within your care
For you're everywhere I've ever been and you're where I long to be.
For there's something about who you are that grows inside of me.
For if I just pause to look –you're already there
And if I just pause to hear –you'll whisper in my ear
You're the words that rhyme my heart as it sings a melody
And you're the something my spirit sighs in peaceful harmony.
There's something about an eagles cry as it soars upon the air
That lifts my spirit upward as I climb on heavens' stair
There's something about the prairie wind as it greets another dawn
That gives my spirit the courage and strength to carry on
There's something about an old tin roof as it's splashed with gentle rain
That gives me gentle healing from the past and all its pain
There's something about a loving kiss from a friend that has been true
As all of this reminds me of the faithfulness that's you.
For you're everywhere I've ever been and you're where I long to be.
For there's something about who you are that grows inside of me.
For if I just pause to look –you're already there
And if I just pause to hear –you'll whisper in my ear
You're the words that rhyme my heart as it sings a melody
And you're the something my spirit sighs in peaceful harmony.

Dane heavily sighed, "Well, Sunny, I guess this was all in vain. I wish you well."

"Dane," Marge buzzed him. "Norma is here to see you. Can I send her in?"

Norma and John had been on a much-needed vacation in Aruba and had just returned home. Dane got up to meet her.

"I hear we're not having a party." Norma said sadly. "That really comes as a shocker."

"How did you find out so quickly?" Dane asked. "We just found that out not less than an hour ago."

"Oh," Norma replied. "I saw Stephanie as I was coming in and could tell she was bothered about something so I pried and she told me Sunny had declined the invitation."

"Yeah," Dan tried to slough it off. "We never saw that one coming, but no one can say we didn't try."

"You call that trying?" Norma got right up next to him and stared. "Dane, you have been a politician long enough to know that when things make no sense on the surface, that something behind the scene is going on. Who in the world turns down a party thrown in their honor by the Governor of their state? Even though Sunny is shy, she is not rude and would not turn that down unless she really felt like she had a good solid reason to. You ought to know better than that. She thinks you've done something bad to her."

Dane suddenly felt silly. Of course there was something else going on he wasn't aware of. Why did it take his sister coming in and chiding him like they were little kids again? What on earth could Sunny imagine that he had done to wrong her?

"Dane, I know you better than anyone in the world and I will tell you what I know to be true- you are in love with Sunny. I know it as sure as I live that sweet person captured your heart and right now you can't figure out what to do about it. You're like that little school kid with a crush on the new girl in class and you can't think about anything else but that little prize that captured your heart."

Dane smiled wryly. He knew better than to argue with Norma once she got on her soapbox.

"Furthermore," Norma shook her finger at him. "I bet that you have already written her a poem, a letter, a short story, or something that speaks of your heart issues and you are considering wadding them all up and throwing them all away, aren't you?"

Again, Dane smiled that kind of bashful smile a little kid caught with a valentine hidden in his book.

"Well, don't be a fool!" Norma chided. "When John and I were in Aruba, I had a dream one night and Sunny was out on the prairie in a four walled structure that was covered in lattice. It didn't have a roof on it and it had one door and she was dressed in white sitting on the edge of a white fainting couch. You walked up and called her name but she just sat there. And no sooner had you left than she got up and ran to the door, opened it, then ran outside looking for you, but you were already gone. She went as far as town looking for you, asking people if they knew where you were."

"Dane," Norma encouraged him. "Please go to her! And be patient with her. She's as confused as you are about life and she doesn't have a clue about your affections. Just be patient. If she doesn't answer the first time, know that her heart will be stirred that you even reached out."

Chapter Thirty-Seven

"Chris," Jennifer Conroy whispered to her husband across pine plank floor of master suite in the log cabin. "Come here- you need to hear this."

Chris groaned as he crawled out of bed, exhausted from spending the day with two new clients in the river. Ron Moore called and asked if Chris would guide him and two others, but Chris's rule was only two at a time so he hired another guide to take care of Moore. Chris didn't want to fish with Moore anyway and figured Old Pete McCann would be the best for Moore. Old Pete heard only about half of what anyone said and the other half didn't matter because Pete didn't like people much. He liked fishing but needed some extra money every now and then. But this day had been too much for Pete, too, and he told Chris that the next time he was charging double and working only half the time. Old Pete didn't have many standards but he protected them like a sow grizzly protecting her cubs.

Moore promised to pay Chris double for any trophy trout that his new business associates caught. Moore bragged about a new enterprise he was working on with the two new partners and wanted to bring all of them to the lodge for a three-day fishing trip. "I want all the biscuits that wife of yours can bake!" Moore shouted into the phone when booking the trip.

"That wife of yours," Jennifer overheard, "has a name- it's Jennifer!"

Moore went on about how special this trip was and how big a business deal he was going to land and how much money they would make and he might just offer Chris a part of the deal when he saw him next. Chris let him know that he was doing just fine with the lodge and not interested in any capital ventures.

Moore and his two associates arrived a few weeks later in the evening, blasting in the door with his loud mouth yapping about Jenny's biscuits and trout the size of your leg. The two men with Moore were about as opposite in appearance as they could be. One had long brown hair tied back in a ponytail with shorts and open toed sandals. The other had a short-cropped businessman look and wore a pair of khaki pants and a lime green polo.

Chris handed them the registration cards while Moore was spouting off about the fish he caught and how many times he and the governor of Kansas - his brother-in-law don't you know - had been there fishing.

Chris inadvertently sucked in air as he read the cards:

Daniel Morgan
Cal Morgan

He immediately recognized the last name and realized they were relation to Sunny's brothers. Jenny flashed anger as she looked at the cards. Chris was right; they were Sunny's brothers.

Chris and Jenny were friendly, but reserved as they checked in their guests for the evening, pointed out the amenities of the lodge, shared information about what time breakfast was served and how to prepare for the next day of fishing.

The next two days fishing were the most miserable Chris ever had. Oh, the fishing was fine with trout rising to ants and grasshoppers splatting on the river, but having to fish with Cal and Daniel was a strain more because of Chris's curiosity and suspicion. He thought at first about mentioning that Jenny went to college with Sunny, but something in his gut checked him from doing that. He felt like he needed to act innocent and listen. He would bet a dollar to a donut that whatever Moore's business plans including the Morgan boys had something bad in mind for Sunny.

Chris was his typical, friendly professional fishing guide instructing the Morgan brothers on the ways in which trout feed, understanding the aquatic lifecycles of certain insects like stoneflies and how certain minnow look-a-likes were made with streamers.

Chris nudged the conversation towards Kansas. "I'm assuming since you share the same last name, you are brothers. Where do you guys call home?"

"Well," Cal responded. "We're originally from Kansas but haven't been back to that godforsaken place since our parents died. I live back east in Philadelphia. I own several businesses and have a cottage in Maine and a house on the beach in Florida."

He continued, "Once I left Kansas, I vowed I would never return to small-town living with narrow-minded people, most of whom never traveled outside of their own zip code. I have a sister that still lives there but haven't heard from her in ages. After our parents died, we just didn't have much reason to see each other since we were never close. Daniel and I have kept in touch with each other but my sister holds grudges so long they turn her brittle. It's too bad, too, she had such promise but then she got dumped at the altar by some redneck schmuck and she's holed up in the hills like an old hermit."

Chris was a bit surprised that Cal didn't mention Sunny rescuing the governor. He seemed like the kind of guy that would ride the coattails of anyone for fame and fortune.

Chris complimented Cal on his technique and pointed out a few more places to fish then excused himself to wander downstream to Daniel. He liked Daniel more than Cal; Cal lied to him so that was a strike against him. Chris deliberately dragged his feet in the river to dislodge little insects clinging to the rocks. As they drifted by Daniel, they became food for the waiting trout so his fishing would be sure to improve.

Daniel easily cast the fly rod and successful strikes proved it. Daniel's rod bowed and his line drew tight with an eighteen-inch rainbow. Chris watched as Daniel drew it near and held it gently in the water. Chris took a quick photo then Daniel slid the fish back into the water.

"Nice catch!" Chris said. "Only the second day here and you're already getting the hang of it!"

"You're a good teacher," Daniel responded. "I didn't know a thing about fly fishing until Cal called said we had an expense paid trip to the Rockies for guided fishing. I couldn't pass a deal like that up."

"Are you from back east, too?" Chris asked.

"Good grief, no!" Daniel gasped. "I'm from California. The east coast is too darn cold for me."

"I kind of like the Rockies," Chris replied. "I've lived here all my life so it's home to me. Cal says you guys grew up in Kansas?"

"Yeah, we didn't live at the end of the earth but you could see it from there. Our parents raised us out in the middle of a pasture a hundred miles away from civilization. Could only get one channel on television and two country radio stations. It would get so hot in the summer you could fry crawdad tails on a pickup hood and so cold in the winter polar bears asked for a campfire. I hated Kansas. Still do. Mom and Dad are dead so Kansas doesn't hold anything but bad memories for me."

"Yeah, that would be pretty rough. You ever go back there?"

"The only good memory I have of Kansas is in my rearview mirror. There is no reason on earth I could ever want to go back. I have a sister that still lives there and she's drying up like a shriveled old spinster out on the plains. We never got along very well and after Mom and Dad died, we have no reason to talk. She was always a loner and would rather be with her horse than people."

Another fish straightened out Daniel's fly rod so the conversation ended. Chris was surprised that neither of them mentioned Sunny rescuing the governor. Surely Moore told them that the Governor was at the lodge earlier the day of the crash.

For two days, Chris tried coaxing conversation out of them about their past, but anytime the talk neared the Kansas border, they were hostile towards their sister and their home. There was no way they knew that Dane was a partner in the lodge. Dane protected that secret more than Chris.

"Chris!" Jenny whispered again. "You have to come over here *now!*

Chris groaned under the covers when Jenny whispered to him. Standing in a mountain river all day left him tired and cold so the comforter pulled up around his neck felt good.

Jenny's urgency lumbered Chris over to the grate along the wall. When they built the cabin, Chris strategically placed metal grates that allowed the heat to rise in their bedroom. He closed the grates during the summer and opened them when it cooled.

Jenny was in an old rocking chair with a blanket draped over her lap when she heard Moore and the Morgan brothers talking below unaware that Jenny and, now Chris, were listening in.

"So, the Governor and I were talking about your sister and what a wonderful thing it was to rescue us. Although you've heard that Dane was the worse off, the truth was I was nearly dead and would have certainly died if it were not for your sister's rescue," Moore said.

"Well, it's about time she did something positive with her life," Cal sneered. "She's a loser and hides out on the prairie like an old spinster. She bugs us for money to help her pay for the taxes, but we don't owe a dime. We don't want the ranch and never did, so why should we pay for it?"

"I gotta admit," Daniel said sipping a glass of cabernet. "I am impressed she finally did something with her life. She's dumped a lot of money in that horse; 'Bout time he earned his keep."

Moore chuckled, "So that's what she's spent her money on? It sure isn't the house or the barn! Those places look like they'd burn to the ground in the next prairie fire. Were they always like that?"

"They've looked like that ever since I can remember," Cal complained. "Dad never spent any money on fixing things up. Then again, Dad never had any money. He inherited the place from his folks and, being the only son, got stuck with it. I sometimes wonder if his desire to keep the place in honor of grandma and grandpa Morgan is what drove him to such depression."

Daniel agreed, "I was told Grandpa Morgan didn't think Dad could handle it and wanted to sell it off before he died, but Grandma wouldn't let him. Dumbest mistake they ever made. Now Sunny's as hardheaded as Dad and thinks she needs to keep it alive. But I figure one day we'll get a call and find out she's committed suicide in the same spot as our dear old Daddy!"

"What do you reckon that land's worth?" Moore asked. "My wife's family owns some pasture land in Oklahoma and it's only worth about a five hundred dollars an acre. How many acres do you all own out there?"

"We don't own anything!" Cal retorted. "Sunny inherited that land when our parents died."

"Was there a will?" Moore probed.

"I never saw one but I just assumed Sunny got it all; that was Dad's wish and I thought she signed the deed while he was still alive. And it's not worth anything since it's just old pastureland with a bunch of rocks on it. Can't farm it at all so it's not got much worth."

"Well," Moore already went to the register of deeds and found out that all three of the children's signatures were included. "It might surprise you if you checked around a little bit. You see, I really can't share this in public since the Governor is such a public figure, but he and I are brother-in-laws and we do everything together as a family."

"Dane and I feel badly that we landed on the prairie and all those folks coming out tore the land up. We can tell Sunny's loves the place but doesn't have the resources to fix it up. So we were thinking maybe we could buy the place and then just let her stay there as long as she wanted."

"So have you asked her to sell it to you?" Daniel quizzed Moore. "It seems like she's the one you need to talk to about buying it, not us. If I recall, Dad said the Governor had tried to buy it off of him but Sunny got madder than a hornets nest and wouldn't let him. Pouted like the little brat she always was."

"No, we haven't asked her yet. We thought we'd ask you two if you wanted to sell your parts first, then we could make a deal with Sunny on the rest. We just want to take care of the place. The Governor already owns those big sections to the south of your land so this would just meld into his. He's really just trying to do Sunny a favor."

"But we don't own it!" Cal repeated. "That's all Sunny's decision."

"Oh," Moore lied again. "We just figured the three of you owned equal thirds so thought if we offered you three thousand dollars an acre for you shares, you might be interested."

"Six times what it's worth," Cal almost shouted. "Why would you give that kind of money for that old pasture land."

"Well, truthfully, the place has a lot of meaning to both of us since it was a place of our near death experience. It's become a sacred spot for us and we just want to make sure that we can repair the land and make it a pristine place for the future."

"You mean you're going to make a shrine to your family?" Daniel queried. "That's kind of creepy."

Moore adjusted, "Oh, no, if we buy the ranch, we'll sign a 99 year lease with Sunny to stay there so she never has to worry about paying taxes again. We just think that piece of land is something pretty special to us and we want to preserve not only our history, but the history of the land as well."

"Well, I still don't think we own it, but if I did have a third share in it, I'd be more than happy to sell it to you!" Cal almost leapt out of his chair. "What do you think, Daniel? You will make some cool cash you didn't even know you had!"

"Dad always said if something was too good to be true, it probably was. I'd like to check and see if we even own it before I get too excited." Daniel's eyes darkened with suspicion, "But it appears the Governor and Mr. Moore might know a bit more about it than I do. I reckon that's why we got this free trip to this lodge."

Moore waved his hand with indifference. "No, boys, we just want to do what's best for your sister, what's best for the land, and what's best for the future of the Lonesome Star. But I will ask one particular favor of you. In fact, if this gets out in the wrong hands it will be a deal breaker since of the high-profile nature of the Governor. Here's the deal: no one, and I mean no one except your attorneys and ours will know about his deal. The Governor doesn't want his name mentioned at all and it will be purchased by one of our holding companies that our family has, but is far removed from any association with the Governor. Dane thinks it's best to keep it as clean as possible."

"I have an attorney friend who will get on this as soon as I can make a call tomorrow," Cal said. "I can't wait to tell my girlfriend about this."

"No one is to know," Moore said. "For if this gets out the deal is off. I'm sure you have the most wonderful girlfriend in the world, but if you want this deal to go through, then only your attorney should know until you get the check. Is that understood?"

"Completely," Cal replied gripping Moore's hand in a vigorous shake.

"Do we have a deal, Daniel?" Moore turned to the younger Morgan boy.

"I reckon," Daniel replied more slowly than his brother. "We have a deal."

"Great," Moore said "I will get my, er, Dane and my attorney on this as soon as I can call him in the morning."

As the three men broke towards their rooms for the night, Chris and Jenny sat in the stony silence of their room.

Soon, Jenny whispered, "What shall we do? Shall we call Shauna and have her warn Sunny? Or shall you call the Governor and ask him if Moore's telling the truth? Something tells me the Governor has nothing to do with this."

"I suppose," Chris spoke softly. "We ought to sleep on it. I still have a full day of fishing ahead with those guys. I'm sure they'll want to use our phone so I'll just fix them breakfast in the morning and tell them you're not feeling well. As soon as I clean up and go outside to gear up for the day, they'll want to use our phone. Good thing it's right below the grate. This might be the first and only time I ever tell you to eavesdrop!"

Chapter Thirty-Eight

Spook and Mackenzie rumbled down the drive to the Lonesome Star in anticipation of cooking hamburgers on the grill and watching the autumn sunset. Mackenzie bounded out of the truck and showed Sunny her new ring.

"I'm going to be Mrs. Spook Masterson!" Mackenzie squealed.

Sunny hugged Mackenzie then admired the ring. "Well, Spook Masterson!" she teased, "Where did you get a rock this size? You been telling me for years you ain't nothing but a broken down cowpoke that ain't got even two nickels to rub together!"

"Well, dagnabit," Spook groused. "That feller behind them pretty glass things are at the jewelry store robbed me blind! I had to trade him old Maybelle my .357, my old red truck, and half of my retirement account!"

"Oh, Spook, you old grouch," Mackenzie giggled as she snuggled up to him. "Not one of those things will feel as good on a cold winter night snuggling with you under the covers as I will."

Spook blushed crimson, sputtered something about being horsewhipped and hogtied and took off to the barn.

Mackenzie saw the forlorn look in Sunny's eyes and comforted her. "I won't take him away from you Sunny. Spook and I have long discussions about our future and we've put an offer in on the old

Hinnen place. He'll actually be closer to you than he has been."

"Oh, I am so glad for the both of you!" Sunny recovered. "I'm not worried about you taking him at all. He's been there for me through thick and thin. He's been my anchor through all the dark storms of my life. I'm glad he's found such an incredible woman like you. Spook is a prize. I wish I could find one half his age."

"Spook is a prize. He covers up his savvy with his country slang but he's the most amazing man I've ever met. There is quietness in my heart when I'm with him that I didn't know could exist. When I'm with him, my heart feels like those mornings on the prairie when the cool breeze of spring dusts the dew off the brome and the sun makes all things grow. I've never been more alive."

Mackenzie saw the dark shadows rush across Sunny's eyes and realized she had gone too far, that romantic talk only increased Sunny's loneliness. Mackenzie blurted, "Spook thinks the Governor's interested in you!"

Sunny's eyes grew dark. "I wouldn't give that man the time of day," she almost shouted. "He's like every other man I've known that comes into my life and tears everything up, lies about what he's going to do to make it better, then leaves. I don't care if he's the Governor of Kansas or the President of the United States, he's just another arrogant jerk that thinks he's God's gift to women."

Mackenzie was taken back by the sudden hostility. "I'm sorry, Sunny," she stammered. "I didn't mean to upset you. I just wondered if maybe you had any feelings for him."

"Oh, I have feelings for him alright," Sunny growled. "And if he ever steps foot on my property again he'll understand very clearly just what those feelings are. I've waited to tell a man off for a long time and he'd be a good one to start on. His pretty little secretary called the other day and invited me to a party at the mansion in my honor and it felt so good to tell her no! Jerks like him get anything and any woman they want but he will never get me!"

"Well, I done thought you fillies woulda had the burgers done cooked by now," Spook drawled as the wandered from the barn. "I guess I'll have to start the f'ar myself and grill them cow patties." His interruption calmed Sunny's nerves.

Mackenzie was surprised by the hostility Sunny expressed in her voice and eyes. Sunny had a lifetime of men disappointing her.

"I have more good news than Spook and I getting married, Sunny!" Mackenzie changed the subject. "Spook told me I should tell you the good news for you first, and then tell you about us, but I couldn't help it. I just had to show off my ring!"

"Oh, I noticed it as soon as you got out of the truck!" Sunny exclaimed. "We ladies are pretty sharp about those kind of things." She playfully kicked Spook in the shin.

"So what's my good news?"

"We are about 99% sure we have a book deal. Gordon Chapman has a friend in the publishing industry and they have one of the best ghostwriters around who thinks this is a terrific book. She and Gordon presented a proposal to Briarcliff Publishers and they are going to ink the deal on Monday!"

"A ghostwriter?" Sunny queried. "I'll have to have someone tail me around and ask me questions all the time and pry into my personal life? If it's a man, I'm not interested."

"Oh, no!" Mackenzie exclaimed. "It is a woman! In fact, I met her once in N.Y. and I really liked her. I think you will, too, but it will be your decision. If you want to sign the contract on Monday, then you basically would interview as many writers as you wanted until you found one you liked."

The thought of someone invading Sunny's private life mortified her. The last thing she wanted was someone telling all about her personal troubles.

"I don't know," Sunny started. "I know we've talked about this, but now that it's close to being real, I'm not sure I want anyone around. I really like it out here by myself with no one but Spook bothering me."

"W'all, Missy," Spook said with a hurt look in his eyes. "If'n I'm that much of a bother to you I guess I'll just hang out down at the co-op more."

"Oh, quit it," Sunny teased him again. "You know I was just kidding. But I really do like the ranch getting back to normal without people around. I am so happy I decided not to let those artists come out. I just want to be alone."

"Well, Sunny," Mackenzie set her up. "How much is it worth to you to put up with someone around for a little bit? Just how much is your isolation worth to you?"

Sunny looked puzzled. "I'm not sure what you mean. Are you talking about how much money isolation is worth?"

"Yes!" Mackenzie shrieked. "They are going to offer you five-hundred-thousand-dollars for the rights to a book and a movie."

Sunny was stunned. Numbers like five-hundred-thousand-dollars were dangled but she was so suspicious she had given up that anything like that would ever happen.

"Five-hundred-thousand-dollars?" Sunny said slowly, in disbelief. "Why would anyone give me that kind of money?"

"It's really quite simple, Sunny, because they will make a hundred times that amount off of your story."

Sunny sat down in the faded web of the old aluminum framed lawn chair and stared across the prairie. Her mind raced with all the things she could do for the ranch. New fences. Put a new corral up at the barn. Paint the house and put some decent windows in that didn't let the cold in. Put in a furnace and an air conditioner. Fix the land the crash tore up. Buy her brothers out.

The rest of the evening was a blur. Sunny was numb as the old screen door battered shut behind her. She sat down at the old yellow laminate kitchen table piled high with bills and rubbed her thumb mindlessly on an old knife gouge on the surface.

Five-hundred-thousand-dollars. She could not get her mind around that number. The most she ever had at one time in the bank was twenty-five thousand, but a drought drove the cattle prices down and the hay prices up so that money disappeared quickly.

The old stairs creaked as she made her way up to her bedroom. She drew the covers over her as Jasmine snuggled in to her side. She lay there staring at the crack in the ceiling illuminated with the soft blue glow of the full moon bouncing off the prairie. Cottonwood leaves fluttered just outside her window. Falling to the ground to welcome fall, they whispered her to sleep.

At first, Sunny felt the tug of a little hands pulling at her leg and she looked down into the bright eyes of a little girl with ebony skin and ivory teeth. Suddenly, dozens of small children clamored around her laughing and asking her to play on the red dirt of a foreign soil. Sunny lifted her gaze and saw an old cream and red-dirt colored cinder block building with large windows with open-air iron grid frames sitting with several other similar buildings in clearing surrounded by massive trees. Beyond the trees were lion-colored grasses of a savannah. Noisy school children voices echoed in the buildings as students sat at their simple metal desks.

Several children gathered under the shade of a baobab tree jostling for the position near a metal wheel rim off an old truck. One child grabbed the head of a cast metal hoe that hung on a wire and began striking the rim with the hoe. Sunny thought it must be the school bell calling all the children to school. The hollow gong rang more loudly than she expected and around the perimeter of the buildings adults began to emerge. Men with dark blue pants and snow-white shirts with thin black ties and horn-rimmed glasses carried well-worn leather satchels. Ladies with dark blue skirts and snow-white blouses marched beside them as each one found their way to their classroom. The children were calling the teachers to school!

No teacher entered the building at the far end where acacia trees huddled around as if to lend their beauty to this building in particular. Little faces peered through the metal grid work of the windows.

"Mwalimu," the children chanted. "Mwalimu."

Sunny felt heat of the African sun warm her face. She bent down to pick up one of the little girls and, when she did, was surprised when the little girl licked her face.

"Jasmine!" Sunny swatted the cat licking her face. "Leave me alone and let me sleep some more." Her eyes slowly opened to the sun peeking in the window.

Reaching for her journal on the nightstand, Sunny yawned and sat up in bed. She wrote dreams down quickly that seemed to have meaning. If she let time go, she would forget all about them. She wrote down a word she never heard before.

"Mwalimu," she wrote. "I wonder if that is even a word?" She described her dream in detail and later would see if that was even a word or just some weird thing that happened in a dream.

She quickly thought of the money that Mackenzie had mentioned last night. What would she do with that kind of money? She saw Rose McKinley in town win a big jackpot from the Kansas lottery and went on a buying spree for her and all of her family and friends. It wasn't more than two years and Rose was out of money, her family had quit talking to her and most of her friends disappeared. Money could sure ruin folks. But it would be nice not to have to worry about things like taxes and a cow getting killed by lightning or how to pay for all the things the crash tore up.

She scooted Jasmine off the bed, slipped into her work clothes and unraveled her tussled hair in the faded mirror of the antique dresser. She was surprised to see the sadness in her own eyes. "I'm getting old right before my very eyes. Something must be wrong with me. I was told I'm going to have more money than I ever dreamed of and I look like I've been dragged across the prairie by a wild bull."

She made her way downstairs and out to the barn. Starbuck whinnied affectionately as the rusted hinges of the barn door creaked in the early light of dawn. He nuzzled Sunny as she drew near, throwing her arms around his neck and caressing his mane.

"Starbuck, my friend," Sunny wept into his thickening coat. "I wish all of this would go away. I wish the Governor had never crashed here. I wish the prairie looked as pretty as it did before the crash. I wish that people like Radcliff would leave me along. I wish I could have someone like Spook does. Five-hundred-thousand-dollars will buy us a lot of things. Except love."

Chapter Thirty-Nine

"Ladies and gentlemen, I present to you the Governor of our great state of Kansas, Governor Dane Richards!"

Dane walked to the podium with camera flashes and a spotlight beading a thin line of sweat. He unfolded his speech from his pocket—which event was this? Who was he campaigning for? What bill was he trying to convince people was the best?

Once on the stage and the spotlight in his face, he remembered why he got into politics to begin with: he wanted to effect change. He saw the bumbling policies of self-serving politicos and knew his integrity would withstand the rigors and temptations of holding such a prestigious office. Although he loved the job, he was not disappointed that he was at the end of his second term and there was no possibility of re-election. His party approached him about a run for the presidency, but he didn't feel the time was right nor did he have the passion required. He knew others to run for the Presidency, but it was an all-consuming, cutthroat mudslinging circus he didn't want to buy tickets for. Although idealists encouraged running a positive campaign, election after election gave evidence that negative smear campaigns simply work. The masses love hateful mudslinging. Ancient Romans loved to watch the lions devour people; something in humanity has a sick desire to destroy people.

He finished his speech to thunderous applause and later milled around the reception meeting people and telling the story of the crash again. His popularity was at an all-time high: however, his passion for politics and public life faded with each bill signed, each high level meeting, and each battle with the legislature.

Making his way around the room, he thanked people for asking about his health and recovery. As he visited with people, an elegant lady sparkling from her diamonds approached him and asked for a brief moment of his time. Excusing himself, he stepped away from the crowd.

"Governor," she barely spoke loud enough for him to hear. "My name is Lucy Sinclair and I am married to Judge Malloy Sinclair in Oklahoma City. Could I visit with you privately?"

"Certainly," Dane led her to a private room adjacent to the hall.

"Governor Richards, I have a story to tell you that I think you need to hear that involves that cowgirl that rescued you and your brother-in-law, Mr. Moore."

"You have my undivided attention," Dane said. "I've heard of your husband- a fine man. Isn't he some kind of relation to Ron's wife?"

"Yes," Lucy replied. "They are cousins. Will you promise me that you will never tell anyone what I'm about to tell you? The information I'm about to share could destroy a lot of lives if you're not careful. But I tell you so even more lives won't be destroyed."

Dane responded with rapt attention. "I promise."

Several years ago, about a year after I married Malloy, we decided to separate because it just wasn't working out. I went to a party one night and had too much to drink. You're brother-in-law, Ron, was at the party, too. His wife was there - an unpleasant person who constantly berated him - and she left in a huff and, well, one thing led to another and nine months later I had Ron's baby."

Dane was stunned. Moore's admission during the final descent that he had been unfaithful startled Dane, but Dane had no idea that Moore was the father of another child.

"Does Moore know?" Dane asked.

"Yes," she replied. "I was so scared after we had our affair that I immediately went to Malloy's house and seduced him. I wasn't on any contraception and was afraid that I might get pregnant. I wasn't sure if Malloy and I would make it, but I was afraid if I got pregnant during that time, it would indicate I had an affair."

"So how do you know it's Moore's child?" Dane asked.

"I had a private paternity test ran to find out. I just had to know myself who Samuel's father was. I told Mr. Moore because I felt he had a right to know, but I swore him to secrecy. There are only three people who know about it; me, Mr. Moore, my sister, and, now, you."

She went on. "He knew Mrs. Moore would divorce him if she ever found out. Malloy and I got back together and, when he found out I was pregnant he assumed it was his baby and he became a changed man. He was so excited to be a dad and our marriage has been marvelous ever since."

"So why are you telling me this?" Dane asked.

"There is a conversation that you need to know about. It is in regards to a business deal with Mr. Moore and the brothers of that cowgirl that rescued you. I'm here to tell you of the deal."

"Business deal?" Dane was surprised. "What kind of business deal?"

"Mr. Moore is working on a deal to purchase that ranch and turn it into some kind of tourist destination dude ranch that ties in with some kind of a book and movie deal he is working on. He's approached Miss Morgan's two brothers who have already agreed to sell him their portion."

Dane was stunned. "I appreciate this information more than you know. But I am still perplexed. You run incredible risk in giving me this information and I am uncertain why you would even tell me."

"It's really quite simple, Governor Richards." Lucy said with a mischievous smile. "I'm doing this as a favor to my sister. I think you know her."

"My apologies, ma'am, but I'm at a disadvantage. Who is the sister to whom you refer?"

"Jennifer Conroy. She and Chris are your partners in the Fishing Lodge."

"Mrs. Sinclair," Dane grabbed her hand and shook it warmly. "I promise that your secret will go with me to the grave. I appreciate knowing this more than you could ever realize."

Dane continued to visit with others but he was distracted. A million scenarios rushed through his mind to keep Moore from continuing on with his greedy efforts. He was surprised that Ron and Cheryl weren't at the event that evening because that was the type of event they always attended. Now it made sense.

Dane was reminded of Norma's words. "It's your turn to rescue Sunny." It was his turn. She had no idea that her brothers were, literally, selling the ranch out from under her. What were they getting an acre? Were they even owners? Every time he visited with Sunny's Dad before he died, he left with the impression that Sunny would get it all that her brothers weren't interested. Had he left a will? Should he drive out to the ranch to warn her? What if she wanted to sell?

Dane had to be cautious; he couldn't call up the courthouse to see who was on the deed. He couldn't get his attorneys on it without raising suspicion. He could ask Norma or Stephanie, but it put them in an awkward position. If the press knew he was prying, they would pry, too.

Dane fumed on the ride back to Cedar Manor. He had tolerated Moore for Debbie's sake for the last time. The sniveling, conniving, liar had to be stopped. Dane made a promise to Debbie's father, but Moore had crossed the line and cashed all the checks on any relational equity he had on Debbie's account. As he crawled into bed, he spoke to the photo of Debbie. *Debbie, my love, I know you will understand, but this is the last straw. Moore has crossed a line and I will do everything in my power to stop him.*

As he walked into the office the next morning, Marge handed him the list of his appointments for the day. He scanned over the list to see which ones he could postpone. "Marge," he buzzed from his office. "Can you reschedule all my appointments up until 10 o'clock?"

"Ron," Dane said into the phone. "I know you're in the Capitol today working on that farm legislation, can you stop by for a quick chat. I've got something I'd like to run by you."

"Sure!" Moore exclaimed. He loved personal calls to the Governor's Office and would be bragging about it all morning. "Would 8:45 work? We don't meet until 9:30."

"Yes," Dane replied. "8:45 would be great. I'll see you in a few minutes."

Dane looked out the window at the cottonwood and oak trees dropping leaves on the Capitol lawn.

"Marge," Dane buzzed her again. "Please cancel all my appointments today and reschedule them tomorrow."

"Certainly, Governor," Marge replied. "Is everything okay? Is there anything else I can do for you?"

"Yes," Dane said. "Call Norma and have her meet me at Cedar Manor at 10:00. Tell her to bring get my Dad to meet her there with his pickup. I'll need to borrow his truck and she'll need to take him home."

"Yes, Governor," Marge said. "Headed out for a day trip are we?"

"Marge," Dane replied. "That is none of your business."

"Yes, Sir," Marge said. "It is none of my business, but could you stop along the way in Teterville and get me some of Maude Johnson's sand plum jelly? I hear it's to die for."

Dane resumed looking out the window. This was his chance! He could go out and warn Sunny and help protect her from losing the ranch. But first he had to deal with Moore.

"Governor," Marge said with disgust dripping from her voice. "Mr. Moore is here to see you."

The door swung open and Dane invited Moore in. Although Moore was excited to be there, he knew that Dane was unhappy with him so he was justifiably cautious.

"Have a seat, Ron." Dane motioned to the leather chair in front of the desk. Dane sat in his big leather chair and looked across the desk at Moore. Dane understood the intimidating effect of the position.

"I ran across an old friend of yours last night," Dane began as Moore fidgeted in his chair. "A lady by the name of Lucy Sinclair. Do you know her?"

Moore squirmed in his chair as if a dentist was pulling a tooth without Novocain, "Well, as a matter of fact she's some kind of relation to Cheryl. I'm not sure how; we never see her except at a rare family reunion."

"Ron," Dane stood up and placed his hands firmly on the desk and leaned over. "Do the names Daniel and Cal Morgan mean anything to you?"

Moore began stammering and admitted to knowing they were Sunny's brothers but denied knowing them personally.

"Does the name Samuel Sinclair mean anything to you?" Dane glared.

Moore grew white and began to shake.

"Let me tell you how this plays out from here on out just so you understand me as clearly as possible."

Moore began to protest but Dane held his hand up to stop him.

"I've been trying to treat you like family but it is abundantly obvious that you are nothing but a liar. You have gone behind my back numerous times and I simply will not turn my head away anymore. I understand you're trying to buy the Lonesome Star. If you do that, I will force you out of the committees that you serve on because of my connection and will take over your part of the company. And I will make it perfectly clear behind the scenes that you no longer represent my views and interests. In effect, your power in this city has been because of me. Your Dad had enough sense to put conditions in my contract that I could control all the holdings if you started acting like a total idiot. I'll take a lot of power away from you if you go through with this deal on the ranch.

Furthermore," Dane handed Moore a paper. "I'd like to you sign this acknowledging that you are giving up any pursuit of purchasing the Lonesome Star. Please sign it, leave my office and drop this whole matter, and you can keep you position and power."

Moore wadded up the paper and threw it across the room then lunged out of his chair towards Dane. In his rage the veins popped on his neck and forehead like fat night crawlers writhing on a sidewalk as he spit. "You can't do this! I'll call my lawyers and drag you through every slime-hole and sewer pit I can find. We'll ruin you, you self-righteous bastard!"

Dane stood up ready for Moore to take a swing. Marge had security waiting just outside the door in case she heard a scuffle because Moore reacted the way Dane predicted. Dane wanted nothing more than to take this fight out behind the woodshed and settle it the old fashioned way but he had an office to protect, a position to dignify.

"Ron," Dane stood three inches taller and looked down on Moore as he spoke. "You always disappoint, but never surprise. You are acting the way any spoiled brat would. Your parents and Debbie would be so ashamed of you."

"You leave them out of this!" Moore screamed. "We were a perfectly happy family until you came along and ruined it. I've spent the last fifteen years listening to 'Dane this and Dane that' like you're some sort of god that we all have to bow down and worship. You fooled Dad and you fooled Debbie, but you can't fool me. I have been collecting dirt on you for all of these years and now I'm going to make it public."

Dane's smile was almost a smirk. Moore took a swing but Dane and anticipated it and the punch swung wildly through the air causing Moore to lose his balance and stumble. "I'll get you for this," Moore shrieked. "Come on and fight me you chicken." Moore poised like a boxer ready to fight.

Dane looked down at his watch and smiled again; it was 9:15. He had already delivered the knockout punch earlier that morning and

Moore was too stupid to know it. Dane met with his attorneys the day before and at this very moment they were at the courthouse with specific instructions; if you don't hear from me by 9:00, file the lawsuit against Moore stripping him of any holdings in the company.

"I'll not disgrace the honor of your family by trading blows like a barroom drunk." Dane sat back down on the edge of the desk. "You've lost, Ron, you've blown the last chance for dignity and honor that I'm willing to give you. The best gift that I can give you is not the power and position that comes with money and politics, but the opportunity to do what is noble and decent. Instead, you've repeatedly chosen a path of duplicity and dishonesty."

Moore's defiance was so palpable it was like the room was crawling the rattlesnake as he hissed. "You will eat those words Mr. Grand and Mighty Governor of the State of Kansas. I will bring you down so far you'll be living in the gutter with that cowgirl whore."

Dane's face chiseled into granite. "Mr. Moore, please find the door and excuse yourself. Security will escort you out of the building. You will not be allowed back inside."

Chapter Forty

"Sunny," Mackenzie said over the static on the phone. "I hope you're not disappointed, but they didn't offer the five-hundred-thousand-dollars like we hoped they would."

"Oh, that's okay," Sunny said. "I didn't have any money to start with so not having any now isn't going to change much. Besides, my Daddy used to quote a proverb that said money that comes quick brings destruction with it. I've seen enough shows about people winning the lottery then totally ruining their lives. But it would be nice to have some money to fix some fences and paint the barn."

"Well, you had better sit down Miss Sunny Morgan because they didn't offer you five-hundred-thousand-dollars, they offered you a million dollars."

Sunny sat down on the old wooden stairs that creaked with her weight so stunned she could barely breathe.

"One million dollars?" Sunny said. "I can't believe it."

"Aren't you excited?" Mackenzie asked puzzled. "I thought you'd be screaming?"

"Oh, I'm very excited!" Sunny perked back up. "But I'm also really scared. If people know I have money, there'll be crawling out of the woodwork like rats."

"Well," Mackenzie inserted. "Spook and I were talking about this and we think the first thing you need to do today is to go see a financial advisor and an attorney. You can set that money up, Sunny, to where it's really out of reach yet making you more money. It all starts with a good financial planner, but you also need an attorney to figure out what you want to do with your brothers and the ranch."

"Well, they each own 1/3ʳᵈ just like I do, but they haven't been helping to pay the taxes or anything. I'd like to buy them out."

"Then get an attorney and call your brothers today with an offer. Once this gets out, there will be a bunch of greedy people, including your brothers, who will try to take you for all your worth. Tell them Spook fell into some money from marrying a rich wife and he is going to loan you the money to buy them out. That way it won't look suspicious like you've fallen into a lot of money. I've got the numbers of a couple of people who will help you a lot. They're both lady friends of mine and are as smart as they come."

Sunny hung up the phone and put fresh clothes on to go into town. She decided, at the last minute, to take Spook. He made things feel better. She told him of the ruse of calling her brothers and pretending like he had the money to loan her and buy them out.

"Hot dang!" Spook shouted in the phone. "I been wanting to calf-rope and hog-tie them coyotes ever since they done went off and left you on the ranch. It'll be my pleasure to help you smoke them out of their den."

"Sonya Hutchinson," Mackenzie met them at the attorney's office. "I'd like you to meet a couple of friends of mine. This is Sunny Morgan and Spook Masterson."

"Sunny," Sonya hugged her. "It is such a pleasure to meet you! I've been watching all of this unfold and it is just amazing. And Spook! Congratulations on your upcoming wedding! Mackenzie is a great find for you."

Spook settled uncomfortably in the big leather chair as Mackenzie explained the situation to Sonya. Sonya wrote notes and occasionally asked questions about the particulars.

"So, let me understand this," Sonya said to Sunny. "You want to call your brothers and make them an offer on their part of the land? What is the current value of pastureland? Five hundred an acre?"

"Yeah," Sunny said. "That sounds about right."

"So is that what you want to offer? What are you willing to go up to?"

"Well, right now I don't even have any money so until I get that money I can't really do anything anyway." Sunny said, slumping in her chair.

"Well, there are several ways we can do this, Sunny, but if you want this done today, we can make a call and get a contract on it that gives you a certain period of time to come up with the money."

"W'all," Spook groaned. "But too much time would give dem fellers time to thing up something to put a monkey wrench in the machine. What would happen if you guaranteed we could get that money to them right this here very day if they agree? Sunny, we'll loan you the money until the check comes."

"Well, that settles it, "Sonya put her pen down. "We'll make an offer that has to have an immediate acceptance with a guarantee we will have the money to them in two hours."

Sunny picked up the handset and dialed the number. The speakerphone was on so all could hear.

"Hello?" Cal answered.

"Hi Cal," Sunny twirled her hair as she talked. "This is Sunny. How are you?"

"I'm good, Sunny. Long time, no talk to," he said. "What gives me the pleasure of this call so early in the morning?"

"Well," Sunny stammered. "I – I- uh, I'd like to make you an offer for your part of the ranch."

"Really?" queried Cal. "You get a book deal did you?"

Sunny ignored the bait. "Spook has offered to loan me the money to purchase your share of the ranch. He's listening in. And to prove we mean it, we have an attorney listening in ready to send you a contract and you can have the money by noon today."

"Hi Spook," Cal said. "How's the old cowpoke doing today."

"Better than most," Spook spit.

"So what kind of offer are you two making to me?"

"Well," Sunny hesitated. "I was thinking about $600 an acre. That's what pasture land is going for around here now."

"Nah," Cal said arrogantly. "I kind of like that old piece of land and want to keep it. It's going to take a lot more money than that to buy me out."

"How much?" Sunny sat up rigidly, trying to stifle her anger.

"Five thousand dollars an acre," Cal laughed.

"Five thousand dollars an acre," Sunny shrieked. "That's robbery! You've never cared for the land before."

"Well, I already have an offer for three thousand so if you want it, you can have it for five thousand."

Sunny looked angry and helpless. Who had offered him three thousand? The Governor? That would be like that smarmy jerk to buy it out from underneath her.

"Cal," Spook drawled, "If'n I was to give you thirty-two-hundred-dollars an acre, would you take it right now and put your John Hancock on the paper. I can get you that money to you now but you have to agree right now."

"Cal," Sonya interrupted. "This is Sonya Hutchinson, an attorney for Miss Morgan. If you will agree to this immediately, do you have a witness there that can listen in to this conversation? A verbal agreement over the phone as long as you have a witness will suffice and we will begin the transfer the money immediately. We will need your bank account number."

"Spook," Sunny whispered. "That's too much money! I love the ranch but this feels like extortion. I'm not sure I want to live on it if I have to pay that much an acre. Our parents would be so ashamed of us."

Sunny wheeled and blurted to Sonya. "Put the speaker phone back on. Cal, you can sell your portion to whomever you want, but there is no way on God's green earth that I'm paying you or Daniel thirty-two-hundred-dollars an acre for pastureland. Mom and Dad would be just as ashamed of me as they would of you for a trick like this. I won't do it."

Sonya concluded the call as Sunny sat fuming. Sunny thanked her then began a conversation about managing the money in such a way that it didn't become a temptation or a hindrance to Sunny.

"W'all, Miss Sunshine," Spook said. "I know thirty-two-hundred an acre is way too much money, but don't you want to buy it? You're a millionaire now and that ain't nothin' but chump change."

"Spook," Sunny replied. "It's quite simple. I love the ranch, but what I love most about the ranch is that it holds the dreams that my Momma and Daddy once had. I stay there because I love the prairie and I love the ranch, but I also do it to honor my parents. I have to realize that what used to be no longer is and it would be a dishonor to our parents for me to allow Cal and Daniel to bully me into giving them an obscene price. I would never feel good on the prairie again if I had to pay that outrageous sum."

"I'd rather buy another ranch somewhere else that is just mine and not full of the horrible memories of the Lonesome Star. I want to live on a different prairie and listen to new voices whisper to me."

As simple as that, Sunny welcomed the realization that this change in her life was good, not for the money that she would make, but the awareness that she was now empowered and free to make decisions that were best for her and not bound by trying to keep the dreams of her parents alive.

"Sonya," Sunny changed the subject. "I need your help with this money."

"There are a variety of ways to tie up the money so it is not easy to get at." Sonya's appreciation of the character and quality of Sunny increased. "It just depends on what you want to do with it and how long you want it to be tied up. I can help with the particulars of protecting yourself and the ranch considering that your two brothers might be selling out, but you really need a financial advisor to help with long-term strategies."

"What about a foundation? Like a non-profit? Or one that means to help others? Do you know anything about that?" Sunny asked.

"Certainly," Sonya had a puzzled look on her face just like Spook and Mackenzie had on theirs. "Just what kind of work are you wanting to do?"

"I keep having dreams about poor children in other countries. I wake up and its almost like I'm there with the children. I love that ranch and I love being alone, but I'm wondering if that ranch is keeping me from being who I'm supposed to be. I wonder if I'm just hiding and it's time to let go. I wonder if my dreams are telling me to move on. Something inside keeps telling me I'm supposed to go to Africa."

All four sat in silence at this turn of events. Just a few minutes before, Sunny was willing to pay outrageous amounts of money to keep the ranch and now she was talking about Africa. Sunny was as surprised as they were at what she said.

Sonya broke the silence, "Sunny, I think that is a marvelous idea. I've been to Africa several times and, if I didn't have a profession and a family, I'd probably move there myself. I'd love to help you set up a foundation. In fact, I know a lot of people who'd like to be involved with you in whatever you want to do."

"W'all, I'll be a gol-danged cow what just got zapped by a cattle prod." Spook said. "I would never once have thot your purty little head was full of such crazy idears as moving to Africa."

"Sunny," Mackenzie said slowly. "It seems like a great opportunity to talk about a lot of things. I think we need to sit down and make a plan, not only about what you do with the ranch now that your brothers want to sell their part, but about what you want to do with Africa. They have cows and horses in Africa, right? Maybe I can get this hard-headed old cowpoke here to join me and we'll go to Africa with you sometime."

"W'all, I suppose I might consider going as long you two are going. God knows purty little fillies like you two need someone a watchin' over you so you don't get dragged into the bush by a lion or a tiger. Neither one of ya have the sense God gave a goose when it comes to danger so I'll take ol Maybelle with me and shoot the first varmint that moves toward ya."

Sunny settled. "That sounds like a deal, Spook. You've been taking care of me since I was a little girl and I'd hate for you to stop now."

Chapter Forty-One

Sunny turned down the drive, stunned by the day's events. She had no idea when the day started that by the end of it she would be talking about moving to Africa. Where did that come from? What had those dreams been about? Was she just crazy from being alone so long on the ranch? Had the bizarre happenings since the crash turned her into a lunatic?

She noticed a strange truck sitting in her drive. She recognized all of the vehicles that belonged around the area, but she had never seen this one. Strange vehicles always made her a bit nervous. As she drew closer, she saw a man leaning on the hood of the truck, looking down the lane at her as she pulled up.

Good grief, well this is a fine way to end the day. The last person I want to talk to today is Mr. Governor of the Fine State of Kansas. He probably is out here to gloat about buying my brothers out. Well, he and them can have this ranch. I'm done with it.

He smiled as she drew near but she kept driving past and up to the barn. She had feed sacks to get out of the back of her truck and the sun wasn't too far from setting. If he wanted to talk to her, he could walk out to the barn.

She shut the truck off and grabbed the first sack of feed for Starbuck. He did like his oats and molasses and whinnied softly as she dumped the feed into the big metal barrel. Starbuck shifted his gaze to the open door where Dane was carrying a sack of feed as well. Sunny felt her face blush- silhouetted against the door, with tight jeans and the short sleeve shirt revealed his well-toned body. His thick black hair with sprinkles of gray near his sideburns was rim-lit with the setting sun. He was amazingly handsome.

"Looks like you could use a little help," Dane said.

"Been doing it for years by myself," Sunny retorted. "You're welcome to help if you want, but I don't need it. I can manage it all by myself just fine."

Dane could tell he offended her again. He had always been at ease around women and was not accustomed to such curt behavior.

"I'm sure you can," Dane replied. "I thought I'd just be neighborly and give you a hand."

"So are we neighbors or do you own part of the ranch now?" Sunny put her hands on her hips ready to fight.

"What do you mean?" Dane asked. "How could I own part of the ranch?"

"Well, someone's offered my brothers six times what it's worth to buy them out and you been pestering my Daddy for years so I figure it's you. So is that the deal? You're going to wait and fix it up after you buy it? You lied to me once when you told me you'd fix it up and you never did!"

Dane was reeling, "I never lied to you! I have been working on plans to fix it up and fund it with my own money. I tried to send someone out to talk to you about it, but you wouldn't listen to them."

"Moore?" Sunny shouted. "Moore told me you weren't going to do a darn thing about it since you were going to have to pay for it out of your own pocket. Men like you have lied to me to for so long I'm just used to it. So don't try to tell me now that you want to fix it up. You are the high and mighty Governor of the Great State of Kansas and you think you can do whatever you darn well please, but this is one dame that isn't going to buy your good looking smile and sweet-as-pie charm. You're a liar just like every other man I've met except Spook Masterson.

"I didn't send Moore," Dane defended himself. "I had a private firm send you some letters and try to come out. I even had a helicopter fly over to take photos so we could assess the damage."

"Oh, sure," Sunny continued fuming and walked close to Dane. "So it's been months now since you two idiots crashed your plane on my land and it's been nothing but a heartache for me. You're the big hero Governor who has used the crash to move up in the polls and you think you can come out here and push me around. You tried for years to push my Daddy around and you're one of the reasons he killed himself was because of arrogant rich men like you that treated him like crap. You people with all kinds of money think you own anyone and everything and you can get what you want just by offering money. Well, I don't need your damn money and I can't be bought."

Sunny was surprised at the way she talked to him. She had never talked to anyone like this, but it felt so good she couldn't help it. The volcano of anger erupted and it felt good for the lava to flow.

"You know what makes guys like you so hard to stomach for folks like me? You have never had anything go wrong, have grown up with great, rich parents that gave you everything you wanted and spoiled you rotten. You've combed your hair and flexed your muscles and got any girl you wanted to spread their legs for you. You wrote big checks and played politics so well you get everything you want and then you have the gall to come out here to the ranch and think you can do whatever you damn well please. Well, if you want this damn ranch, you can have it. I'm sick of you, I'm sick of my brothers, I'm sick of every man I've ever met so you and my brothers can have this place and make your own dude ranch and turn it into a playground for rich idiots for all I care. Now get out before I call Spook and have him shoot you!" She began to turn back to the truck for more grain.

Dane reached out to touch her arm. "Sunny, you have it all wrong."

Suddenly she wheeled and uncoiled like a tightly wound spring and slapped with full force across the face. She hit him so hard her hands stung beneath her leather gloves and it sent him reeling into the stall. Starbuck lunged to the side.

"I have it wrong?" Sunny shouted. "How could I have it wrong? You've been bugging my Dad for years to sell you this place. You crash your plane on my land with your idiot brother-in-law who pissed and puked all over himself and then got every Tom, Dick, and Harry with four-wheel drives to tear the place up. You promise me you're going to fix it then you send Moore out to tell me you're not going to fix it after all but then he's cooked up some deal with a Hollywood movie guy to trick me into giving up the rights to the story. Then you have your secretary invite me to a party supposedly in my honor just so you can get your picture in the paper again. Then I find out today that you offered my brothers five times what the land is worth so you can buy their share and force me out. Tell me, oh Great Governor of the State of Kansas, just exactly what did I get wrong? Starbuck and me should have just let you idiots die out on the prairie. Had I known all of this was going to happen, we would have headed back to the ranch and called in that fat sheriff. You both would have been dead by the time he found you and I would have been a lot better off."

The left side of Dane's face was red and a welt started to form. He was speechless, as Sunny stood toe-to-toe with him angrier than any protestor he had ever seen. He didn't know where to begin; he had never seen a woman with such fury.

"I, uh, well, I don't know where to begin," Dane stammered.

"Well, I don't want to hear anything that you have to say. You are a liar just like every other man I've known so please just leave now. I can't call the sheriff on you because that fat little weasel is probably your friend so it's just Starbuck and me. He saved your life once, but he'd be more than happy if I roped you and dragged you kicking and screaming down the driveway so please just go."

"Okay," Dane said. "I'll go. I promise, I'll never come back. Next week, there will be a man driving an Eco-Prairies truck that will show up with a contract that guarantees every inch of the land will be restored and personally paid for by me. His name is Dale Zimmerman and I'd encourage you to take the contract to your lawyer to have he or she look at it. And it was Moore that offered to buy your brothers out, not me."

He followed Sunny out to the back of the truck as the sunset cast a soft yellow glow against her face. Behind her, a full harvest moon cast a soft blue light on the prairie rimmed her auburn hair. Her beauty transfixed him.

"Sunny," Dane said. Would you please turn and look at me? I have one more thing to say before I go."

Sunny turned around with her hands on her hips. "Well, it better be good because as far as I'm concerned you're like every other politician; we can tell when you're lying because your lips are moving."

"Although you won't believe me, I never have lied to you." Dane said as Sunny rolled her eyes.

"And of all things I've said," Dane went on. "This is the most true; I am in love with you and will do everything I can to prove that to you."

Her eyes burned with confusion like the spring fires that sweep thru the hills.

Dane locked his eyes on her dark anger. His presence in her life was like a blast of oxygen on a smoldering flame that gave breath to an inferno. He was startled at the hostility, but knew he was the fuse that detonated the shed full of dynamite.

"Sunny," Dane said. "I am not like any other man in your life. I came out here today with a crazy hope that I would tell you I loved you and you would fall into my arms and say you loved me, too."

Sunny pulled away and folded her arms and leaned against the truck. The pupils of Dane's eyes had catch-lights in them from the moon, the iris popping with full color. He was strikingly handsome, but she would not be fooled by good looks and charm. But the confidence in his eyes cracked open the sealed door to her heart.

"But obviously you don't feel the same way about me. My Mom said the heart wants what the heart wants and my heart wants you. You are the last flutter of my eyes as they close for sleep each night and you are my first cup of coffee when I wake up. Many times a day, without even thinking, your name finds its way from my heart and whispers through my lips. I gaze outside my office window and hear your voice rustling in the leaves of the cottonwood. I sit in meetings with powerful people, yet my mind makes the trip south to this ranch and I dream of you and I on saddled horses galloping across the prairie."

Sunny softened as golden words tumbled from his lips. When love dances with truth, the universe moves. She began to believe him.

"People closest to me told me I was in love with you before I even knew it. After my first wife died with cancer, I never thought, nor did I think it was possible, to ever love again. I didn't mean to fall in love with you; but I did. I will drive away tonight and respect your feelings, but it will never change the way I feel about you and the way I feel about us. You see, Sunny, I believe there is some destiny that awaits me that I will never find without you by my side. I don't know what it is, but I have powerful dreams about my future that look very different from my past, and you are always in them. I can't help but believe that my future is with you and will not give up hoping no matter how many times you slap me in the face."

He took the letter out of his back pocket and handed it to her. "When you are not so angry with me, would you please read this letter?"

Sunny sat in silence. She reluctantly took the letter. "Maybe. I don't know. I'm confused. Please leave. It's getting dark and I want to go inside."

Chapter Forty-Two

The Letter. It sat unopened on top of the worn yellow laminate kitchen table for several days. Sunny covered it with other mail, but even hidden it whispered to her. She wanted to read it, but was afraid.

His words stunned her; his eyes even more. She was furious that night. She had never raised her hand against another living soul and did not know why she slapped him. She tried to sleep but the anger turned to sorrow that swallowed her up like a blizzard covers the land. Within a 48 hour period, she discovered she was going to be a millionaire and slapped the Governor; proof that money didn't buy happiness.

Almost two weeks passed since Dane handed her The Letter. Sunny thought about tossing it into the wood stove one chilly evening.

Cal called asking if she would give two-thousand-dollars an acre for the ranch. He acted like he was giving her a deal and, after she refused, he dropped the price to one-thousand-dollars; his other offer had fallen through. She did believe Dane that he wasn't the one behind the scheme, but it didn't matter. She offered him six-hundred-dollars like she originally did. She decided to fix the ranch up a little bit, but she was no longer tied to it as emotionally as she had been. That day in the attorney's office was a turning moment when she realized that she had been fighting to keep her parents' dreams alive, not hers. It was a battle she wasn't sure she wanted to fight anymore.

She asked a heating and air contractor to give her a bid on putting in a forced air system. For years it was either an old wood stove or a gas furnace in the floor that heated the drafty old house. Little electric space heaters in the bedrooms and bathroom kept the snow off the inside windowsills. She promised herself no major purchases for a year. She'd pay some back taxes, get new tires for the truck and fill the propane tank to the top- something she couldn't usually afford to do. Frankly, she was afraid of the money. But it was nice not worrying about buying feed this winter or if the cattle market was going to collapse.

Spook agreed to come out today. He spied the lumber in her truck when she was at the co-op and surmised she was fixing the barn. The crew from Eco-Prairies was supposed to come out today, too. True to Dane's promise, they showed up about a week after he left. She was excited to see something finally good happening to the ranch.

She didn't tell anyone about the visit from the Governor. Nor The Letter. If she wanted advice, plenty would tell her what to do one way or the other. But so much had happened; she just needed to time think.

The Letter. Even though she hid it under a pile of other mail, it was always there. She knew what it would say. She knew it was his love letter to her. So it wasn't like it would surprise her to read it; he had been pretty clear in his feelings towards her that night. She didn't know how she felt about him. She wondered if it was some kind of weird attachment he felt since she saved his life, like some kind of obligation to return a favor. But she didn't need him or his money.

Why was she afraid of The Letter? Since the night with him by the barn, she found the lonesomeness on the prairie unbearable. What would it be like to kiss him, to be held close and smell his body next to hers? And those eyes! She noticed their intensity when he came out to the ranch after the crash. She couldn't make eye contact with him then.

He was handsome, but like her Momma said, handsome is as

handsome does. Shane was handsome, too. He left her at the altar so handsome didn't matter. Momma said you could tell what a man was like by looking at his Daddy and Dane's father, Johnson, was a true gentleman and Dane's mother a saint.

She surprised herself with the talk about Africa at the attorney's office. She picked up some books when in town about Africa and what people were doing to help. Was it a crazy idea? She could either spend all the money on herself and ensuring her future or maybe she could help people in real need. She read about non-profits and foundations in the evening and went back to town once to see the attorney, Sonya.

She grabbed The Letter and stuck it in the back pocket of her tight blue jeans and strode out to the barn; she did her best thinking in a saddle astride Starbuck. Spook wouldn't be out until he finished coffee at the Wrangler so she saddled up and rode by the newly tightened fence. She'd finally replaced some of those old hedge posts with metal ones.

She zipped her Carhart jacket tight and slid her buckskin gloves on as the wind wove leaves from the hedge and oak trees along the fence line. She avoided the crash site where the Eco-Prairies crew was working and ambled down to the old Clatterbuck place to spy on the ancient ruins. Maybe she could find an old arrowhead shining on the ground.

Dipping over the edge of a rocky rise into a little valley and out of the breeze, she reached to her back pocket to take out the letter. Pausing by the spring fed stream with sycamore leaves canoeing across a rock ledge, she peeled off her buckskin gloves and unfolded the paper. She breathed deep.

It was handwritten. She admired his penmanship and began to read,

Dear Sunny,

I realize the great risk I take in writing this letter. You might toss it out onto the prairie the next time the pastures are burned, use it to start a fire in

the woodstove, or you could show off my silliness to Spook for the sake of a good laugh. I heard someone once say that you have to risk the slap in the face for the pleasure of a kiss; I'm more than willing to take that risk. While I'm certainly not asking you to kiss me, I do hope this letter is met with at least some small amount of favor on your part.

Even as I write this, I find it awkward to even explain to you why I'm writing. Perhaps the best thing I can do is to express it as a poet. So I'll begin to describe the mysterious machinations inside me using a few of lines from a poem I wrote some time ago that was inspired by the Flint Hills.

"The wind lays soft against the prairie, and gives it breath to a new day

This winding road I'm traveling on's a memory of a place I've been and a place I'd like to stay

But a voice in the distant hill is calling, from the shadows it whispers my name

And the winding road I'm traveling on will take me to a place I'll never leave again."

Sunny sat in stunned silence. Dane was THE anonymous poet? Either he was lying or he really was the poet whose words she fell in love with. He couldn't have known she had memorized this poem. No one knew that. No one. Her heart trembled.

She remembered the night she fell asleep reading this poem and the dream came back to her as lucid as the night she had it. While asleep, Sunny was transported to a dark, green, lush part of the prairie where she could look over a vast valley. She was sitting in what seemed to be a patio out in the middle of nowhere. She looked down at her sandaled feet and found them resting on exquisite flagstone that had been skilled quarried and expertly laid. Surrounding her was a fence of pearl white lattice work that reached about eight feet in height and resting on top of finely turned wooden poles was an open air roof made of boards crossed in a square pattern. A late spring breeze drifted across her skin warmed by the overhead sun. Suddenly, she heard her name being called by a deep male voice. Her heart raced at the voice of her lover, her friend. Her mind didn't recognize the voice, but her heart did. This was her man. Her lover was calling her. This was her friend! She turned to peer out the lattice at the direction of the voice, but all she saw was a shadow fleeting across the prairie.

That voice was Dane's! His voice spoke to her heart that night and made her feel so alive.

Starbuck whinnied softly as Sunny read the letter. Tears spilled like the gentle fall rains that melt the leaves into the earth. She read line after line.

I love you, Sunny. And while it might not seem that I know you well enough to say that, I beg to differ. I believe that the fathomless part of me that is not bound by reason is connected to you in such a way that we are to be eternally joined.

You are my first thought as another day tugs at the covers to waken me; I spend the day making decisions on matters of the State and wonder if you'd agree with them; I sit down to eat and wonder if we would like the same meals; I fall asleep at night imagining you wandering in to the house from having just tucked Starbuck in for the night. You consume every waking and, often, sleeping thoughts.

Sunny, I love you. Plain. Simply. Consumed.

I am not asking you to marry me. Yet. I will, in time. I promise that. But it will be much more of a surprise than just to write it in a letter. But I am asking for a chance to prove to you what I feel in my heart. I do intend to marry you if you will let me. But I intend, first, to romance you with all the creativity in me and get to know you in such a way that you would trust me with every aspect of your being. I'm in a hurry for you to know; but I'm patient to wait for the evening your breath whispers 'good night' in my ear. I know that takes time.

And above all, I will become your friend.

I love you, Sunny.

Dane

P.S: If you ever want to talk, my private line is: 316-555-1212. Call anytime. Day or night. Anytime. I would appreciate knowing – one way or the other - if there is a chance for me to win your heart.

Sunny's tears splashed on the saddle horn as Starbuck snickered, shimmying his coat as he sensed the change in her. Years of abandonment rushed out of her like a Kansas wind blowing through open doors of an old farmhouse, clearing winter's ash off the furniture. Finally, she was loved. Something in her soul knew this was real; something in her spirit knew that this was truth and truth can never be changed.

"Oh, Dane," Sunny spoke to the wind. "I don't know what you see in this plain old cowgirl but I think I love you, too.

The gentle squeeze of her knees turned Starbuck towards the house.

Chapter Forty-Three

Sunny turned the lamp on as the evening shadows began to snuggle her into the night. Dane included the poem he wrote for her:

There's something about the water lapping gently at my feet
That stirs my soul with wonder and makes me feel complete
There's something about a sunset throwing violets on the lake
That sets my mind a-soaring and breathes my heart awake.
There's something about a summer wind that rustles in the trees
That calms my anxious spirit and drives me to my knees
There's something about the candle glow as the moon rises in the east
That quiets raging fears and gives me gentle peace.
For you're everywhere I've ever been and you're where I long to be.
For there's something about who you are that grows inside of me.
For if I just pause to look –you're already there
And if I just pause to hear –you'll whisper in my ear
You're the words that rhyme my heart as it sings a melody
And you're the something my spirit sighs in peaceful harmony.

She did not see this coming. Spook suspected; Mackenzie teased. But if you had asked her six hours ago if she ever thought the

347

Governor was the poet whose words had taken up residence in her heart, she would have told you to get back on your medicine. Yet, here she was trembling with this sudden awareness that she was loved by one she loved as well.

Did she love him? This morning she was warming to the idea. But The Letter whispered to her a possibility she wanted to believe but feared to accept. Even though The Letter was just another piece of paper piled in the bills, it became a force that slipped into the backdoor of her mind and teased her with fearful curiosity. Unwittingly, she had let The Letter unlock the chains she laced across her heart's dungeon like a spider web.

Sunny pulled the comforter up over the chilly night as Jasmine purred beside her. Could this be real? She was not a goofy little girl reading dime-store romance novels; she was an educated, tough, independent rancher who was able to keep a struggling business afloat with hard work and smart business moves.

Yet, since she read the letter clarity of purpose came as fresh as the smell of a fresh cut alfalfa field and as sweet as the fragrance of the wild roses outside her kitchen window after a rain. Like the misty fog that rose off the dew-kissed prairie as sunlight glitters millions of water beads, life suddenly made sense.

Jasmine jumped down as Sunny threw the covers off. She slipped into her heavy cotton robe and sheepskin slippers and made her way down the creaking wooden stairs to the phone. She lifted the phone and began dialing.

"Hello?" his voice melted her heart and glued her tongue to the top of her mouth. "Hello? Hello?" She couldn't speak. "Hello?"

She put the phone back on the receiver and collapsed on the kitchen chair. What was she going to say? What was she going to tell him? Her mind raced like a bobcat running from a coonhound.

She started back up the stairs, stopped, and went back down to the phone.

"Hello?" he answered the phone.

"Yes, may I speak to Dane, please," Sunny stumbled.

"This is Dane." She could tell he recognized her, but he waited for her next words.

"Dane, this is Sunny. I'm sorry if I wakened you."

"Sunny!" Dane said with great affection. "No, you didn't waken me; I was writing. It seems like I spend all my free time writing; it slackens the tornado in my mind to a nourishing rain that brings life instead of a raging storm that wreaks havoc."

"Besides," he continued. "I find myself staying up late hoping you will call."

"First off, I need to apologize for slapping you. I've never laid a hand on a person in my life and I don't know what got into me. That's not who I am."

"Sunny, if I had been you I would have slapped me to. You had no way of knowing that Moore was lying to you and all the shenanigans he tried to pull. He convinced you it was me letting you down and sneaking around behind your back to buy the land when it was him all the time. You had a right to be angry."

"Thanks, but I'm still sorry. I don't have a temper, but something tripped in me that night and I took it out on you. I also wanted to tell you that it's taken me a while, but I finally read the letter. I've been very confused and needed some time to think, but I did get around to reading it tonight."

"And?" Dane asked.

"Well, I really don't like talking on the phone. Are you free to come out to the ranch on Saturday?" Sunny queried. "I'd like to talk to you in person. I don't do well on the phone and this kind of conversation is best face-to-face."

"Absolutely," Dane said. "What time?"

"How about three o'clock? I'll saddle up a couple of horses and we'll go for a ride. I think and talk better when I'm on the back of Starbuck and out on the prairie."

"Great, I'll see you then," Dane said. "And, Sunny, I meant every word that I said and wrote."

"I know you did, Governor. You see, I've read your writings before. I didn't realize you were the anonymous poet I've been reading. I'll see you on Saturday." Sunny hung up the phone.

Governor? Sunny Morgan, you just called him Governor? Sunny caught herself; how was this relationship going to work? He was a man of state and national prominence and she was a cowgirl who just happened to rescue him.

This was not just about her and Dane; it was about a rescue of one of the most famous men in Kansas and the nation. This was already news and now would become even more prominent once the press found out.

The press. I need to call Mackenzie and ask for her advice. If the press finds out about this, that's going to make it that much more difficult.

"Mackenzie?" Sunny's hand shook as she held the phone. "Can I talk to you?"

"Of course, Sunny," she replied. "What is it? Are you okay? Is something wrong?"

"Can you come out to the ranch tomorrow? There's nothing wrong, but I just really need someone to talk to."

"I'm on my way," Mackenzie said. "You want me to bring Spook?"

"Oh, heavens, no!" Sunny laughed. "This is just girl talk. Him giving me advice right now would be like Irene Jones preaching on Sunday about the sin of gossiping. She wouldn't know what she was talking about and no one would listen. He has his place in my life and this time it's just out of earshot."

Mackenzie laughed as she put down the phone. If Sunny didn't want Spook in on the conversation and if it was about girl talk, then Mackenzie could surmise it had to be about another man. Was she having second thoughts about Radcliffe? She brushed him off a whole lot faster than anyone would have guessed. No, he wasn't the kind of man Sunny would be happy with, but he was handsome so maybe Sunny was thinking about him again. Lord knows loneliness makes people do crazy things. There is no heart as confused and blind as a desperate heart yearning for love.

Early the next morning, Mackenzie headed towards the Lonesome Star. The new ring from Spook on her finger reflected light as her hand turned the steering wheel. Years of loneliness for her disappeared as if they'd never happened. Yet, during that loneliness, a deeper sense of her own worth sunk deeper roots in the soil of faith and she felt more secure in herself than ever. A few lacerations on her heart from youthful impatience kept her from rushing into the arms of someone prematurely so she bided her time. She had resolved to live the rest of her life single unless the right one came along.

Spook was the right one. She long admired the real cowboys of the Flint Hills and could spot what Spook called a *goat-roper*. Spook was authentic, like a mint-condition truck kept in the barn and polished each Sunday.

The Governor! Mackenzie shrieked to no one in the car. *Surely it's not the Governor! Sunny can't be falling for the Governor; she can't stand him!*

Mackenzie drove a bit faster, excited to wonder what Sunny wanted to talk about. Each passing fence post down the gravel road leaned towards the road like a little kid's arms stretched out to be held.

Mackenzie reflected on the previous months and the dust devil of activity that swept across the prairie. First the crash; then the trip to New York; then Spook proposing; then the book deal: it was almost unbelievable.

Mackenzie recalled that moment when she promised Sunny she could trust her; that sacred moment was wrapped in the angelic light of heaven meeting earth. Sunny had given away her trust; something she was not easily separated from. And Mackenzie cherished that gift for what it was; the most divine part of any human treasure - trust.

So the cowgirl angel is falling in love with the Governor. Well, that ought to make the news!

Mackenzie groaned as the realization that Sunny would not only have to work thru the complexities of love, but she and Dane would be walking into a public and political field full of landmines. He was quite popular, but had his enemies nonetheless. His detractors would load their cannons with any kind of shrapnel. Dane would expect that as a Governor, but Sunny would be especially vulnerable. Falling in love with a famous figure was going to be tough on her.

Mackenzie smiled to herself and gripped the wheel a bit tighter as she turned down the long graveled driveway. *But that's why I'm here! I can help Sunny in ways that almost no one else can because I know how media works!*

If Mackenzie was right and Sunny was interested in the Governor, then it wasn't a matter of *if* it became public, it was a matter of *when* it became public. Mackenzie began thinking about the strategy for putting such an announcement in place. How would the public discover the romance? It was important that the discovery be staged and not some paparazzi taking a grainy photo for a tabloid publication.

Holding hands at the crash site! Mackenzie could stage that easily by getting the right journalist to cover. People would immediately see the connection between the crash and the romance; it would make such a great story.

But, when? The delicate thing would be the timing. Dane and Sunny must develop a relationship on their own without the prying eyes of the public, but Dane was a public figure and had a lot of eyes on him at all times. And a lot of cameras, too. Some photographer with a powerful lens could be a hundred yards away with his camera trained on every move of Dane and Dane not even know it.

Sunny was so private for so long but the crash made her a famous person, too. Although she was able to retreat back to the isolation of the ranch, a trip to town drew a lot of admirers. However, there were people jealous of her as well.

Mackenzie turned off her car as Sunny bounded out of the house. Her gait was like a fine Tennessee walker- lively, powerful and smooth- as she strode to the car. She had some papers in her hand and a smile like a sunrise on the prairie sparkled her eyes.

"Mackenzie," Sunny embraced her and held her tight. "I'm so glad to see you!"

"Here, read this letter. It's from Dane," Sunny said breaking away.

"Now?" Mackenzie replied. "Aren't you going to invite me in?"

"Oh, I'm sorry," Sunny laughed. "Sure, come on in!"

Mackenzie chuckled as she walked into the kitchen. Sunny still had the same old yellow dining room table with the chrome legs. Sunny sat a cup of coffee down for Mackenzie.

Mackenzie read the letter then put it down on her lap. Mackenzie's suspicions were right. Dane was deeply in love with Sunny and, judging by her enthusiasm, she was, too.

Sunny was looking at her like a little kid waiting to open a present. "Well, what do you think?"

"I think the real question here is; what do you think? Did you see this coming?" Mackenzie asked.

"No, I honestly never did. I was mad at him for crashing that stupid airplane out here and kept getting angrier with him for not fixing the place up that he helped destroy. But it turns out, his brother-in-law, Moore, has been doing a fair amount of lying to me. He's pulled a lot of shenanigans that I didn't know about."

Mackenzie was curious. "So how did you find out about Moore? Did Dane tell you this? Have you guys been talking?

Sunny's face blushed. "Well, yeah, once."

"Have you been up to see him or has he been down here?" Mackenzie asked.

"He was here once when he gave me the letter. I kind of blew up at him before he gave it to me and slapped him. I felt terrible about it as soon as I did it. I've never slapped anyone before in my life."

"You slapped the Governor?" Mackenzie's eyebrows furrowed. "Did he make unwanted advances?"

"Oh, heavens, no," Sunny laughed. "I thought he was lying to me about fixing the ranch again and, well, we were standing in the barn and the next thing I know I slapped his face. I still feel horrible about it. Then he told me he loved me, no matter what."

"He told you he loved you? Wow! So tell me, what did you do after he gave you the letter?" Mackenzie was fascinated.

"Actually, I didn't want to read it for a long time. I knew what it said but I just didn't think I was ready to be in a relationship with the Governor of Kansas. Then I read it and realized he is the anonymous poet I've been reading and his words have already found their way into my heart. I don't know how many times I've read his poems and wished that I could know a man who would feel that way about life. So it's almost like I was in love with him and didn't know it."

"Sunny, I am so happy for you!" Mackenzie reached across the table and held Sunny's shaking hands. "Spook knew the first time the Governor was out here that something was going to happen between you two. He told me later he'd threatened the Governor with severe bodily harm if he ever hurt you! But he also said he'd be a might bit proud to walk you down the aisle."

Sunny laughed. "Leave it up to Spook to threaten the Governor! I haven't told him yet. I wanted to talk to you first. It's good to know he will support us. I trust Spook and if he thought a relationship with Dane was bad, I would have had a hard time with that. He sure didn't like the artist, Radcliffe. My gosh, I've never seen Spook dislike anyone that much, even Sheriff Mitchell."

"So what do you want from me?" Mackenzie asked. "What can I help you with?"

"Mackenzie," Sunny said. "I don't trust easily but you have proven to me that giving you my trust was the right thing to do. I need advice. I feel like a giddy teenager and would marry him today if he brought a justice-of-the-peace along. But I'm scared to death. Dane is so handsome and could have any woman he wanted. He's a powerful, debonair, handsome man that could easily be president of the United States. What would he want in a simple country girl like me?"

"Well, first off, he sees the Sunny almost everyone else but you sees.

I wish I could give you the gift of seeing yourself as others see you. You won't have a traditional relationship. You have to play by different rules because you are both such public figures. You don't get a choice in the matter; you can't have a nice quiet romance just between the two of you. You marrying the Governor will be national news."

Sunny's shoulders slumped and she leaned back in her chair.

"I don't want this to upstage any of the political things that Dane is doing," Sunny explained. "Or to make this some political ploy meant to make Dane look good."

"It won't if you play it right. The fact is this; Dane is a political figure so everything he does has political implications. And with you by his side, everything you do will have political implications. There is no right or wrong about this, it just is what it is."

"But for the sake of your relationship, you have to be politically smart about this. The last thing you want is a grainy picture on a sleazy supermarket tabloid of you and Dane holding hands on a beach in Cancun. You need to be strategic for the sake of your relationship. You don't have the luxury of being private."

"So what would you advise?" Sunny asked.

"Well, first, we need to tell Spook," Mackenzie laughed and mimicked Spook's drawl. "If'n he finds out 'bout you two young'uns getting frisky from Irene Jones, he'll be madder than a preacher at a cussin' contest."

"Then what?" Sunny probed.

"Then we announce to the world that you and the Governor are in a relationship."

"You've already thought this through, haven't you?" Sunny realized. "You knew what I was going to talk about before you even got here today!"

"Let's just say a woman's intuition is something a person ought to pay attention to." Mackenzie said. "You're right, I was thinking about it and I believe we ought to invite a journalist I know out to the ranch. You and Dane holding hands at the crash site will announce to the world that you two are romantically involved."

"But won't the questions start about engagement and a wedding?"

"Of course they will. There will be several reporters who will even ask if you're pregnant and how long you've been having sex. I'll have to work with you and prepare you."

"He said in the letter that he would someday and I don't know that I want to wait on *someday*. Any kind of love is risky and we are not hormonally laced teenagers in the backseat of a car; we are adults and I think we shouldn't say we are romantically involved; I'd rather say we were engaged."

"But you're not, officially," Mackenzie replied. "He hasn't actually asked you."

"So what if I ask him?" Sunny wondered. "Who says he has to be the one that proposes? What am I supposed to do otherwise? Waste a bunch of time and energy waiting for him to pop the question? I want to go into this relationship knowing it's for the long haul. He loves me; I love him; the rest is detail as to when, not if. I don't want to play games; I want to live the rest of my life with him and I'll be a lot better off knowing we are going to get married sometime rather than wait for him to ask."

"Well, Sunny," Mackenzie admitted. "I guess I'm more old-fashioned than I thought. That just doesn't strike me as being the right thing to do. I must admit, when I first met you several months ago, I never thought I'd be having this conversation with you. The Sunny I met was shy, bashful, and afraid of her own shadow."

"I am not the same person I was then," Sunny said. "I'm much stronger. I'm willing to risk; I've been stuck here on the prairie with negative voices keeping me imprisoned like a herd of cattle in a holding pen. I am loved. I am worthy. I am going to marry the lover of my soul.

Chapter Forty-Four

"You slapped the Governor?" Shauna shrieked. "The Governor of Kansas told you he was in love with you and wants to marry you someday and you slapped him? Well, he is pretty easy on the eyes."

"No, it wasn't in that order. I slapped him first, then he told me he loved me." Sunny explained.

"Well, you could do far worse than that. I must admit I've had a few fantasies about him - he is a very good looking man."

"Yes, he is quite handsome. Even though I've been mad at him, after that first day on the ranch I wondered what it would be like to kiss him. I wanted to run my hands through that wavy salt-and-pepper hair of his, but, you know me, I'd shut down any kind of thoughts like that and just be mad at him again."

"So do you love him?" Shauna asked. "It wasn't just a couple of weeks ago you couldn't say a nice thing about him."

"I don't know, Shauna, after he told me he loved me I felt something shift inside me. It was like someone came into my house and cleaned all the dust and dirt and grime. I don't know if it is love or if it is just hope. I didn't realize how depressed I had become. I know, I know, you've been telling me for a long time I needed to get some help. Three weeks ago I could barely drag myself out of bed in the morning and now I wake up bright and early. And happy. I've been through so many changes in the last few months and I'm very excited about the future, but I don't want to confuse hope with love."

"You realize, of course, that this will make the news. Are you ready for that?"

"I've already talked with Mackenzie about how to handle that."

"And what did she suggest?"

"We're still trying to figure that out."

"What do you think about marrying him? You know when the press gets ahold of this, that'll be the first question. And the next will be, 'Are you pregnant?' And they'll go interview Shane and want to interview me. It's going to be very difficult to romance the governor with reporters and photographers sneaking around. I can't believe you, the little-miss-leave-me-the-hell-alone-on-the-ranch cowgirl is going to handle the public scrutiny. It will be really hard to date the Governor of Kansas."

"I know. I actually have a way around that, but Mackenzie didn't like my idea."

"What is that? You just going to elope to Vegas?" Shauna sneered.

"Dane's coming out on Saturday and we're going to saddle up the horses. I'm thinking about telling him the answer is, 'yes,' but I want to get married next month.

"What? Have you lost your mind? Two weeks ago you slapped him and now you want to be his wife? You have been out on the prairie too long! What are you thinking, girl?"

"You are right. We can't have a normal relationship. It didn't start off normal and it can't ever be normal in the sense of boy-romances-girl. He's the anonymous poet whose words I fell in love with a long time ago. No, I don't know how his kiss tastes or what it would be like to press against his strong chest. I can't wait to feel his hands on my body and his hot breath in my ear. But can't you see I already know his heart? His words became a part of me a long time ago."

"Sorry, girlfriend, but you won't be able to marry him. Spook will shoot him first." Shauna laughed. "But seriously, don't you think this is rushing it?"

Sunny chuckled. "Well, Mackenzie is going to help soften the blow with Spook. She also told me that Spook already suspected and that the first time he met the governor here at the ranch, he warned him not to hurt me but said he'd be happy to walk me down the aisle whenever we got married."

"Spook Masterson said that to the Governor?" Shauna clapped her hands. "I've heard it all now. But you didn't answer my question; do you think this is rushing it?

"If I had just met him, yes. But here's my rationale. First, we can't have a normal dating relationship. Like you said, the press will be hiding out everywhere, so we have a choice; if we string a courtship along while I'm waiting on him to pop the question, then we'll have the prying eyes of the press on us *all the time*. Frankly, I don't want to have to wait for him to ask; that makes me feel like I'm some fawning, helpless teenager waiting with bated breath for a man to make a move. I'm a confident woman; I won't be put in a position to have to wait. He and I will be equals."

Sunny continued, "So if we get married in the next month, there will be plenty of press during that time, but after we get married it will settle down. They'll leave us alone; they have a short attention span anyway."

"But," Shauna argued, "You're going from hating him to living with him 'till death-do-you-part. Don't you think you guys are starting off with a lot of difficulty?"

"Of course we are, but from what I've heard you say, you've had difficulties in your marriage and you guys keep working them out. I don't think marriages are successful because they don't have struggles; I think marriages are successful because two people learn how to overcome the struggles. Granted, I've not been married, but it seems to me that the most important thing in any marriage is the commitment to be together at the end of the day. If you know that at the end of the day you'll be crawling in bed beside the person you are fighting with right now, then you will find the solution to any problem."

"Shauna, I've seen a lot of people with great romances to begin with soon fall apart under the strain of everyday life. I've wondered how people can fall in love and can't keep their hands off each other than a few years later pay lawyers big bucks to call each other names. So romance can't be all that keeps a marriage together. It seems to me that commitment, trust, and respect are the fabric that binds it together. I've heard, too, that in many relationships one person loves more than the other, that no couple ever loves equally."

"You're absolutely right, Sunny, Roy and I started off behind the eight-ball because I got pregnant. I went from being his girlfriend to the mother of his child in the first year of our marriage. That was hard on us. The first few years of dating were all romance, but after I got pregnant the romance just slowly got replaced by working, feeding babies, taking care of the house, and life in general."

"So what keeps you together?" Sunny asked.

"Exactly what you just said. At the end of the day, we know we are going to be sleeping with each other and we've promised never to go to bed angry. I respect Roy a lot- he travels and works hard to provide for us. And I trust him. And, when we finally get a chance, the sex is really good, too. That makes up for a lot of frustration because he's really good in bed!"

"So are you going to have sex with the Governor before you marry him?"

"Shauna!" Sunny threw the dishrag at her. "That's not very nice!"

"Well," Shauna laughed. "Like Spook always says, 'If 'n yore gonna buy a pick-em-up-truck, you better look under that thar hood to see if 'n it's got a six-banger or an eight-banger."

"I have to confess something," Sunny's cheeks flushed. "The night out in the barn after I slapped him, he walked to the truck and the setting sun was silhouetting him, I was so turned on. I wanted to throw him down right there and make love to him."

"I'll bet he thought you were going to shoot him!" Shauna laughed.

"He would not have had a clue you wanted to make love to him."

"I called him up after I finally read The Letter that he left. I think he knows that I'm warming to the idea, but I told him I wanted to talk about it in person. I invited him out later today so we can talk face to face. I thought I'd be petrified but I'm not. I feel like I'm in control of this in some way. I waited forever for Shane to ask me to marry him and I remember how helpless that felt. I know I'm pretty old fashioned, but I'll play it by car today and, if I feel like it, I'm going to tell him I want to marry him."

"Sunny, I completely trust you that you know what you want. I have to get back into town and rescue the kids from Roy or Roy from the kids. I never know which starts the trouble, Roy or the kids. I'm really happy for you. Really happy for you."

Shauna went on, "Remember that day you called me right after the crash and woke me from that dream?"

"Oh, sure," Sunny replied. "It was the dream about me being a lily among thorns. How could I forget that? You are one of the few positive voices on the prairie that I listen to over and over."

"If you recall," Shauna explained, "That lily among the thorns was also laying among twisted metal. Sunny, you literally are a lily among thorns and you're beauty is going to be on display for the world to see. The world needs to see your beauty. It already has and is begging for more. So go marry the Governor and shine, honey-child, shine!"

Sunny sat at the secretary her grandmother handed down to her when she graduated from middle school. She was used to reading, not writing, but suddenly she felt an urge to make sense - as Dane said - of the tornado raging inside.

For the first time, she was thankful for the crash. Although the changes were imperceptible and even unrecognized, she was changing for the better.

Was she a different Sunny than when the plane crash happened? She let Shane change her; no, no one could change her; she had chosen to change because of his rejection. She let Shane's fear and insecurities become hers; she let her Daddy's fear and insecurities become hers; she let their voices define her. But, no more.

Was this just because Dane loved her? Was she now defining her worth because the Governor of Kansas loved her? Would she cower back into the recluse she had been if Dane left her at the altar, too?

No. The Sunny she was now is the Sunny she had always been and wanted to be. She let the opinion of others dictate her own worth and she would no longer do that. She was strong, smart, creative, and resourceful. She would no longer look horizontally for someone else to define her value. She would give no one the power to determine her worth but herself.

She would love Dane with reckless desire but without need. She didn't need his love, but she cherished it. What his love released in her could never be stopped. He could help it to flourish and grow, but if he rejected her it would not diminish her resolve to walk with confidence and strength. While she thought about life with him and all things they could do and places they could go, she wasn't dreaming those dreams because she suddenly had a man in her life. Rather, his admission of love for her unlocked a torrent of love for herself, a raging river of self-acceptance and power that would never be dammed again. That's what love does; it unlocks love in others.

The ink flowed as she wrote of who she was and who she purposed to be;

I am the wild rose splashing across the prairie that surprise the casual observer
and pique the curiosity of the adventurer
I cannot be tamed, but allowed to grow free I will bring beauty
and fragrance to your life
I am the gentle spring that trickles down the limestone cliffs into deep
shimmering pools of delight that will refresh and nourish
I am the raging storm that sweeps through the prairie that cannot be
predicted or controlled

but bring sustenance and clarity

I am the newborn foal yearning to frolic on the hillside so I can grow with joy and purpose

to a marvel of beauty only with you as my only rider

You are the eagle that soars in the Kansas sky

Majestic and bold; regal and daring

You are the stallion that races across the plains with mane flowing dark and wild

Magnificent and resplendent in beauty

I eagerly await the moment you claim me as your one, and only

You are the sunlight that kisses me awake and the stars that kiss me goodnight.

You are the one whom my soul loves

I am the one that ravishes your heart

And I say, Yes!

Chapter Forty-Five

Dane turned down the long driveway to the Lonesome Star. He chuckled, half expecting Spook to somehow have discovered the plan and be waiting on him with his .357.

After Sunny's call four days earlier, the week lasted a dozen years. Meetings were interminable; he didn't listen to a thing that politicians rambled about; he hardly slept.

He didn't sleep at all the night she called. He recognized her number on the caller ID, but when she didn't speak the first time, he froze in fear and hung up. He asked her to give a definitive answer and, when she didn't speak, assumed it was negative.

And her second call was so unlike anything he ever imagined that he spent the night reliving the conversation and examining any clues he could to help him understand. She insisted that he come out today.

I wonder if she changed her mind?

He was pleased to know she read his poetry. He knew better than to submit it under his own name or even a made-up name. He didn't write about the way things were; he wrote about the way things ought to be.

He spent all of that first night after she called writing a proposal. He told her he would wait to ask, but why? He was not a child or a hormonally driven teenager. He knew what he wanted; he wanted to marry her and didn't care when.

Dane struggled writing the proposal because each version sounded cliché. He wrote lines that sounded like words that every man from the creation of earth had penned to woo a woman. Finally, on the third day he stumbled across an old marriage custom in cultures where families practiced betrothal ceremonies. He heard that word used in wedding vows in a church when he was a kid as the preacher would have the groom quote, "… and hereby I do betroth you my love," but he never knew the full meaning.

He discovered that at the betrothal ceremony, the groom-to-be took a glass of wine and offered it to his bride-to-be. When he did, the groom would make a speech about who he was and what he was offering to the bride. He would conclude by saying, "Please take this wine; this is all of me. The bride-to-be accepted the offer by drinking the glass of wine and said, "I accept all of you."

That was it! That was how he would propose to her!

He parked near the house and turned the truck off. Using his Dad's truck was the only way to sneak out without anyone following.

Both horses stood hitched at the rail. He heard the kitchen door open first then Sunny came out the back door. Should he hug her? Should he grab her and kiss her?

She settled the question. "Hello, Dane. Are you ready to ride?"

"Sure!" Dane slid his boot into the stirrup and swung his leg over the saddle. Sunny climbed on Starbuck and they made their way east across the pasture.

"It looks like they're finally getting this land back in shape. That's some good looking soil they filled in those ruts with," Dane commented.

"Yes, and thank you." Sunny replied. "I'm glad you had them bring dirt in and fill it up instead of trying to plow or disc the ground around it. The prairie ecosystem is so fragile and these grasses have grown for centuries. I didn't want any more land destroyed."

"We had the best environmentalists study the proper way to do this. They say a year from now you'll never know there was a plane crash here, except for the new steel fence posts to replace the old hedge posts."

"One thing I am glad of," Sunny admitted. "Is that no one is going to fix that old dirt road that got tore up so badly. It's traveled a lot by trespassers and four-wheelers going mudding in the rain, but it's so tore up now and of no future use that neither the county nor the township want to pay for fixing it up."

"So it sounds like there's been a few good things that came out of my crash after all?" Dane fished.

Sunny moved Starbuck closer to Dane and reached out to touch his arm. "I can't tell you how annoyed I was when I saw your plane coming down. I know that sounds selfish of me, but I just didn't want you or anyone else crashing on my property. I didn't want you hurt- I just wanted you to go on a few miles and crash somewhere else."

Dane laughed, "I didn't want to crash anywhere! But I don't blame you - I didn't want the prairie tore up either. I never expected to survive the crash. Moore was screaming like a little girl and I assumed it was the end of me."

"It might have been if Starbuck and I hadn't been here. You were in pretty bad shape."

Dane wanted to hear more about the day of the crash. Why was she out on the prairie? When did she notice he was in trouble? What was she thinking as she saw the crash? How did Starbuck manage to keep his calm in all the chaos? How long did it take for help to arrive?

These questions - and the answers - filled the time as they sauntered across the prairie. The afternoon was clear: the air crisp as a bite of mint.

Sunny spread the blanket on the ground and retrieved the bottle of wine and the dinner from the saddlebag. Dane listened with rapt attention to her detail of that day when he crashed and the days following. He became increasingly aware of how much he had truly wreaked havoc on the land and on her life. It was a miracle he was alive, but after listening to her story he knew it was more than a miracle; it was a destiny. On the blanket under the setting sun in the west and the rising moon in the east, two lonely people intersected history in such a way that the world would forever become a better place.

Dane watched every movement, desiring to touch her skin, to run his fingers through her hair, to taste the succulence of her lips as they kissed, to feel her body next to his. She was getting nervous; her cadence picked up and she lost her train of thought several times.

"Sunny," he said reaching out to touch her hand. "Can I pour us some wine?" She fumbled around for the corkscrew and handed him the bottle and two glasses.

"Dane, you said in your letter that you wanted to marry me and would some day ask. Most people who are interested in dating each other have an end goal in mind of marriage so the courtship is the combination of romance and a duel as people try to determine if that person is the right one. You changed that game when you told me in your very first letter you wanted to marry me."

Dane halted, "I realize that was pretty forward. I'm sorry if it scared you."

"Oh, no, just the opposite," Sunny replied. "It didn't scare me; it settled me. Most courtship starts with a question of *will this end in marriage;* we are starting with the question of marriage already settled. I don't know how, but that changes things. Marriage seems to be a finish line for most courtships; however, it's like we're starting at the finish line. That takes a lot of the stress of the romance out of the way. I don't want to invest my heart into you for a period of time then go through the heartache of a breakup. I will give you my all. Some couples strive to be *one* as if it is destination to be reached; what if we started our marriage with being *one* as a place of origin?"

"Hmm. That's very good," Dane said. "So it's like our marriage would start assuming our souls are meshed in oneness rather than something we're always trying to attain? I like that; because oneness would then be about two diverse people assuming they are unified instead of trying to become unified. It doesn't mean we'll always agree; it means that we're always in it together. At the end of the day, we'll be together no matter what."

Dane continued, "Sunny, you know I've been married before. Debbie was a wonderful woman and I loved her and always will. Her death was hard on me and I never thought I'd love again. So I know what love feels like; I know how to listen to my heart. And my heart is totally captured by you. I wake up thinking of you, I can't pay attention during the day because of you, and I fall asleep thinking of you."

"Is there room for me in there with Debbie?" Sunny asked.

"Funny you should ask that," Dane said. "Because Debbie told me before she died that she wanted me to find someone again. I couldn't bear the thought of losing her and didn't want to have the conversation at all, but she insisted. She didn't want me to rush right out and find someone, but said that in time the right one would come along and she wanted that for me. She told me the right one would ask me this question; is there room for me in there with Debbie?"

A sacred silence fell on their conversation.

"Someday, I want to learn more about Debbie," Sunny said. "I needed to hear you say that you loved her; that tells me something about who you are that I needed to know. I know you will tell me the truth and the most important thing I ever want from you, Dane, is that you always tell me the truth. We make decisions based on what we believe to be true, but when we find out we've based our decisions on a lie, then all crumbles into a pile. I was so angry with you because I thought you lied to me. I based my feelings on the lies of others. I'm sorry."

"Sunny," Dane replied. "Writing that letter to you was the scariest thing I've ever done because I felt completely naked and more vulnerable than I've ever been in my life. I didn't realize it until afterward, but it dawned on me that the letter wasn't so much about me being head over heels for you in love, but it was more about trust."

"Trust is the key to any relationship," Dane said. "It is the most sacred part of any human being and to give it away is the most precious gift you can give or receive from anyone. There are hundreds of conversations of discovery that you and I will have in the years to come, but if trust is the key that holds us together, then we can weather any storm. Trust knows at the end of the day we will be snuggled under the covers. Trust knows that my name is safe in your mouth."

"There have been a lot of changes since you crashed here on the prairie," Sunny said. "And I know there are going to be a lot of changes that come our way. I love this ranch and want to keep it. I don't even know where you live, but I want us to live here some. But you should know before you marry me that I have had dreams of helping children in Africa. I want us to make our marriage more than just about us; I want our marriage to make this world a better place in which to live. I had a dream some time ago and African children were chanting *Mwalmu, Mwalimu.* I discovered later it is a Swahili phrase that means *teacher.*"

"Sunny," Dane replied. "I've had similar dreams. Being the Governor has been a great honor, but I believe it's provided me a platform to do something international. I had a dream and children in Central America surrounded you and they were looking at me but pointing at you chanting *epousa, espousa!*"

"Dane, you said in the letter that you would someday ask me to marry you. I have something I want you to read."

She reached into the saddlebag and handed him her letter. He turned so the light of the campfire illuminated the words on the page.

I am the wild rose splashing across the prairie
surprising the casual observer
piqueing the curiosity of the adventurer
I cannot be tamed, but allowed to grow free I will bring
beauty and fragrance to your life

I am the gentle spring that trickles down the limestone cliffs into deep
iridescent pools of delight that will refresh and nourish
I am the raging storm that sweeps through the prairie
that cannot be predicted or controlled
 but bring sustenance and clarity
I am the newborn foal yearning to frolic on the hillside so I can grow with
    joy and purpose
 to a marvel of beauty only with you as my only rider
I am a lily among thorns
You are the eagle that soars in the Kansas sky
Majestic and bold; regal and daring
You are the stallion that races across the plains with mane flowing dark and
    wild
Magnificent and resplendent in beauty
I eagerly wait the moment you claim me as your own
Your one
Your only
You are the sunlight that kisses me awake and the starlight that kisses me
    goodnight.
You are my lover
You are altogether my friend.
And I say, Yes!

The moon swathed the undulating prairie with an umber blanket of light and firelight tickled the sides of the wine glasses. The last of the meadowlarks warbled in the grass and a newborn colt whinnied in the distance as Dane rose to his feet and lifted Sunny to hers.

"Sunny," Dane said as he poured more wine. "There is a tradition in some cultures called the betrothal ceremony. It is a party by the two families of the couple getting married. At this party, the man holds up a glass of wine and gives a speech to his bride-to-be. When he is done, the woman – if she so chooses - drinks the wine both as a way of saying she accepts and a way of saying she returns the request to him."

Cradling the glass of wine in one hand and holding her hand with his other, he spoke into her heart:

The evening shadows on the prairie wrap us together, again
The stars kiss the day goodbye as the meadowlark lullabies the hills to sleep
Providence once united us here in torrential tempest as death beckoned me
But was denied by because of the angelic heroism of a woman and her horse
With this wine, I offer you everything that I am
This nectar of life is filled with all of my past
With all of my failures and all of my successes,
All of defeats and all of my triumphs.
It is filled with all of my future
With all of my dreams and all of my hopes
Which now have become entwined with you
My dreams now have you as my purpose; my failures have you by my side
My hope draws its breath from you and all of my fears long to be held in
    your arms.
I ask you to marry me,
We will dream, together
We will fail, together
We will triumph, together
We will breathe, together
Will you drink all of me?

Sunny put her hand on the glass still in his hand and lifted it to her mouth and moved it close do Dane's lips. Breathing deeply of the wine, she then blew gently across the top, the fruity smell of wine circulating between them, she whispered.

I drink all of you. And I say yes.

Tipping the glass, the wine exploded each taste bud with delight. Pulling away she spoke to Dane.

I accept you and all that you are; all other voices on the prairie grow mute and yours alone is the one I hear.

Will you drink all of me?

Dane lifted the glass to his lips as a tear splashed in the wine.

I drink all of you. And I say yes.

Wine glistened lips met as passion drew them into the lover's embrace.

The taste of love melted their hearts into unshakable contentment.

The End

Purchase other Black Rose Writing titles at www.blackrosewriting.com/books
and use promo code PRINT to receive a 20% discount.

BLACK✿ROSE
writing™

CPSIA information can be obtained
at www.ICGtesting.com
Printed in the USA
FSOW04n0148300715
9224FS

9 781612 965574